LOVE
AND
WAR
IN THE
LAND
OF
CAIN

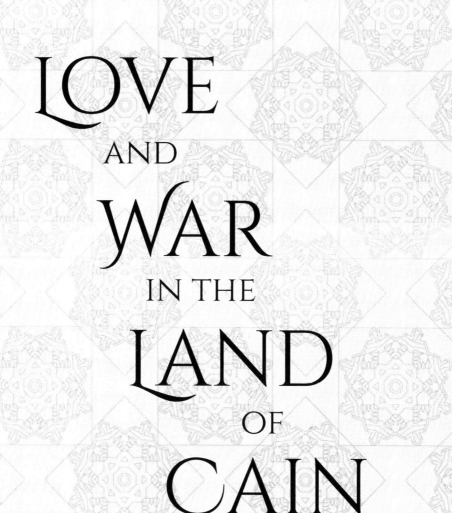

LOVE
AND
WAR
IN THE
LAND
OF
CAIN

DEBRA DENKER

Love and War in the Land of Cain
© 2021 by Debra Denker

This is a work of fiction. Names, characters, places, and incidents are either the product of the author's imagination or, if real, used fictitiously.

Previously published as *War in the Land of Cain* by Synergy Books in 2011

Paperback edition published 2021 by Catalyst Artistic Productions
ISBN for paperback edition
978-0-9991252-3-6

Cover design, interior design and formatting by

www.emtippettsbookdesigns.com

Author photo by Tara Waters Lumpkin

Published by Catalyst Artistic Productions
www.catalystartproductions.com
www.loveandwarinthelandofcain.com

Praise for

LOVE AND WAR IN THE LAND OF CAIN

Debra Denker paints the human side of war that is often forgotten. Denker's riveting novel is more than entertainment; it is also a wake-up call. It asks us, as a nation, to go beyond the stereotypical, cartoonish notions that dominate our thinking about the peoples whose nations we've invaded in recent years. Denker has made an important contribution and her novel merits a wide readership.

—Larry Dossey, MD
Author of *One Mind*, *The Power of Premonitions,* and *Healing Words*

I was blown away by *Love and War in the Land Of Cain*. I didn't expect Debra Denker (or anyone else) to be able to capture the spirit of Afghanistan and the Afghan people, but she has done so. She cleverly sets her story during the Soviet occupation of the 80s, so as not to politicize her tale and bring in the reader's bias towards the current conflict. She manages to show us Afghanistan through Afghan as well as western eyes. We learn what the Afghans have been fighting for all these years and the tragedies they continue to face. Most important, we are shown forcefully the toll that ALL wars take on non-combatants and especially on the most defenseless members of society, women, children and the elderly.

All the characters are real and human, struggling to figure out what they feel and want. I couldn't wait to get back to this thoroughly engaging book every day I was reading it.

Love and War in the Land Of Cain brought back my experiences in Afghanistan in 2002 more than anything I have read since I was there. Denker knows the country and people deeply and writes with refreshing honesty, so these people are all real. Her observations on human behavior and desires are wise and the book is filled with the love of humanity in all our foolishness so that you read through the book with hope, amazingly. Highly recommended.

—Bill Megalos,
documentary filmmaker specializing in
global health and development issues; film instructor

Only someone who knows Afghanistan intimately could write such a beautiful and profound story set in the early years of the ongoing conflict. Debra Denker, a journalist in Afghanistan in the 1980's, weaves a passionate and yet sometimes tender tale of the often tragic unfolding of life in this country, which has been at war since 1979.

I am the founder of the multimedia platform Voices for Biodiversity, which focuses mostly on the field of environmental journalism. However, I spent a decade of my life working as an anthropologist in post-conflict countries such as Namibia, Panama, and Rwanda. I am familiar with the emotional territory of people and places that have been affected by war. War leaves an indelible mark on its people and the land itself.

This novel is entirely engaging and truthful. Quite simply, I couldn't put the book down. The novel powerfully shows how war in Afghanistan has affected its people and others who came to be there. But this novel is not just about Afghanistan, it is also a story that could take place in many countries that have been or are approaching a crossroads. To read this book is to peer into the heart and mind of possible opportunities for change and choice.

—Tara Waters Lumpkin, PhD
Founder, Voices for Biodiversity

Also By
DEBRA DENKER

Sisters on the Bridge of Fire:
One Woman's Journeys in Afghanistan, Pakistan, and India
(a memoir originally published in 1993, reprinted 2001)

Weather Menders
(a cli-fi time travel novel published in 2017)

I dedicate *Love and War in the Land of Cain*
to the people of Afghanistan.

I especially want to honor the courageous
Afghan women and men
who have worked for decades
for human rights and women's rights.
This novel would not have been possible without the inspiration
of Fatana Syed Gailani and her husband Syed Ishaq Gailani.

*Afghan and other Central Asian legends hold
that the Kabul Valley is the Land of Cain—
the Biblical Land of Nod, East of Eden where Cain fled
after murdering his brother Abel.
Some claim there is a tomb of Cain outside the city of Kabul,
which Cain is said to have founded.*

PREFACE

The seed of *Love and War in the Land of Cain* was planted in a cave in Afghanistan. It was April 1983. I was a young freelance journalist who had crossed the border from Pakistan into Afghanistan disguised as an Afghan woman, armed only with an open heart and a passion for truth. I wanted to tell the stories that were usually not covered by other correspondents, overwhelmingly males, who preferred to focus on battles and warriors. I wanted to give voice to the Afghan women and children living their precarious lives in the war zone of Soviet-occupied Afghanistan.

To this end, I had requested my friend Syed Ishaq Gailani, to set me up with a party of Mujahedeen freedom fighters who would lead me several days' walk into Kunar Province to a remote village where a volunteer Afghan doctor had set up a clinic.

The first night of walking I seriously injured my knee, probably a torn ligament, when I tripped in the dark over a furrow in a cornfield. I had no choice but to grit my teeth against the pain and keep going. Early the next morning, just as I had drifted off to sleep in what seemed a safe cave, the sound of explosions startled me awake. One of the Mujahedeen came running and urged me to move quickly as I scrambled in pain to a higher, deeper cave.

I had no idea if the cave really was safe. Unlike many of my colleagues, I had hoped to avoid actual battlefields, but here I was. Time took on a surreal quality, stretching and contracting and wrapping itself around me. Though I sympathized with the Afghan people defending their homes against a foreign invader, at that moment I could only see the absurdity of war.

It was not unlike living through the COVID-19 pandemic. I just wanted it to be over. I wanted to fast forward the film and get to the good parts, the peaceful, nourishing, hopeful parts.

I journaled, and amused myself by fantasizing about the doctor I was going to meet. If only…I conceived the character of Dr. Yusuf, a dedicated Afghan-born doctor, the perfect bridge between traditional Afghan and Western culture. Let's make him a Sufi mystic, and he must deeply respect women of course. So in that cave, as shells fell in explosions of dust and rock across the narrow valley, Dr. Yusuf was born.

I am not Elizabeth. Creating characters in a novel or screenplay is almost like Method acting. Who would I be and how would I feel if I were a woman journalist from Bethlehem, Pennsylvania, or an Afghan doctor who had lived in San Francisco, or an idealistic Afghan socialist who ended up compromising with the Soviet invaders?

Though Elizabeth's background and story are very different to mine, our sensibilities are similar. When I returned to my Afghan friends' house in Pakistan after eight days in Kunar, I wept with survivor's guilt, having witnessed both horror and heroism firsthand. How could I relax into relative luxury when the people I'd left behind in Kunar were daily facing the threat of bombing, strafing, arrest, betrayal?

Unlike Elizabeth, I initially couldn't get any of my articles published. I spent the summer of 1983 in Pahalgam, Kashmir, writing a novel originally titled *War in the Land of Cain* while receiving rejection slips from a variety of publications that were not interested in Afghanistan.

I finished the first draft in two months. It subsequently went through many, many incarnations over a period of years, decades actually. Elizabeth, Yusuf, and Yusuf's brother Ayub were just as rejected as my early efforts to get stories of daily life in a war zone published and to open the hearts of the American people and the world to the plight of Afghanistan.

After a frustrating year, fate, circumstance, and synchronicity led to the opportunity to do my second freelance article for *National Geographic*. In the fall of 1984, the magazine sent me to cover the refugee situation in Pakistan, with instructions that if I felt it was safe I could also venture again into Afghanistan's war zone.

Four months of traveling around Pakistan to various refugee camps, with a brief foray into Afghanistan's Jaji province, resulted in the June, 1985 cover story "Along Afghanistan's War-torn Frontier." Many will remember Steve McCurry's famous cover photo of the Afghan girl with green eyes that illustrated the story.

I used my 15 minutes of fame to speak as much as possible about the dire situation that ordinary Afghan people were facing. I wrote more drafts of the novel and pursued literary contacts offered by Charles McCarry, *National Geographic* editor and author of spy novels, and other colleagues. All to no avail. I recently burned the rejection slips that I had for some reason kept for over 30 years. It was satisfying. Some of them were quite mean-spirited.

My theory at the time was that agents and publishers found the plot point that turned on the Soviet withdrawal to be implausible. After all, the Soviets didn't actually withdraw until 1989, years after I was shopping the manuscript around New York and London.

In retrospect, it's entirely possible that I wasn't as mature and brilliant a fiction writer as I thought I was. The novel has benefited immensely from both my lived experiences and my honing of my skills as a storyteller. The comments of other writers helped me to see what needed strengthening and what needed cutting.

There was a flurry of interest in Afghanistan in 2001, after September 11th and the subsequent U.S. invasion of Afghanistan, but I still was not able to find a publisher. I continued my speaking and fund-raising work, and let the manuscript lie fallow.

Ten years later, in 2011, a friend told me of a small press looking for manuscripts, and I contracted with Synergy Books to publish the novel. It didn't become a best seller, but my dad was able to hold the book in his hands and take a moment of pride in his daughter's achievement before he sank into the long journey into dementia.

Another decade later, as the tragedy of the fall of Afghanistan to the Taliban unfolds, it is time to rebrand the novel as *Love and War in the Land of Cain*. The story hasn't changed, but the emphasis has. When I was a young journalist horrified by war, the drama of conflict was what I saw—between the Afghans and the Soviets, and between the two brothers, Dr. Yusuf and Governor Ayub. With the benefit of nearly four decades' hindsight, during which the book has become an historical novel, I realized that the most important story is a love story—not just between Elizabeth and Yusuf, but between Elizabeth and her Afghan women friends Salima, Malolai, and Maryam, and between all of the characters and Afghanistan itself, and finally, between the shadow of war and the bright dream of peace.

As that bright dream recedes from the immediate future, a Sufi story comes to mind:

"There was once a king who commanded his wise advisors to make him a ring that would make him happy whenever he was sad, and sad whenever he was happy. They thought and thought, and finally decided that the ring should simply be engraved with the words, 'In hamah b'guzerad—This too shall pass.' Thus these terrible times for Afghanistan must pass, as all previous occupations, invasions, coups, and cruel regimes have passed."

So, dear reader, I hope that you will lose yourself in this story of love, even in what seems the darkest of times. The most transcendent Sufi poetry speaks of Lover and Beloved as One. As you read this novel, may you find a glimpse of the peace that comes from the recognition of the ultimate union of all existence.

Debra Denker
Santa Fe, New Mexico
August 15, 2021

PROLOGUE

Summer, 2001
Peshawar, Pakistan

T he two women clung to each other sobbing while the two bewildered boys looked on. Occasionally one of the women would pull back her head and look at the other's tear-streaked face, laugh, and then start to sob again and hold the other even tighter.

Outside, brilliant lightning flashed, swiftly followed by thunder grumbling its baritone promise of the monsoon's sweet relief. Inside, the two old friends were so intent on their reunion that they barely noticed the stifling heat that enfeebled the room's small air conditioner.

Finally, breathlessly, the American woman pulled away from the Afghan sister she had not seen for so many years. She shook her head, not wanting to say what she was thinking.

But as always, Salima read her mind. "I know. I have gotten old," she said softly.

"These years have not been easy."

"Not for either of us."

"But easier for me than for you I think."

"Are you saying you look younger than me, Elizabeth *jan*?"

Elizabeth was startled for a moment by her friend's directness, then saw the familiar and long-missed impish grin. "Hardly! This boy of mine runs me ragged."

Salima stepped towards a tall, dark-eyed boy of about twelve who hung behind Elizabeth, looking from woman to woman and occasionally suppressing a shared snicker with the other boy in the room, who looked close to his own age.

"So this is Yusuf's son," the Afghan woman said with a mixture of emotions Elizabeth could not define.

"Yes," said the proud mother. She turned towards her son, wiping tears from her face. "Come here and meet *Khala* Salima. I've told you about her so many times."

The boy extended his hand as he had been taught, bowed slightly in the Afghan manner, and said perfectly, "*Salaam, Khala* Salima."

Salima was delighted. "*Wa aleikum salaam. Namat chist?*"

Elizabeth's son ducked his head with the awkwardness of his age. "Jawad. But most people call me Joe."

Salima burst out laughing, but squeezed the boy's shoulder to reassure him. "Here you will be Jawad, if you don't mind. Come, meet your cousin, my son Karim."

The other boy had been sidling towards the TV and was within a hand grab of the remote when Salima's words pulled him back.

"Is he my real cousin? And do I have to speak English to him?"

Salima pinched his shoulder gently. "Real cousin or not, it doesn't matter. Elizabeth and I are like sisters, so she is your *Khala*, and Jawad becomes your cousin."

"*Man Farsi khoob mefahmam*," said Jawad proudly, then pulled a funny face.

Karim's dark eyes grew wider. "Cool," he said nonchalantly. "Wanna go play games on the computer?"

Jawad narrowed his own eyes slightly. "Yeah. Cool. *B'rim b'kheir.*"

The two boys ran out of the room like the best of friends, without a second glance back at their mothers.

Salima led Elizabeth to the couch. They sat down and stared at each other, then hugged silently for a very long time, feeling the beating of each other's hearts. Finally Salima reached to the low table in front of her and began to pour tea. Her hand shook so badly she had to set the china pot down.

"No more servants," she said apologetically.

"Salima, you're not ill?" asked Elizabeth urgently.

The other woman shook her head, wiping away new tears with her hand and trying to smooth back her graying hair.

"Why? Because I do not color my hair anymore?"

"Salima, stop it! Your situation is worse than you let me know in your letters and calls."

Salima took a deep breath, steadied herself, and went back to pouring tea. "My sister, you have been gone for a long time." She laughed softly. "Remember how hard we thought life was then? It was nothing compared to now."

Elizabeth sipped her tea, a flood of memories cascading through her mind at the familiar cardamom-spiced taste. "You are in danger. I saw it on your Afghan Womens' Freedom Alliance website. Nothing like finding out that your best friend has a death threat against her from surfing the net."

"It's not so bad. Massoud is under the same death threat."

Elizabeth winced. "Maybe it's time for you to leave Peshawar. There's no way you can live in Afghanistan under the Taliban, and you're not even safe here. Ask Massoud to call in some old favors and get you visas to come to America. Come live with us in California. It's not Afghanistan, but we have nice mountains there."

Salima's eyes flashed with passion. "No!" she said vehemently. "Massoud won't go, and neither will I. We are needed here. No one inside Afghanistan is safe to speak out against the Taliban for human rights, or for women, who cannot even leave their house to work or go to school. We are close to our country here, close enough to smell the lilacs of the homeland in spring, and the melons in summer. We have the girls' school, the clinic for women and children, the Afghan Women's Freedom Alliance. We can't leave all these people now, not after twenty years of fighting."

"But what about Karim? Your whole family could be killed. Or what if it's just you and Massoud? Then he'd be an orphan."

"And then you, my sister, can come take him to America. But not before. Remember, Elizabeth, this is not the first time we have been threatened. You were here."

Elizabeth put down her cup, unable to enjoy the sweet tea. "I hope the security is better in this house than in that one."

Salima smiled, her stress showing in the lines around her eyes and the tightness of her lips. "Yes. Now we rate the official protection of the Pakistani police."

"Great. We know what that's worth."

"It is not exactly the same as house arrest. And anyway, I am not as famous as Aung San Suu Kyi."

"Not yet, anyway. We do have Amnesty International and other organizations working on it. And my camera crew will be here tomorrow. It will be a big story. The media attention should help keep you safe."

"*Inshallah*." Salima said the word automatically, but Elizabeth could tell that the faith that underlay it was still strong, though sometimes wavering. "My dream is to do something for my country," she continued softly, "to be a hero in some small way, just as Suu is fighting for the freedom of her own people. You know I heard her son speak on her behalf when I went to the Women's Conference in Beijing."

Salima faltered and fell silent. The two old friends looked at each other, their faces still nearly a mirror of each other across cultures, distance, and a decade, though in Elizabeth's eyes Salima's strong and beautiful face showed the premature aging of extreme stress and sadness. As one, they shook their heads, and said the same words: "How did it ever get this bad?"

PART I

SPRING, 1984

CHAPTER 1

ELIZABETH

Spring, 1984

Kunar Province, Afghanistan

Elizabeth wondered what she was doing in a cave in Afghanistan in the middle of a war. She caught her breath at the sound of a particularly loud concussion echoing between the stony walls of the narrow valley as an exploding tank shell landed a hundred yards away, kicking up a cloud of dust. Her faithful bodyguard Sharif, stretched out on a sleeping bag spread out on the dirt floor of the tiny cave, didn't stir. Elizabeth sighed and shifted slightly in an effort to find a more comfortable place, or at least a space where she didn't feel as if she were about to slide down the mountain.

Her right ankle throbbed, and no matter what position she sat in every movement seemed to jar it. She raised the loose purple silk trousers of her borrowed disguise and tenderly probed the bare and bruised skin of her swollen ankle. Sharif's massage with salt water had helped; Ebrahim's more clumsy massage had been, much like him, well-meaning but painful.

She couldn't believe it was only yesterday that she had woken up in Dunahi. She checked the watch she'd tucked into her fanny pack. April 12th. She wondered how Massoud and Salima were doing back in Peshawar, and if the Mujahedeen leader and his wife were praying for her as promised.

She winced with embarrassment at the thought of them finding out she'd been sidelined by a stupid injury her second night behind enemy lines. Some journalist. She'd wanted to be heroic in her stamina, or at least keep up just like any male journalist. Now she felt like nothing but a burden to her Mujahedeen escort.

Another explosion. She jumped slightly. Would she ever get used to this? It was still early, and birds twittered in the bushes near the idyllic stream, their treble voices counterpointing the bass continuo of the river. The explosions were a more modern dissonance.

She hadn't realized how gun shy she was. Her father was a member of the National Rifle Association, but to his lasting irritation she and her brother the conscientious objector had never liked the weekend hunting expeditions, even as children. She was always glad Mark preferred long walks in the woods to killing defenseless animals.

She smiled at the thought of him. He was a good older brother for the precocious pre-teen she had been. She had been only twelve when he turned eighteen and went off to college. Even then she had envied him for escaping Bethlehem with such apparent ease. Mark wasn't going to end up in the Steel, nor was he going to take over Dad's construction business. By the time she'd gone off to Philly to college, Mark was already working in film production in New York. When she'd left on this trip, he'd just finished a stint as first assistant director on a feature. He had all kinds of offers, and was writing his own scripts too.

Mark had really been there for her, had believed in her. When he'd seen her off at JFK last month, he'd given her a big grin and a thumbs up, and told her she was just as good a photographer, and a much better writer, than "the famous Tom," her successful and competitive recently-ex-boyfriend. Elizabeth smiled at the memory. Mark was her best friend, closer in some ways than her girlfriends, always ready to listen patiently to her endless complaints about

Tom as she cried into Vietnamese or Ethiopian food. She'd seen him a lot when she lived in New York, and spent more than one night at Mark's place after she'd walked out on Tom "for the last time." He'd made her laugh, and never judged her for her choices.

Nor had she judged him for his. His sexual preference remained a matter of discretion in the family. Mark had tons of friends, but no long-term lover, male or female. He was a classic workaholic, far too busy to seek out intimacy, and seldom seeming to notice its absence.

He was a lot more honest than Tom, she thought, gritting her teeth. For a moment her anger flashed, and she blamed Tom's selfishness and fear of intimacy for her being in this cave under shellfire with an injured ankle that made her a hazard to herself and her companions.

No, it was her choice. A lot of people ran away to get over rotten relationships. They just didn't usually run away to war zones. She kind of wished they'd been married. At least it would have given her the dignity of claiming a nasty divorce.

An explosion brought her back to this cave in Afghanistan. She glanced at Sharif, envying the Afghan ability to sleep any place, any time. Carefully, she scooted backwards to her camera bag, which was wedged in a cleft above her.

She unwedged the bag, taking care not to awaken Sharif. He looked rather sweet, lips slightly parted, his camel cap planted firmly on his head, hands crossed over his bandoleer like a sleeping cat's paws. His snore even sounded a little like a cat's purr.

She sneaked a picture, then sighed in irritation. She should be with the Mujahedeen down in the valley taking close-up pictures as they attacked a tank convoy on the road below. But no one could be spared to look after a slow-moving journalist.

An hour ago she had been awakened from a brief sleep by the sound of a nearby helicopter and Ebrahim's urgent insistence that she move to this cave. The cave wasn't far from the Mujahedeen camp where they had arrived at dawn, but it was around a bend in the valley, and higher. Ebrahim said it was both safer and offered a better view.

She didn't know about the safety, but she had to admit it was a cave with a view. When she leaned forward she could see all the way to the mouth of the valley, where a chalky line of road was occupied by tanks that looked like locusts with singular antennae. They were not that far away, perhaps less than a mile. She could not see the Mujahedeen, but heard the sound of their guns, and saw the flash of fire and the puff of smoke whenever a tank fired towards the valley.

She attached the 300-millimeter telephoto lens to her camera and leaned forward, ignoring the pain in her ankle. With one elbow braced against the rough wall of the cave, she steeled herself for the next inevitable explosion. She shot off a couple of frames, missed the tank's firing, and cursed under her breath. That tank turned and moved on, under heavy but probably useless fire from the Mujahedeen. She hadn't noticed any shoulder-fired missiles amongst the group they had joined with at the camp.

Two more tanks passed, but before the third there was an explosion in the road as a mine ineffectually went off. The tank turned slowly, like a monster in a horror movie. This time she caught the tank as it fired, and then decided she'd had enough of perching on a rock ledge and wondering how far shells could reach.

She set the camera down and took out her notebook. She felt dazed from their all-night walk, but didn't think she could sleep. The situation had a strange unreality to it, like watching a movie on video late at night. Maybe that was why she was thinking so much of Mark, and Mom and Dad. They were something familiar to hang on to. Shit, even Tom the arrogant abuser looked good from this place.

She began to write. "April 12th, Babur Tangay. Note: *Tangay* means 'narrow valley' in Pashtu."

She paused, wondering where to begin, then plunged into describing the terrifying night walk that had brought them to this cave.

She had not expected the land to be so clearly divided between free zones and occupied zones, but there were definitive though unmarked boundaries. They had passed with quiet bravado within a kilometer of an Afghan government post manned by Soviet and Afghan soldiers, and then had to walk a long way south to find a point where they could safely cross the river.

It was clear that the night belonged to the Mujahedeen. By day the helicopter gunships flew, but at night even large groups of people could travel undetected. The Mujahedeen attacked government posts by night, and the darkness of their journey had been frequently punctuated by gunfire as small groups of men moved ghostlike through Kunar's fertile fields.

The worst part had been when they had left the safe house where they had waited for someone to find an inflated skin raft so they could cross the river. Every dog in the village had started yammering as they walked through the fields towards the river. Then two loud shots had sounded. Elizabeth shivered as she heard again the pitiful whimpering, which had soon fallen silent.

She rubbed her ankle absently. Unaccustomed to darkness and the exhaustion of long night walks, she had twisted it badly on the way to the river, falling repeatedly into unseen pits and muddy channels. She was furious at herself for her carelessness. Now these Afghans would probably think that all women were weak.

She described the raft in detail. Nothing but a few wooden poles lashed over rows of inflated cowskins came between them and the river, fed by the snowmelt of the Hindu Kush and now in the full spate of spring. She was acutely aware that she was a lone foreign woman crowded onto the raft amongst her warrior companions, and felt vulnerable as they pushed off from the dubious safety of the shore into the wide, swiftly flowing river.

The dedication of these simple villagers had moved her greatly. Her party of Mujahedeen had shown up at the safe house well past midnight, yet the lady of the house had given them tea while her husband had gone off in search of a raft.

Elizabeth sighed and tapped her pen on the page. Some villages were safe for the Mujahedeen, others were considered the province of the fundamentalists, and still others were pro-Khalqi or pro-Parchami. Why? Ebrahim said that the

Communist government offered people money to support their factions, but it couldn't be quite that simple.

Ebrahim always seemed to be afraid of spies. He warned her that a foreign woman journalist would be as great a prize for hostile fundamentalists as for the Communists. Disconcertingly, he found it necessary to walk with a grenade in his hand, but Elizabeth had decided that Ebrahim just enjoyed drama.

Certainly there were real dangers. The most frightening part of their walk had been through a stony moonlit meadow, which Ebrahim said was a minefield. He told her the path itself should be safe, as many had passed over it recently, but not to take one step off the path, for any reason.

Then this morning she had seen bright green plastic fragments in the grass by their path. They were the remains of a small anti-personnel mine in the shape of a graceful butterfly, the ones her friend Salima had told her about. She wondered whether a child had picked it up, or a goat had lost a leg, or maybe the Mujahedeen had seen it and exploded it with a stick from a safe distance. She clutched at her swollen ankle, in sudden thankfulness that she had only sprained it.

A very loud explosion sounded, and she glanced out the cave to see a white puff just down the mountain from her sanctuary. A few dislodged rocks rolled into the path and down to the river. Her heart pounded, but she forced herself to concentrate. She felt oddly detached. There was nothing she could do, nowhere she could go that was any safer than where she was.

She hoped the Mujahedeen would all come back safely. They had been so solicitous when she and her escort had arrived. There were about twenty of them at this camp, ranging in age from fourteen to seventy. Most were from Massoud's party, but a few supported other moderate leaders. Elizabeth didn't know if they argued politics, but there seemed a camaraderie between them, and they had gone off together to fight the common enemy.

The youngest boy, who didn't even have a beard yet, had baked delicious whole wheat *nan* on a griddle. The Mujahedeen had given her a choice of black or green tea, and had pressed lump after lump of raw brown sugar on her. She stopped writing and looked fondly at the man sleeping near her. Sharif had insisted that she wear his blanket when they walked. He had reassured her by joking with her. Ebrahim had seriously translated Sharif's question, "What will you do if we meet the enemy? Will you fight?" But Elizabeth had seen the smile on Sharif's lips, and had replied that she would be as likely to shoot herself or a friend as the enemy. Sharif had laughed, while Ebrahim had looked affronted.

And after she had sprained her ankle, it was Sharif who offered to carry her when they had to cross outlying branches of the river. Of course she had refused at first, but after she stumbled in the icy water she had relented and allowed him to carry her on his back. Though this had been embarrassing, she had to admit it was gallant.

A smile played on her lips as she looked at his face now. It was a good question to ask a prospective lover: "Will you carry me across dark rivers on your back, through a war zone?"

Tom wouldn't have, she thought angrily. She would have carried him to the ends of the earth, would have–and had–sacrificed anything for his happiness and success. But an oblivious or cruel Tom used to walk way ahead of her in the New York subways at night, disappearing around the bends of the tunnels. He used to lecture her on the virtues of self-sufficiency, while she'd argued vainly for the merits of mutual consideration.

She laid down her notebook and rested her chin on her knees. This semi-fetal position comforted her. Sharif was still asleep, and she suddenly felt very alone.

She again picked up her notebook and wrote: "I wish Sharif was the one who spoke English. I find myself strangely attracted to him, because of his kindness I think. Like picking me that flower, the *shin gul* (which means "blue flower" in Pashtu). Not that Sharif's not extremely good-looking as well, in that macho Afghan way. And not that I'm going to do anything about it. It would certainly be foolish in a Holy War with fundamentalists around every bend in the valley. I think he likes me, but looks on me as a sister. Maybe that's why I'm thinking of Mark so much. But I'd sure rather be with Sharif in an emergency than with Ebrahim. Sharif strikes me as cooler and calmer, the kind of person who would stop to aim. Ebrahim would fire wildly."

She started at the sound of a stone being dislodged just below, and saw Ebrahim climbing up towards her. She slipped her notebook inside her camera bag.

"*Staray mashay,*" she greeted him enthusiastically in Pashtu.

Sharif stirred and sat up, rubbing his eyes. "*Staray mashay,*" he muttered. Ebrahim crawled into the cave, and Sharif sat up to give him room. They spoke in Pashtu for awhile, then Ebrahim turned to Elizabeth.

"Did you sleep?"

"No. I've been writing. And taking a few pictures."

"Are you afraid?"

"Are we in danger?"

Ebrahim merely laughed.

"What is happening down there?"

"Good fighting. The Mujahedeen are okay. They've been fighting for three hours now. It's a big convoy."

Sharif said something to Ebrahim, who shifted to let Sharif out of the cave. Sharif smiled cheerfully, waved to her, and shinnied down the cliff.

"He's gone off to war," said Ebrahim.

An explosion echoed, and Elizabeth felt empty and scared.

"This one was close," Ebrahim remarked. "See the dust up on that side of the mountain."

"But we're in no danger," she remarked dryly.

Sarcasm didn't register with Ebrahim. She decided to pretend to sleep, and curled up on the sleeping bag. She was actually dozing off when Ebrahim shook her. Before she realized what was happening he had thrown Sharif's camel-colored blanket over her. "Parchami spies," he hissed. "Hide under the blanket, like you are a sleeping Mujaheed."

Her heart beat unbearably loud. How did he know they were Parchami spies? She hoped every part of her body was covered. She covered the camera bag for good measure. The fact that she lay under Sharif's blanket somehow comforted her. She listened as Ebrahim scrambled down to the river, and fell into conversation with the alleged spies. Their voices receded, to be replaced by the roaring of the river.

She didn't know how long she remained in that position. She was afraid to move or peek. She forgot the pain in her ankle. She heard the crunch of footsteps, the sound of someone coming nearer, climbing up to the cave. She held her breath. It must be Ebrahim coming back. Suddenly a hand grabbed her injured ankle. She shot up with a cry, and the blanket fell from her shoulders.

CHAPTER 2
AYUB

Approaching Chagaserai,
Afghanistan

Ayub Khan peered out of the thick Plexiglas helicopter window, looking down upon his ancestral homeland and following the helicopter's swift shadow as it moved along the valley floor. He savored the news of his appointment as Governor of Kunar. It was a great honor to be able to serve the homeland.

General Lermontov had dozed off in the seat beside him, but now stirred and looked down disinterestedly upon the wide, placid valley.

"I think the Central Committee has made a good choice," the Russian observed. "I am familiar with your records, and with your loyalty. But you realize that you are taking over this position at a most difficult time."

Ayub nodded seriously and adjusted the headphones that made conversation possible. He answered in Russian that closely approximated the general's well-educated Moscow accent. "Yes, but I have no doubt that I am capable of keeping the situation well under control."

"We, that is our friends in the Central Committee of the People's Democratic Party of Afghanistan, have great confidence in your abilities. Not, of course, that the bandits are winning, but they do pose a serious threat to our security, and a challenge to our efforts at pacification."

"They only need a firm hand. The revolution cannot be reversed."

"Well spoken." The Russian put a beefy hand on Ayub's shoulder, in a fatherly gesture. "Incidentally, did you enjoy your course of study in Moscow?"

"Tremendously. I had been there before, as you know, for two years while I was studying at the university for my master's degree. It was a great pleasure to see the city again, and of course some old friends."

"Old friends?"

Ayub evaded the question. "Fellow students."

"Female fellow students?" asked the Russian conspiratorially.

Ayub's face tightened. He could never quite get used to the Russian openness on these matters. Though he admired Lermontov greatly, and regarded him as his mentor and "Russian uncle," he hardly wanted to tell him about his hot and cold affair with Sonia. Anyway it was over now.

Ayub faked a smile, and craned his neck to look out the window. "What's going on down there?"

Lermontov glanced, then settled back down in his seat. "Another bandit attack, I expect. They like to harass our convoys."

Ayub continued watching the strange scene being played out far below. It looked like a silent film shot from a radical high angle. Along one edge of the valley a light scar of road ran along the foot of the mountains. A convoy of tanks was stretched out along this road, moving more slowly than the helicopter. Occasional flashes of fire spewed forth from the long slim guns of the heavy tanks, but above the roar of the chopper's blades he could hear no sounds of war.

"Can we go down lower?" Ayub asked. "I'd like to see how they do this."

"Your training was in ideology, not military tactics," the Russian replied shortly. "If you have any ideas about improving our methods, you had best leave that to those who are trained to evaluate strategy and tactics."

"I would like to observe," said Ayub firmly. "As Governor of this province, security is one of the issues that concerns me, correct?"

The line of the Russian's heavy black brows raised slightly. "I see. Correct. Well, I don't think any harm can be done by observing for awhile." Lermontov shouted orders to the pilot, who put the craft into a stationary hover.

Ayub knew he had won his first test of authority, and was pleased. He watched with the same keen powers of observation he had applied to his studies all his life. The bandits had apparently planted mines in the path of the tanks, but they always seemed to go off too soon, or too late. The heavily armored tanks were almost invincible.

So were the bandits. The tanks fired blindly, and he knew the bandits who called themselves Mujahedeen were hidden in the unfriendly rocks and ridges of the hills, just as tribal bandits had hidden in less enlightened centuries, waiting to prey on innocent travelers.

"My father was a soldier," commented Ayub. "So I grew up with stories of heroic wars against British imperialism. You might say I have a special interest in these matters."

"Where is your father now?"

"I don't know," answered Ayub evenly. "And you know that I don't know. I have been asked many times by many people."

"Strange that he should disappear so suddenly from Kabul."

"Indeed."

"Where are the rest of your family?"

"My mother and sister, I think in Pakistan. My brother is in America. I think he will sponsor them to go there as…" He stopped before he added the word "refugees."

Lermontov nodded. "Most of the bourgeois and petty bourgeois classes have fled to the capitalist countries."

"Their hearts have always secretly longed to be there," said Ayub cynically. He thought of his own brother, the doctor, who had only come back to Kabul twice since he had gone away to school in California in the late 60's. Ayub had still been a child then, though a precocious one, and had looked on his elder brother as someone who could do no wrong. Gradually, though, as Yusuf became more estranged from his family and from Afghanistan, Ayub too had become disillusioned with family ties.

Lermontov smiled at the young man beside him. "But your heart will always be an Afghan heart, and a socialist heart."

Ayub relaxed and enjoyed the Russian's verbal stroking. Far below, three helicopter gunships had caught up with them and were circling above the hills, occasionally firing their machine guns, or firing a rocket at one of the small mud brick houses in a village near the scene of the attack.

"Can we go down lower?" asked Ayub again. "I would really like to see better."

Lermontov sat back in his chair and burped. "It is really not advisable."

Ayub assented, reasonably. He smiled charmingly. "I will leave the military matters up to you. Thank you for staying here for this long so I could see. We should proceed to Chagaserai. I am eager to meet my staff."

Lermontov ordered the pilot on to the provincial capital. As they passed high over a ridge, a streak of fire curved over the green-tinted hills below them, and impotently dived to its own destruction.

"Was that aimed at us?" asked Ayub in surprise.

"We are perfectly safe," answered the Russian. "No matter if it were aimed at us or at the heroic soldiers and pilots in those ships below us. We have the power of the skies, and the bandits do not have the weapons to fight us in the air. The Americans will never risk relations with Moscow by giving missiles to a disunited rabble led by fanatics and terrorists. Don't worry."

Ayub laughed at the impotence of the well-hidden bandits far below him, but he felt sad to think of the ignorant tribesmen who were resisting the benefits of the revolution. It was unfortunate that sometimes villages needed to be destroyed in the process of pacification, but the villagers had to learn not to give refuge to criminal elements, even if it were claimed under the ancient Pashtun code of asylum. Education, thought Ayub, that's what they need. A little education, and they will be pleased to give up backward superstitions and substandard ways of living, in return for the benefits of a strong economy in an industrialized socialist society.

"Governor. Governor Ayub."

Ayub became aware that Lermontov had used his title for the first time. He turned to the general and smiled.

"Do you like the sound of your new title then?"

"Very much, General."

"We knew you would. Governor, there is one matter I must discuss with you. We have information that a new bandit chieftain plans disruption in Kunar. Commander Rahimullah Khan. Have you heard of him?"

Ayub thought. "Rahimullah Khan," he repeated slowly. He shook his head. "He is not one of the hereditary chiefs."

"We must build an intelligence file on him. You must find out all you can. We have a network of patriotic citizens who were of assistance to your predecessor. We will put you in contact with them. And I will be here much of the time, for your assistance. Do not hesitate to call on me at any time."

"Thank you. That's very kind of you. I'm sure we will be in close contact."

"Ah, there is Chagaserai now." Lermontov drummed his fingers nervously on the arm of his seat, as the helicopter and its escort of two other transport copters lowered towards the landing field.

Ayub ran his fingers through his moustache, took up the silver karakul cap from his lap, and adjusted it on his head. He had long affected this cap, a sign of high status in Afghan society, but now he really knew he deserved it. He smiled to himself and zipped up his leather jacket against the chill spring breeze.

"I hope you do better than your predecessor," remarked Lermontov, as if thinking aloud. The general sat up straight, adjusted his hat, and brushed off a speck of dust which had settled on one of the medals he wore on his chest.

Ayub raised his eyebrows quizzically. "Governor Safiullah? Wasn't he transferred to Farah?"

Lermontov cleared his throat. "He met with an unfortunate accident upon the way. But then, he had not had much success in subduing criminal elements."

The helicopter touched the ground, and its rotors kicked up a cloud of dust. The motor shut off and the rotors slowed to a stop. Ayub looked out the window and saw a line of Afghan Army soldiers standing at attention while several official-looking men in Western-style business suits stood waiting to greet their new boss.

Lermontov put a protective hand on Ayub's shoulder. "Trust no one," he said, smiling. "Governor Safiullah spoke far too much, to all the wrong people. Trust no one, and you will be a credit to your homeland, and to the great tradition of socialism."

CHAPTER 3

ELIZABETH

Babur Tangay,
Afghanistan

For a moment the surprised Afghan man stared at the terrified woman. The man Elizabeth saw was a rough-looking character, even by the standards of the Mujahedeen. A couple of weeks' growth of heavy beard made his face swarthy, and disheveled black curls peeked from beneath a rolled cap worn tilted at a careless angle. Across his chest was a bandoleer, which made him look even more warlike. His dark eyes cut through her like a laser, but she noticed a faint trace of amusement in them. She hoped she hadn't been discovered by a spy.

"*Staray mashay,*" she said uncertainly.

He nodded, and heaved himself up into the cave. "*Staray mashay.*"

Elizabeth backed against the rock wall, involuntarily gasping at the pain as she moved and instinctively reaching for her injured ankle.

"Shall I take a look at that ankle?" A perfect American accent.

"Wait a minute! Are you American?"

"No."

"You're not Afghan."

Surprise accentuated the arch of his dark eyebrows. "But I am Afghan. Don't I look Afghan?"

"Yes, you look Afghan. But so does everybody else. Your sure don't sound Afghan."

He said something in what she thought was Pashtu, followed by something in what she recognized as Farsi. "Now do you believe me?"

"You could be a Russian for all I know. Speaking the language doesn't prove anything."

"You Americans are such skeptics. I'm sorry I don't have a business card on me."

He extended his hand. "Then let me introduce myself formally. Dr. Yusuf Hakim, M.D., College of Physicians and Surgeons, Columbia University, New York. You can call me Yusuf if you want, or if you prefer to be more formal, Dr. Yusuf. That's what the people here usually call me.

"I was last seen working at UC San Francisco Medical Center, but I was born in Kabul, so I think I qualify as an Afghan."

She shook his hand feebly. "I think I've heard of you. But no one told me you'd studied in America. I've never met an Afghan with such a perfect American accent. You ought to work for the State Department."

"How do you know I don't?"

Again caught off guard. "Do you?"

He shot her a look of injured annoyance. "I work for myself, and for my people."

"Only joking." His face reminded her of an insulted cat. She almost laughed, and realized he hadn't yet let go of her hand.

"Who are you, by the way, and what's a nice girl like you doing in a war like this?"

"Elizabeth Owen, free lance journalist and photographer." She wished she could say she was on assignment for some prestigious publication. "I work through an agency. They sell to *Time* and *Newsweek*, as well as international news magazines around the world."

He squeezed her hand, and let it go. "Nice to meet you, Elizabeth. You didn't say it was nice to meet me."

Typical cool San Francisco. His smooth manner belied his rough appearance.

"Actually, I've come to interview you. All the way to Kunar."

He ran a hand over his stubbly chin. "I hope you'll let me shave first. My agent didn't tell me there was a journalist coming."

"Oh, I'll be here for awhile," she said, pointing to her ankle. "By the way, I thought you were either a Mujaheed or a spy. Are you?"

"Which, a Mujaheed or a spy?" He laughed, showing a fine set of teeth which contrasted with his beard. "I thought *you* were a sleeping Mujaheed. Imagine my surprise at seeing the face of a terrified woman. I thought you were Afghan at first, even after you spoke."

"Really?" Terrified woman indeed! "It's been a trying day." As if to confirm this, another explosion sounded nearby.

Dr. Yusuf leaned forward out of the cave. "Oh, that one was rather near."

He took off his hat and hit it against his palm to shake off the dust, then replaced it on his head. He settled back into the cave and gestured at her. "Let's see that ankle."

He placed his large hands on her ankle. The fingers were long, the touch firm yet gentle. The backs of his hands, she noted, were neither too smooth, nor too hairy.

She bent over, closely examining his every move. He looked up at her, amused. "I really am a doctor."

"I don't doubt that."

"I would say this was recent. Last night? How did it happen?"

"Repeatedly falling into irrigation channels, and hidden pits in the dark. I'm not as sure-footed as an Afghan."

He probed gently, manipulated her foot, then pressed two fingers hard on her ankle. She gasped, but didn't cry out. She leaned back slightly, gritting her teeth and trying not to think of the pain.

"Elizabeth. What are you doing in a *sangar* by yourself? You didn't get to Kunar by yourself."

"The Mujahedeen are all attacking the tank convoy down on the road." She flinched at the sound of another explosion. "I guess the battle is still going on. Abdul Sharif stayed with me for awhile, then Ebrahim came back, and Sharif went. Do you know them?"

His hand stopped its massage for a moment. He looked up at her. "Ebrahim and Sharif. Yes. My father owned land in their village. Narang. It's not far from here."

He continued the massage, working up the calf and shin with one hand while supporting her foot with the other. Surprisingly, it seemed to be helping. "Is this what they teach at Columbia these days?" she asked.

"No, it's what I learned in Afghanistan from my uncle when I was a teenager. Mixed with a little acupressure picked up in San Francisco."

"I suppose San Francisco's the place for it."

"Why don't you tell me more about how you came to be here alone?"

"About half an hour ago, Ebrahim said there were Parchami spies around, and I should hide under the blanket. He must have gone off with them. Eventually you came. You scared the hell, uh, you scared me to death. I thought you were a spy."

"Lucky you didn't have a gun."

"Lucky for you I didn't."

He had stopped his massage, and was rummaging in the cloth bag he had been carrying over his shoulder. He produced a tube of analgesic balm and gently rubbed some into the skin of her swollen ankle.

"I'm sure I can learn to do that myself," she said. "Anyway, you still haven't told me how an Afghan-born doctor trained at Columbia and living in San Francisco ends up in the middle of Kunar. In other words, what are you doing here?"

"What do you think I'm doing here? Taking my annual two-week vacation?

But you already know more about me than I do about you. I don't even know where you're from."

"I'm the journalist. Who's interviewing whom? You first."

He patted her ankle and sat back against the rock wall opposite her. He looked at her appraisingly, one eyebrow raised slightly. "Promise you'll tell me your story afterwards? Can't have this all one-sided."

She nodded impatiently.

He looked out of the cave as if studying the mountains, or waiting for other shells to fall. "I was working in San Francisco. There was a war in Afghanistan. I had the money, so I decided to come back here. Pretty place, don't you think?"

He was too glib. She studied him. Despite the scruffy beard, or perhaps because of it, he had an attractive profile, with clearly chiseled features, a long nose, high cheekbones, and a strong chin. Definitely photogenic.

"There's got to be more to it than that."

"Oh yes, there always is. But we Afghans don't tell our entire life story on first meeting. Especially not to a journalist. That's one habit I didn't pick up in America."

"How long were you in America?"

He looked back at her, one side of his lip curling laconically. "That's not a fair question. Maybe *you* ought to work for the State Department. You've broken our agreement. But I'll give you one free question. I was eighteen when I went to college in America. UC Berkeley in the late sixties. An Afghan teenager in Berkeley. I'm thirty-five now. I think you can work it out."

Eighteen years in America. A lot must have happened between eighteen and thirty-five. "There's got to be more to it than that," she pressed.

"Of course, Miss Elizabeth. I take it it's Miss. Or do you prefer Ms?"

"Ms. to you."

"I thought so. Why don't you tell me at least a little about yourself? Let's start with where you're from."

"I was born in Bethlehem, Pennsylvania. Steel Town, U.S.A., and one of the first places to be hit by any recession. They say it's a dying town now. But we have more churches per capita than any other community in the U.S. That's where all the people laid off during the recessions are supposed to go.

"My mom and dad still live there. I have one brother, six years older than me, and he lives in New York. That's where I was living until…" She didn't want to tell him about Tom. "Until I came here."

He sat back against the wall, and dug in his pocket for a package of cheap Pakistani cigarettes. He offered her one, which she refused, then lit one himself, slowly, deliberately drawing on the first puff.

"It's always doctors who smoke."

"We feel we're immune. Besides which, the war may get me first."

She watched him blow out smoke, first in a stream, then in precisely-formed rings. His face was now pensive and quiet, and he watched the smoke rings with relaxed curiosity. She still could not reconcile his appearance with his conversation.

The valley was growing chilly as the sun's rays receded. There hadn't been any explosions for a long time. "What's happened to the Mujahedeen?" she asked nervously. "I hope they're all right. You're a doctor. Shouldn't you go and see?"

He blew out another stream of smoke, but didn't look at her. "I don't feel I should leave you alone. Especially if there might be Parchamis around."

"I'll be all right." Now she was really getting worried. What if somebody was wounded? "I can hide under the blanket. I really don't mind. Somebody might need you."

He crushed out the cigarette on the rock wall, and flung the butt out of the cave. He looked at her seriously, and she noticed the pronounced lines in his high forehead, and the hint of silver in his hair. A strangely noble face, she thought. Though she wouldn't dare describe it that way in print.

"They'd love to catch an American journalist," he said bluntly.

"But it's not likely, is it? Not at this time of day. Please go."

He gathered up his bag, and lowered himself down the cliff. "Don't go anywhere," he said casually. "I'll see you later. *Inshallah*. I owe you an interview.

"Oh, and about that ankle, I don't think it's a true sprain. You really shouldn't walk on it, but I don't suppose that can be helped. Just keep applying that balm. *Khoda hafez.*"

"Pashtu?"

"Farsi." He looked up at her. "You'll learn. It means 'goodbye.' Literally, 'God be your protector.'"

CHAPTER 4
ELIZABETH

Early April, 1984

Peshawar, Pakistan

Only two weeks before, and a world away, Elizabeth had been in the home of Massoud Khan, the famous leader of the Afghan Resistance, inquiring about accompanying a party of Massoud's Mujahedeen into the war zone of Afghanistan's Kunar Valley. She had eagerly leaned forward, pointed chin cupped in thin white hands, sharp elbows resting on jeans-clad knees, as she listened as if her life depended on it.

The sounds coming from the shiny Sony boom box were sounds no boom box should emit. A sustained low-pitched roar grew louder, closer, then gave way to the sounds of automatic rifle fire, and shouts in a language Elizabeth did not understand.

The group of men on the other side of the low table clustered tensely around the tape player. A long-faced, somber man with a bushy black beard and an over-sized white turban spoke into a microphone held by Dr. Nasir. Elizabeth winced slightly at a burst of particularly loud fire. "Mujahedeen," the man said stoically. The freedom fighters. More distant fire. A word Elizabeth didn't know, but supposed meant "the Russians." The sound of jets, muffled explosions, then what could only be a chopper's blades. The turbaned man grinned and gestured as if holding a rocket launcher. The sound of the chopper stopped, and was replaced by something unidentifiable and infinitely more terrifying. The tape ended and the machine clicked off.

Elizabeth wondered with horrified fascination what she was getting into. A chill stirred the knotted pit of her stomach. Did she really want to get that close to the action? These guys were fighters, and she was just a journalist who hoped to bring back a good story and some great pictures. Maybe better to hole up in a safe place with a 300-millimeter lens.

The small group of men had broken into an animated conversation. Elizabeth looked expectantly at Dr. Nasir, her only link with the English language. Brow furrowed, he peered at the young freedom fighter who was telling a story, and occasionally nodded. Elizabeth thought how old Dr. Nasir looked, much older than when she had interviewed him and Massoud Khan in New York last year. And how gaunt, though he still appeared dignified and distinguished.

Dr. Nasir sighed, set lips curling into a thin smile. "Kandahar," he said. "My clinic was near there. These Mujahedeen have come from there, just yesterday. There was lots of fighting while I was there. Now it is worse. They say sixty Mujahedeen were martyred, and a number of women and children as well, in the bombing." Dr. Nasir looked at her directly, unflinching.

"It seems every day you get news like this."

The doctor brightened. "But not all bad. They did shoot down a helicopter, and some Afghan Army forces surrendered. The POW's are still across the border."

Elizabeth nodded. She had never been near a war before, and it all seemed a little incomprehensible, especially listening to a tape in the safety of the Pakistani border town of Peshawar.

"What was that about?" she asked, nodding towards the handsome young Mujaheed. "Was he telling a story?"

"Yes, a most unbelievable story." Dr. Nasir hesitated again, then smiled. "Perhaps you will not believe it. But I think it may be true."

"Tell me."

"This man says that during the battle a small bird, I do not know the name in English, landed on his hand. The bird looked at him in the eye, to see if the Mujahedeen wanted to harm him. The man looked back at the bird, and when the bird saw no harm was intended, he hid here, beneath the crook of his arm."

Elizabeth repressed a smile. This sweet story brought out an innocent side of these rough fighters, even if it was made up.

The doctor continued. "When the Mujahedeen left to go back to their *sangar*, their stronghold, the bird followed, flying after them. But it was hit by a Russian bullet."

Elizabeth's smile faded. Cute stories were not supposed to end this way. But villagers were not supposed to be bombed either, and farmers, merchants, and students were not supposed to take up Kalashnikov rifles and go off into the hills to fight.

"So you see, even the most innocent are being killed in this war," concluded Dr. Nasir.

Elizabeth said nothing. She had known it would be this way, but knowing from friends in New York who had gone "inside" to take pictures, or from Massoud Khan's press conferences in the States, was quite different from being so near the war.

Dr. Nasir had turned back to the small band of Mujahedeen. He was playing back the tape he had recorded, with the black-bearded man's commentary now laid over the roar and rumble of war. A servant, a thin country boy, poured scented tea into the glasses on the table, and offered a plate of toffees to the guests. Elizabeth absently took one, and watched the doctor.

He was indeed distinguished, she reflected. Tall, thin, elegant, the slightest trace of an accent. Pale skin, deep-set black eyes, jet black hair blending to silver on the sides. She could easily imagine him in Paris in an Armani suit. He had in fact trained in France, spoke fluent French, and could probably have had a lucrative private practice had he remained in Paris. But he had gone back to Afghanistan, and had lived in Kabul, supplementing his private practice with volunteer work in rural villages, and making his services available to the poor people of the capital's Old Town. She imagined he had lived well in Kabul, but at least he had remained Afghan, unlike some of the highly Westernized professionals she had met at Massoud Khan's talks in New York and D.C.

Dr. Nasir worked harder than any of the other doctors she'd met. President of the Afghan Medical Association, and chief of surgery of a small but busy Mujahedeen-run hospital in Peshawar, he still found time to set up clinics inside Afghanistan, in areas "liberated" from Soviet control by the Mujahedeen. She admired him for the risks he took. He didn't stay safely behind the lines at his clinic, but accompanied the freedom fighters to the front. He hadn't told her this, but she'd heard it from others, many others.

Strangely enough, in a gossip-ridden and factionalized city like Peshawar, no one seemed to have anything bad to say about Dr. Nasir. He maintained good relations with all the feuding Afghan political parties, from the moderate Islamic nationalists to the extreme fundamentalists. She wondered how he managed to stay above politics in such an essentially political city.

Elizabeth sipped her tea, which had cooled down slightly. Pleasant tea, not too strong. One could drink it all day, and often did. It had a faint aroma of cardamom, which reminded her of Danish pastries.

Dr. Nasir and the Mujahedeen were still occupied, so she studied the room about her. Massoud Khan's home gave a first impression of opulence. The terrazzo floor was covered with thick red Bukhara carpets, a color TV sat on a low table in the corner, and two large speakers, normally hooked up to the boom box, sat at opposite ends of the room.

But when Elizabeth looked more closely, she could see that everything was a little run down. The gold cushions of the couch and chairs were slightly stained and worn, the carpets were not of the fine quality that someone like Massoud would have had in Kabul and the tables and TV were scratched. Still,

Massoud and his family lived better than three million refugees in tents and mudbrick.

Dr. Nasir and the Mujahedeen stood up, and Elizabeth, realizing belatedly that Massoud Khan had entered the room, stood hastily, spilling her tea. The five Mujahedeen rushed to kiss Massoud's hand, and he greeted his men warmly, embraced Dr. Nasir, then turned to Elizabeth.

He offered his hand in Western fashion. "I'm sorry I'm so late. We had an emergency at the office. Please sit down."

"Please don't worry. I know you're busy. We've just been listening to a tape of the war in Kandahar."

Massoud Khan's face suddenly looked drawn. He too had aged since New York, she thought with a pang of sympathy. He was perhaps in his mid-thirties, but already had traces of frost in his black hair and well-sculpted beard. He'd obviously been out in the sun a lot, as his fair skin was burnt dark, and his expressive eyes nested in a fine network of lines

The young leader had a commanding presence, yet there was something entirely ingenuous in his manner. She didn't remember him joking much in New York, but he had been much more relaxed in America. Now he frequently rubbed the furrowed expanse of his forehead as if he had a headache.

The Mujahedeen and Dr. Nasir waited expectantly. At last Massoud spoke. Elizabeth couldn't tell which of Afghanistan's two major languages he spoke, Persian or Pashtu, so she merely observed the intent faces of the Mujahedeen. And old man in a blue-gray turban. Leathery skin, sharp eyes and nose, a long silky white beard. A dark and beautiful youth with a thin new moustache, his delicate features like a face in a Persian miniature. A quiet, middle-aged man with mournful light brown eyes, wearing a pink and gold embroidered pillbox hat, inset with tiny mirrors, over his close-cropped hair.

It was strange to see Massoud in Afghan dress. At the conferences in the States he had worn a dark gray suit. When she had interviewed him at his brother's apartment, he had worn casually elegant slacks and a cashmere sweater. Now he was dressed all in white, a well cut knee-length shirt over loose trousers, and a short vest over the shirt. It suited him, made him look more tragic and lost at the same time. Black eyebrows arched over sad eyes, which seemed to contain all the sorrow and hope of thousands of years of victories and defeats, the history of a nation.

Massoud and the others stood up, so she also stood, uncertainly. Massoud motioned her to sit down. "I will be right back, and we will talk about your trip. You must stay to dinner tonight also. It is already late."

He and Dr. Nasir followed the men outside. Elizabeth couldn't remember the word for "goodbye," so merely smiled.

Massoud Khan and the doctor returned and resumed their former places. Massoud called for a servant, said something about *chai*, which Elizabeth recognized as the next inevitable round of tea, and sat back in his chair. A few years fell from his face, and he looked more like the man she had photographed in New York a year ago.

"So, Elizabeth, it's been a long time. How are you? And how is Tom?"

Elizabeth flushed at the mention of her ex-boyfriend. "I'm fine. We're, uh, not together anymore." Massoud was probably thinking of the instability and brevity of Western relationships, especially those unsanctioned by marriage.

But Massoud looked concerned. "I'm very sorry. Are you all right?"

"Yes," she assured him quickly. "And so is Tom. His career is going very well," she added in what she hoped was a neutral tone. Damn bastard hadn't missed a beat, was off to Nicaragua the day after she moved out, and then the Thai border for three weeks, shooting pictures for *Time*.

"And your career?"

"Not bad." Not as good as Tom's, but that was a matter of her being less aggressive. She gritted her teeth at the memory of how she had submerged her career, if not her whole personality, in his for the past five years. She was glad she'd finally gotten up the courage to leave. And yet she still missed the bastard. Go figure.

"Thank you for sending the pictures, and the copy of the interview," Massoud was saying. "You write well."

"I'm really glad it got published. Being freelance isn't always easy." Unless you're Tom Dunne.

"Are you working for anyone now?"

"I'm working through a photo agency, and a news agency is interested in syndicating some of my stories. Unfortunately, neither of them were willing to advance any money, so I'm on my own."

Massoud Khan regarded her with an expression she could not quite read. "What do you hope to accomplish by going inside Afghanistan?"

Elizabeth was taken aback. She sat up straighter, feeling like a child being asked, "What do you want to be when you grow up?"

"Well, first of all, I want to see the situation for myself," she said carefully. "I only know what I know from you."

She couldn't bring herself to tell him that part of it was that she just wanted to get away from New York and from the agony of her breakup with Tom. Against the backdrop of the suffering of the Afghan people, her desire to escape to Asia, gambling her savings that the trip would pay off professionally and financially, seemed petty and self-indulgent.

"Lots of reasons. For one, you invited me"

"We invite everyone who has an interest."

"You sound like a travel agency. Adventure tours inside Afghanistan with the freedom fighters." She immediately realized that her attempt at humor had fallen flat. "Massoud, I'm sorry. I don't mean to make a joke of it. I came because you and Dr. Nasir have made me care about your people. I want to see the way the war is affecting the life of the Mujahedeen, and the ordinary people too. I want to tell the world the truth about it, whatever that is." She wondered whether she sounded more insincere, or more pretentious. Maybe Massoud would respect her more if she just said, "I'm a journalist, and I'm here to do a job."

Massoud looked at her keenly, but noncommitedly. "Very few women have gone inside. It is a rough journey, and dangerous. Some also find our customs very difficult."

She met his gaze evenly. "I can handle it." *I hope.*

Massoud held her gaze for a moment, then nodded. "Okay. I'll be happy to arrange your trip for you, if you wish. Do you have any idea where you want to go?"

"Where can I go?"

"Anywhere you wish. We control some 80% of the country, more at night. We can even get you into Kabul city."

Elizabeth looked skeptical.

Massoud's eyebrows raised ever so slightly. "We've got a tour leaving for Mazare Sharif next week, two hundred Mujahedeen, all expenses paid. That one is a minimum one month though." A smile had begun to show through Massoud's beard.

"I don't know if I'm in any condition for a month of walking. I was thinking of Kunar Province. It's close, and Dr. Nasir says the Afghan Medical Association has a clinic there. I thought that might be a good place to start."

Massoud Khan looked questioningly at Dr. Nasir, who nodded. "Deh Wagal. Dr. Yusuf Hakim."

"Ah, yes. I should think that can be arranged."

"How far is it?"

"Deh Wagal? Only a few days. How long do you want to go in for?"

"As long as I need to do the story."

Massoud nodded. "We would be able to get you out quickly if anything happened. It's near enough to the border."

She hesitated. "What about payment? I mean, do you need some money in advance, for guides and things?"

Massoud waved his hand. "Not from you. If you were working for a big magazine, we would ask some payment in advance. After all, it is expensive to feed so many people, and some risk to our men to take care of people who don't know their way around a war zone. But you are one person, and you are our guest. Please, don't worry."

Elizabeth looked doubtful, and resolved to give whatever she could to help Massoud's fighters. "Thank you. One more question." She tried to sound nonchalant. "Will it be very dangerous there?"

"Not very, I shouldn't think. There is always a lot of fighting in Kunar, but it changes from day to day. There has been fighting in Kunar since even before the Soviet invasion. It was one of the first places to declare *jehad*, and the Kunaris are proud of this.

"The Mujahedeen of Kunar will know the current situation, and can advise you. Although one can never be certain. We say it is *naseeb*, *qismet*, fate, the will of Allah."

"I know. *Inshallah*, if Allah wills it."

"That is the only reason we keep fighting," he said tiredly. "Faith that Allah will one day decree our freedom. But you will see that for yourself, decide why hungry people keep fighting, and decide..." He paused, and looked at her with a trace of irony. "You can decide if you think our friends, the freedom-loving nations, are arming us well enough. And also whether they are arming the right people, the ones who will respect democracy and human rights and women's rights, or the wrong people, like the fundamentalist hypocrites who disguise their abhorrence for freedom in religious garb."

Elizabeth was surprised at the bitterness in Massoud's voice. "I have no power to influence American policy, no matter what I decide," she said quietly.

He sighed. "How well we know that. And how little power I had myself, even talking to the Congress in Washington." He stared beyond her for a moment, then fixed his eyes on her. "Tell me, Elizabeth, are you afraid?"

She wanted to say no, jauntily, but the word stuck in her throat. "I've never been in a war before. How do I know?"

"A good answer. But Elizabeth, everyone is afraid. I am afraid, Dr. Nasir is afraid, and those five Mujahedeen who were here are afraid."

"They didn't look afraid."

"No, that's part of our culture, not to show fear or weakness. I think you call it 'macho,' don't you? But I assure you, we're only human. We're called courageous, but perhaps we're just more willing to do what we are afraid to do. You see, we don't feel as if we have been given a choice. It's true we believe that if we die in this *jehad*, this Holy War, we will go to Paradise. So we are not afraid of death. But we *are* afraid of dying, and of pain, and of leaving wives and children and mothers behind, alone. Most of us are neither the religious fanatics nor the faultless heroes that some of you people have tried to depict."

"I..." she protested.

"No, not you. But enough others. I want you to understand before you go. Tell me, Elizabeth, do you write poetry?"

"Oh, not seriously. I've never even tried to publish." But how she had dreamed in high school, even in college, of publishing books of poetry, short stories, novels. She thought of the locked drawer in her old room at home, now filled with the flotsam and jetsam of five years with Tom. No poems in the *New Yorker* or *American Poetry Review*. She had been sensible, had studied journalism, had taken an internship, and one thing had led to another. The other, unlocked drawer of the filing cabinet was filled with published clippings, first of Knights of Columbus dinners, in the *Parish News*. Then local swimming meets, campus politics, and human interest stories about housewives who had helped police solve hit and run cases by looking out their windows at the right time. Finally there were pictures of mayors, senators, even the current president. And some interviews of Massoud Khan. Journalism had achieved its purpose and had gotten her out of the confining embrace of her mother's house, and the small town, small-thinking pettiness of Bethlehem, Pennsylvania.

"I thought you might write poetry," said Massoud after a pause. "You have the eye and tongue of a poet. It takes an Afghan to know a poet. Professor Dupree, who lived amongst us for so many years, wrote in his book that 'Afghanistan is fundamentally a nation of poets.'"

"Yes, but poetry doesn't pay the bills."

"That does not matter so much, as that a person with a poet's eye should come to our country. You will care enough to write the truth."

"Certainly I will try."

"So, to the details of your trip. It can easily be arranged. I have many men in Kunar, and they have good cooperation and coordination with the other parties. When do you want to leave?"

"As soon as possible."

"It make take a little time to find someone who speaks English."

"That doesn't matter," she said quickly, hoping she sounded brave. "I'm sure I can manage."

"Good, we'll see who we can find. Meanwhile, I hope you will both stay for dinner. I would like you to meet my wife."

Massoud rose and drew the red curtain that hung at one end of the room. Elizabeth was assailed by rich aromas from dishes displayed on a dining room table. "Please," Massoud gestured. He seated Elizabeth, then seated himself at the head of the table. "Have you ever had Afghan food before?"

"Only once, with you and Dr. Nasir and your brother in the Afghan restaurant in New York. But it was hardly like this." She gazed at the array of dishes: browned rice with raisins and nuts, platters of white rice, bowls of meat, potatoes and vegetables, and a pitcher of what she recognized as *doorgh*, a delicious cooling drink made of yogurt mixed with water and dried mint.

He laughed. "You won't be eating like this in Afghanistan, so I thought I would fatten you with a few good meals before you go. Tonight you are our special guest. My wife cooked all this for you. Ah, here she is."

A striking woman entered the room from a door at the back, carrying a platter of oranges and bananas, which she set down on the table. She smiled graciously and extended her hand.

"*Salaam aleikum*," Elizabeth greeted her politely.

"*Wa, aleikum salaam.* I am delighted to meet you at last."

Comprehension was slowly dawning. Massoud Khan's wife looked uncannily like Elizabeth. The same pointed face and slightly Roman nose, the same pale skin and wide almond-shaped eyes fringed with black lashes and framed by arched eyebrows. She also had similar black curly hair, which in

Elizabeth was the mark of Italian blood. Only their mouths were different, the Afghan woman's full and wide, while Elizabeth's was thin and petite.

"My wife, Salima."

"I've heard a lot about you," said Elizabeth. "But I didn't know..."

"Didn't know you looked Afghan?" finished Massoud.

"It was Massoud who told me he had met a ravishing American journalist who looked like me," said Salima.

"I suppose looking like an Afghan may come in handy," murmured Elizabeth embarrassedly. Suddenly she understood the occasional strange glances Massoud had given her. She was glad to learn that her resemblance to his wife was the reason. She hadn't wanted to think that this pure and upright Mujahedeen leader might be planning to proposition her.

Massoud, Dr. Nasir, and Salima all burst into laughter, and Salima put her arm around Elizabeth's shoulders and squeezed her affectionately. "You're very sweet. I can't help liking someone who looks so much like me. You must stay with us until you go. We have plenty of room. Move your things here tomorrow."

"Yes, please do," said Massoud. "It will be safer for you, and easier for you to leave when we have everything arranged."

CHAPTER 5

ELIZABETH

Peshawar

S till in Peshawar. Apparently everything was taking longer to arrange than Massoud had anticipated.

Elizabeth had been staying at Massoud's house for five days now, and had come to know him and Salima quite well. Though their lives were so different, Elizabeth found that she and Salima had more in common than similarity of appearance. They were close in age, though Elizabeth at nearly thirty had never been married, and Salima at twenty-eight had been married for eleven years. Salima, Elizabeth discovered, had a wicked sense of humor and loved to tease. She seemed to look at life, as Elizabeth did, with a mixture of compassion and acid sarcasm.

Elizabeth found a sympathetic sister in Salima, and told her in detail about the relationship with Tom, all five years of it. Salima wasn't judgmental, and for this Elizabeth was grateful. In retrospect, she had a lot to be judged for. The first year had been good, but the other four had been years of self-effacement bordering on abuse. She didn't know how she could have missed it. She supposed her Catholic upbringing had been stronger than she had thought. If you loved a man, even if you weren't married to him, you stuck with him forever. Tom hadn't been the first, but there hadn't been many others. A few guys in college, a couple of one-time sexual experiences with close friends afterwards. She'd never been promiscuous. Nonetheless, she avoided mentioning the others to Salima. Though love seemed to justify a lot in Salima's eyes, there might be a limit to her tolerance.

As Elizabeth recounted how she had helped Tom establish his career by sacrificing her own, she grew more and more angry. She bitterly remembered all the times she had stayed up late printing pictures for Tom when he was away, before he had an agent, and how she had neglected her own work to make the rounds of New York editors on his behalf. And how Tom's appreciation grew less and less, until she had been taken for granted. True, Tom had claimed to be a liberated male, and had made an effort to wash dishes, help clean, and even cook a meal occasionally. But he had expected her to be a superwoman, available whenever he wanted. Over and over, he had repeated, "We have a mature relationship. We see each other when we want to." Which translated into when *he* wanted to.

Elizabeth was often on the edge of tears as she talked to Salima, but she never let herself go entirely. The break was too new, and though it had been a clean one, it was still more painful than she had realized. Salima seemed to sense her discomfiture, and never pressed. Whenever Elizabeth fell into brooding, angry silence, Salima shared her own experiences, which were, admittedly, limited.

When she spoke of Massoud, Salima became giggly like a teenager. After eleven years of marriage, Salima was still deeply in love with her husband.

"We knew each other as children," she reminisced. "We played together until we got too old, and boys and girls were not supposed to play together anymore. Then he was in high school, a brilliant student, also a football player, the game you call soccer. But he was always very serious.

"We didn't see each other very much for a few years. His family went to Jalalabad, to their land, for holidays, and my family was mostly abroad, as my father was a diplomat in India.

"When we finally came back to Afghanistan, I was sixteen and Massoud was twenty-two, and in university in England. His family had a party for my family, to welcome us home. Massoud was on holiday then, and was in Afghanistan. He had always been good-looking, but when I saw him at that party, I couldn't believe how handsome he had become. He was studying political science and economics then, and had big plans to develop Afghanistan. He might have gone into the foreign service, or worked for the UN or the USAID in a development project."

Salima had fallen silent, her soft gaze drifting off to what might have been. "But that was not in our fate. I am only grateful to God that He gave me such a good and loving husband, who also loves his country so much. *Nam-e-khoda*, we say, that means 'in the name of God,' we are lucky for such good fortune. Only," she hesitated, "I pray to God we may one day yet have children. Eleven years, and we have tried. My husband is very patient."

Salima looked up, tears brimming over her dark lashes. "Massoud is gone so much now, to the front, or to Europe or America for conferences. Even when he is here, he leaves early and comes late, and then is always so tired he falls asleep before I can even talk to him."

Elizabeth hugged her friend. "When the war is over, and Massoud has more time to be with you, maybe then you'll have a baby."

Salima sat up straight and quickly brushed the tears off her cheeks. "*Inshallah*. We Afghans live on hope. Perhaps you are right. In all the years we have been married, Massoud and I have had little time together. At first he still spent most of the year in England at university, and I was in Afghanistan. Then we have been in exile."

"How long have you been in exile?"

"Since just after the first Communist coup, when Taraki took power in April, 1978. We had to come walking for two weeks, through the mountains. At least there was not fighting then, but the order had gone out to arrest Massoud's whole family. If we had been discovered, they would have killed us then. Massoud wore an old turban and ragged clothes. I wore a borrowed *chadari*, the kind that covers from head to toe."

"You are very brave."

Salima had smiled at this. "Life does not leave us much choice."

Now Elizabeth was in her room, reflecting on that conversation. She examined the two sets of clothes provided by Salima, and wondered if she would be warm enough, if there would still be snow this late in April, if there would be rain and mud, and how she would be able to walk wearing the awkward baggy clothes. Impulsively, she tried the Afghan clothes on over her jeans and plaid shirt.

There was a knock at the door. "Who is it?" she asked, startled.

"Salima. May I come in?"

Elizabeth was embarrassed. "Sure."

"You look wonderful! These clothes suit you."

"I like the colors," Elizabeth admitted. She was wearing an enormously wide pair of purple pants, topped by a loose pink and green floral print shirt that fell to her knees. She'd wrapped the black cotton shawl over her head and around her shoulders so that it covered her to the hips. "Did I wrap the *chadar* right?"

Salima surveyed her. "Yes, here, just hold it up like this, over your nose. And you must wear some *surmah*."

"What's that?"

Salima gestured gracefully. "Black. For the eyes. I'll get a bottle for you."

Salima returned with a small glass bottle and a tiny wooden stick. She expertly applied the black powder to Elizabeth's eyes, and Elizabeth blinked at the smarting sensation. "It's good for the eyes, as well as looking beautiful," said Salima. "Come into my room and look at the mirror."

Elizabeth was startled at the transformation wrought by the simple dress. She hardly knew herself, and indeed wondered who she was becoming. Certainly someone different than the Elizabeth Owen, moderately successful journalist and photographer, who had been "Tom Dunne's girlfriend" for the past five years.

"Come and show Massoud," said Salima wickedly. "Go in first. Maybe he'll think you are me."

Elizabeth hung back, but finally allowed herself to be pushed into the salon, where Massoud was poring over a book in Persian. For a moment, it did seem as if he mistook her for his wife, then he burst into laughter.

"Do I look ridiculous?"

"No, no, it's precisely because it suits you so well that I was laughing."

"It's more comfortable than I thought it would be," said Elizabeth. She took a few steps around the room. "I think I'll actually be able to walk in it."

"Our women do," said Massoud. "Certainly you will be doing a lot of walking, even as they do. Can you be ready to leave tomorrow?"

Elizabeth's heart took a flying leap over a cliff. "Sure. Are your people ready?"

"They can be ready to leave tomorrow if you wish. Or you can wait a day and meet them first. I am sorry, but they are busy today with briefings and reports, and collecting ammunition."

"That's fine. I'm more than ready to go." She avoided asking the question she really wanted to, which was, "Did you find anyone who speaks English?"

"I'll send a message to them. Is seven tomorrow morning all right for you?"

"Yes." Heart pirouetting in space somewhere, trying not to look down or around.

"You must have things to do to get ready," said Salima. "You can leave whatever you want here. I will arrange for breakfast early. And Massoud and I will get up to say goodbye."

"Oh, that won't be necessary," she protested. "It's too much trouble."

"You're beginning to sound like an Afghan, always worried about trouble. But the proverb says, 'You make me a sinner if you stop me from giving you hospitality.'"

Elizabeth retired to her room, and packed and repacked, checked and rechecked the rolls of film, her camera equipment, her small tape recorder and cassettes, notebooks and pens, and her few clothes and toilet articles.

It seemed very little to take into a war zone, but she knew they would live off the land. Massoud had said there wouldn't be much to eat, and Dr. Nasir had advised her to bring some snacks in case she went into a hypoglycemic condition. She and Salima had gone to the bazaar and bought some milk toffees, as well as several packets of salted peanuts to counteract dehydration. And her water bottle. She must remember to fill it in the morning.

Again a soft knock, and Salima came in and sat on the bed. "I'm sorry, dinner will be delayed tonight. Some Mujahedeen have come to talk to Massoud. We can't go in until they leave."

Elizabeth sat next to her, again in her familiar jeans and loose plaid shirt. "When you come back," said Salima, adding an "*inshallah*," which failed to reassure Elizabeth, "you must buy some *shalwar kameez*. Not like the ones you will wear in Afghanistan, but some nice fashionable ones like we wear here. We'll go to the bazaar and pick out some cloth, and I'll have my tailor stitch it. I think you will find them more practical for here than your jeans."

"What did you used to wear in Kabul?"

Salima laughed. "Jeans. But that was when I was young. Before the coup, life was good for us, at least in our class of society. Perhaps we did not appreciate either our comforts or our freedom, and that is why God has chosen to test us in this way. My husband always felt a social responsibility, and I think he and some others like him could have helped our society improve, but our fathers and our leaders had already made terrible mistakes."

She stopped and considered. "In Afghanistan we were never as permissive as Iran was during the Shah's time. But the upper and middle classes were quite liberal in their outlook. Many people were not really practicing Islam anymore. They had become very far from the people. Too many of our men, especially those in positions of power, were drinking too much alcohol. And when an Afghan drinks, he doesn't drink to enjoy himself, but to get drunk. I am thankful to God that my husband never drank, even after so many years in England.

"My family were always good Muslims, but never fanatics. My sisters all were educated. I married early, but I still might have done further studies if this coup had not taken place. We women were free to come and go, within reason. Not as free as you people, but as free as we wanted to be. I wore blouses and skirts, jeans and sweaters. I dressed modestly of course, but we didn't have to cover our heads unless we went into the villages."

Salima sighed. "Look what our life in Peshawar has become. We cannot even go out, and anyway there is nowhere to go. My Pathan friends, who were born in Peshawar, have the same complaint. If we do go out, no matter how hot it is, we have to wear these big white *chadars*, and I wear dark glasses, so no one can see the wife of Massoud Khan. When Mujahedeen come, unless they stay outside in the garden, I am confined to my room, and must wait until they have eaten first. But," she dismissed her troubles with a gesture, "it is the only way we can fight now. I know I could do more, if I were free. I could collect clothes from my Pakistani friends, for the refugees and for the Mujahedeen. But coming from this family, I cannot be free. It would be too dangerous. So I am happy to help my husband in the way that I can. I envy you though."

"What does Massoud think of all this?"

"He is trapped. It is what the people expect of him. Most of our Mujahedeen are simple people, uneducated village people. But they are the people who are fighting and dying. Most of our educated people have gone as refugees to America or Europe. Only my husband and some others have stayed. He and his father, Mohammed Akbar, began fighting even before the Russian invasion in December of 1979. My husband goes to the front as often as he can. He loves to be there with the people."

"That must be difficult for you."

"Very difficult. You don't know how difficult. Sometimes I hardly sleep for months at a time, but I know I have to be strong. I believe that God will protect Massoud, and one day may give us a child, if His will is turned to us in kindness. That faith is all I have.

"Once Massoud's foot was wounded. I saw it in a dream the night that it happened, or maybe before. It was not clear, but I knew something was wrong with his foot. He was thrown when a bomb exploded near him, and he fell onto his ankle and broke it. But it could have been much worse."

Salima sighed, troubled at the memory. "Promise me one thing. Don't go off the paths. Follow behind the Mujahedeen. Put your footsteps exactly in theirs. They will guide you well, they know which ways are safe. After all these years of war, there are many mines, and I have heard that the Russians have dropped small bombs from the air, all along the mountains on the border. They look like butterflies half buried in the ground, and so sometimes children will pick them up with curiosity. They have blown off so many people's hands and feet…

"But don't be frightened. I will pray for you, every day and every night, that you may have a good *qismet.*"

CHAPTER 6

ELIZABETH

On the way to the
Pakistan-Afghan border

Elizabeth stood alone on the dusty edge of a busy street in a part of Peshawar she didn't recognize. She clutched the black *chadar* more closely about her, covering her face despite the strong spring heat. She was thankful for the dark glasses Salima had given her this morning when she left. Not only did they help conceal her identity, but they protected her eyes somewhat against the glare.

Where had her two Mujahedeen gone? They hadn't yet said a word to her, in any language. They'd shown up an hour late, and then Massoud had rushed her into a three-wheeled motorized rickshaw, speaking to the two men in Pashtu. She was starting to differentiate the sounds of Persian and Pashtu: Persian was what they called "sweet," while Pashtu was harder.

Elizabeth's companions had crowded with her into the tiny rickshaw, her camera bag and small backpack concealed under blankets on their laps. They had careened through the early morning rush hour, the smoke and haze, the din of horns, bicycle bells, motors, horse's hooves and shouts, to this even more chaotic section of the city.

She looked around her nervously. Hardly any women on the street. Lots of turbaned men, mostly young. Ostentatiously large turbans, full moustaches, some beards. All dark, handsome faces. Enjoy the view, she thought. A few women, squatting and waiting, their veiled faces turned away from the road. A few others in black *burqas* with heavy chiffon veils over their faces. Some wore Afghan-style pleated *chadaris* with crocheted grillwork in front of the eyes. These stifling garments were at least colorful, she thought ironically: shades of powder blue, malachite green, chocolate brown.

She took a quick step backward as a rickshaw screeched to a stop near her foot. She almost cursed in English, and looked away to keep from glaring at the driver. She wondered if she looked authentic, or if she looked like what she was, an American journalist dressed up as an Afghan.

She wished she could take pictures of this crazy scene, the buses, trucks, and auto-rickshaws. All were painted with scenes of lions, Taj Mahals, martial arts, slightly distorted female faces, mountain lakes and Mujahedeen brandishing rifles. As if this were not enough decoration, many of the vehicles had Day-Glo decals on the windows, advertisements for batteries, oil, or airlines. Alongside these were lines of graceful Arabic script, invocations to Allah and Prophet Mohammed painted in hot pink, chartreuse, or Islamic green. From what she had seen of driving in Peshawar, Elizabeth supposed these invocations were the only thing that kept the vehicles on the road.

Someone touched her elbow. She nearly jumped, but was relieved to recognize one of her companions. At least she thought it was one of her companions. She hadn't really gotten either of them fixed in her mind yet. This one was the handsome one. He reminded her of the sweet hippie guy she'd dated in college, back in the 70s. Long thick black hair, and a full beard that sometimes gave way to the flash of a grin that revealed a faultless set of teeth. She couldn't guess his age, but his face was a mature one, its lines carved by weather and the vagaries of life. He wore a rakishly angled camel-colored cap, and had deep-set, kind eyes rimmed with black lashes so thick that it looked like he used *surmah*. The eyes were large, and expressed lexicons of experience. Elizabeth hoped he spoke English.

His hand on her elbow, the man guided her to a well-worn cream-colored Toyota sedan. It too had religious decals on the window. Her other companion, a clean-shaven but otherwise unremarkable fellow in a white crocheted skullcap, was sitting in the front seat. Several men she had never seen before were in the back. Her friend with the beard held open the front door for her, and she got in next to Skullcap. Good-looking put both her bags, still wrapped in their blankets, in the trunk.

She settled in next to Skullcap. Good-looking got in the back seat with the others, said something to the driver, and they lurched off into traffic.

Elizabeth maintained her vise-like grip on her *chadar*, afraid it would slip and reveal her identity. She wondered when they would reach their fist checkpoint, marking their entry into the Tribal Areas of Pakistan, the border regions subject only to Pathan tribal law, where foreigners were officially forbidden.

Skullcap put on a cassette of what Elizabeth guessed was Pashtu folk music, and cranked it up. The other four people in the car engaged in an animated conversation. She watched the changing scenery, the thinning traffic, as they reached the city's outskirts and buildings gave way to low-lying fields, occasional marshes, and the ubiquitous refugee camps. Miles of yellow UN tents, taupe-colored mud brick, and pools of water which reflected the bold sky beautifully, but made life miserable for the inhabitants of flooded areas.

Skullcap turned to her. "You can speak now." He grinned. "We're in a car of friends. All Mujahedeen. The driver is from Peshawar, but he is also a friend."

"You speak English!"

"Yes. Didn't Massoud Khan tell you anything about me?"

"Well, no, I suppose there wasn't time."

"I am educated. I was born in Kunar, but educated in Kabul. I studied in the Faculty of Engineering of Kabul University for two years. I learned English in the American Center, and speaking with the tourists. I was always with the tourists in Kabul. I like Americans very much. I have many American friends. Maybe one of them will give me a visa to go to America. But now I am working with the Mujahedeen, to make my beloved motherland free."

"I see." She pondered the man's various and contradictory sentiments. "Does anyone else here speak English?" She looked around the car hopefully.

"Only me," said Skullcap proudly.

At least she wouldn't be caught in an emergency without a translator. "What is your name?" she asked.

"Mohammed Ebrahim Khan. You may call me Ebrahim."

"And the others?"

Ebrahim introduced Good-looking as Abdul Sharif, Commander of Deh Wagal. She was glad he was a commander. She liked something about him, and felt safe with him. The other two were a callow, dreamy-eyed youth with a wispy beard, called Karim, and a taciturn mountain man of about fifty named Alam Shah.

Once Ebrahim had found his voice, he chattered incessantly, occasionally breaking to translate to the others.

"What is your name?"

"Elizabeth."

"Lizbet."

"You can call me Liz."

"I like Lizbet."

Elizabeth was resigned.

"Where are you from?" asked Ebrahim.

"America."

"I know America. Where in America?"

"I was born in Bethlehem, Pennsylvania. But I've been living in New York."

Ebrahim nodded eagerly. "New York is a very great city. I would like to go to New York. Do you like New York?"

"Yes and no. New York is very exciting. Also very big, crowded, noisy, expensive, and dirty. You might not like it."

"I would like to see it. I wonder if I can get a visa. I can help my country there too. I can make good propaganda in New York."

"Visas are hard to get, even for refugees."

"But if someone were to sponsor me?"

"Do you have any family in America?"

"No, no family. My family are in Kabul. My mother, two sisters, one small brother. My father is dead. I worry about my family night and day. It is not possible for me to get a visa without family?"

"No, the laws are very strict now. Unless you worked for an American company, or you are considered in 'specific personal danger.' I think that's the phrase."

"I was in Pul-e-Charkhi for a week."

"What's that?"

"You don't know what Pul-e-Charkhi is?"

"I'm sorry."

"Pul-e-Charkhi is the worst of the prisons kept by the Russians and their Afghan slaves. It is in Kabul. There they take the people they have arrested in demonstrations. They torture people there, and they kill many. Too many. If you are captured, they will take you there too." He grinned.

Elizabeth wondered if all Afghans had such a macabre sense of humor. "Why were you in prison?" she asked quickly.

"Why? You ask why? Does there have to be a why? Like so many other students, I was arrested for no reason. We were all brought to the jail and kept for one week. When we were released, I came over the mountains to Peshawar. That was four years ago. I have not seen my family since."

Elizabeth felt a pang for Ebrahim. She wondered how many others had similar stories. There were at least three million refugees in Pakistan, and perhaps another million in Iran.

"Tell me about New York. What is it like? I have seen pictures. What kind of work could I do?"

"New York…New York is mostly buildings, very tall buildings. And a few big parks. There are lots of banks and offices. All kinds of great restaurants, from big fancy restaurants to little cafes and diners, sort of like the stalls in the bazaar, or the tea houses, *chui khanas* you call them?" She hoped she didn't sound patronizing.

"Do they have big bazaars in New York?"

"Well, I wouldn't call them bazaars. But lots of shops, yes, selling everything you could ever want, and a lot of things you would never want."

"Like Barra."

"What's Barra?"

"A smuggling center near Peshawar. You can get anything there, but it's very expensive." He lowered his voice. "You can even get drugs. You like hashish? Heroin?"

"Heroin!"

"All right, hashish then. Most Americans like it."

"Uh, no thank you." Elizabeth was aware of the harsh drug penalties for foreigners in Pakistan, despite the blind eye the government seemed to turn to poppy cultivation. She was also aware that she was about to set off for a Holy War with a party of rather orthodox Muslims.

"Never?" Ebrahim persisted.

He was beginning to annoy her. "No, honest, I really am not interested in hashish or heroin. I need to be thinking clearly in order to work."

"We can get whisky in the bazaar in Bajaur Agency, near Sharif's house."

"No, thank you." Alcohol, she knew, was forbidden under Pakistani's strict Islamic laws.

"Our first checkpoint is coming," he said dramatically. "Hold your *chadar* over your face. Don't say anything. Let me do the talking."

A chain blocked the road. A uniformed man stood by the chain, chatting to two men in gold-embroidered caps. He looked disinterestedly at the Toyota, and indifferently let the chain drop.

Elizabeth breathed again. This might be surprisingly easy. A slight thrill of victory tickled her. She was someplace she Wasn't Supposed to Be. "Where are we?" she asked.

"Mohmand Agency. We will pass through here, and then Bajaur Agency. We will stay there the night, at the house of Sharif's mother, and will go in the morning to the border."

He made it sound so simple. Ebrahim slipped into a lively conversation with the others, and she gazed out the blue-tinted windows. They had begun to climb, the road snaking along rugged, rocky hills. Where the land dropped, it led to green valleys dotted with *qilas*, the fortress-like, high-walled enclosures of Pathan villages. Each *qila* had a tower. Most of them were square, but a few were rounded and massive, reminding Elizabeth of Rhine castles. Occasionally the green sweep of wheatland was broken by carefully tended fields of tall, graceful flowers, blood red, or gaily striped cream white and reddish-magenta. They looked rather like tulips, but Elizabeth knew they weren't grown for their beauty. This was her first sight of opium poppies.

She wondered what Massoud Khan would think if he knew Ebrahim was offering her hashish, heroin, and whisky. Ebrahim was either very naïve or very trusting, perhaps both. Maybe he was only trying to be helpful, in his own peculiar way. Perhaps other journalists had accepted his offer.

"Ebrahim, how well do you know Massoud Khan?"

"Oh, Massoud Khan is a very great man. He is the leader of our party, and we are loyal to him. He is a very right man."

"Have you known him a long time?" she tried from another angle.

"I know all the leaders of all the parties. I am not a political man. I worked with others, and now I work with Massoud Khan. I have been a member of his party for six months now." He dug into the pocket of his long tan-colored shirt and produced a battered plastic wallet. "This is my membership card. The Afghan Muslim Front."

It was indeed his picture, but she couldn't read the script.

"Farsi and Pashtu," he remarked, putting the wallet away. "I speak both. Do you know any words?"

"*Salaam aleikum* and *khoda hafez*. That's 'hello' and 'goodbye,' isn't it?"

"That's Farsi, or Persian, which we also call Dari. In Pashtu, the true Afghan language that we call Afghani, we say *staray mashay*. It means, 'may you never be tired.'"

"*Staray mashay*," she repeated. "May you never be tired. I like that."

"*Staray mashay*," said Sharif, following it with something she didn't understand. But he was smiling.

"Good, I'll try to learn a little Pashtu and a little Farsi each day. In Kunar you speak mostly Pashtu, don't you?"

"All Pashtu. Only the educated people, the people who have been in Kabul or gone to high school, speak Persian."

"Where did you go to school?

"I went to high school and university in Kabul. Before that I was in school in my village of Narang. *Inshallah*, you will see it, but from far. The Khalqi and Parchami traitors who daily sell our country to the Russians are in control of it now.

"Sharif and I are both from that village. We are like brothers, because we grew up in one place. Sharif speaks Farsi also. He has finished twelfth class, but his family had some problems, and they couldn't afford to send him to Kabul to university, so he had to work. He is literate in both Pashtu and Farsi, so they hired him on the road project. Now we are destroying the same roads he built." He spoke to Sharif, and Sharif laughed, but not, Elizabeth noted, without a tinge of bitterness.

"Where is Sharif's family now?"

"You will meet them tonight. His mother, his three unmarried sisters, and younger brother. Two other brothers are in Kunar with the Mujahedeen. His father was martyred in Kunar, near Asmar. He was a brave man, a whitebeard, but a commander." Ebrahim's face lost its excitement, and he fell into brooding.

Elizabeth wasn't sure she liked Ebrahim much, but she felt sympathy for him. Death seemed to be an ever-present, even likely possibility for these people. Maybe people got tired after a while, dreamed of the magical towers of New York and London, of an imaginary world labeled "the West," where there was no war and no danger.

She'd seen the Afghans in America, the ones who came when Massoud Khan and Dr. Nasir were giving lectures and press conferences. The men in nice suits, the women in fashionable clothes, gold earrings and bracelets, their nails flawlessly polished. She'd gone to one of the receptions for Massoud, where all forms of alcohol were served. Massoud had abstained from both alcohol and comment. She wondered how long Ebrahim would keep on "making propaganda" if he got to New York.

She hated her own cynicism, but couldn't help feeling that if all the educated Afghans went to America there would be no one to rebuild the country if it ever was free again. Afghanistan would be a country made free on the blood and backs of the peasants, who might not welcome back an intelligentsia who had fled when convenient. And that could easily open the way to fanatics, she thought uneasily, like the faintly hostile and well-armed fundamentalists that stalked Peshawar's back streets and bazaars.

She liked Sharif, she mused. She wasn't sure why, as she couldn't even speak to him. But he seemed to have a natural sympathy with people, a calmness, and a protectiveness that did not overwhelm. Perhaps in the next month she could learn a few words of his language.

The drive began to seem awfully long. The weather was hot, but not yet the stifling heat that would come in another month. The ancient Toyota labored up grades and coasted down, doing a dangerous ballet with painted trucks and buses coming the other way.

They passed through two more checkpoints. At one, the guard thoroughly scrutinized each member of the party, while asking Ebrahim questions.

Elizabeth looked straight ahead through her dark glasses, wondering if she would be asked to unveil her face. But the guard merely shrugged and let them pass. When they were out of earshot, Ebrahim turned and chuckled. "I told them you were my wife, and that we are all refugees from Kunar."

Ebrahim didn't ask her any more questions. No one spoke much. The men in the back smoked cigarettes, and Ebrahim tapped the dashboard in rhythm to a tune from a Hindi film.

The tired Toyota chugged into a comparatively large town in the late afternoon. Ebrahim said it was called Khar, which meant "city" in Pashtu, and that Sharif's house was nearby.

Ebrahim spoke quietly to her. "Don't say anything once we get down from the car. Just follow me. The others will go a separate way."

To Elizabeth's horror, they stopped right under a fort-like wall with a sign reading, "Headquarters: Political Agent, Bajaur."

Ebrahim paid the driver, and the men said their endless goodbyes. Then they set off into the crowds of people who milled about the main road. There were mostly men, but a few women in various head-to-toe shrouds glided by. Everyone appeared to be rushing somewhere, and a faint haze from cooking fires hung like gossamer over the baked-brick town and the fields of green wheat beyond. Looking straight ahead, Elizabeth followed Ebrahim, who moved irritatingly fast along the rough potholed paths through the town.

They came to a wide, sluggish river. Ebrahim removed his shoes and socks, and so Elizabeth likewise removed her shoes, rolled up her loose trousers, and followed him into the stream. The water was no more than knee-deep, but she nearly lost her footing on the slick mud-covered stones, and her pants came unrolled. She bit back a curse, noticing a small boy watching her from the opposite bank.

On the other side of the river, they followed a path which led towards the distant mountains. Finally, Ebrahim took a steep side path up a hillock toward a cluster of enclosed dwellings. He led her along a channel of lazily flowing water, past a border of flowering trees, to a rough wooden door which gave onto a courtyard filled with children, chickens, and a few women who smiled and looked up curiously.

Ebrahim paused at the door. "This is Sharif's house. I can't go in because of the women."

Elizabeth was surprised. After all, hadn't Ebrahim and Sharif grown up together, and weren't they almost like brothers? "How will I talk to them?"

"Don't worry. If you have any problems, I will be with the others in the guest house. Just ask Sharif to take you to me. It is safer that you should be here."

Elizabeth stepped over the threshold and closed the door behind her. Sharif emerged from an inner doorway, smiling. A middle-aged woman and three young women stood shyly in a corner of the yard, whispering behind their hands and giggling. Sharif said something, and the older woman, her handsome face framed by a gold-bordered black veil, came forward, followed a few steps behind by the others. The older woman put her hands squarely on Elizabeth's shoulders, and reached up to kiss her on both cheeks. "Mother," said Sharif. He pointed to the three younger girls, ranging in age from perhaps eighteen to fourteen. "Sister, sister, sister." Elizabeth smiled and let them kiss her as well.

One of Sharif's sisters dragged a string-bed from the corner of the courtyard out into the sun. Another ran into the house and emerged with an armful of colorful cotton quilts, which she arranged on the bed. She motioned for Elizabeth to sit down.

"*Chai?*" asked another sister, a very pretty, brown-faced girl with a large, flower-shaped brass ornament through the right side of her nose.

At last, a word that Elizabeth understood. She nodded gratefully, and was glad when the sweet milky tea was set on a rough wooden table before her. It was steaming, and she could only sip slowly, but Sharif quickly downed his, and poured himself another cup from the chipped turquoise enamel teapot.

Elizabeth watched the women baking bread. The youngest sister, who wore jingling silver coins pinned to the bodice of her full, rose-printed overdress, took balls of dough from her mother, who was busy kneading the mixture. The girl patted them between her hands, and slapped them on the inside of a beehive-shaped clay oven.

Elizabeth looked at Sharif, who was still sitting on the bed. "Camera?" she said hopefully, and made a gesture of clicking a shutter.

Sharif nodded eagerly, and called to one of his sisters, who came out of the house carrying Elizabeth's camera bag and a photo album. Sharif set the album on his lap and opened it to the front page. It was filled with pictures of solemn portraits and unreal, hand-colored portraits, mostly of small boys and family groupings minus the women. There were one or two of the women of the family, heads veiled but faces uncovered. Sharif pointed toward his mother and youngest sister. "Photo, post?" he asked.

"Yes, yes," promised Elizabeth. "I post."

She quickly unpacked her equipment and set about taking pictures of the women at work. At first they were shy, then they posed, but she waited patiently until they finally became engrossed in their work and ignored her.

A frantic squawking came from across the yard, accompanied by wildly flapping wings. The squawking stopped abruptly, but the flapping continued, and out of the corner of her eye, Elizabeth saw Sharif standing with a bloody knife, laughing as a white headless chicken flew a few feet before collapsing and twitching. Better get used to it, she thought. She might see much worse things in a war zone.

Sharif squatted and began plucking the chicken. A teen-age boy came into the courtyard, carrying a small package wrapped in newspaper. He set it on the table and ceremoniously unwrapped a yellow cake loaf.

The boy cut the cake into slices and pressed two upon her. She slowly chewed the sweet raisiny cake, and again sipped tea while the boy sat next to her, leaning on the table, his chin cupped in his hands. "I am Sharif's brother," he volunteered.

"You speak English?"

The boy turned shy. "Little."

Elizabeth spoke slowly. "From where?"

"School."

"Where? Khar?"

He nodded. "What is your name?"

"Elizabeth."

He looked puzzled, then said, "Lizbet."

Lizbet it would be in Afghanistan. "How old are you?"

"Fourteen."

"Good. What is your name?"

"Nazif."

She debated where this conversation might take her, but the boy asked, "You go Afghanistan, with Mujahedeen?"

"*Inshallah.*"

"You go Kunar?"

"Yes. With Sharif and Ebrahim."

The boy shook his head seriously. "We come from Kunar. Bombs. Every day. And many helicopters. And jets."

"Every day?"

Solemnly. "Every day."

She hoped the Mujahedeen knew what they were doing. "God help us."

The boy looked blank. Elizabeth seized the moment to re-open the photo album which lay on the table. "This is your family?" she asked.

The boy nodded and turned to the last page, a large black-bordered photo of a handsome white-bearded man in a karakul cap. "My father," he said proudly. "Martyred in Kunar."

Elizabeth was not quite sure what to say. She shook her head, hoping her face conveyed the right expression. The boy did not seem sad, but uncertainty lurked beneath his pride.

The scent of frying chicken and spices mixed with the aroma of freshly baked wheat bread, and engulfed the courtyard. The shadows had lengthened, and Elizabeth thought the sun must be near the horizon by now. Perhaps she had better ask about a toilet before it got dark.

"Toilet?" she said to the boy, rather gingerly.

He spoke to one of his sisters, who had been squatting in a corner washing clothes in a shallow aluminum basin. The girl got up, dried her hands on her veil, and motioned to Elizabeth.

Outside, the land had been transformed by the last rays of sun. The sun balanced on the distant mountains, which marked the Afghan border, and its long rays cut through the haze which hung over the immense valley. Elizabeth followed the girl out into a field of knee-high corn, which she soon realized was the local toilet. She stood for a moment gazing back at the now golden city of Khar, and wishing her escort would go away. But the Afghan girl continued to stand sentinel, and Elizabeth finally squatted facing the city. From this distance, and at this time of day, there was nothing of the twentieth century in it, nothing of any recent century.

Elizabeth stood up to face the hills just as the sun dipped below them. The sky was a transparent white, and a few clouds to the west were edged with gold. The mountains were a slate-blue silhouette, softened by haze. Tomorrow she would be in those mountains, perhaps beyond them.

She glanced back towards the east, toward the city, now dark but for a few faint lights that might be either electric bulbs or lanterns. In the translucent evening, the sounds of children crying, people shouting, a donkey braying, and a man singing rose above the land. But above them all soared the varied notes of the evening call to prayer.

The sky had turned a deepening blue, and already the evening star shone. Elizabeth knew it was only Venus, but some childhood part of her remembered long summer evenings in the Poconos, the evening star reflected in a pale lake. She wished now on the same star, fervent, hopeful wishes for a safe journey for herself and her companions.

CHAPTER 7
ELIZABETH

On the border

Elizabeth panted as she labored up the last slope to the cat's-back ridge that marked the border between Pakistan and Afghanistan. Above her the Mujahedeen crouched on the ridge, looking towards their country. Sharif squatted and smoked thoughtfully, while Ebrahim gestured dramatically.

They had picked up a few more men in the Tribal Areas on the way to the border. She hadn't quite caught their names, and still wasn't sure how many people were traveling with her. There seemed to be about ten people, all armed, but rather poorly.

Most of the day had passed in a blur of fatigue and heat. She remembered dimly the serious portioning out of arms and ammunition in Sharif's guest house that morning. With the solemnity usually reserved for a sacred ritual, the men had gathered around a *charpoy* string bed, had prayed for the success of their *jehad*, and then had unwrapped the burlap bundle that Alam Shah had brought from Peshawar.

Someone had brought in several Kalashnikov AK-47s, which Ebrahim said had been taken from the bodies of dead Russian soldiers. Privately, she wondered if they were really some of the American-supplied arms that had made their way from Egyptian stockpiles of old Russian weapons through Pakistan, and then to the leaders of the various Afghan political parties. And therein seemed to lie the problem, as far as Elizabeth could see. Not much seemed to be filtering down to rank and file fighters, at least not to those supporting more moderate parties like Massoud's.

To the Mujahedeen accompanying Elizabeth, the source of their arms was of far less concern than their effectiveness. Ebrahim owned one of the Kalashnikovs, of which he was very proud. Young Karim took another. Alam Shah carried a long heavy rifle with the legend, "Longbranch, 1941." Ebrahim said it came from the open arms market in Darra, the gun-making town in the Tribal Areas which had provided weapons for all the tribal wars of the past hundred years.

Sharif, to her surprise, had only a pistol. This he wore on a black bandoleer filled with golden bullets, which made him look like a Mexican outlaw of the Old West, and decidedly photogenic.

Elizabeth smiled ironically at the memory of the anti-climactic beginning of their journey, in a battered Toyota pickup. She had worn a blue-gray *chadari*, loaned to her by Sharif's mother. It had been hot and uncomfortable, and she had gasped for breath through the closely woven crocheted netting. Still more frustrating was the vision of the world as if broken up by a screen.

Elizabeth had tripped over the *chadari* as soon as they got out of the truck, and was glad when Ebrahim told her they were well past the danger of Pakistani border guards, and it was safe to wear her lighter and less awkward *chadar*.

They had lunched on sugared rice and tea, in a *qila* belonging to a *malik*. The village headman had relatives across the border in Afghanistan, and was sympathetic to the Mujahedeen. In the dark cool room, Elizabeth had unveiled, and had gratefully changed from her Peshawari sandals to her hiking boots.

As her eyes had adjusted to the dimness, she had studied the faces of each of her companions in turn. One had a hooked nose and an amused smile. Another was quite fair, his beard and hair tending towards brown, his eyes a startling shade of clear green, like a mountain river. Though she had known there would be light-skinned, light-eyed people in Afghanistan, the faces never failed to astonish the photographer in her. Afghanistan's ancient name had been Ariana, and here in the crucible of Central Asia, where northern steppes met western deserts and subcontinental plains in the uplift of the Hindu Kush, the Aryan race had met Mongols, Turks, Persians, and Indians. They had mixed, culturally and racially, to produce a vital and varied race, famed in equal measure for their hospitality to guests and their hostility to foreign invasion.

After fond goodbyes and endless thanks to the *malik*, Ebrahim had requested one of the many posed group pictures which Elizabeth hated but felt obligated to take. They always stood in bright, contrasty sun that cast dark shadows under their eyes and noses, and either stared straight into the camera, in the manner of nineteenth-century British officers posing for portraits, or brandished their weapons at imaginary enemies.

Right now, on the ridge that formed the border, they were posing again. As Elizabeth stumbled the last few steps to the crest, ignoring Ebrahim's proffered hand, she became aware that Ebrahim was asking her to go back down to take pictures of them.

"Just let me rest a second," she panted. Sharif produced her water bottle, and she drank slowly and deeply, as she stared down at the wide emerald valley below, and was enchanted by her first sight of Afghanistan.

A brown river snaked along the valley floor, and the hills dropped beneath her feet in descending rank till they leveled out into farmland, then rose again into echoing hills on the western side of the valley. The sun had already set in the valley, and the mountains cast long shadows. Up here the last rays were golden, and as they caught the faces of the Mujahedeen, they conferred upon them the quality of a fine and timeless oil painting.

She stood up, realizing how quickly that light would go, and backed down the path until she found the proper angle. The Mujahedeen again brandished Kalashnikovs, rifles, and pistols, pointing them towards their captive homeland.

"Where will we be tonight?" she asked Ebrahim when she again reached the crest of the ridge. He stood next to her, resting his hand on her shoulder. With his right hand, he pointed to a village by the river, now in darkness.

"There. That is Dunahi. *Inshallah,* tonight we will reach there, and stay in the house of Sharif's uncle. We must hurry now. It is a long way."

Elizabeth could see that much. It looked forever down to the cluster of houses near the river. She couldn't even imagine a path down off this ridge.

There was a path, of sorts. After a few minutes of slipping down a steep, narrow goat track, they came out onto a small plateau of flat earth, where the men set down their loads. "We will just pray here," said Ebrahim. "It is the time of sunset prayer."

She watched as each man spread his camel-colored blanket on the ground. They lined up in two rows, standing, as one man faced them and intoned prayers in a chanting, rising and falling voice. As one, they performed the motions of the prayers: the prostrations, the standing, the graceful but precise gestures filled with meanings she did not understand. The prayer was at once an intensely private act and a communal one. They had laid their weapons before them, as if offering them to God.

She felt an intruder on a sacred moment, so she turned and walked a few yards down the path, to an open spot from which she could see the land below dropping into shadow. The hills on this side were far more wooded than on the Pakistani side. All day she had been expecting cross-border incursions by helicopter gunships, and wondering where they would find cover amongst the stones and few scrubby bushes. Ebrahim had laughed at her fears and pointed vaguely to boulders that looked as if they might be able to shelter a cat in a pinch. But these oak and olive trees would provide more substantial shelter, she thought with some relief.

She heard a step behind her just as the concussion of an explosion echoed through the hills. She gasped at both. Sharif put his hand on her shoulder reassuringly, and smiled. "Tank." He said something in Pashtu, and waved his hand towards the distance.

She sighed. The valley had looked so deceptively peaceful.

Ebrahim slapped her between the shoulder blades, nearly causing her to lose her balance. "Are you afraid? You must get used to it."

"How far away is it?" She studied the land, but could see nothing.

"Approximately…" He paused in thought. "Twenty kilometers."

"It's very loud for such a distance. I guess it echoes."

Ebrahim shrugged, and took the lead down the narrow path. Elizabeth followed silently, Sharif and the others behind her. The sun had long since set, but the sky had been collecting light all day, and now shined softly on the thousands of delicate wildflowers strewn like gems alongside their path. Her favorite was a tiny blue flower which looked as if its five petals were carved from lapis lazuli.

To Elizabeth this was the color of Afghanistan. It was the color of the sky above mountains, the color of gems in the earth, and the color of ceramic tiles that mingled with pure turquoise and gold on fluted domes and slender minarets of mosques in ancient and exotic cities with long histories of invasion and empire. Genghis Khan had passed through these lands, had destroyed the great cities of Bukhara, Balkh, and Herat. But out of dust and ashes had risen new cities, a new Herat and a reborn Samarkand, rebuilt in greater splendor in a Renascence of art, science, poetry, and architecture, under dynasties of first Timurids, and later the Moghuls who were to rule the Indian subcontinent for centuries. Wars passed, and tyrants died, and so surely in time the mongers of this war would also pass.

In the thickening dusk, Elizabeth stooped to pick one of the lapis flowers, but Sharif, with the quickness of a cat, reached to her feet and plucked a sprig of three tiny blossoms. Standing, he pressed it into her hand and said, "*shin gul*."

She repeated the words, which meant nothing to her. She wanted to ask Ebrahim, but he had gone far ahead, disappearing into the dusk, so she scrambled after him. He seems to have no regard for the rest of us, she thought in some irritation. Unlike Sharif, who seems so sensitive. How could such different people be best friends?

As the light faded, the path grew harder to see, and Elizabeth stumbled with exhaustion. She no longer leaped from boulder to boulder as Ebrahim did, but went down on her haunches, cautiously trying to maintain her balance. Behind her, she felt a hand grasp her upper arm and steady her every time she felt about to slip. Sharif's grasp was firm, but spoke of nothing but brotherly concern.

It was late when they emerged from the foothills onto the valley floor. They all walked more slowly now, but Sharif touched her elbow reassuringly, spoke to Ebrahim, and hurried on ahead. Though the path had become easier, she felt deserted.

In darkness and silence they reached the outskirts of the village. High walls rose on either side of them. Elizabeth looked up and was rewarded. Beyond the tops of the earthen walls, the spring stars shined bright and hard in a soft velvet sky, blazing like fierce fires creating new worlds. Were all lands at war so dangerously beautiful?

They rounded a corner under the low-hanging branches of sweetly-scented trees, to meet Sharif, who led them down a lane between two high walls to an open wooden gate which led into a tiny courtyard. Elizabeth started to follow, but Ebrahim stopped her.

"No. Tonight you will be in the house of Sharif's uncle. It is there. Are you tired?

She nodded. "Where are my things?"

"Sharif will bring them after. You go with him. Eat, sleep, rest. We will be here tomorrow, and tomorrow night we will cross the river. Good night."

We cross the river at night? Sharif closed the gate behind him, and softly scratched on the twin gates across the lane. After a long time it was opened with a creak by a round-faced woman in a black veil. She fervently embraced Sharif, then kissed Elizabeth on both cheeks and led her by the hand across the dark courtyard into a room lit by lantern light. A tall, white-bearded man rose and grasped her hand warmly. Elizabeth could make out perhaps ten people in the room, toddlers, young women, two young men, and an infant in a hanging cradle rocked by an old woman pulling on a rope.

Sharif led Elizabeth to a *charpoy*. He signaled to one of the young women, who helped Elizabeth remove her shoes, then vigorously massaged her aching calves.

Sharif's aunt set a small table beside the bed, and a young girl brought a full teapot and a wooden bowl filled with mealy bread crumbled into milk and flavored with sugar. Elizabeth was almost too tired to eat, but the mixture quickly filled her up.

The old man, the woman, and the grandmother watched her eat. She gazed back at them, wishing she could say something, wondering if anything at all could be said. They seemed a normal village family, the kind she had seen in villages in India and Nepal. They worked their land, the women baked bread, and they all sat around the fire and gossiped and told stories. And now they talked of war.

Hardly aware of what she was doing, Elizabeth stretched out on the *charpoy* and allowed the black-veiled woman to cover her with a flowered quilt. Behind a low wall, cows mooed and stirred in the straw. The last thing Elizabeth saw before she fell asleep was the old man sitting on the floor, his dark face pensive, his beard golden in the lanternlight, holding in his hands a rosary that appeared to be made of liquid amber.

CHAPTER 8
ELIZABETH

Babur Tangay

E lizabeth watched Dr. Yusuf, the strangely non-Afghan Afghan doctor she'd just met, disappear around the bend in the valley. She'd never met an Afghan like this one before, not in America and not in Peshawar. She wondered how he'd looked in San Francisco. Probably wore expensive warm-up suits and went jogging in between shifts. I'll be he had lots of girlfriends and took them all out to charming cafes in Sausolito. Did he have a tastefully-painted renovated Victorian in the City, or a rambling redwood in Marin? He probably drove a black Porsche, played tennis, and drank Margaritas.

She crouched back under Sharif's blanket, but left one eye uncovered. This Dr. Yusuf was certainly not at all what she'd expected. She'd met most of the young doctors at the Afghan Medical Association office in Peshawar. Some had trained in Kabul, some abroad, but they were all very Afghan. This doctor, on the other hand, sounded like an American dressed up as an Afghan.

What would motivate an Afghan – or anyone else – living a comfortable upper middle class life in San Francisco to come to this crazy war zone? He seemed too holy to be true. There were Albert Schweitzers and Mother Teresas in the world, but they were few and far between. This one might make a good story, if she could pin him down.

She heard voices, and was infinitely relieved to see Ebrahim rounding the bend of the valley, closely followed by Sharif.

Sharif was grinning, and had one finger bandaged. His bandoleer was empty, and he held up the empty cartridge of a Kalashnikov.

"We had a good fight!" shouted Ebrahim. "Ten Russians killed."

"Really? How do you know?"

"We saw them fall."

"Wait a minute, how could you see them if they were inside tanks?"

"They came out of the tanks. And we shot them. They were dragged back into the tanks by their evil friends."

"So they were either dead or wounded?"

"No, no, they were dead."

"What about the Mujahedeen?"

"No one martyred, not even wounded. Only Sharif's finger, hit by a piece of flying stone."

"Where are the others?"

"Come. They are all in the *sangar* cleaning their rifles. Then we will pray. And you will take pictures."

"What about the Parchami spies? Do you think they could have found out that I'm here?"

Ebrahim laughed. "Oh, they were not spies. I didn't recognize them at first. One was Najeeb Khan, from Chagaserai. He comes and goes freely into Chagaserai, and he helps the Mujahedeen with information."

Elizabeth was relieved. "I was terrified."

"No problem. How is your foot?"

"Better. I met the doctor, and he gave me some medicine."

"I know. He came to us, and we met him on the way."

"You didn't tell me he'd lived in America."

Ebrahim looked surprised. "I didn't think it would interest you."

"It gives the story an American angle," she said icily. "I find it very interesting."

"Of course. As you like."

Why did Ebrahim remind her of a snake when he grinned that way? She chastised herself. Poor man had been off fighting and might have been killed. But that didn't mean she had to like him.

The band of fighters greeted her exultantly, brandishing the weapons they were cleaning, calling out, "Photo! Photo!" She obliged them by taking pictures as they dismantled their rifles, ranging from Kalashnikovs to antiques. She concentrated on one middle-aged farmer who wore a sprig of yellow flowers in his cap and proudly showed her the insignia of King Edward on his long rifle.

Ebrahim was standing on a boulder, holding a Kalashnikov. "Lizbet! Take a photo of me!" She shot off one frame, and faked a few more, hating to waste the film on such asinine poses.

"Where has the doctor gone?" she asked casually.

"Back to the clinic. He'll be expecting us when we get there. As soon as he saw that none of us were wounded, he went another way."

"But I didn't see him go past."

"He took the path up the mountain. That side." Ebrahim pointed, and Elizabeth made out a faint track on the opposite cliff amongst the bushes. "We will also follow that way, later, when we have eaten."

"How many days to the clinic?"

"For him, one night and part of tomorrow. For you, perhaps three days."

"My ankle seems better now," she said hopefully.

"Maybe from my massage," grinned Ebrahim. "What did the doctor do?"

"Massaged it, like Sharif did. Then gave me analgesic balm."

"I will also massage your foot, whenever you need." Ebrahim leaped down from the boulder. "We will pray now. I will gather the Mujahedeen."

A young man with a bullhorn cried the call to prayer, which echoed in the hills as the sound of shellfire had echoed hours before. Elizabeth moved discreetly in and out of the scene, not wishing to distract. Sharif glanced at her for a moment, eye to eye, as he turned his head for the ritual *salaam*. She knew instinctively that she had an outstanding photograph.

CHAPTER 9
YUSUF

On the way to Deh Wagal

Dr. Yusuf Hakim plodded slowly up the steep path and into the dying light. The wooded valley below had long since fallen into shadow. He did not feel the weight of his bag, and his feet seemed to find the path by themselves.

Four months inside Afghanistan had wrought changes in him, but he wasn't yet sure how deep or irrevocable they really were. Four months ago this path had been hard. He had struggled to keep up with the Mujahedeen who were leading him to the spot the Afghan Medical Association had chosen for the clinic he had volunteered to staff. He had struggled even harder not to let them know he was struggling.

He had thought that tennis and jogging the steep hills of San Francisco had made him fit for anything. But it had been a long time since he had walked the mountain paths of his native land, and he hadn't realized how soft he had become. Or was it that the war had hardened his countrymen?

He'd walked a lot in the past months, from valley to valley, to villages on hilltops, to battle sites, to the twisted aftermaths of bombing raids. He had lately come to know the paths he might have been learning all his life, were it not for the accident of birth that had caused him to be born to a wealthy family of Kunari landlords settled in Kabul rather than to a family of poor tenant farmers in a village. That accident had set him on a course that had taken him far from his home, his family, and even his culture.

It was late in life to be rediscovering his own culture, and these were strange times, times such as no one had ever thought would come. But they should have known, he thought. We should all have seen it, my father and his friends in the army, and my generation, who might have been able to change it. I thought it didn't matter if I stayed in America, because I was just one person. Then I met Janet, and that decided it.

He didn't know which had come first, the disintegration of his marriage, or the destruction of his country. To him, they both seemed to have come at the same time, news of an invasion at Christmas, followed by one of his and Janet's fights that never quite made sense afterwards. But this time, despite the years that passed pretending they had made up, and the subsequent wearying months of wrangling over property, the rift had never quite healed.

He remembered her sneering, "You don't even care about your own country, or your own family, let alone me." There had been endless variations on that theme. Janet had never been particularly interested in Afghanistan before. She had always complained when they had Afghan friends over or went to "boring Afghan parties." And she always forgot to send pictures to his parents in Kabul. But she had carefully probed his psyche until she found his weakest, most tender spot, nurtured in the dark of years by cumulative guilt. She had deftly cut it out and exposed it to public view, like a high priestess triumphantly displaying the heart of her sacrificial victim.

Maybe he was here because of her, he thought as his feet trudged unfailingly up the steep path. Maybe she had unwittingly goaded him into proving something, to himself if no one else. "You're a doctor," she'd said sarcastically. "I thought you took an oath to help people. The only person you've ever helped is yourself."

He'd thought he was helping people at the hospital. After all, he hadn't gone into private practice, as Janet had with her psychology practice. And he'd continued to volunteer time at the Haight Free Clinic, which she hadn't.

But it was true he hadn't done what his father had hoped. He'd never gone back to live in Afghanistan and work with his own people. Now he was back, and his father didn't know. His father was in Kabul, out of reach. And Janet didn't know. After years of fighting over petty details of finances, she had gotten the house in Mill Valley and he had quietly moved into a renovated Victorian in the City, and never seen her again. Maybe if this American journalist published a story on him, Janet would see it and know he was here. His lips stretched into a smile against his will.

Dr. Yusuf reached the top of the hill and continued along the ridge till he came to a spring flowing out of the mountain rock into a natural stone pool. It used to be the water supply for the *malik's* house that used to be on top of this hill. The house was now in ruins. Heaps of stone and piles of splintered wood were all that remained of a complex of several houses.

The fields were green in the day's last light, and looked as if someone had been tending them. But Dr. Yusuf knew they were only weeds. No one knew what had happened to the Malik and his family. If anyone had been there the day the helicopters shot rockets at the place, they were probably still buried under the rubble.

The doctor rested at the spring for a few minutes and let the light fade. He drank deeply and listened, without thought, to the frog chorus which was testing its evening voice. It must have been a beautiful place when the family lived here, he thought. Girls must have come here every evening to fetch water, and shepherds and travelers would have stopped to slake their thirst. There was something very Biblical about it. Maybe the whole life of his nation seemed Biblical to Americans. Even to him, steeped as he was in American culture. Afghanistan had only really begun to develop in the post-war era. About all that was left of rural development now was a few radios on which the Mujahedeen listened to the BBC and Voice of America. The only mechanized things left in Afghanistan were highly sophisticated machines of death.

Dr. Yusuf removed his shoes and methodically completed his pre-prayer ablutions. Hands to the elbows, face, mouth, nose, behind the ears, and feet to the ankles. What was now mere ritual had once had a serious hygienic purpose. And still did now, he reflected, when one was reduced to this basic life.

He spread his blanket and faced toward Mecca. Before he'd returned to Afghanistan, he hadn't prayed his *namaz* for more years than he remembered. A few months at first, in Berkeley, but his roommate's friends used to stare. The formal motions and words hadn't seemed so important under the circumstances. But in this place, in this time, they again had assumed an importance to him. Perhaps it was the influence of all those around him fighting a Holy War. He'd become a born-again Muslim. The phrase made him smile.

The prayers, which he'd had to strain to recall from his childhood, now came easily, and the Arabic flowed through his life like a current. It gave him the comfort of familiarity. He finished the last prayer, stood up, and shook out his blanket. Throwing the blanket over his left shoulder, he continued on his way.

One star glowed in the western sky, which was now the color of faint rosewater. All was quiet now, after the day's long battle. Dr. Yusuf could see the pale white road running along the foot of the mountains, distant and remote in the Kunar Valley. It was deserted now.

As he walked, slowly, steadily, the thinnest crescent moon faded into view, its arms open to embrace the evening star across a wide patch of sky. Separation, he thought, longing for Union. A few lines of Persian poetry came to his mind, from the *Masnavi* of the mystic poet Maulana Balkhi, known outside Afghanistan as the Sufi philosopher Rumi. And there before him in the darkness he saw a sudden vivid image of his proper balding father. Baba had always dressed in an immaculate Western suit or in his Brigadier's uniform, except when he went to mosque on Fridays or when they went to the village in Kunar, where he had worn Afghan dress.

In his vision Yusuf saw Baba intoning poetry to the wide-eyed boy he had been, then asking Yusuf to explain the meanings. This had always frightened him a little. Baba had insisted that his children be educated in both Farsi and Pashtu, that they should speak both languages with proper accent and grammar, and be well-versed in the literature of both. "If you speak Farsi and Pashtu perfectly," he had said, "you can speak to anyone in Afghanistan. And you can serve them better." The old man, who really hadn't been so old then, had drilled him, Ayub, and their young sister Maryam mercilessly. He had seemed inflexible, but had delighted in poetry, and had encouraged Yusuf when the boy had shyly brought his father his first efforts at quatrains and couplets.

"A man should be a warrior and a poet," Baba had said. "All else is superfluous. But when you have achieved these things, you must learn, and improve yourselves in all other manners. And you must always serve your country and your people."

All this talk of serving had soon palled for Yusuf. It had kept him away from Afghanistan, but had planted the seed of guilt that had sprouted in San Francisco and now was bearing fruit in Kunar.

He wondered if his younger brother Ayub, the new Governor of Kunar, knew where he was now. It was supposed to be a secret, but Yusuf knew the Communists had their sources, just as the Mujahedeen had theirs.

Ayub had taken all the talk about serving very seriously, but not quite in the way their father had intended. Ayub had studied political science, had learned English assiduously, had faithfully read *Time*, *Newsweek*, and *Soviet Life* from an early age. He had admired leftists like Noor Mohammed Taraki and Hafizullah Amin, and had thought they were much too harshly treated by King Zaher Shah and later by President Daoud. Ayub had voiced these opinions at the dinner table, much to their father's disgust.

Ayub had stated his opinions ever more loudly as he grew older. Yusuf had tried to have a talk with him when he'd gone home to Kabul in the summer of '74. Ayub had accused his brother of being out of touch with the realities of the Afghan nation. He had spoken frequently of "the people" and used catchphrases common to dogmatists everywhere. Yusuf, who considered himself a liberal Democrat and had taken part in a good many demonstrations against the Vietnam War, had gently explained that socialism was all very well, but that Afghanistan was slowly changing and modernizing anyway. In his view, the People's Democratic Party of Afghanistan had far too close ties to Russia, which could cause Afghanistan to lose its national identity. After all, its natural gas resources were already being sold to the Soviet Union at less than the production cost. Yusuf had used his own catchphrase, "Self-determination for all people." Both sons had upset their father badly.

Ayub had taken part in university demonstrations, but had somehow stayed out of jail. He'd won a scholarship to do a master's degree in the Soviet Union. When he returned to Kabul, he'd become a professor of political science at the university, where he was regarded as a brilliant and sincere apologist for Marxism. He'd cut all family ties, and hadn't seen their father for years. Two weeks ago, Yusuf had heard that Ayub's sacrifices had finally been rewarded with the post of Governor of Kunar Province. Ayub now sat in Chagaserai, presiding blithely over the destruction of his ancestral homeland.

Yusuf wondered what his brother thought of his work as a doctor with the Mujahedeen, if he knew of it. Ironically, Yusuf had never listened to his younger brother's pleas that he return to Afghanistan and "serve the people." Ayub had thought Yusuf should settle in a village somewhere, at least for a few years. "Afghanistan only has one doctor for every 20,440 people," Ayub had intoned. Yusuf hadn't known how to answer that, except by putting off the whole issue by reminding his brother that he still had two more years of medical school, and two years of internship after that. He'd never seen either his brother or his father again after that 1974 visit.

Now he was serving the people, much in the way his brother had envisioned, but on the opposite side. And if Ayub wasn't so damned dogmatic, he would be on the same side. Yusuf wondered how his brother's oversensitive conscience justified bombing villages, cutting off water supplies to villages the government couldn't control, and arresting and executing people, some of whom he had known as a boy.

It was too late for any of the Communists to come over now. The Khalqi faction now claimed to be anti-Russian, and disowned the butcher Hafizullah Amin and the Parchami Babrak Karmal. But the majority of the Afghan people had no sympathy for "godless communists" of any persuasion. Deserters from the Afghan Army were welcomed by the Mujahedeen after a probationary period, but they had been conscripts, not volunteers. Afghan Communists had to know that there was only one way for them anymore, and that they'd chosen it a long time ago. Ayub was obviously making the best of it. But Yusuf, having known his brother as a sensitive child who couldn't bear to harm another living being, didn't suppose he was very happy.

Walking like this was a good way to sift through half-remembered phrases and scenes, to brush the dust off the mirror. That image too was from the poetry of Rumi. The mirror of his own soul had grown both dusty and rusty with the years. San Francisco fog and years of adulterated culture had corroded it. It would take a long time, and a lot of careful polishing, to get it back to normal.

Though Yusuf wondered what "normal" was. How could he even know which language to think in? When he thought of Janet, of American friends, or of the hospital, he thought in English. When he thought of his father and his brother, he thought in Farsi. And when he thought of the people with whom he came in contact each day, he thought in Pashtu. He read at night in Farsi, and he listened to radio broadcasts in both Farsi and English. But the American woman, Elizabeth, was the first person he had spoken English to in four months. This must be the journalist season, he thought wryly. The snows have melted and it's not too hot yet.

Still, he was looking forward to meeting her again. She intrigued him. Or perhaps he was just lonely for an American. Thank God she didn't remind him of Janet. Janet had been classically tall and blond, sure of herself to the point of being a know-it-all. This woman seemed to have a softness underneath the journalistic grit, and compassion to match her wit. She didn't like to admit that she was in any pain, or having any trouble. But she seemed the kind of person who would admit a mistake, and that was something Janet had seldom done. The only mistake he could ever remember her admitting to was marrying him.

Yes, Elizabeth Owen would be a welcome diversion. She seemed the kind of person who would be eager to learn about the Afghan people. She wasn't just doing a job, though doubtless she'd do a damn good one. He smiled at the memory of how he had met her. "*Staray mashay*," he murmured. It was probably the only Pashtu she knew, but her pronunciation had been excellent. He must have scared the hell out of her, grabbing her ankle like that. And it had to be the injured one, he remembered in shame. He hadn't even apologized to her.

He wondered what he had looked like to her, with his unshaven face, grimy clothes, and bandoleer. But she must be used to it by now. He had been as surprised by her as she had by him. He really had thought she was an Afghan, and had momentarily wondered what an Afghan woman was doing in a Mujahedeen *sangar*. Remarkable, her resemblance to an Afghan. His ideas of beauty really had been formed in childhood, not by the American media, no matter what Ayub said. He had considered Janet "California attractive," and had loved her very much at one time, but had never thought her beautiful, as he did his mother, sister, and cousins.

He wondered why Elizabeth had come to Afghanistan. Most journalists came for their careers, and there were even a few out and out adventurers who thought war was fun and exciting. But virtually all the journalists he had known, adventurers, professionals, and the few idealistic dreamers, had been men.

He knew his country had a way of enchanting certain personalities, mostly loners, much as America had initially enchanted him. Elizabeth seemed ripe for enchantment. Perhaps she was running away from a broken love affair, he thought with an odd mixture of cynicism and hope. Or was he just assuming that because she was a woman? Perhaps she was finally doing something she'd always wanted to do, taking a gamble that a gutsy story about an obscure war might catapult her into the bigtime job she really wanted.

Yusuf saw the faint warm glow of fire through the door of a mudbrick house just below the crest of the hill, and decided to stop for tea. A few old men sat on the floor, smoking tobacco in a *chillum*. Everyone knew the doctor, and greeted him warmly. He refused food, but accepted black tea with a few lumps of sugary *gur*. He also asked if they could shelter a small party of Mujahedeen who might arrive that night. The men agreed to put them in the mosque, a simple structure that housed a few *charpoys* on a straw-covered floor. The doctor hesitated, then added that a woman was with them, an American journalist. The owner of the house smiled and said, "Then she will be our guest."

The doctor went his way under the stars, until he came to the house of a *malik* he knew. There he ate *nan* and ladled yogurt out of a wooden bowl with a wooden spoon. He shared a *chillum* of tobacco with the *malik* and his friends, finished a whole pot of tea, and slept deeply for a few hours.

CHAPTER 10
GOVERNOR AYUB

Chagaserai

Governor Ayub wiped his fingers on the delicately embroidered linen napkin, then raised it to his lips and patted his brushy moustache. The kebabs had been excellent tonight. He was lucky he had such a good cook. In a mere two weeks he had made his Chagaserai headquarters quite comfortable, he thought with satisfaction. Though it was true he didn't dare go out at night, and was compelled to keep a detachment of guards around the perimeter of the compound at all times.

Mousa, the aging, unmarried servant Ayub had had since he was a boy, knocked discreetly at the door and brought in an envelope on a silver tray next to Ayub's tea. Ayub was relieved to see that the note was in Pashtu, not Russian. At least it was not that tiresome Lermontov. Ever since his arrival in Kunar the Russian's manner had become more and more arrogant, and his constant "suggestions" grated on Ayub's nerves.

He tore open the envelope, scanned the note, and directed Mousa to show his caller in. Najeeb Khan was already proving to be one of his best informants. Ayub didn't know how Najeeb maintained his network in the villages controlled by the rebels, and he didn't particularly care as long as the spy provided reliable information. Najeeb was paid well for his services, and seemed quite prosperous. Ayub suspected that he played both sides. He probably got arms from the rebel parties in Peshawar and sold them at a profit in the arms market in Darra in the Tribal Areas. He probably sold information to the rebels too. He had a rough manner, but his usefulness compensated admirably for that and for his doubtful loyalty.

Mousa showed Najeeb in and quietly set out an extra cup and saucer with a plate of *noql*, sugar-coated almonds that were difficult even for someone in Ayub's position to procure. Najeeb, a middle-aged, black-beared man in a dirty gray turban that matched his dirty gray *shalwar kameez*, kissed Ayub's hand. Caught by surprise, Ayub quickly drew his hand away.

"Comrade," reproved Ayub, "you must get over these old backward ways. There is no need for these, uh…" He stopped, unable to find a word, then smiled in an attempt at natural hospitality. "We are all equals now in the People's Democratic Republic of Afghanistan."

Najeeb returned an ingratiating smile, as if he didn't really believe the Governor and was humoring him. "Yes, comrade."

Najeeb declined the overstuffed armchair indicated by Ayub and instead sat on the floor on the plush red Bukhara-patterned carpet. Mousa lingered, sprinkling ground cardamom into the teapot and pouring the tea back and forth until it had steeped to just the proper color.

Ignoring Mousa, Ayub turned his attention to Najeeb. Mechanically he asked the lengthy formal inquiries as to Najeeb's health and the health of all of his family members. Slowly he worked his way round to the subject of Najeeb's visit.

Najeeb slurped his tea and Ayub winced. "I have some news," the man said deliberately.

"So you say in your note." Ayub wondered if a scribe had written it, or perhaps one of the soldiers outside.

"This news will be of great interest to you."

Ayub waited, sipping his tea quietly, savoring its flavor.

"There is an American journalist in Kunar."

"Really?" he asked politely. Another American journalist. What was special about this one? Was he definitely CIA?

"A woman. Lizbet. She was sent by Massoud Khan, and was at Babur Tangay during the ambush."

"All of your information is useful to us, and proves your loyalty to the Afghan nation," said Ayub non-commitedly.

"She is planning to interview your brother."

Ayub looked up sharply. "My brother?"

"Everyone knows your brother is on the side of the rebels, and is helping the bandits in the hills," said Najeeb, punctuating his remarks with loud slurps.

Ayub's heart pounded. "Your information is incorrect. My brother is in America."

Najeeb regarded him with hooded eyes. "No, your brother is in Kunar, for four months now, at a place called Amrau Tangay."

"I know the place. Why was I not informed before?"

"You were not Governor before, so your brother was not so important. You must have a good *qismet*, or this fact would have made it impossible for you to become Governor."

Ayub clenched his teeth. "And what in God's name, uh, what does my brother Yusuf think he is doing here?"

"He is being a doctor, I think, for the bandits." Najeeb sipped his tea disinterestedly.

At that moment Najeeb reminded Ayub of a bearded snake. What did this man expect him to do, hunt down his own brother in those rather hostile hills? He would have to think and prepare a plan of action. When Lermontov heard of this information, which could not be kept from him indefinitely, the general might make an unpleasant "suggestion" on which he would be compelled to act.

"Who else knows of this?" asked Ayub.

"Only yourself, *sahib*."

"I will give serious consideration to the matter," said Ayub frostily. "In the meantime, tell no one. I will bring it to the attention of the proper authorities."

Najeeb lingered longer than necessary, appearing to enjoy the luxurious atmosphere of the Governor's Residence. He had three cups of tea and half a plate of *noql*. Ayub suspected that some of the *noql* had disappeared into the copious folds of the informant's blanket for later consumption.

Ayub was relieved when Najeeb left. He slipped a cassette into his Sony tape player. Beethoven's Third. The Eroica. He had developed a taste for Western classical music when he lived in Moscow while working on his master's degree. He'd also developed his taste for vodka then. It had been hard enough to satisfy when he'd returned to Kabul, and was even harder now, though not as difficult as for the foot soldiers of the Red Army.

Why did Yusuf have to come back to Afghanistan at this stage, and in this manner? He probably saw himself as serving the people, though he was too late and on the wrong side, thought Ayub sulkily. Where was Yusuf when the people really needed doctors, before the revolution? In America, drinking whisky and marrying American women.

Yusuf really hadn't cared about his people, not like Ayub had. Yusuf was so damned short-sighted. What would happen if these rebels won? Did he think Afghanistan would go back to the status quo, or that the king would return? Couldn't he see that there would be a bloody civil war if the Soviet troops weren't here? Probably the most right wing fundamentalists would gain control, and then the country would be cast back into the Dark Ages. Where would Yusuf fit in then? Ironic that the Americans were giving most of their aid to the most right wing orthodox rebels. The Americans always tried to bet on winning horses, just like the Russians. And neither was averse to switching horses in mid-race.

Mousa cleared the tea and Ayub dismissed him for the evening. When the servant had shut the door behind him, Ayub removed a small key from the pocket of his French-cut trousers and opened a wooden cabinet. He took out a bottle of Stolichnaya and a shot glass and poured himself a nightcap. He drank it quickly, just like a Russian, he thought, and just as quickly locked up the evidence.

He had nobody to confide in. He thought back to his childhood, as he often did these days, to all those dreams of social equality, land reform, internationalism, rights for women. No more veils, no more women behind the curtain of *purdah*, and education and health care for all. An end to the abuses of feudalism and an end to ignorance had been his twin unchallengeable ideals.

It hadn't quite turned out that way. The Communist Saur Revolution had provoked a religious reaction in the villages, and an intellectual reaction among the educated elite. Perhaps they had handled things badly, in hindsight, but the Communists had had to seize power when the chance presented itself, and when they were offered fraternal support from the Soviets.

The first year hadn't been so bad. There had always been political prisoners in Afghanistan. Now there were different prisoners than in the days of King Zaher Shah and President Daoud Khan. It was true that some had been the same luckless souls arrested by every regime, but for the most part Taraki had arrested only fanatical mullahs and their followers, the ones who were holding Afghanistan's progress back.

If Yusuf had been in Afghanistan during those years, he might think differently. How had Yusuf fallen in with such fanatics when he had such Western ideas about women? Now his brother had sided with those who would keep all women ignorant and in *purdah*.

Ayub paced toward the cabinet again. Just one more quick drink, he told himself as he hastily gulped another shot. No harm done.

Ayub hoped he would not be forced to move against his brother. He loved Yusuf, though Yusuf, as the eldest, had always been their father's favorite, and had always told him what to do.

Ayub wondered where their father was. He had disappeared from Kabul some time ago. Some people said he had gone to the mountains to join the rebels, others said he'd been arrested, taken to Pul-e-Charkhi and killed in prison. *Baba* was an embarrassment, but had not seriously harmed Ayub's career. Ayub was taken on his own merits, and on proven loyalty. Discreetly, he had made inquiries about his father's disappearance. Nothing. The wily old man must have gone to the hills. All that physical training, hunting, shooting, not to mention his military knowledge, would be useful somewhere.

Ayub would have tried to protect his father, if only he'd stayed put in Kabul and out of trouble. He owed that much filial duty to his own father. But now there was nothing he could do. He wished Najeeb, or one of his informants, would find out where the old man was. Hopefully not anywhere in his jurisdiction.

But Yusuf, as he'd just been so unpleasantly informed, was in his jurisdiction. As long as Yusuf wasn't actually fighting, perhaps he could safely be ignored. One doctor wouldn't make much difference to the rebels. It was only a matter of time before they were beaten down.

But maybe before too many other people died, maybe the Geneva talks would be successful. Pakistan looked ready to make a deal. The country couldn't go on forever playing host to three million refugees. If Pakistan cut off the flow of arms to the rebels, the resistance to the revolution would crumble. The damn Russians would be off our backs and we would still be in power.

Ayub slammed the liquor cabinet shut and locked it decisively. Damn you, Yusuf, keep your head down. Don't give me a reason to look for you. Even in those hills, we'd find you eventually.

CHAPTER 11

ELIZABETH

En route to Amrau Tangay

The moon had long since set when they reached the spring where Dr. Yusuf had stopped to pray. Sharif filled Elizabeth's water bottle and they spread their blankets out to lie down. Elizabeth could see the shell of a half-ruined house silhouetted on the hilltop against a bright mist of stars.

"Ebrahim, what happened here?"

"Bombs."

"But when? How? Why?"

"There was a lot of fighting in Deh Wagal two years ago. We shot down two helicopters and destroyed many tanks. You can still see pieces of them. But then they bombed our villages from the air with helicopters and jets."

"I never thought the war could reach here," she said quietly. She could not imagine bombs and rockets raining down upon such a remote and beautiful place.

The men were silent, resting on their backs and looking up at the stars, which hung in the black sky like frozen lightning bugs.

Sharif propped himself up on one elbow and said something, which Ebrahim translated for her. "You Americans have been on the moon, haven't you?"

She nodded.

"Sharif wants to know what they found there."

She thought. Not God. At least she didn't think so. What they did find was rather prosaic. "Rocks," she recited. "No air. One side, the side we see when the moon is full, is too hot for life, the other side is too cold. There is a lot of dust and stone. Like Kunar."

Ebrahim translated and they all laughed. "Sharif wants to know if there are other planets like Earth," said Ebrahim.

"Not like Earth. But there are other planets. Eight others. We don't think any of them have life. But you see all those stars? Some of then would take years to get to, even if we traveled at the speed…no, just tell them even if we traveled in the fastest ship it was possible to build. But maybe those stars have planets that have life, because each star is a sun just like ours."

"I know all this," said Ebrahim with a superior air.

"I know. But Sharif asked. Please translate for him."

Ebrahim translated to Sharif, who was now sitting up in the darkness to her right. Sharif nodded eagerly, and raised his face to the sky like a small child filled with wonder. The Big Dipper tilted in the black sky, pouring its milk out toward the north. Sharif's finger traced it and then he said, "*Charpoy.*"

"*Charpoy,*" she repeated, and suddenly saw the constellation in the shape of a bed instead of the familiar pot which her own culture saw.

Sharif again traced the constellation with his finger and pointed off north to the polar star, saying something in Pashtu.

Ebrahim had lost interest and didn't translate until Elizabeth had asked him twice. "Only he says it is a way to find north."

"Tell Sharif he is very wise and knows much about the stars."

No one said anything for awhile. Elizabeth listened to the frogs, now in full voice. She thought of the ponds back home in the summer, with frogs chirping all night and lightning bugs flashing. She smiled at the memory of how she and Mark used to catch fireflies and put them in jars. Sometimes they'd touch their glowing wings and paint their faces with the bright stuff on their fingers.

Sharif spoke again, quietly. "Sharif wants to know if you know any *ghazals*," Ebrahim translated.

"What are *ghazals*?"

"Love songs. He wants to know if you know any American love songs."

She was touched. Tom had never liked her to sing, not even at home and certainly not in public. But she knew she had a good voice. As a teenager she had often had solo parts in the parish choir, but Tom's criticism had shaken her confidence.

"Is it safe to sing here?" she asked.

"Yes, yes, no one will hear. We are in the free area now."

"Okay. It's not exactly a love song. It's something better, a song about hope and victory. By a sort of hometown boy, from my part of the country. His name is Todd Rundgren, though I'm sure you've never heard of him. I think you'll like the words. It's like a prayer.

Shyly at first, Elizabeth began to sing one of her favorite songs, "Just One Victory." Like the frogs that sang into the night, she found her voice.

When she finished singing, she found she had tears in her eyes. She was glad no one could see her in the thick darkness.

Ebrahim translated, and there were murmurs of approval. "Again," commanded Ebrahim.

She sang the whole song again, louder and with more confidence. She almost laughed as the Mujahedeen clapped in time. Near the end of the song she saw the flash of a weapon being fired across the mountaintops on the opposite side of the valley, near the border. She faltered for a moment, then came back even louder, ending on a defiant crescendo.

The Mujahedeen applauded her. Ebrahim slapped her on the back. Sharif seemed to be staring at her, though she could not tell for sure in the dim starlight.

"Shouldn't we go?" she asked Ebrahim suddenly. "It is very late."

"If you are ready."

As she stood up a pain shot through her ankle and up her leg, causing her to stumble. Sharif caught her arm as she cursed under her breath.

"I can go on," she said shortly, taking a few limping steps. Someone spoke behind her but she couldn't tell whose voice it was.

"Alam Shah says we should get you a stick," said Ebrahim.

"From where?

As they passed the ruined farmhouse, Alam Shah turned off the path and poked around the remains of an animal shelter until he found what he wanted. He broke off a long stick that might once have supported a ceiling. With his knife he expertly whittled it down to the proper length and sharpened one end to a point. Karim carefully wrapped his handkerchief around the top end and tied it firmly to make a solid hand grip.

Elizabeth tried out her new walking stick and found it a great help. "Thank you," she said earnestly, "*mehrbani.*"

They walked on along the ridge and began to descend, slowly, circuitously. The stick helped Elizabeth keep her balance and Sharif remained at her elbow, careful not to touch her unless she was about to fall.

She was beginning to worry about Sharif, who was paying altogether too much attention to her. It was strange to be the only woman in this male world. Though she had been made to feel like everyone's favorite sister, she supposed it was inevitable that someone would start to feel lonely.

Ebrahim didn't worry her much. It was always easier to rebuff someone who made a direct approach, especially if you didn't really care whether you hurt the person's feelings.

The last thing she wanted right now was to get involved with anyone, especially so soon after leaving Tom. She had plenty of work to do and didn't need any distractions. She wanted to spend at least a few days at the clinic. That doctor Yusuf would make a good article. She wondered what his real story was. She would have expected anyone dedicated enough to give up a comfortable life in the States and return to Afghanistan in wartime to be, well, different. Heroic. Idealistic. So far Dr. Yusuf didn't appear to be either. He existed in a vacuum, with no family and hardly any background. And, more important, what motivation? He had been irritatingly glib, and she hoped he wouldn't be a hard interview. Snappy answers could smack of cynicism when they appeared in cold hard print.

Yet the doctor was kind. He just didn't want anyone to know he was kind, and probably equated kindness with weakness. Mark could be like that sometimes.

Her father was even more so. How he had ranted and raved when she had moved in with Tom. But there had been an especially generous Christmas gift that year, and Dad had been gruffly friendly to Tom. Tom had of course been banished to separate sleeping quarters, but he had enjoyed beers with her dad, and the two had watched the New Year's football games together, cheering loudly. Tom probably had more in common with Dad than he did with her, come to think of it.

Mark, on the other hand, had never really liked Tom, but he'd respected his sister's choice and kept his opinions to himself. From the beginning, though, he had kept a certain distance from Tom, and had given Elizabeth a key to his apartment and let her know the spare room was available any time.

Mark would like this place, she thought. He'd really appreciate the beauty. Also the black humor. And the tragedy. She would have to start a letter to him. He'd laugh when she told him she sang *Just One Victory* to the Mujahedeen. Mark had always been the one to go to concerts in Philly with her, and the one who had convinced his energetic younger sister to sit down and listen to the lyrics. Tom had never had time to listen to music, and hated concerts because they were crowded.

She wondered what kind of music Dr. Yusuf liked. Probably something very California. Laid-back music, which he'd listen to while driving through redwoods in his black Porsche. Or maybe he liked singles bars and disco music. She grimaced. She couldn't imagine him ever listening to Afghan folk music.

But then if she hadn't seen him here she probably couldn't have imagined him working in a clinic in Kunar either. Although he sure did look the part. It was the accent and the offhand manner that had jarred her.

Her thoughts were increasingly disturbed by a growing awareness of the pain in her ankle and her own exhaustion. She hadn't slept all day and she knew it was well past midnight. Though she didn't want to appear weak, she finally asked, "When are we going to stop for the night?"

"Soon," said Ebrahim. "It is very near."

She had learned that Ebrahim's concepts of "soon," "near," and "easy" differed widely from her own. She walked more and more slowly, resenting Ebrahim's lack of concern, but just when she thought she would collapse a hamlet materialized against the stars.

The *malik* with whom Dr. Yusuf had shared a *chillum* led them into a one-room structure, carrying a kerosene lantern. "Mosque," said Sharif reverently, gesturing to her to take off her shoes.

Sharif guided her to a *charpoy* in the corner. In the dim light she saw six or seven string beds scattered around the square room, and felt straw beneath her feet. Painfully, she raised her legs onto the bed and fell immediately into sleep. She half heard talk of *chai*, and it was Sharif who roused her and handed her a steaming glass and two lumps of raw brown sugar. She had not finished her tea when she fell asleep again, one hand dangling off the bed reaching for her glass on the floor.

CHAPTER 12

YUSUF

Near Amrau Tangay

Even from a distance Dr. Yusuf could see that the boy running towards him was in a hurry. The child leaped over boulders and splashed frantically through the river. Yusuf hoped that no one had been seriously wounded, and steeled himself for bad news. As the excited boy got closer, the doctor recognized him as the son of the *chowkidar*, the caretaker and watchman of his village clinic who had been with his family as long as Yusuf could remember.

"Doctor *sahib!*" the boy shouted.

"*Staray mashay*," Yusuf greeted him.

"*Staray mashay.*" Struggling to catch his breath, the boy respectfully inquired after the Mujahedeen, the villages the doctor had visited, and the success and comforts of his journey.

Yusuf then inquired in some detail as to the boy's health and that of his household, then anxiously asked if anything was wrong in the village.

The boy grinned. "Commander Rahim has arrived. He is eager to see you, and was disappointed to learn that you had gone to Babur Tangay."

"Commander Rahimullah Khan? I have heard of him. What is his business?"

"He says he is your father."

"But that's impossible. That is not my father's name. And my father is in Kabul."

"He said you probably would not believe him, but he insisted that I tell you to hurry."

"What does he look like?"

The boy laughed impishly. "Like a man who would be your father. The same shape of the face, the same eyes and nose. But his beard is white."

Dr. Yusuf couldn't believe that his missing father could have suddenly reappeared in the guise of the famous Mujahedeen commander. He quickened his pace. "Tell me more"

The boy scampered ahead. "He just arrived this morning from Peshawar, after walking in the night. He has a nurse with him, sent by the Afghan Medical Association. A girl from Jalalabad. And a foreigner, Mr. Michel. He is a journalist. And many Mujahedeen, with Kalashnikovs, and even rocket launchers, and rockets, and mines."

Yusuf hardly noticed the last hour of the journey. His feet found their way as if he were walking in a trance, and his mind was nearly numb with excitement. He had not seen his father in ten years.

He did not pause for breath as he hurried up the last steep slope to the village. For there on a rooftop, prostrating in the humble posture of prayer, was a man Dr. Yusuf Hakim recognized.

The young doctor rushed up the path, but paused at the edge of the roof and, tears in his eyes, waited until the older man had completed his prayers. His father, Yusuf knew, was aware of his presence, but refused to break the sanctity of prayer. Finally the old man stood up with dignity, picked up his blanket, and tightly embraced the son he had thought lost to him.

For a long time the two stood that way, tears spilling from their eyes and choking speech from their throats. Every time they loosened their embrace, fresh emotions would well up, and they would hold still more tightly.

At last the old man wiped his eyes with the end of his turban, took his son's hand, and led Yusuf down into a courtyard under a mulberry tree. Commander Rahim called to the boy-messenger, who was watching from a respectful distance, and asked him to bring tea.

"*Baba*, Father, I should be offering you tea," protested Yusuf. "You are a guest in my home."

"Praise be to Allah that I have found my son here, where I had never expected to find him."

Yusuf was confused. "But surely you knew I was here?"

"I did not mean that. I meant only that I did not think you would ever return from America. Especially in these times, when it is so important that our educated people should return. I am proud of you, my son, for you have heeded me at last."

The wiry old man embraced his son again, and Dr. Yusuf hid his embarrassment. His father was speaking Farsi to him, and as usual, it was literary, exact Farsi. In all these years, Yusuf knew the boy he had once been had forgotten how to speak that way except when he recited poetry.

Commander Rahim settled onto the *charpoy* that served as a couch, his son close beside him. The boy brought a pot of tea and two glasses. Dr. Yusuf waved his away and served his father the tea and accompanying lumps of *gur* himself. "I am sorry that I have nothing more to offer you on this occasion," he murmured in apology.

"This *gur* is sweet, made sweet by both the occasion and the fact that it is the food our people must eat in the time of *jehad*."

Yusuf watched his father affectionately. "I was afraid I might never see you again. And Mother is afraid of that all the time. Where have you come from now? Kabul?"

Commander Rahim laughed, white beard and turban setting off teeth not dulled by age. "Sit, drink your tea, and listen. I left Kabul some months ago, in the Haj season. I had official permission to go on pilgrimage, but I did not go on the Haj plane. That was only my excuse to leave the house with some luggage. I went straight to the mountains, where I met a small party of Mujahedeen with whom I had been working in Kabul. After two weeks we came to Pakistan, by way of Ghazni…"

"But why did you not contact me then? Or at least send a message to Mother?"

"Be quiet a moment. You have always spoken before your turn. There were reasons why I could not. But put your mind at rest. Your mother knows I am here, and I have seen her. I saw her only five days ago in Peshawar."

Yusuf was stunned. "Is she well?" he asked anxiously. "And is Maryam well?"

"They are both well, do not worry. They are more worried about you, and send their fondest *salaams*. I promised them I would come first to you, and then go to my other work. But I will tell of them in time.

"When I first reached Peshawar, I went to Mohammed Akbar and his son Massoud Khan, and told them of my proposal. Mohammed Akbar advised me to go first to Haj, and obtained a Pakistani travel document for me. I thus went on Haj to Holy Mecca."

"Blessings to you," said his son, kissing his father's hand.

"And blessings to you, my son. I think you have become a Muslim in your old age."

The son was abashed. "I never really forgot my faith. I just…"

Commander Rahim laughed. "I know. You just thought that many rituals had become only hollow forms empty of all substance and meaning. And so they can be. But they do not have to be, if you keep safe in your heart the meaning of the words and motions, and live these words in your life. Do you pray your *namaz* now?"

"Not always five times a day, but I pray."

"In these times it seems the right thing to do," Commander Rahim observed. His sharp face tightened, and his pursed his lips. "After freedom will come the struggle for interpretation, between those like Mohammed Akbar and Massoud Khan on the one hand, and the fundamentalists on the other.

We will probably have a civil war for some years, and that will be a tragedy to witness. But at least when the Russians leave, it will be our own disaster, an Afghan disaster, not a Russian or an American disaster."

"We already have civil war," said Yusuf tiredly. "Every day Afghan boys are dying in the army as well as among the Mujahedeen. Most do not want to be in the army, but some do support the government."

Commander Rahim sipped his tea thoughtfully. "You mean like your brother Ayub?"

Yusuf nodded, feeling as if he were betraying his younger brother.

"May Allah guide Ayub rightly. But we must remember that Allah guides those to Him whom He will. And remember that Ayub thought he was serving the people of Afghanistan, as I had always exhorted you children to do. Neither of us knows Ayub's mind now."

"But do you know where he is now?"

"Yes, of course I know that he has just been made Governor of Kunar, just as I knew you were the doctor of Deh Wagal. But you did not know that Commander Haji Rahimullah Khan was your old father. And *inshallah* Ayub will not come to know."

"But surely there are few secrets in Afghanistan."

"True, but there are some." He leaned forward and spoke in a low voice. "When I returned from Haj, Mohammed Akbar was prepared for me. We have a camp where I put my military training to good use."

"And what do you do in this camp?"

The old man smiled broadly. "We train commandos."

Yusuf's expressive eyebrows, inherited from his father, rose into fine arches. "How?"

"You know I had extensive military training in Britian. Also, ironically, in Russia. And your grandfather fought the British in the Third Anglo-Afghan War, and his father fought them in the Second. When I was a child, I learned a lot from both of them. Now I am applying it.

"We have three hundred specially picked men from all over Afghanistan. First they take an oath of secrecy and loyalty on the Holy Koran. Then we put them through strict physical and spiritual training. We alternate feeding them well, to build up their bodies, with fasting to build up their spirits. Of course most of them have been through hunger and fighting before, but not at the level we demand of them. We put them through the most strenuous physical training – obstacle courses, rock climbing, rappelling. There is target practice, and some weapons training, but you are aware of our problems obtaining high quality weapons. We instead stress self-reliance and strategy. We Afghans have always been rather weak on the latter. We are brave fighters, but we have too often thrown all to the wind for a dramatic sortie that has ended in disaster. It is better to take less, but to take correctly and hold.

"Of course we don't have the resources we had in Britain or Russia. We must make do with what we can. But we have made a relief map not of concrete or plasticine, but of earth, with a few plastic soldiers and houses." He chuckled. "I wish you could see it. It is quite effective. We change it every week. We have done simulations of Asmar, Chagaserai, Jalalabad, Kandahar, and Kabul. Kabul was enjoyable, an attack on Pul-e-Charkhi, where we freed the prisoners. Also attacks on the airport. *Inshallah*, these will be carried out shortly.

"I am of course not the only trainer. Some of my former colleagues have joined me. Two have returned from America for this service. We have finished the first course. Now I have led a party of fifteen picked men into Kunar. We will see what we can do." He sighed. "I only wish the Americans were supplying us to the extent that the Russians accuse them."

Yusuf poured another glass of tea for his father. How had their lives come to this talk of killing and commando attacks on prisons and airports? Before the war, the talk of old battles, strategies, and defense had only been a diversion, a game of chess with ideas. His father should have been allowed the dignity of growing old as a gentleman, sitting in his garden, hunting with his Afghan hounds, and writing poetry for others to sing.

"Will you really attack Chagaserai?" asked Yusuf. He could not look at his father.

"Only if we can win. There are many other targets, easier ones, and thus better ones. But circumstances change. God grant that the Geneva talks should succeed first."

Yusuf thought of his brother sitting in the Governor's Residence in Chagaserai, and wondered if Ayub would have the same compunctions their father had. Yusuf knew of other families split by ideology. In most cases, political differences had resulted in the death of one or more family members. There was the Kabul Mujaheed who had attacked his own cousin's house. The beautiful pro-Soviet television announcer who had been killed by her husband, who had then fled to Peshawar. And the Communist who had ordered his own father executed, though he had spared his mother and sisters.

"Have you fought alongside the Mujahedeen?" asked the father.

"I have fought," said the son. "I do not know if I have killed anyone. I don't think I want to know. It is better that way. We all shoot, and we all share the credit." He hesitated. "And the guilt. I am sorry, Father, I know we must fight. But I am a doctor. I cannot take joy in death. I fight when I must. You taught me how to shoot as a child, so I wear this pistol, and I can use it well. Now I know how to use a Kalashnikov too, and even an anti-aircraft gun. If the helicopters come over this clinic and I have a weapon, I will use it. But I fight my *jehad* with a stethoscope."

"Well spoken. A true soldier takes no delight in killing. It is our duty to fight the enemy, and desirable to minimize casualties on both sides. It is desirable to take live prisoners, though we have trouble to feed them. It is desirable to prove to the world that Mohammed Akbar's party, at least, abides by the Geneva Conventions regarding the treatment of prisoners of war. Even Russians. Not all of us are so scrupulous, but we must abide by the laws of God and man, and we must be honorable fighters, so that we are morally better than our enemies. We must remember that Allah is first of all compassionate, merciful, and forgiving. Does not every chapter of the Holy Koran begin with 'In the name of Allah, the Compassionate, the Merciful?'"

"Not everyone thinks as you do, Father. You are an idealist."

"And so are you, my son. If I have taught you right."

Yusuf rubbed his stubbly cheeks, suddenly feeling very weighted down by his idealism.

"But why have you taken this new name?" he asked his father. "Only to hide your presence from Ayub?"

The old man's dark eyes smiled, and the lines around them deepened. "Think of the meaning of the name. 'Mercy of Allah.' It is, you might say, my private joke with those who will listen and think."

Yusuf smiled. His father had so many aspects to his personality, and they unfolded with the years like the multihued petals of an exquisite flower. He loved the old man now as he never had in his youth, or even in his childhood.

"Of course I wish my identity kept secret," Commander Rahim continued. "Your mother knows, Mohammed Akbar and Massoud Khan know, and now you know. The small boy also knows, and his father, who has been with me since he himself was a boy. But no one else, even in the village. Those who have seen us now will think only that a young man has greeted an elderly commander with respect."

"It's much safer that way," agreed Yusuf. "We all have much work to do."

"Yes, and we have brought a young woman with us to help you. She is a nurse from Jalalabad, called Malolai."

Yusuf looked up with interest. "Does she sing like the girl in the legend?"

"I don't know." The old man laughed. "The Malolai of old did sing, of course, but the new girls urge us on in other ways. In Kabul they stand against the guns, the high school girls march in the streets, and in the prisons they defy their captors and spit upon them. One girl opened her own veins with her nails and died slowly and horribly in Pul-e-Charkhi."

Yusuf's expression betrayed his shock.

"I can see you have not been back here long, or you would have heard many uglier stories. We know this one is true. I have talked to one of the girls who was in prison at that time and saw the girl dying in her own blood the next morning. That is why we are fighting, son."

Yusuf shook his head. "I have seen the bombings, the wounded. Some horribly wounded. But a young girl taking her life in that manner…you must know the pain and the will involved."

Commander Rahim looked at him steadily. "And the faith. God grant that no one need ever do it again. God grant a swift end to this genocidal war. We must fight beside our women. This Malolai will be a great help to you. She was a medical student in Jalalabad, but of course was not able to finish her studies. She came across to Pakistan with her cousin only recently. Her parents are dead, and her brother is in Kabul with elderly aunts and uncles and younger cousins. He works with the Kabul Mujahedeen. When Malolai came to Peshawar, she came straight to the Medical Association and asked to be sent to a clinic at the front."

"Where is she now?"

"She has gone down the valley to meet some of the villagers and to assess the health needs of the women. The Frenchman, Mr. Michel, has gone with her."

"She wastes no time."

"And neither does the Frenchman."

"Who is he?"

A young man. A free lance photographer and writer. He has no experience in this part of the world, but he is interested in everything. Including, perhaps, our women. We must be careful with him."

"Will he be staying here long?"

"I think he will follow our commandos for a little while. We plan to be based in Badel."

"I do not want you to go soon, but neither do I want the Frenchman here for long. It is distracting to our work. And there is another journalist, an American woman, who should be coming tonight or tomorrow. She has come especially to write a story on me."

The father looked up sharply. "On my clinic," Yusuf corrected himself.

"Did you know her in America?" The father's white eyebrows were every bit as expressive as the son's black ones.

"I met her only yesterday, in a *sangar*." He omitted mention of the way he had grabbed her injured ankle by mistake, and the later massage. "Poor thing had twisted her ankle. That is why it will take them so long to reach here."

"From where?"

"Babur Tangay."

"And the attack there?"

"They say they killed ten Russians. No one martyred, or even seriously wounded, by the grace of God. How did you know there had been an attack?"

"News travels fast. You must know that. Or were you in America too long?"

"I have been here now four months. I am no longer tired by the journeys, and no longer weak from little food. Maybe I have become Afghan again."

The old man mused, chewing on his lower lip. "An Afghan is always an Afghan. One changes, one adapts like a chameleon. Ideally one adopts the best manners and ideas of the other civilizations. Too often we have taken the worst. But we are always Afghans." He paused. "Yusuf *jan*," he began, using the Persian term of endearment, "what has happed to your wife? Janet? Your mother said only that you are well and had made a decision to come here. She said she knew nothing, but I do not believe that."

"Mother would never lie, especially to you. Just as I cannot lie to you. Janet and I are divorced."

He didn't know what kind of reaction to expect. Divorce was not unknown in Kabul, but it was rare and had not stained their own family until now. He could not look at this father, who he knew had disapproved of his marrying an American.

"I'm very sorry," said Commander Rahim. "It must have been very hard for you."

"Yes. But it was not all her fault. It was my fault too." He shocked himself by admitting what he had never admitted before, even to himself. "But don't think that all marriages between Afghans and foreigners end in divorce. I know some very happy people. Janet and I were not two of them. I don't know why. Perhaps I picked someone who was very American, and tried to become like her. If I had become a little American, and she a little Afghan, it might have worked out." Her parting sneer echoed in his brain: "You'll never go back." He had come back, but how could he explain to his father, or even himself, why?

"Are you running?" asked the old man.

"I don't think so."

"Good. Because when running we only trip over ourselves. Perhaps it is *qismet* that your marriage ended when it did. How long ago did it end?"

"About a year ago. It took some months to settle. Luckily we had put off having children. It took me some more time to make the decision to come here, and then to clear up my affairs in America. I realized I no longer had any excuse not to be here." And no one to care if he didn't come back, least of all himself. His neatly capsulized story had left out a lot, all of the pain, the neurotic mutual accusations, the drinking and occasional soothing cocaine. Yes, he had indeed taken up the worst of the California lifestyle: cocaine, recrimination, and divorce. Even suicidal ideation. That had been the phrase Janet used, hadn't it?

"Don't look for death," said the old man. "It will find you when it is time."

Yusuf stared at his father, shocked at the old man's ability to read his heart. Was he looking for death? He thought he had gotten over that. He was reckless, true, but one had to be reckless here. Maybe they were all suicidal, every crazy bastard involved in this war.

Commander Rahim took his son's hand and pressed it to his own eyes. "I thank God for you, my son, for I have lost my other son. I thank God that you have at last returned to your home and to me. You know they say, 'things that come late come right.'"

"Yes. And 'patience is bitter, but bears a sweet fruit.'"

"May we all live to taste the sweet fruits of freedom, and of peace in our beloved land, without conflict, but with unity." When Commander Rahim took his son's hand away from his face, Yusuf's hand was wet with his father's tears.

CHAPTER 13
ELIZABETH

Near Amrau Tangay

Elizabeth wished she were anywhere else. She fervently wished she were in New York sitting in Mark's apartment listening to music. Or even with Tom in the Den of Doom. Or back home in Bethlehem, listening to her mother talking about the latest bake sale for the right-to-life movement. She'd rather be listening to her father loudly bemoaning Japanese trade competition and illegal immigration above the too-loud television.

She smiled fondly at the thought of her opinionated father. Dad would never change his views. But he was a fair-minded man, and he really was an equal opportunity employer. He had a soft spot for all his employees, blacks, Puerto Ricans, and poor Bethlehemites from families of European immigrants who had not become rich and successful even after several generations of honest hard work in America.

It was time to get some perspective on her sentimental though conservative mother and her kind-hearted though conservative father. They'd been very understanding about her going to Afghanistan. They didn't know much about the country, but they did know that peasants were getting Russian bombs dropped on them.

Of course they didn't exactly know she was going into the war zone. She'd told them she was going to Pakistan to "cover the situation," and that there were three million refugees, several political parties in exile, and a city full of spies. She'd made it sound exciting, but not *too* dangerous.

Mark knew the truth though, and was proud of his little sister. He'd done a Tarot reading for her the night before she left, and had assured her it would be a good trip. It was just the change she needed in her life. The Wheel of Fortune as the subconscious factor, or something like that.

She hadn't bothered to tell Tom she was going. He was probably out of town anyway, covering some war or other. She only hoped the pictures she was taking here would get published, and her stories too. Her writing ability was something Tom neither shared nor appreciated, and it was something she had held on to through the seasons of denigration.

Perhaps all along the conflict between her and Tom had been an unbridgeable difference in modes of communication. Tom was essentially non-verbal. Maybe if she'd been similarly inclined it would have worked out. But she needed someone capable of thinking and communicating both verbally and visually.

Oh hell, she didn't really need anybody. She was just tasting freedom, maybe for the first time in her life, and she enjoyed the sensation of having chosen her own fate. Though perhaps she hadn't been all that clear about what she was getting into. Still, when she really thought about it, she realized she didn't want to be anywhere other than where she was right now, twisted ankle and all.

The ankle was troubling her, but Ebrahim had assured her about two hours ago that they were nearly at Dr. Yusuf's clinic. Then he had assured her again, and again. They had turned up a narrow valley and were now, thankfully, walking on a level, long disused dirt road littered with the orange-painted debris of a bulldozer. A neat stair-step village clung to the side of a gorge. She didn't dare ask if this was Amrau Tangay.

"You see the village?" asked Ebrahim.

Am I blind? "Yes."

"That is our destination."

"*Al-hamdulillah*. Doesn't that mean 'thank God?'"

Sharif smiled and repeated, "*Al-hamdulillah*." He said something in Pashtu that she recognized as "long way." She was quickly picking up the words used most often.

They found Dr. Yusuf at work on a rooftop. A group of men sat under a mulberry tree in the courtyard below, and another group watched from an adjoining roof. A huddle of women were more discreetly positioned among a jumble of large boulders on the outskirts of the tiny hamlet. Children dressed in deep pinks, rich reds, and bright greens ran back and forth between the groups. A very beautiful, oval-faced woman in a maroon *chadar* appeared to be assisting the doctor. Elizabeth wondered who she was, then let her eyes wander to the tall, thin, sandy-haired man who was taking pictures.

"*Staray mashay*," she greeted everyone, casting a slightly resentful glance at the doctor. He *knew* it had been her idea to do a story on the clinic, and now he was letting someone else do it first.

Dr. Yusuf smiled broadly when he saw her. "*Staray mashay*. How is the foot?"

"Oh, nothing that about a year's rest won't cure."

"Then you will have to stay with us for awhile. Sorry." He went on with his examination of an old man's ears.

"Hopefully not too long."

"I'll do what I can to avoid prolonging your stay."

He was going to be a difficult subject. "Seems a popular story these days," she observed.

He gave her a look of warning which she could interpret any number of ways.

"Meet Mr. Michel Dubois, from France. Like yourself, he is free-lance."

"Please to meet you," she said sweetly, extending her hand to the tall man who stepped forward to greet her, Nikon dangling from a long strap about his neck. He was handsome. Gray eyes, an aquiline nose, fair skin, and one of those Mujahedeen mountain caps slightly askew on a head of thick, sandy hair. His gray *shalwar kameez* matched his eyes, and with the de rigeur blanket thrown over one shoulder he almost looked the part of the dashing *mujaheed*.

"*Enchanté*," he said quietly, taking her hand. She found his gaze disconcertingly penetrating. "I hope my presence will not be any trouble to you."

"Oh no, not at all." He was certainly disarming.

Dr. Yusuf was watching with barely concealed amusement. She noticed that he had shaved, and didn't look quite so rough with only a moustache. "Her name is Elizabeth Owen, by the way," said the doctor. "She seems to have forgotten her manners."

She fixed him with a frozen smile. "I beg your pardon, I'm terribly tired," she said lightly. "And as I mentioned, my foot does hurt."

"Please, sit down here," said the Frenchman, quickly clearing his camera bag off a string bed.

Ebrahim had also been watching. "No, no," he said as she sank gratefully onto the bed. "It would be better if we went into the courtyard so we don't disturb the doctor."

"Oh, if it's all right with the doctor I'd like to watch. But only if it's all right with the doctor. And his patients of course."

"By all means stay," said Yusuf. "You're not bothering me. Not any more than the entire village watching from the rooftops. All I ask is that you request permission before taking pictures and do not take pictures of women if they object."

"I don't think I'll be taking pictures of anybody today. Just observing. I prefer to take my time, so I'm not a threat to people. And it's not my policy to take pictures without people's permission." She looked at him severely, but he went on with is work, bent over a ledger. Ebrahim appeared to grow bored and wandered off with a group of men to have a smoke, as she sat patiently, watching.

The maroon-veiled woman spoke to the doctor, then to Elizabeth's surprise, spoke in lightly accented English. "I will make some tea for your guests." She looked at Elizabeth and smiled. "You must forgive my bad English. You are most welcome." The woman smiled shyly, the smile lighting up her startling eyes, green flecked with amber. Elizabeth wondered if this woman was the real reason Dr. Yusuf had returned to Afghanistan.

"Thank you." Was she the doctor's wife? Elizabeth watched the woman, who walked gracefully and with confidence, then returned her gaze to Dr. Yusuf, who was now listening to the heartbeat of a baby girl held by her anxious mother. Elizabeth waited until he looked up, then asked, "Who is she?"

"A village woman. Her baby has a bad case of diarrhea, very common here, and is in danger of dehydration. The woman herself also seems to have some sort of intestinal trouble."

"Thank you, but I meant your..." she hesitated, "assistant."

"Oh, her name is Malolai." He wrote some notes in the ledger. "She has just arrived, a few days ago, with my father and Mr. Michel..."

"Your father!"

He shot her a look of warning that she at once understood, though she didn't know the reason. The Frenchman had not reacted and seemed to be out of earshot, and no one else was close enough to hear. "So Malolai is a nurse?" she continued hastily in a slightly raised voice. "She is from which place?"

"You don't have to speak pidgin with me. I lived in America for eighteen years, remember?"

"Sorry." She was crestfallen. "I guess I've just gotten into the habit."

Dr. Yusuf gave her an odd look. The Frenchman, seeming oblivious to all, continued to move around with his big Nikon. Elizabeth gazed for awhile at the river far below and watched him out of the corner of her eye. Why was he constantly shooting into the sun? She strolled up behind him, careful not to get into his line of sight, and looked over his shoulder as he knelt for a low angle of Dr. Yusuf.

"What speed film are you using?" she asked.

"I am using high speed film, black and white, for special effects, artistic effects."

Leave it to a Frenchman to be pretentious. "Who are you shooting for?"

"Gamma-Liaison. And you?"

"Black Star. So I suppose we're in competition."

"*Ouf, merde!*" The Frenchman's camera appeared to have jammed.

"I think you're at the end of the roll," she observed.

"*Ouf,* yes, what a fool I am. I am simply too engrossed in my work. And I left my film in the room downstairs. *Pardon.*" He stepped lightly across the roof toward the doorway leading down the stairs.

Elizabeth hobbled back to the string bed. Dr. Yusuf had turned his attention to the baby's mother, a middle-aged woman with a black veil and nut brown skin. Elizabeth couldn't see much more of her, as she wore voluminous skirts over voluminous trousers.

Dr. Yusuf was discussing something with the woman. He gestured toward Elizabeth and gently directed the woman to sit down on a string bed beneath an overhanging roof.

"Elizabeth, I need your help."

She limped across the roof. "To do what?"

"To examine this woman. Orthodox Muslim women, and especially their orthodox Muslim husbands and fathers and brothers, don't like women being examined by male doctors. This is Malolai's job, but she's busy making tea and I don't want to wait. You'll do. You're female. Know anything about medicine?"

"I've read a copy of *Where There is No Doctor.*"

"You can learn a great deal if you stick with me. Come here, I want you to examine this woman's belly and tell me what you find." The doctor retreated a few paces and faced away from the woman on the bed.

"How...?" asked Elizabeth, uncertainly approaching the woman. The woman looked at her pleadingly and slightly raised the full frilled skirts of her tunic. Elizabeth sat down on the edge of the string bed and placed one hand on the bare skin of the woman's abdomen. Suddenly she remembered a picture in a book of a person listening to someone's belly. She leaned over and placed her ear to the woman's navel. To her relief she heard gurgling, lots of gurgling. "Sounds like lots of gas."

The doctor started to turn his head, then caught himself. "What are you doing?"

"I'm listening to her stomach. 'A silent belly is like a silent dog,' right?"

"Where did you read that? It's true that silence can be an ominous sign, but…never mind. Can you please continue the examination and tell me where the sound appears to be concentrated. Touch the navel first, then go clockwise, starting at noon and continuing on around. I will ask her at each spot if it hurts, and what sort of pain it is. First touch each spot lightly, then when I tell you, press a little."

Elizabeth did as she was told. Most of the pain and gurgling seemed to be concentrated in a horizontal line between three o'clock and nine o'clock.

"Thank you, Elizabeth. Tell me when she's completely dressed again." Elizabeth helped the woman adjust her drawstring trousers and smooth her skirts.

"Okay."

The woman sat up, still with the pleading look in her eyes. She walked over to her baby, who she had left near the doctor's chair, and picked her up, crooning. The doctor returned to his table and again wrote notes. "Elizabeth, can you go over to those boxes and pick me out some belladonna?"

"Is it labeled?" She really wished Malolai would come back.

"Nothing so fancy as labels here. They are pink and green spotted pills. You can't miss them."

"Okay. How many?"

"Ten should do it."

"What do I put them in? I don't see any bottles."

"What do you think this is, *General Hospital*? We are, after all, in a war zone. We don't have the luxury of bottles, much less childproof caps. Bottles are heavy, bulky, and breakable. We wrap tablets in papers." He deftly tore a square from a sheet of paper on a pad, folded the tablets in the paper, and handed the packet to the woman, who clutched it tightly in her hand. He said a few words to her, and she backed away, thanking him profusely.

"How does she know when to take the pills?" Elizabeth asked.

"I'm hoping she was listening. At least she was content with tablets and didn't beg for an injection. Too many of our own doctors, who want too much money, have given injections when a pill, or even no medication, would have been better. Now the people think only injections will cure them, and so our doctors too often bow to their whims. I refuse to do this. But sometimes I worry that they aren't taking their medicine." He took off his stethoscope and laid it on the table in front of him, then rubbed his temples.

"Headache?"

He looked up. "Always. I don't believe in taking too many drugs."

She smiled. She was almost beginning to like him now that she saw the conditions he had to work under.

He got up and started towards her deliberately. "Let's have a look at the old ankle."

"The old ankle is aging rapidly. I don't know if there's anything you can do about it."

She sat lengthwise on the *charpoy* and raised her right leg onto the bed. He perched on the wooden frame of bed and palpated her ankle, an expression of concentration, or possibly concern, on his face. Again she was struck by the delicacy of his touch and the warmth of his hands.

"Nothing a few days rest can't cure," he said off-handedly. "And a few massages. I'd suggested you stay off it for a few days, and enjoy our hospitality. Get to know the place and the people, and don't walk far for at least a week. You did say you like to work slowly."

"It seems a relatively peaceful place. And your work interests me. I hope Ebrahim and Sharif and the others won't mind."

"You can send them away." He was massaging her ankle and calf, which she found somewhat distracting, but once again his healing hands seemed to be working a minor miracle.

"I don't think so. Massoud Khan commended me to their care."

He slapped her on the ankle and she jumped. "I have a lot of patients waiting. I can work on this later. Over dinner."

"You make it sound like a date."

"Just you, me, and the Mujahedeen." He stood up, looked at her with an unfathomable gaze for a moment, then went to the doorway and called out for the next patient.

A gaunt man of about thirty shuffled across the roof and squatted next to the doctor's examination table. "He's one of my TB patients," said the doctor.

"Do you have many?"

Perhaps thirty-five identified cases in the nearby valleys. We can't treat them properly here of course, but we do what we can when we can get medicine. You can mention that to the Medical Association when you get back to Peshawar."

She took her notebook out of her camera bag. "Was Malolai sent by the Medical Association?"

He was listening to the man's chest. She started to repeat her question.

The doctor sat up. "Elizabeth, have you ever listened through a stethoscope?"

"No, why?"

"Do you have any idea how loud it sounds when someone else is talking?"

"No. Sorry, I'll be more careful," she whispered.

"Good. I'll teach you how to take blood pressure and listen to a heartbeat and then you'll be as useful as Malolai."

"I doubt that. You didn't mention that you had a woman working with you." Just like him to slight the value of a woman.

"I told you she had just arrived."

"Oh, that's right. With this Frenchman, what's his name, Michel? And... someone else?"

"A slip of the tongue. You didn't hear it. And I hope no one else did."

"Why?" And why was she pressing the matter like some paparazzi?

"His wishes," he said shortly. "You will meet him soon. But you won't know that he is anyone but Commander Rahim. Please." He cast his gaze directly at her in a conspiratorial moment, then glanced quickly at the doorway. "Elizabeth, one more thing."

"What?"

"How is Ebrahim with you?"

"What do you mean? I mean, I don't know if he's interested, if that's what you mean, but he's been a gentleman."

"A quaint way of putting it. But that's not what I mean. What does he say about Massoud Khan?"

"Only good things. Why? Are you questioning his loyalty?"

"Ebrahim was at university with my younger brother, who was a member of the Khalqi faction of the Communist Party, and is now collaborating with the Parchami faction that is in power. He also happens to be the present Governor of Kunar."

"Oooh…"

"I'm not saying that Ebrahim is pro-Russian. But he was a Shola'i then."

"A what?"

"Pro-Chinese Communist party. Maoist. From *shola*, the flame."

She quickly rifled her memory for any indiscreet statements in Ebrahim's presence. "Does Massoud Khan know?"

He shook his head. "I'm sure not. Massoud Khan meets too many people. His only failing is that he takes people too often on their word. He thinks everyone is as good as he is. Perhaps Ebrahim's sympathies have changed. Lots of people's have. But be very careful."

CHAPTER 14
AYUB

Chagaserai

Ayub felt relaxed as he lounged in a comfortable woven-rope chair in the garden. Mozart filtered out from the house, and thick bushes of lilacs in bloom infused the garden with the scent of spring. On a low, carved wooden table by his side reposed a silver tea set.

He was reading reports. Things had been thankfully quiet since the attack near Babur Tangay, and that had only been a minor harassment of a supply convoy. Maybe the war was winding down. If the rebels would only give up their resistance. Not even completely, but just enough so that the Russians would think they were in control. Maybe then the bloody Russians would withdraw. Or at least leave the Afghans to their own mess. Maybe the government could work out a compromise with the rebels. Marxist Islam, or Islamic socialism. Whatever they wanted to call it. But the Russians would never leave as long as these damn fanatics kept harassing them. Why were they fighting a war they couldn't win?

Ayub heard the sharp salute of the guards, followed by the creak of the compound's steel gate opening. A dark green army jeep hove into view. Think of the Russian devil and he appears.

General Lermontov waited for his driver to open the door for him, then descended ponderously. His gray-salted moustache and well-fed face reminded Ayub of a stock Russian villain, the kind he and his fellow Afghan students used to make fun of in their Moscow dorms.

Ayub stood up respectfully. At least he didn't have to salute. "My dear General," he began in fluent, Moscow-accented Russian, "how good of you to come today."

Lermontov returned the greeting perfunctorily and sat down opposite Ayub. The general's small eyes flicked around nervously. "Ayub, are we alone here?"

"Yes. There are guards outside, and the only others in my house are my servants." Lermontov's manner presaged more than the usual dose of doom.

"I have serious business to discuss with you. We have been informed of something that concerns you."

Ayub wanted to fidget, but did not. "Would you like some tea first?"

The general laughed. "You Afghans. Tea sweetens everything for you. I suppose I have the time."

Ayub rang a small brass bell on the table and was relieved when Mousa appeared almost immediately. Mousa quickly cleared the tea set and returned to the kitchen for a fresh pot.

"I hope nothing has gone wrong?" began Ayub. "I have just been reading through these reports, and our pacification program seems to be achieving its goals. We have contained the bandits in several locations, and…"

"We have discovered the whereabouts of your father."

Russians didn't mince words. Ayub could hardly trust his own voice. "Oh? Is he well?"

"I can see you really don't know anything about it. Fortunately for you. He is very well indeed. He is now using the name of Commander Rahimullah Khan. Commander Haji Rahimullah Khan, the warlord I warned you about," the general said slowly, as if he expected Ayub to take notes. "He is known to the rebels as Commander Rahim. He now commands an elite group of men who he has trained in guerrilla tactics. An ungrateful sort of man. He is using our own training against us. But that might make him easier to predict."

"Where is he?"

"He is headquartered in Badel."

Ayub's face blanched. He didn't notice Mousa pouring tea, but automatically took the proffered sweets.

"I realize that makes things awkward for you. A pity he didn't consider his own son's position. If he must make mischief, he should do it outside your jurisdiction."

Ayub held his breath. What did Lermontov expect him to do? "Has he taken any action?" he asked coolly.

"Most unfortunately. Nothing irremediable, but he has been surprisingly effective. Our troops had captured one of your brother's health assistants, the one who works in Badel."

"Ismail Jan."

"That is correct. The next night, this Commander Rahim and his trained terrorists raided a village. They entered the home of a patriotic Afghan and kidnapped his wife and children. They also stole a small quantity of weapons."

"When did this happen?"

"Last night. Doubtless you will soon receive a report."

"Doubtless. How long has my father been in Kunar?"

"We think about seven days. We didn't expect you to know about it unless you had been in contact with him."

Ayub felt a chill, and his emotions struggled between fear of his Soviet mentor and rage at his betrayal by his father.

"Oh, nothing intended by that," said the Russian hastily. "Your loyalty has never been under question, despite your bourgeois background. We know that the first generation of leadership in any post-revolutionary society is bound to be comprised largely of bourgeois intellectuals.

"We can afford to overlook the activities of your brother, as he is a doctor and not a terrorist. As far as we are concerned, as long as he does nothing directly to provoke us, he is doing a service to the Afghan people. But your father and his activities are quite another matter."

"I understand," said Ayub briskly. "What happened to the patriot's wife and children?"

"Our local authorities received a note this morning. It offers the wife and children unharmed in return for the release of the health assistant."

"I see." Ayub pondered, his heart pounding. "Is there any hope of releasing them in any other way?"

"Not alive. We think the bandits would kill them before letting them go."

"Then our choices are either to keep the health assistant and stall for time, to attack and risk the hostages' death, or to negotiate with them."

Lermontov sipped his tea.

"Is it a civil decision or a military decision?" asked Ayub.

"We will abide by your decision as Governor."

Ayub slammed down his glass with a bang. "I see no real choice. Send the bandits a message that as soon as they release the patriot's wife and children and return the stolen weapons, and only *after* they release them, this Ismail Jan will also be released. But we must increase security so that this intolerable sort of incident will not be repeated."

"You would trust the bandits?"

Ayub fixed the general's gaze. "As they would trust us. Honor among thieves."

Lermontov tapped his heavy fingers on his glass. "Mozart's Clarinet Quintet," he commented. "You have excellent taste." He thought for a moment. "I think we can accept your decision. If they betray us, we will shoot them on the spot. If they deal fairly, we will nevertheless punish the village that sheltered the bandits." Lermontov got up to go.

Ayub walked him to his car, numbly. He watched the general drive out, heard the gates clank shut behind the car, and cursed the fate that had imprisoned him behind these gates.

CHAPTER 15
ELIZABETH

Amrau Tangay

Three days had passed, and Elizabeth was growing impatient, but resigned to her fate. She had not yet had her "date" with Dr. Yusuf, nor had the mysterious Commander Rahim appeared, and she didn't feel she was getting much accomplished on her story.

The day after Elizabeth's arrival, Michel had left for Badel to join the commander and his men, who had been delayed. Elizabeth had wheedled Ebrahim into accompanying Michel as a guide, convincing him that she didn't need a translator while she was at the clinic. Ebrahim had at first refused, citing his responsibility for her to Massoud Khan, but had finally relented when she reminded him that Sharif would remain with her to protect her.

Since the others had left, Elizabeth had at least learned a great deal about the doctor's day-to-day work, and had used up a number of rolls of film. Though Dr. Yusuf seemed to be studiously avoiding granting her an actual interview he had, as promised, taught her how to take blood pressure and what to listen for in a heartbeat. To his amusement, several people had asked if she was a doctor, which she had begged him to tell them she was not.

With only four of them at the clinic, Sharif had been pressed into service as a dispenser of medicines. The four got along well, though they did not have a common language, and despite her frustration Elizabeth was beginning to enjoy the daily routine. It helped that her ankle felt better every day.

She also enjoyed her growing friendship with Malolai, who had a wicked sense of humor and loved to tease. Most of her practical jokes were at Dr. Yusuf's expense, and Elizabeth derived a wicked and somewhat guilty pleasure from this.

Yusuf lived in a small house opening onto the clinic's courtyard below his rooftop office. Inside it was simple and orderly, with six *charpoys* tucked against the rough mud walls and a colorful woven carpet spread over the earthen floor. This carpet was swept every day by the boy Rahman. He and his father Farid were employed by the Medical Association as servants and watchmen. They slept inside the dispensary and Farid cooked for the doctor and his guests. Rahman's mother and sisters were all in the relative safety of a refugee camp near Peshawar, Elizabeth discovered, and the Medical Association paid a stipend directly to the family for the father's and son's work.

Malolai worked tirelessly beside the doctor and ate lunch with Elizabeth on the days when there was time for a lunch. In the evenings she went to a house up the valley where she lived with a family, as was proper for an unmarried woman. Elizabeth missed her in the long slow evenings when she and Sharif retired with Yusuf to his small room lit only by a small kerosene lantern. It was hard to read and write in the dim light. Sharif sat for hours quietly murmuring as he slid the amber beads of his *tasbeh*, the Muslim rosary, between his fingers. Elizabeth often grew tired of straining her eyes and watched Sharif pray and Dr. Yusuf work endlessly, bent over Persian script. She wished she had the simple faith to pray endlessly, but when she tried to say the rosary it still felt hollow to her, so she comforted herself with the memory of her innocent childhood love for the Virgin Mary and fell asleep with gentle thoughts.

The third morning of Elizabeth's stay there had been few patients at the clinic. Around noon an old man had come up from a village in Deh Wagal, requesting the doctor's urgent presence to tend to his infant grandson, who had a high fever and was too ill to move. Dr. Yusuf had left Malolai in charge and had gone with Sharif down the valley.

Malolai was in the dispensary taking inventory of the medications and Elizabeth sat on the *charpoy* under the mulberry tree writing to her brother Mark. The smell of the cooking fire wafted across the courtyard as Farid baked pancake-like flat breads on a large black griddle. She reread what she had written.

Her narrative was terse, detailed, and even humorous. But she was dissatisfied. She seemed to be missing a crucial point.

She gazed out over the gorge and across to the steep mountain wall, which she followed up to the cloudless sky, then back to the intense green tracery of tender new mulberry leaves just over her head. How could she describe the beauty of this scene?

She wrote decisively, "I can't seem to find the words to make this real to you, or even to myself. Afghanistan is a land that demands poetry."

Malolai came out of the low dispensary building and yawned as she stretched, then laughed, making a face. "Boring work, to list the medicines."

Elizabeth closed her writing pad. "Come and sit down. I think lunch is almost ready."

Malolai sat beside her. "You have been writing a letter?"

"Yes, to my brother in New York. I won't be able to mail it till we get back to Peshawar, but I don't want to forget anything."

Malolai cupped her chin in her hands pensively, just as Elizabeth often did. "Are you close to your brother?"

"Yes. He's like a best friend to me. We used to have great times when I lived in New York."

Malolai continued staring out towards the mountain wall. "I am close to my brother also, but I haven't seen him in such a long time."

"Where is he now?"

"In Kabul. It's really only a few months since I have seen him, but it seems longer because I don't know when I will see him again. Everybody is separate now, like leaves in the wind. It's hard for us. We are used to close families. Are your parents living?"

"Yes, in Pennsylvania."

"Do you live with them?"

"No, I was living in New York, a few hours away. I don't know where I'll live when I get back."

"Are you close to your parents?"

"Yes and no. I love them of course, but they don't understand what I want from life. I usually only see them on holidays. But when I'm in trouble they're always there for me."

"We say *nam-e-khoda* in Farsi when we talk about our families. It means 'in the name of God,' and keeps the evil eye away from loved ones, or from someone who is beautiful. I am glad you have a nice family. I only have my brother. My mother died soon after I was born, and my father was imprisoned during the time of Daoud and died in prison. I was just thirteen then, and my brother Habib was in his twenties. Habib and his wife took me in to live with them."

Elizabeth was always shocked at the casual way Afghans discussed tragedies like death in prison. She stayed silent for a moment, then asked, "How old are you now?"

"Twenty-three. And you?"

"I'll be thirty next month, in May."

"You don't look thirty."

"Thank you. You don't look twenty-three."

Malolai blushed and laughed nervously. "For that I am happy. For an Afghan girl this is an old age not to be married. Maybe if this stupid coup had not happened I might have been married by now. But I went to the Medical Faculty in Jalalabad and lived at my cousin's house. I wanted to be a doctor.

Maybe someday, *inshallah*, I can finish my studies, when the war is over. Our country, as you can see, needs women doctors."

"Do you want to get married?"

"Yes." She was surprised. "Don't you?"

"Well, yes, someday. But…I suppose in America we marry much later."

"Every Afghan girl wants to get married. But if we are educated we don't want an arranged marriage. We dream of a love marriage."

"Didn't you meet any nice doctors at the Medical Faculty?"

Malolai blushed again. Her skin was fair and her hair very black. Her green eyes completed a striking combination. Elizabeth was surprised that such a beautiful and intelligent woman wasn't yet married.

"There was someone I liked. He wasn't a doctor yet, but a student like me. But I had to leave Jalalabad quickly. I refused to work with Russian doctors and I was warned I was going to be arrested. I don't think he knows what happened to me."

"Is there any way you can reach him to let him know?"

Malolai shrugged. "What good would it do? He is there, I am here, and it is my *naseeb* to be here."

Elizabeth envied Malolai her calm certainty. "Malolai, what made you decide to come here?"

"I didn't decide to come here. I went to the Medical Association as soon as I reached Peshawar and asked them to send me back to Afghanistan to work with any doctor who would allow a woman to work beside him and would arrange a family for me to stay with."

"And Dr. Yusuf agreed. How is he to work with? You seem to work well together."

"Oh, he's a wonderful man and such a good doctor. He never orders me about. He really loves the people here. And he is so much fun to tease because he is so serious."

"Serious" was not a word Elizabeth would have chosen to describe Dr. Yusuf. Perhaps he had a different personality when he spoke Pashtu.

"But he is an unhappy man," continued Malolai. "He is torn between Afghanistan and America. He can never really be either. Maybe someday he can be both."

For a woman who had never been beyond Peshawar, Elizabeth thought, Malolai was quite perceptive. She must have seen Afghans like Dr. Yusuf return to Kabul sometimes, helplessly flapping oversized wings in a home grown too small for them.

"But he has come back," said Elizabeth. "He has made a choice."

"Yes," agreed Malolai. "Perhaps it will make him happy one day. He seems happy only when he works."

"Well at least he spends most of his time working. He certainly doesn't talk much about himself. All I know is that he went to medical school at Columbia University and lived in San Francisco before he came here."

"Then you know more than I, and more than I even want to know. It is enough for me just to work with him."

Farid had draped a red cloth over the low table next to the *charpoy* and had placed two large *nans*, still hot, on the cloth. He offered them a tin plate of pale butter and poured tea into two glasses. As Elizabeth watched him solicitously serve them, she for a moment envied the Afghans their certainty of social roles, and felt uncertain of her own place. Why did Yusuf interest her so much? She could not think of a person more different than herself, and one she would be less likely to talk to had she met him in the States. Perhaps it was merely her curiosity. "Curiosity killed the cat," echoed her mother's voice. "Satisfaction brought him back," answered a small girl's voice.

"What do you think of Ebrahim?" asked Elizabeth to distract herself.

"We should not talk about our friends when they are not here. But really, I don't like him much."

Elizabeth was interested. "Why?"

"He is like this." Malolai stood up and puffed out her chest, an arrogant expression on her face. She said a few words in Pashtu, which Elizabeth recognized by sound if not meaning.

Elizabeth laughed. It was an excellent imitation. Farid laughed as well. "What does that mean?" asked Elizabeth.

"He's always asking, 'what has happened here?' as if he must know everything. He thinks he is too important."

Elizabeth tended to agree. "But I think he means well. He is difficult to travel with though."

"Is that why you made him go away with Michel?"

"I didn't…well, I thought we could all use a vacation."

Malolai laughed a full laugh. "And what do you think of Michel?"

Elizabeth stood up and postured, posing as if with a camera, gesturing to people to move out of the way. "Pleeze, pleeze, thees way a leetle."

Malolai and Farid were both laughing uncontrollably. "Malolai," she mocked Michel, "you are so beautfeeful in the peetures." Malolai burst into fresh peels of laughter. Elizabeth sat down and put an arm around Malolai's shoulders. "Seriously, why don't you marry Michel? I do think he likes you, and you could go to France."

Malolai wiped away tears of laughter. "Michel likes every woman. And I think he likes men too."

"Ahh. I wondered about that."

Malolai giggled. "Do you think he and Ebrahim…?"

Elizabeth doubled over with laughter at the thought of Ebrahim's expression of shock if he could hear their conversation. Finally their giggling subsided and they began to eat.

"What do you think of Sharif?" asked Malolai shyly.

Elizabeth glanced at her sharply. "He's a very sweet man. He's like a brother to me."

"I also admire him very much. He is a good Mujaheed. Very honest. And he loves the people very much. He admires you as well."

"Admires me?" Her bread suddenly tasted like sawdust.

"Only, he speaks well of you. He says you are very brave, that he knew you were in much pain with your ankle."

"I'm not at all brave," said Elizabeth. "You are. What else does he say?"

"That is all, of you. But he talks of many things. He wants to learn about the world. He would have been educated, but his family had ill luck and then the Communists came. He is very intelligent and kind-hearted. He has compassion and knows a lot about our traditional medicines. I wish there would be time to teach him more of first aid. The Mujahedeen need men who know what to do. I wish you could understand Pashtu or Farsi. Then you would know what kind of man he really is."

The two women ate in silence. By an unspoken mutual agreement, neither of them joked about either Sharif or Dr. Yusuf.

"Elizabeth?"

"Yes?"

"Act like Michel again. You really make me laugh."

Elizabeth screwed up her face into an approximation of the Frenchman's offhand smile. "Malolai, may I make you some tea? You work so hard. Just a leetle beet?"

Neither of them heard Dr. Yusuf and Sharif come up behind them. "Malolai," Elizabeth continued her mockery, "I will publish many peectures of you in beeg magazines in Paree."

Dr. Yusuf dropped his bag on the ground. The two women turned, and at the sight of the expression on the doctor's face, stopped laughing.

"How was the baby?" asked Elizabeth. "Is it all right?"

"The baby died while I was there. The high fever was cholera."

"We have some vaccine," said Malolai.

"Not nearly enough. All we can do is vaccinate high risk patients and send someone to Peshawar to try to get more vaccine. And pray."

"How many days before someone could return if he left now? And with how much vaccine?" asked Elizabeth.

"Enough, if one person carried only vaccine." He calculated. "Seven, eight days. It's a long time, but it might save some lives. If we can even get the vaccine.

We're lucky the weather isn't too hot yet. It would be impossible to preserve it in the summer. But who can we send?"

Malolai looked at Sharif, who nodded in answer to her unspoken communication and spoke in Pashtu to Dr. Yusuf. They conversed for a few minutes while Elizabeth watched, not daring to ask a question.

Finally Dr. Yusuf turned to her. "Sharif will go. He was worried about his responsibility to take care of you, but I have given him my word that I will answer to Massoud Khan for your safety." The doctor clapped Sharif on the shoulders. "This is a brave man, and a dedicated one."

Yusuf took a pad out of his bag, wrote something in Persian script and put the folded note in an envelope, which he left unsealed. He spoke to Sharif in Pashtu, and Elizabeth picked out the words "Dr. Nasir" and "Afghanistan Medical Association."

Peshawar seemed another world, unreachable. For a moment she wished she were going as well. "Dr. Yusuf?" she asked hesitantly.

He looked up, his brow deeply furrowed.

"Can you ask Sharif one thing? Only if he has time. I know he will be in a great hurry and I don't want to cause him any more trouble."

"What, Elizabeth?" he asked tiredly.

"Will he be seeing Massoud Khan?"

"I don't know. Yes, he can. What do you want him to say?"

"If he can, ask Massoud to mail this letter to my brother. Otherwise just say that I am all right. Not to worry. Don't mention my ankle. Work is going well. The Mujahedeen are all being good with me."

The doctor smiled and shook his head. "Silly girl. Woman. Of course he will say all these things, and will ask Massoud to send your letter." The doctor translated for Sharif while Elizabeth found her letter and addressed it.

She handed the letter to Sharif and looked at Yusuf. "Tell him thank you."

"Tell him yourself. *Inshallah*, you will see him after seven days."

Elizabeth shook Sharif's hand. "*Mehrbani*," she mumured. "*Mehrbani*." She hoped her eyes would convey what her words could not. Sharif squeezed her hand and said something in Pashtu, pointing at her ankle.

"He says be careful of your ankle," said Dr. Yusuf. "For God's sake, Elizabeth, don't act as if he's not coming back." But the doctor embraced Sharif with emotion.

Elizabeth all at once sensed how tenuous was their hold on life, yet how tenaciously they clung to fraying branches of hope.

Sharif threw his blanket over his left shoulder with natural grace and set off. Elizabeth said a silent "Hail Mary" for him as they watched him stride down the path. At the bend in the road, he turned and waved. For a moment his gaze lingered on Malolai, and then he was gone.

CHAPTER 16
ELIZABETH

Amrau Tangay

The quiet of the plum-colored dusk was shattered by a distant Pashtu song as Elizabeth sat under the mulberry tree writing in her journal and worrying about the night to come. Malolai had gone to the house where she stayed and Dr. Yusuf sat at his worktable on the roof catching up on records. Rahman and his father Farid were preparing the evening meal. They had obtained two eggs from somewhere and she could smell them frying.

She wondered if she should offer to sleep outside in the courtyard now that Sharif was gone and Yusuf was the only other person in the house. In America it wouldn't matter, and this doctor was certainly American enough to understand platonic friendship. But the villagers might see it differently. It was perfectly acceptable for her as a foreign woman to be in a house or cave with more than one Mujaheed, as the men acted as de facto chaperones for each other, but being alone with one Westernized doctor might be seen as immoral or at the least improper.

As she watched Rahman shake out the table cloth, she knew she'd have to make a decision soon. She saw the doctor get up from his table, spread his blanket on the ground and perform his evening prayers. Watching him pray, no one could guess that he had lived in the States for all those years.

He came down the steps, blanket wrapped around him against the night chill. He looked haggard. "Let me get you another blanket," he said kindly. "You must be cold." He went into the house and returned with a neatly folded camel blanket, which he draped over her shoulders before sitting down next to her. "Now you look like a Mujaheed," he said with a slight smile on his face.

"Thank you. So do you." She knew her conversation sounded inane. She wanted to comfort him, but his sadness tonight seemed too overwhelming to touch. "It was so good of Sharif to volunteer to go," she began.

"Yes, Sharif is a good man. He has a pure heart. That sounds ridiculous in English, but it is the way we speak. I wish you understood Farsi."

"So do I."

An awkwardness fell between them like empty space. He filled it by pouring tea and breaking her bread into small pieces. A lantern in the doorway of the house was their only light as the sky deepened to the violet blue of new plums, and a few stars glowed faintly.

"Dr. Yusuf…"

"Please, call me Yusuf. There's not much point in formality between us."

"Okay, Yusuf. I was thinking, it's such a nice night tonight. I'd like to sleep out here if you don't mind."

He half turned toward her in the dim light, and she thought how esthetic his profile looked rim-lighted by the kerosene lantern. A strong, stubborn face.

"You are beginning to talk like an Afghan," he said. "Americans are usually more direct. But I've already decided I will be the one to sleep outside."

"But I don't want to inconvenience you," she said hastily. "You don't look very well today. If you get sick, who will take care of you?"

"I didn't know you cared," he said lightly.

The Pashtu song, which had fallen silent, now broke into their conversation from somewhere nearby. They turned to see three lights coming down the valley, skirting the nearby houses.

"Ebrahim," said Yusuf. "In fine voice tonight. I think our problem is solved."

Ebrahim stopped singing as soon as he saw Yusuf and Elizabeth sitting together. "Where is Sharif?" he asked in surprise.

"He's gone to Peshawar," said Elizabeth. "There is cholera in the valley, so he volunteered to get vaccine."

Ebrahim spoke rapidly to Dr. Yusuf in Pashtu. Their faces, and that of the young Afghan man with Ebrahim, were grave. Michel stood silently on the edge of the circle of light.

Yusuf recounted the story in Pashtu as he poured tea for his guests. Farid brought two more *charpoys* from inside the house. The doctor sat down next to the man Elizabeth did not know, a slight youth with a fuzz of beard on his face, while Ebrahim sat on another *charpoy*, leaning forward to hear every word, occasionally offering comments.

Michel joined Elizabeth. "May I? I don't like to disturb you, but I cannot understand the conversation."

"Of course. Sit down." He was polite if nothing else. "Who is that other man?"

The Frenchman's gray eyes widened. "You do not know that story yet? Of course, he is the health assistant who was captured by the Russians. Ismail Jan. Commander Rahim came to know of it and led a party at night to the house of one Khalqi. They captured the Khalqi's wife and three children, and also some arms. Then they sent a message to the authorities offering to trade the woman and children for Ismail Jan. The authorities agreed to the trade, but only if the Mujahedeen would give the arms back.

"You should have seen! Most of the Mujahedeen wanted to make the trade and promise to give the weapons afterwards, then break the promise and keep them. Commander Rahim said that would not be honorable, can you imagine? He agreed to the bargain and gave back the weapons. Ismail Jan was freed this morning."

She chafed at the thought that her injured ankle had left her sidelined. "It's a good story," she said grudgingly.

"Yes, I have taken many good pictures. From the very beginning, pictures of the Khalqi's wife and children as prisoners, and with the telephoto from the mountain, pictures of the trade actually taking place."

"Aren't you afraid that the Russians will find out that you are here?"

"How?"

"Won't the Khalqi woman tell her husband that there is a foreign journalist in Badel?"

"Anyway I am not in Badel now," he said dismissively. "And I don't think one journalist is worth all the trouble to fight the Mujahedeen."

"You didn't mention any other journalists, did you?"

He looked puzzled. "No, why should I?"

"No reason." She wished he would go away soon. For good. "What will you do now?"

"I will go where the wind blows me, wherever there is fighting. Perhaps back to Badel to see Commander Rahim and follow his men. He doesn't seem to mind. I think I will stay in Afghanistan for some time. And you?"

"Because of the cholera I have to wait here at least a week until Sharif comes back. The rest of the men I came with are in Badel. I really don't know what I should do. My ankle seems better now, and I think I could walk, but I don't want to leave if Yusuf, uh, if Dr. Yusuf needs my help. We have some vaccine here now, and tomorrow we're supposed to vaccinate high risk patients."

"So you have no plans to go to Badel?"

"No, I guess that's your story. I think I should stay here for now."

Michel cupped his empty glass in his hands. His fingers were long and thin, and pale white, the hands of an artist, not a businessman or a laborer. Elizabeth poured him another glass of tea and refilled those of Ebrahim, Yusuf, and Ismail, none of whom acknowledged her. "I think I'm beginning to know what it's like to be an Afghan woman," she muttered to Michel as she sat down again.

"Yes, it is very difficult for them. This is something the Mujahedeen must change, or they will fail."

"But how can they change it? I agree, believe me, but the only way I see is for more women like Malolai to get an education and to work. Liberation can't be forced on them by people like us, and certainly not in the middle of a war. But from what Massoud Khan and his wife tell me, women were getting more freedom before this war started. Once it's over the process will continue. In some ways maybe it's been accelerated by the war. The women of Afghanistan have played too much of a part in the struggle to accept being second-class citizens. Don't you think women like Malolai will demand a say in any government set up after the Russians leave?"

"*If* they leave." The Frenchman frowned. "The Communists gave women equal rights and the people didn't want it. That and the land reform infuriated the mullahs. That is why these people are fighting. It is actually a very backward rebellion, led by religious fanatics."

Elizabeth was exasperated. "Not all of them are fundamentalists. If people like Massoud Khan and his father Mohammed Akbar get into power, things will change for the better. They're certainly fighting for a lot more than the right to keep practicing feudalism and keep their women in *purdah*. They're fighting for their faith, for one thing, and for their very lives," she said passionately. "You can see the destruction all around us."

"Yes, but it is exaggerated. The Pakistani press has exaggerated the refugee problem just to get more money. The war is actually going on at a very low level."

"You almost sound pro-Soviet."

"Oh, no, no, no. Only one must look below the surface."

"Why did you come to Afghanistan?" she asked. "You don't seem to like the place much."

"Oh no, I love Afghanistan. Just I want to see the Afghan people having a good life, an equal life."

"So do I, and so do Yusuf and Massoud Khan. The Russians certainly aren't giving them anything except death and destruction."

"Do you think the Americans will give them any better?

"That's not the point! They're hardly involved. There's virtually nothing in the press about Afghanistan."

"Why did *you* come here?" he asked blandly.

"A broken love affair. The French should understand that."

"Really?" He suddenly looked sympathetic.

"Yes, really. But nobody else here knows about it. It's not my only reason, of course. And I'm not looking for anyone to comfort me, so don't get any ideas. Actually I'd been thinking of coming here since I interviewed Massoud Khan in New York last year. When my relationship fell apart it seemed like a real good idea to go on a trip." She was surprised at herself for confiding in this stranger. Perhaps she just missed the easy camaraderie a woman could sometimes have with a Western man.

Michel looked at her over his glass. His sympathy seemed quite genuine. "Was it a long relationship?"

"Five years."

"I have never had such a long relationship myself. With a woman or a man."

Elizabeth did not react. Malolai had been right. "I think commitment is difficult in Western culture," she said. "We're no longer accustomed to it. It always seems that one person is more committed than the other."

Michel suddenly looked very young and very sad. "Yes," he whispered.

She wondered who he had been in love with. Male or female? "How old are you?"

He hesitated. "Twenty-two."

"You're still young! I will be thirty next month. You've got years to find a partner, if that's what you want."

"Yes, I suppose. But I don't think I will."

"Well if you don't think you will then you probably won't. You have to be open. Did you also come here to escape a broken romance?"

He glanced at the other men, who were still deep in conversation. "Yes."

"Well, you must admit coming here is sure a distraction. It cures suicidal thoughts too."

He smiled faintly. "You remind me of my sister. She is older, and married. I can tell her most things. I lived in her house since I was a child, when my parents were killed in an accident. You are the kind of person people can talk to. I don't think you tell other people's secrets."

"No, I don't betray confidences. But I don't ask for them either." She hoped he was not about to unburden himself of too horrible a secret.

"I am bisexual," he said, not looking at her.

"So is my brother."

He looked up, surprised. "I pity him."

"Why? Mark's perfectly happy the way he is. He avoids close relationships, but so do lots of people. He enjoys life and has tons of friends, both male and female."

"Is it possible?"

"Of course it's possible."

"Where does your brother live?"

"New York. He works in film and theater."

"That is the difference. In France…" He trailed off.

"But I've spent time in Paris. It's one of the most tolerant cities in the world."

"I didn't live in Paris, not until the end. I am from a small town near Lyons. I was not accepted there. I felt that everyone knew what happened, and pitied me." He paused. "How old was your brother when he realized he was gay? And how did he come to know?"

"I never asked him. I was much younger, only twelve when he went off to college. I always thought he was more sensitive than other boys, and I always looked for men who were like him. Well, till I got involved with Tom. Anyway I've got a lot of gay friends. I guess Mark must have known he was gay when he was in college, maybe before."

Michel looked at her squarely. "I was raped by my headmaster when I was twelve. At first I was frightened. Then I knew I enjoyed it. I went to him many times that year. Then someone in the school observed us. One of the boys spied on us, and brought more friends. They talked in their homes, and the whole town came to know.

"Everyone pitied me. Jean-Paul, that was my headmaster's name, was sent to a prison somewhere. They thought I should hate him. I said I did, but I didn't really." He hung his head and stared into his glass. "I feel I betrayed him."

This was out of her depth, but she felt for Michel in his confusion. She looked towards Yusuf, who was still engrossed in conversation. "You were still a child. Children have no power."

He looked at her hopefully.

"You were taken advantage of by an older person in authority. You did what you had to do to survive."

"It was never the same for me in the town. I waited only to go away. For two years I was at college in Lyons, and at last I was in Paris, at the Sorbonne. I made love to women, but I did not enjoy it. I wanted so badly to be normal, so I pretended.

"But last year I had a wonderful professor of political science, a man. We became friends. We spoke for long hours about politics and sociology. I felt attracted to him, but he had a wife and children. Then one afternoon, when it was raining and gray, he put his hand on my shoulder, like this." He demonstrated, and Elizabeth felt uncomfortably like a voyeur. "And we made love. But he became cold after that. He did not speak to me in class, and he no longer invited me."

"We've all been through this, gay or straight," she shrugged.

"I felt that this rejection, this betrayal, was my punishment for betraying Jean-Paul. I no longer wanted to live in Paris. I had heard that many Pashtuns were homosexual, and thought they might be more tolerant here. When I took my degree I decided to come here."

"And are they more tolerant here?"

"Yes, I think so. Gentler. Less judgmental." He looked at her with sadness in his candid gaze. "I do nothing here, only look. But I like to be close to my friends. Here I can embrace a man and no one says you are terrible or filthy. Maybe I love a man here, but I do nothing. Just to be with him is enough."

"It seems a repressed culture," she said with an implied warning. "It could be a big problem if you came on to the wrong man."

"I will be careful." He looked away, up at the sky. "Now you know all my secrets, Elizabet."

"And you know some of mine, so we're even. I guess that means we have to trust each other." She offered him her hand, and he shook it firmly.

"Nice to see you've decided to be friends," broke in Dr. Yusuf. "We may all be here for awhile. I think we should turn in. We've got a long day tomorrow. Elizabeth, I'll need your help. It's too much for just Malolai and me. Will you come with us?"

"Of course," she said with a cheery certainty she didn't feel.

"If I had a melon, I'd give you one to practice on. You'll have to make do with Ebrahim and Michel. At least they can't sue you for malpractice."

CHAPTER 17
ELIZABETH

Amrau Tangay

Early the next morning, long before the sun had climbed over the high rim of hills opposite the clinic, Dr. Yusuf watched as Elizabeth prepared her first syringe.

Ebrahim offered his arm to Elizabeth with a great show of bravery. She felt uneasy touching his hard and muscular arm and was afraid that she might inadvertently jab him harder than necessary.

Michel had had a cholera injection four months before, but Dr. Yusuf thought it wise to give him another shot, so Elizabeth practiced on him too. He offered her his arm trustingly, and looked into her eyes with affection. To her satisfaction, she injected both Michel and Ebrahim without any apparent damage.

"You seem to have a knack," said Dr. Yusuf. "Maybe you should have been a doctor."

"I may end up one yet."

They started off down the path toward the lower villages, the doctor leading, Malolai and Elizabeth following. Ismail came behind, carrying the doctor's bag filled with all the vaccine they had.

"How far is it?" asked Elizabeth.

"About two hours," answered the doctor. "How is your foot?"

"I'll let you know tonight."

"You'll probably feel some soreness. It shouldn't be serious."

The tone of the day changed subtly. Above the ever-present roar of the small river, Elizabeth detected something more ominous. As they walked the sound grew louder, and then unmistakable. Elizabeth looked up to see three Soviet MiG's flying in formation, silver needles stabbing the cottony sky. She froze. Dr. Yusuf kept on walking.

"They are not for us," he said without emotion. "They have other work today."

Elizabeth resumed walking, attempting to control her shaking. "But where are they going? What are they doing?"

"Bombing. They don't do anything else. We can only pray for their targets and be grateful that today, at least, it's not us."

They heard distant explosions, no more than dull thuds. No one spoke. Elizabeth felt numb. What impersonal power decided today one village, tomorrow the next? What person could sit behind the controls of an airplane, and what hand could push the button that unleashed a fiery death on those below, people the pilot and bombardier had never seen?

But Americans had done it in Vietnam, and now Russians were doing it in Afghanistan. And what a price we paid, she thought, remembering all the Vietnam veterans she and her brother knew. Some were alcoholics, others heavily into marijuana, or if they could afford it, cocaine. Most couldn't seem to have a decent long term relationship. A few seemed happy, held jobs, had wives or girlfriends, and only occasionally fell silent for no apparent reason.

Mark had done his service as a conscientious objector, making occupatiional training films for deaf children. The Red Army didn't have conscientious objectors. A conscript's choices would be Afghanistan or Siberia, and Afghanistan was a shorter commitment. All they had to do was survive.

Elizabeth suddenly felt sorry for all those men, here for reasons they didn't understand and perhaps didn't even question, with most of the population of the land against them. She even felt sorry for the men in those planes, men made into unthinking uniformed gods dispensing death.

As if there weren't enough threats to human life. Cholera, malnutrition. As a race we develop ever more effective threats to our continued existence. The Afghans and the Americans said the Russians used poison gas in Afghanistan. Strident voices in Congress indignantly deplored not the suffering of the Afghan people but the technological gap between Soviet and U.S. methods of destruction. In the end, a U.N. inquiry had been unable to establish conclusive evidence of the illegal use of chemical warfare. They could prove the use of toxic gases, but not of lethal gases. It was one of those fine but crucial points of law. Only lethal gases had been banned; the merely toxic had not. And strangely, manufacture had not been banned, only use. It didn't matter, thought Elizabeth cynically. The victim of a bomb or bullet is just as dead as the victim of chemical warfare.

Elizabeth's experience had not prepared her for the scene that greeted them upon their arrival in the village. A small boy showed them into the upstairs quarters of a house, reached by climbing an unsteady log carved with uneven notches. Inside, Elizabeth first heard the sobbing, then as her eyes adjusted to the dark she made out a young woman, barely out of her teens, crouched in a corner of the room, rocking back and forth and wailing uncontrollably. A pretty girl with shiny black hair in many small braids and silver ornaments peeking out from under her loose veil was trying to console her.

A middle-aged man entered the room and started shouting at the woman, making her cry more. He raised his hand threateningly, and Dr. Yusuf spoke sharply. A thin-faced old man entered and gazed disapprovingly on the whole scene. At a word from him, the young girl with the braids looked up, nodded, and with a last reassuring pat on the weeping woman's shoulder left the room and disappeared down the log ladder.

The old man then spoke to the middle-aged man, apparently his son, who left the room as well. Dr. Yusuf, at the old man's invitation, sat down on one of several *charpoys* in the room and gestured to Elizabeth and the others to do the same. Elizabeth sat next to Malolai, who had placed herself near the bereaved woman. The woman's racking sobs had subsided, and now she merely whimpered from time to time. Malolai slid down to squat next to her, took her hand, and spoke quietly.

Elizabeth felt awkward, not knowing how to be of use. She looked from Malolai and the distressed woman back to Dr. Yusuf, who was in conversation with Ismail.

At last Yusuf spoke in English. "Elizabeth, there is a lot of work to do. You and Malolai must vaccinate all the women and most of the children. We will start in this house, as this is where the child died. This is the mother. She is quite distraught, so I may have to give her something to calm her if Malolai does not succeed. You and Malolai will go from house to house and Ismail and I will work outside on the rooftop.

"And one more thing. You are not to eat or drink anything in this village."

"But…" Behind Dr. Yusuf the middle-aged man reentered the room, carrying a pot of tea and a stack of glasses.

"I'll explain to them so they will not be insulted." The doctor spoke at length. The man nodded, but did not look happy. The old man appeared to understand better, and waved his son away.

Dr. Yusuf divvied up supplies, leaving the bag to the two women, and followed the old man and Ismail down the ladder.

Malolai kept talking to the grief-stricken woman while Elizabeth prepared a syringe. Elizabeth handed the syringe to Malolai and watched the woman's face as she offered up her bare arm, uncaringly. Her face was darkly beautiful but now swollen and puffy, her brown eyes rimmed in red. The baby must have been young, for not even the woman's loose clothes could hide breasts swollen with milk.

"It was her first child," Malolai whispered as she and Elizabeth made their way down the log ladder. "It was a son. Her husband, that man you saw, was happy that she had had a son. Now she fears he will be angry with her and blame her. She is his second wife and is afraid he might divorce her. She is all alone now. Her father is dead and her brother was martyred last month."

"What will happen to her? Her husband won't really divorce her, will he?"

Malolai looked up at Elizabeth, who was still balancing down the ladder. "He can. Maybe he won't. We are in a *jehad* now and our families must stay together. I told her she is young and still beautiful and *inshallah* she will have many more sons. What else could I tell her?"

What else? Life went on. War went on, and death went on, and life went on. People married and had babies, and died with more frequency and violence than usual. Yet something drove people to deliver innocent souls into this increasingly uncertain and transitory world.

"I told her the most important thing is to give everyone in this village the vaccine, to prevent this sickness from spreading to anyone else. But we don't know if it's too late or not."

"Surely if we vaccinate everyone here that can stop the spread."

"There are too many uncontrollable factors. The Mujahedeen have passed through this village. The baby's grandfather came to us in Amrau Tangay. And Sharif was here yesterday with Dr. Yusuf." She caught her breath sharply. "Sharif!"

"What's wrong?"

"No one thought to vaccinate Sharif. He might be in danger..." Malolai's oval face faded to white.

Words caught in Elizabeth's throat. "What's the incubation period? Surely there will be time when he reaches Peshawar. Dr. Nasir will ask him and immediately vaccinate him."

Malolai's face was the color of cold ashes. "We can only pray to God. Not everyone gets cholera. And perhaps for some reason he had already received the vaccine before. But if he should get cholera...Elizabeth, you must see the consequences! It is not only Sharif, but the Mujahedeen, the villages, and whoever he meets in Peshawar."

A pattern of horror unfolded before Elizabeth's eyes. "Where is Sharif now? Where will he be today?"

"Still at Babur Tangay, waiting for the night to cross the river."

"Then someone might still be able to reach him. Someone should go right now, with enough vaccine for all the Mujahedeen of Babur Tangay. Let's see, if Sharif has been exposed, he could already be a carrier. If the disease is still in the incubation stage, can the vaccine prevent him from getting sick?"

"At this time, yes. Or it can make the disease less severe."

"Where's Yusuf?" asked Elizabeth quickly. She scanned the village and saw him and Ismail on a nearby rooftop. She ran across the courtyard between the houses and scrambled up another log ladder. "Yusuf, someone has to go after Sharif!"

"What? Why?"

"Did you give him an injection?"

The doctor's face slowly registered. "Oh my God..."

"There's still time. Send Ismail to Babur Tangay, right now."

He looked dazed, and she hoped he was not falling ill himself.

"What made you think of this?"

"I didn't. Malolai did. But don't waste time. Sharif will only be at Babur Tangay until dusk."

Yusuf looked at the sun. "There is a chance," he conceded. "We have to try." He spoke rapidly to Ismail, whose face tightened with concern.

"Give him enough for the men at Babur Tangay," said Elizabeth. "More than enough. We've got to stop the disease now. Malolai said it could go to Peshawar otherwise..."

"She's right." He covered his face with his hands and rubbed his forehead. "And it would be my fault. How could I have been so stupid?"

She wanted to take his hands, but did not. She stood on the edge of the roof. "It will be all right. And it's not your fault."

He looked directly at her. "How not my fault? I am a doctor and should consider all possibilities."

"And Malolai is a nurse, and I am a journalist, and we all should have known better. You are only human, Yusuf." He continued staring at her, and she felt vulnerable and exposed on the village rooftop. "Tell Ismail to go now, Yusuf."

As if shocked into action, the doctor rattled off instructions to Ismail. Elizabeth scurried down the ladder to rejoin Malolai and told her to prepare the bag with enough vaccine for twenty-five people. By the time Ismail reached them it was done, and the young man took the bag with a smile and was soon out of sight, traveling at a run.

The two women, both shaken, continued their work. The crying babies, the stoic women, the frightened young children trying to be brave, were all a blur to Elizabeth. She watched Malolai, who despite her anxiety never made a mistake and injected each person as painlessly as possible. The sun slowly lowered in the sky, tinting the valley with soft gold. Elizabeth was seized by a sense of lost time, as if this had all happened before, and would happen again, natural destruction hand in hand with human destruction. Malolai bent over a large cloth in which she was gathering unused disposable syringes and small vials of vaccine. Elizabeth saw a single tear fall in the dust beneath the cloth and caught her friend by the shoulders.

"He'll be all right," said Elizabeth.

"It is almost sunset," answered Malolai. "If Ismail has not reached, or if Sharif left early…"

"He reached!" said Elizabeth fiercely. "Sometimes I just know things, and I know he reached there."

Malolai looked at her uncertainly. She had controlled the rest of her tears, but her black lashes were wet.

"Anyway, we will know as soon as Ismail returns," continued Elizabeth. "That should be tomorrow, right?"

"*Inshallah.*" Stoically, Malolai returned to her work.

Dr. Yusuf was addressing a circle of village elders on a rooftop. The two women did not approach, but at a sign from the young girl in the first house climbed into the upper chamber and waited. The mother of the dead baby had calmed herself and was at her prayers in the corner. When she finished, Malolai took the roughly woven prayer mat from her and performed her own *namaz*. Elizabeth sat cross-legged on the floor and closed her eyes, praying in whatever words she could call to mind. Most of the formalized prayers of the Roman Catholic Church had long since abandoned her. When she did pray, she tried to communicate directly. She was sorry that it always seemed to be a request rather than pure worship. But right now she prayed that Ismail had reached Babur Tangay in time.

The doctor entered the room and the bereaved mother turned away. "We should go," he said shortly.

Elizabeth and Malolai rose. Malolai embraced and kissed the mother and then the young girl, and Elizabeth followed her lead. Yusuf stood in the doorway looking out at the mountains. In the light of the setting sun the gray in his hair stood out.

They followed him wordlessly down from the hillside village to the path that ran along the river. For a long time no one spoke, then Yusuf said tiredly, "I told them to boil the water, to clean everything, to avoid urinating into the water supply. All of this is something that should have been done years ago."

"Do you think they'll listen?" asked Elizabeth.

He shrugged. "Maybe. It's given them a good scare. Maybe if people like me had come out to the villages ten years ago, maybe if I'd come instead of staying in America, none of this would have had to happen. Some of our family lands were in this very region, but I hardly ever came here."

"You weren't the only one," said Malolai. "Everyone preferred to be in Kabul if they couldn't be abroad. I also would have lived in Kabul."

"And look what we have done to our country," he said bitterly. "We have left it ignorant and uneducated. We left our people open to the sweet promises of social justice offered by the Russians, and we left them unprepared to fight the Russian machines. Which is the greater sin?"

"Stop blaming yourself," said Elizabeth. "And stop pitying yourself. We all do things we regret. What matters is what we do once we realize we regret them."

"If it's not too late by then," he said. "It's not enough that we have war and malnutrition, but now we have an epidemic that could have been prevented. If only we had more vaccine!"

"And more doctors," said Elizabeth. "And more nurses, and health workers. It's not your fault. You are doing what you can. It's up to the world to provide some medicines and a little support. I didn't even know who you were, or what you'd be like, but I wanted to cover this story because Afghan doctors are taking risks to help their own people, and I think people ought to know about it. Everyone hears about the French doctors who go into war zones in Afghanistan and Central America, and famine areas of East Africa. I admire them too, but the world hears only about them and thinks that the Afghans aren't doing anything to help themselves, and therefore deserve no help. I want to tell them differently."

"I'm no hero, Elizabeth *jan*. Don't try to make me into one."

She knew he had used the Persian term of endearment to her, but as she looked at his face she could see no clues to his real thoughts. His profile was sharp and hard in the light of the rising moon. "You're all heroes," she said. "You, Malolai, Sharif, Commander Rahim, whoever he may be and wherever he may be. And every Mujaheed and every villager. You're heroes because you are surviving against great odds."

He smiled slightly. "But you are more heroic than any of us. You don't have to be here."

But I do. You don't know, she thought, but said, "Neither do you."

"You can call it *naseeb*, *qismet*, our fate or portion. Maybe it's atonement for my past sins."

"They couldn't be so awful."

"To deserve this?"

"To deserve the way you are flagellating yourself."

"Flagellating. A good English word."

"For God's sake, I admire you. Why don't you just accept that?"

His hand brushed hers in the darkness and squeezed her little finger. "Be careful. You may compromise your journalistic objectivity."

"But I want people to understand what I've seen."

"Take my advice, write the facts. No one wants to hear about heroes these days, especially foreign people who wear turbans or funny wool hats and run around in mountains carrying Kalashnikovs."

"I'll write the truth," she said vehemently. "As I see it."

"'Truth is like the stars; it does not appear except from behind the obscurity of the night.'"

"Who said that?" she asked, surprised.

"Khalil Gibran."

She said nothing. There were billions of stars, and perhaps billions of corresponding truths, more here in these brilliant skies over the center of Asia than anywhere else on Earth.

"Now, hush," said Yusuf. "It's been a long day. Just walk, and look at the stars above Afghanistan and remember where you are."

The three walked on, like trance-walking travelers in awe of the arching dome of sky.

CHAPTER 18

ELIZABETH

Amrau Tangay

The messenger was waiting when they arrived at the clinic. Elizabeth knew something was badly wrong as soon as she saw Ebrahim's pinched face. A dark youth sat next to him, his face reflecting stark fear. The boy sprang to his feet as soon as he saw the doctor, speaking rapidly, almost hysterically. Malolai gasped sharply and went pale. Dr. Yusuf looked angry, but beneath the anger was a hard fear that squeezed his features.

"They've bombed Badel," he said harshly.

"What! How badly?"

"Some dead. Others wounded, maybe dying. I'm going now."

"I'll come with you."

"You'll only hold us up."

"I will not. My ankle doesn't hurt anymore."

"Why do you want to come so much? You want to take pictures?"

She stared at him, flashing dark anger. "I'll leave my damn camera here," she said, forcing her voice under control. "I thought Maololai and I could help."

He rubbed his knuckles over his forehead, his fists tight white balls of rage.

"Elizabeth, forgive me. This is all coming too quickly. And you know who is in Badel," he said in a whisper.

"I will go. Even if I have to sneak off in the middle of the night and find the path on my hands and knees."

"You don't have to do that," said the doctor quietly. "You and Malolai come with me. Mr. Michel, I will again ask you to stay with Ebrahim. Elizabeth, bring your camera. I think the world needs to know what they have done here. Can you do it?"

"I think so."

"It will be ugly, very ugly. Are you squeamish?"

She really didn't know. She had seen the wounded in the hospitals in Peshawar, and had taken pictures. It had been difficult. "I don't think so."

"Do you think you can help us with the wounded?"

"I will do all I can. It's better than just taking pictures."

"Good. We'll go as soon as Malolai has everything ready. There's no time to lose. I only wish Ismail was with us."

After a quick glass of tea, five small figures set out into the immense darkness. It was not yet 10 o'clock. With luck they might reach Badel in the early hours.

Dr. Yusuf set a fast pace, walking ahead with the youth who had brought the grim message. Malolai came next, and after her Elizabeth, with a Mujaheed from Amrau Tangay bringing up the rear, a silent, blanket-wrapped figure carrying a Kalashnikov.

Elizabeth thought of Sharif, and sensed that Malolai was doing the same. By now he must be across the river, vaccine or no vaccine, and was probably on his way through the hills and meadows at the edge of the wide valley, a solitary, stealthy figure armed with only a pistol. The moon had set. It would be hard going for Sharif, as it was for them.

Soft chill breezes stirred the bushes as they climbed. Occasionally a goat would bleat, or something large would blunder through the underbrush. There was a sharp dampness to the air. As they walked Elizabeth looked up now and again and was disturbed to see whole quarters of the blazing sky blotted out by colorless masses of cloud. The silence was ominous; it spoke to Elizabeth of dishonorable plots, of seductive and sudden dissemblance.

The sky flickered violet from time to time, but there was no thunder until they reached the top of the ridge that divided Deh Wagal from Badel. As they hurried along a path amidst the pines that topped the spiny ridge, a concussion startled them and echoed through the valleys. Elizabeth heard Yusuf mutter under his breath and saw him look apprehensively at the sky, which was now cloaked with cloud. They walked more slowly now, and in utter darkness. The mountains seemed to have been swallowed up. Nowhere in all of this vast blackness was there a single light, of divine or human manufacture.

The small party was forced to go still more slowly as their leader picked out a path step by step. They crunched on the dead pine needles of generations, and passed patches of snow that reflected faintly the dim light seeping through the clouds. Yusuf and the leader stopped for a few minutes and conferred. They seem to have lost the way, thought Elizabeth for a brief moment of real terror.

But they struck a path, a steep goat track that clung to the edge of a hillside. On the downward slopes, Elizabeth's ankle began to twinge, then ache. She wished she had brought her walking stick. Cold wetness began to precipitate, then turned to sleet. Finally the sky cut loose its burden and pummeled them with hail. Elizabeth pulled her soaked woolen blanket up about her face to avoid the sting of the small balls of ice. Hot tears burned in her eyes. She could not understand how they could go on. They might fall into chasms of darkness in this storm.

The path became more slippery as rivulets turned into small torrents. The mountains seemed to have come alive, water and stone hurtling from one place to another with an almost human frenzy. Elizabeth suddenly missed Sharif, who before had always been there to catch her.

She saw Malolai stumble in front of her and instinctively dug in her heels and grasped Malolai's arm. The two teetered, and Elizabeth was thankful she could not see whether they were in any real danger.

The hail turned into a cloudburst. Sheets of water rained down on them and Elizabeth, water dripping off her forehead and into her eyes, thought that surely they must stop and wait for the storm to pass. She could hardly see Dr. Yusuf, but sensed a set in his mind that would not allow him to stop, not when lives might be saved by their early arrival.

It was still raining when they entered the village that had been bombed that morning. The rain had put out the fires, which had burned well into the night. The ruins no longer smoldered, but steamed. The fresh rubble had a peculiar horror about it. These bricks were not long sun-dried in their ruin, but newly shattered, inner structure laid bare to the harsh anger of the elements of Central Asia.

A voice hailed them from a nearby hill, a cry that rose above the rain and fell into the dark chasms below them. Their leader shouted back, another rising and falling cry that seemed to contain no words, then spoke to Yusuf, who nodded and followed. There hadn't been many houses in the village, even before it was bombed. Now only the three that perched on the nearby hill were left standing. A lantern appeared through the rain as someone hurried toward them. Elizabeth could see nothing of the face, shrouded in a blanket, but heard hurried exchanges, and among them the name of Commander Rahim.

They reached the three houses, stacked one on top of another in stairstep fashion, and climbed onto the roof of the lowest one. From there they entered a welcoming rectangle of light, to be greeted by the smell of death.

There were several people lying on *charpoys* and two more on the ground on rough woolen blankets spread on the woven carpet. Various parts of their bodies were covered with makeshift bandages now stained dark with blood. There were soft moans, and harsh, rasping breaths. Somewhere in a corner beyond the reach of the lantern a small baby cried.

A tall turbaned man with white eyebrows and beard stepped into the room from outside. Yusuf turned toward him and with a soft cry embraced him. In the dim light Yusuf's eyes shined with unshed tears as the two men spoke in Pashtu. Then the doctor knelt next to one of the victims, a thin, middle-aged man with a clumsy bandage around his upper thigh. The man's eyes were feverish, and he stared half-comprehendingly at the doctor, who gently removed the bandage to reveal a mass of undifferentiated blood and bone.

Dr. Yusuf spoke in Pashtu to Malolai, and then turned to Elizabeth. "You'll be responsible for sterilizing surgical instruments. I have asked them to bring us hot water, and when that is finished to bring us more boiling water, all night if they have to. It appears there are pieces of shrapnel to be removed. Malolai will assist with the surgery. You may have to dress the wounds after I suture them."

Elizabeth was numb with shock and cold and hoped she wouldn't faint. She knelt beside Malolai, trying to ignore the moans and cries around her.

"Take off that blanket," Yusuf snapped. "And the *chadar*. It doesn't matter here and will only chill you." He spoke to Malolai in Pashtu, and she too discarded her soaking outer garments.

Someone brought a large iron kettle of boiling water, which Elizabeth poured into the small enamel tray Malolai produced from the doctor's bag. Malolai laid out the instruments the doctor would need, and with tongs Elizabeth dropped them one by one into the sterilization tray. Out of the bag appeared a powerful battery-operated lamp, which Malolai handed to the old man in the turban, whose large hands held it steadily.

First, the man with the compound fracture of the femur. An injection of pain killer, and careful cleaning of the wound. Once the shreds of dirty blue cotton were pulled away, the wound did not look quite so horrifying. Elizabeth watched with fascination as the doctor prepared the man for a traction splint. People came and went from the room, dragging in boards of varying lengths until one met with the doctor's approval.

"Elizabeth, tear me some strips from that sheet," he ordered. A shadowy figure handed her a coarse piece of cloth, which didn't tear very easily. Finally she searched the bag for scissors and started each tear with a cut.

"Can you tie surgical knots?"

She followed Yusuf's instructions, tying the strips of cloth in place along the man's injured leg and under the rather damp board which Yusuf carefully positioned while Malolai gently steadied the wounded man's leg. Firmly, the doctor tied off the last knot, around the foot and the notched end of the board. Elizabeth saw him swallow once and concentrate. "*Bismillah*," he murmured in prayer, and then began to twist the knot of cloth. Elizabeth saw the splinter of bone in the man's open thigh move slightly, and then in a soft cry of pain the bone was in place, and the man had lost consciousness. The doctor sighed in satisfaction.

"Elizabeth, can you please dress his wound, carefully and cleanly. I'm sorry; you'll have to do it in the dark."

Yusuf and Malolai moved on to a moaning man with a ghastly-looking head wound. As they unwrapped the bloody bandage, Elizabeth swallowed hard to keep from gagging. It looked as if the man would lose the sight in his right eye, if not the eye itself. In the darkness of the hut, inside the greater darkness of the night, the battery-powered lamp showed the scene with horrifying sharpness.

To Elizabeth, in her exhaustion, the wounded became like symbols in a dream. Two had crushed legs. The doctor cleaned and bandaged and splinted them. Elizabeth winced at a small boy's sobs of pain as Yusuf removed chunks of embedded shrapnel from the child's thin upper arm.

A woman lay in the corner, breathing with great effort. Ignoring all convention, the doctor lifted her upper skirts to reveal an open abdominal wound. Elizabeth's stomach involuntarily heaved and she heard herself gag. The doctor examined the gaping wound, the intestines so very white in the bright light, then looked at Elizabeth expressionlessly.

"Can you…" she began.

He shook his head briefly. "They didn't tell me she was this badly wounded. Maybe they didn't know. It would already have been too late. I'm surprised she's lasted this long."

Yusuf spoke quietly to the woman as he gave her an injection of precious pain-killer. The wounded woman did not appear to be aware of much. Her dark, pain-glazed eyes stared at the ceiling, their expression altering slightly only at the sound of a baby's cries. When the doctor moved on to another patient, Elizabeth impulsively took the woman's hand. She felt an answering pressure, then a weakness, and the grip loosened. The hand suddenly felt very cold. Elizabeth kept watching as the woman seemed to sink out of sight, and her eyes lost their feverish glow, opening very wide, not with fear, but with curiosity. Then the woman's breathing stopped.

A grave voice startled Elizabeth from behind. "Another martyr," said the old man in the turban. "Gone home to God." He shook his head slowly, and it was as if all sorrow in the world were focused on the death of this one woman.

Near the woman who had just died sat an uninjured woman, cradling a silent infant in her arms. On a blanket an older baby lay wailing. The doctor had first picked up the crying baby, and finding it uninjured, spoke to the woman. Slowly she drew aside the veil covering her own baby, to reveal a raw wound recognizable as a face only by its position on the infant's body. Wordlessly, the woman looked down at her baby, and then up at the doctor.

Elizabeth's stomach again heaved, and she looked away and tried to distance herself from this appalling reality. She could see Yusuf's hands shaking as he loaded a syringe, shaking almost imperceptibly, but shaking. Gently, he shifted the infant in the mother's arms and injected the contents of the syringe into the baby's rump.

The doctor spoke quietly to the woman while Malolai busied herself cleaning up the instruments. They had done what they could. Into the doorway filtered a cold white light, the color of all dawns empty of hope. The doctor paused by the dead woman, felt for a pulse in her neck, and closed her eyes with his thumbs. He murmured a prayer over her and then pulled her veil over her face for the last time.

Yusuf looked at Elizabeth. The skin was drawn tight over his facial bones. "Go outside," he said tired. "I'll ask for some tea." She rose to go, picking up her still damp *chadar* and reluctantly wrapping it around her. "Oh, and thank you,

Elizabeth." She looked toward him, but he wasn't looking at her. As she stepped into the light, the battery lamp in the dark room behind her was shut off.

She walked to the edge of the roof. The rain had scrubbed the world clean and the sky over Badel was now a pale blue, a soft blue found in no flower. A gold coin of sun reached up over the valley's steep wall and turned the rain-wet fields into heaps of treasure. But no one would reap this richness, not this year. She looked below, to the ruins, where heaps of freshly broken stone steamed delicately in the new morning. She thought of the woman's intestines and the baby's gaping face and heaved violently and repeatedly. Nothing came up, but the motion doubled her up, and she teetered on the edge of the roof.

A hand pulled her away from the edge. "You should know better," said Yusuf.

"I must be tired," she said feebly.

"You have the right to be. And you have the right to feel sick. Gagging is an involuntary reflex. You controlled yourself well. Especially for your first time."

She looked away down the valley, her heart wrenched by the dual spectacle of destruction and beauty. She glanced up at the sky. "Will they come again?"

"They are finished here. For now."

She swallowed hard, but the tears came anyway. She turned away, crouching on the roof, her *chadar* pulled to hide her face in unconscious imitation of the Afghan women. Yusuf crouched beside her, and gently pulled her hand away from her face.

"I won't say it's all right," he said quietly. "It's not all right. And I don't know when it will ever be all right for Afghanistan again."

She wiped her face with her *chadar* and bit her lips. "What will happen to that baby?"

He didn't answer.

"What kind of an injection did you give it?"

He breathed in and out slowly.

"Did you give it something to kill it?"

He looked at her hard. His jaw was set.

"Did you?"

His gaze went soft and sad. "I gave it a sedative. Under normal circumstances, it would not be harmful, not even to an infant. But when the system is in shock, and very depressed…"

She nodded slowly. "You did the right thing."

"It is up the will of Allah. I relieved its pain. I could do nothing more. If Allah wills, it might recover. I pray that it doesn't."

Here, where the line between death and life was so fine and so sudden, she felt the freshness of dawn pierce her lungs, and felt the energy of life in every cell of her body. The two stared down at the bombed houses below, not speaking for a long while.

At last he placed his hand on her shoulder and stood. "Come and have tea. Then you and Malolai must sleep."

CHAPTER 19
YUSUF

Badel

Yusuf slowly climbed the hill above the village. The path was steep, and still muddy from the night's rain. He knew he should be sleeping. But he wanted to find a place where he could not see the ruined village, a place on top of a hill where he could sit and think and pray only in the sight of God.

He had seen all this before. He had seen it in Peshawar in the hospitals, but it had been more antiseptic there, detached from its cause, and at a later stage. He had seen red blanket cases in San Francisco, gruesome stabbings and mutilations. He had seen a man shot through the heart who had survived due to the most intricate microsurgery. Ironic that the man had been an armed robber who had just killed a policeman. He would recover to face trial for his life, and the endless guilt of having taken someone else's.

Life seemed so chaotic and senseless. Yusuf spoke of Allah's will, yet wondered what was on Allah's mind that He allowed such things to happen. A murderer is shot through the heart and lives. The Soviet Politburo and the generals, and others like them in every country on Earth, are responsible for the deaths of millions, and yet live. These people have access to the most advanced surgery, the most delicate technologies and costly techniques. But a young Afghan mother takes a chunk of flying metal in her belly and dies. Her orphaned baby lives, uninjured, while another woman's baby's face is obliterated.

There was simply no justification for suffering. The philosophers, Eastern and Western, who had so long and so seriously pondered the problem of evil and the inevitability of suffering, were all wrong. Life didn't make sense, and it didn't have to. It was only our embryonic brains that sought to impose order on disorder, or to imagine order where there was none. If there was order, it had to be far beyond the power of our poor human brains to grasp either its pattern or its significance. And from that perhaps humility was born.

Lacking faith, Yusuf nonetheless prayed. He had reached the top of the hill. The village was hidden by a screen of trees. What he could not see need not exist. At a small spring he ritually washed face, hands, and feet. He gauged the direction of Mecca by the sun, and spread his blanket out to pray. As he murmured the Arabic words he felt the warmth of the sun on his back, and felt the vulnerability of his position. When he prostrated himself and his forehead touched the earth, cold and damp through the woolen blanket, he felt a strength in that earth. These mountains and valleys were the spinal cord of Asia, vertebrae and cartilage, encasing nerves that were the source of invisible synapses connecting the hidden and the manifest. He was possessed by a feeling that he was somewhere in the middle of the spinal column, opposite the solar plexus of the planet, at the place that held the continent of Asia together. One serious injury, one severance, and the planet would be paralyzed, unable to stop its headlong rush toward self-destruction.

His father had found the same mountaintop and without disturbing the son had laid out his own blanket. Before Yusuf had finished his prayer, Commander Rahim had begun his. There was an overlap, a sense of continual prayer, and Yusuf thought first of all the Muslims of earth praying in an exquisitely timed ballet as the earth turned, and then of all men and women of all nations and creeds praying at dawn. He imagined Catholics in country churches and grand cathedrals scented with incense, Buddhists in Himalayan temples crouched in deep valleys and perched on sheer cliffs, scattered Jews praying with ancient words not unlike his own, and Hindus standing by wide tropical rivers, saluting the sun and offering fragile leaf boats of flame and flower to this simplest of wonders. And the many tribal peoples still inhabiting the jungles of Brazil, India, New Guinea, worshiping with reverence whomever, whatever they believed to be God. At this moment, Yusuf supposed that all men, women, and children, in Afghanistan, in America, in Russia, had a sense of reverence at the dawn, a sense of powers greater than themselves, a sense of humility and of horror at their own deeds.

Yusuf's father finished his prayers and sat beside his son. The son respectfully waited for his father to speak, but the old man stared out across the ragged undulations of the land, east to the sunrise and the Durand Line that marked the limits of battle.

"Every small victory is marred by these savage attacks upon the innocent," said the old man in slow, correct Persian. "This is our greater defeat."

Yusuf looked at his father. The commander's face, fully lit by the brazen spring sun, showed every line of thought that had animated his mind for the past sixty years. Yusuf wondered if his father would live to see a free Afghanistan, or if any of them would. The old man shook his head slowly, rubbed his temples as if he had an inescapable headache, and sighed deeply. "I don't know how else to fight."

Yusuf spread his hands in a gesture of helplessness.

"You know the story of your health assistant, Ismail Jan."

Yusuf nodded. "He told me everything. I was grateful that he had been freed."

The commander stared down at the dusty ground where they sat. "I thought I was doing the right thing. Had I known the consequences…"

"You could not have known. Our mistake was in expecting the dishonorable to deal honorably. No disrespect intended, Father."

"*My* mistake, not our mistake. I come from a different world, in some ways a harsher world and in some ways a kinder, more honorable world. The British were our enemy before. They were an honorable enemy, in some ways a predictable enemy. Perhaps I am predictable to the Russians. They trained me, and they know that the British, with their conception of honor, completed the training."

"What else could you have done?"

"Allowed Ismail to remain in Russian custody. And most likely to die."

Life these days seemed filled with horrifying moral decisions. In the West, the questions facing Yusuf had been the sophisticated ethical dilemmas posed by euthanasia and genetic engineering. Here the questions were more immediate and fundamental.

"In terms of lives," said Yusuf, "that course of action might have been less costly." It choked him to say this. Ismail had come from Peshawar to work with him, and Yusuf had grown to love his loyal and dedicated assistant.

"It is not so simple. First, Ismail is in a valuable position. So few of us have any medical training. If he were lost, how many others might die? I considered this. And I considered you."

"That you should not have done," said Yusuf bitterly.

Rahim looked at his son gravely. "I also considered Ayub. I conceived a plan that I thought would free your health assistant, show our power to the Communists, and allow Ayub an honorable way of dealing with us. I knew he would not allow the woman and children to die. I gambled that the decision would be left up to him. I think I was right. They negotiated with us. They did not shoot down our representatives. I watched with binoculars from a ridge above the village. The young Frenchman, Mr. Michel, was with me, taking photographs. The exchange occurred, and our men left safely. The next morning the planes came."

"Are you sure it was directly related to the prisoner exchange?"

"I always taught you to be honest with yourself, my son. Fooling oneself is the first crack that leads to many other flaws. The patterns are too obvious.

We attack the road near Babur Tangay. The next day, Baharabad is bomed. We kidnap a Khalqi woman and her children, trade her for a health assistant, and Badel is bombed. We are helpless. We cannot send all our women and children to Pakistan. We need the villagers for support. Otherwise where will we sleep, what will we eat, who will tell us the Russian positions?

"I had contempt for the Khaqis and Parchamis as Communist traitors. But now I understand why they are collaborating, at least in the villages. In Kabul it is different. There it is not a matter of survival. But here it has become so."

"But if the villagers turn against us we can never win," said Yusuf angrily. "Our people must be willing to sacrifice to the last drop of blood."

"Precisely. But we are growing tired. They are destroying our crops, and driving our people into exile."

Yusuf wanted to argue, to say that the Afghans would never grow tired, that they were fighting a Holy War for a way of life and a way of worship, for their families, their land, and their very lives. But he knew the soul-numbing tiredness he felt after only four months, and could imagine the exhaustion of a people who had seen year after year of war.

"We are still willing to sacrifice," said the old man. "But you have seen that it is not a pretty sacrifice. The Khalqi woman knew nothing of politics, and most likely her husband doesn't either. He is a tribesman, just like our Mujahedeen. Probably a good Muslim as well. But for the sake of his family he is an opportunist. Perhaps for himself he wouldn't be. Our feelings for our families are our weakest link in the chain of resistance."

"Ayub appears to have forgotten such scruples."

The old man bowed his head and again rubbed his temples. "I did not think he would allow this vengeance."

Yusuf took the old man's hand, kissed it, and pressed it to his forehead. "I pray to Allah I never betray you. Let us believe that Ayub did not order this, that he had no control."

"Oh God, how I want to believe that."

The father and son sat on the hilltop, hand in hand, in a long silence.

"One son has betrayed me and all I tried to teach him. But the other brings me great joy."

Yusuf ignored the compliment and remained lost in the wilderness of his own thoughts.

"Tell me, Yusuf, where did I succeed with you and fail with Ayub?"

Yusuf smiled briefly. How often the letters had asked where his father had failed with him, that he had no desire to return to Afghanistan and serve his people. How often, in the early years, they had praised Ayub. His father had not been unaware of Ayub's leanings, but had not guessed the extent of his son's covert political activities.

"I am a late bloomer," Yusuf reminded his father.

"But 'what comes late, comes right,'" the old man quoted. "You made a mistake with your first marriage. Perhaps your second will be right for you."

Yusuf looked at his father sharply. "I have no intention of marrying again, *Baba*. I'm sorry. I know you would like a grandson. My sister must marry a fine man and give you grandchildren. Maybe when the war is over I can consider remarrying. But my duty now is to the people, and marriage would only interfere, would make me weak, as you say, in my resistance. It would give me too much to lose."

"You already have too much to lose," observed Commander Rahim thoughtfully, "but you don't know it yet."

"Wife and children would only interfere with my responsibilities," said Yusuf with finality.

"Unless she were committed to the same ideals."

Who could he be thinking of? Malolai?

"You are, first and foremost, an idealist, Yusuf *jan*. So is Ayub, but he fell into an inviting web of false hopes. You too had false hopes, but something has happened that has left you free. Be glad, and pity your brother. Our people are being bled dry while he lives in the Governor's House and eats fine food. But you are far more free than he is. He must bear the guilt for the destruction of our land."

"So must we."

"Yes, even some of the Mujahedeen have turned the tired population away from us, have greedily stripped villages and murdered the innocent. You do not know, but I do, of a small village where only one family remained. For months they aided the Mujahedeen, of all parties. Then one day a commander became suspicious. Why were these people the only family in the village? They must be spies.

"So they killed the woman and cut off the man's nose. They spared the children. The man came to Massoud Khan seeking justice. It was not the fundamentalists who did this, but some of Massoud's own men. They love Massoud, but he cannot always control them. Like zealous children, our uneducated people sometimes do cruel things and then come to those they admire for approval. They disgust us and then they are shocked, sometimes resentful. They murmur against us. Some go to the fundamentalist parties, who sanction these outrages under the mantle of Islamic law. And these few terrible stories, true as they are, give ammunition for propaganda to the Russians. It becomes a little easier to turn the people against us. A little *bakshish* makes it still easier, in the time-honored tradition of bribery as a means to divide and rule a hungry nation. We talk of unity, but we are still a collection of backward and backbiting tribes.

"Yusuf, you are thirty-five. You are a doctor, and you have seen much of the world. But you do not know your own country or your own people."

"Now I must learn," replied the son, humbled.

CHAPTER 20
AYUB

Chagaserai

Ayub nervously fingered his moustache as he read the reports. He had not yet dressed for the day, and wore a blue silk dressing gown over his pajama-suit. From long habit he always slept in Afghan traditional dress. It was the only time he wore it, as he had learned to prefer a more cosmopolitan style for his daily life.

Ayub was a handsome man, not yet thirty and quite resembling his brother Yusuf. And like Yusuf, Ayub had inherited the tendency to go prematurely gray. He now absently ran his fingers through his close-cropped, curly hair, black shot with strands of silver, drawing small circles on his right temple with his forefinger.

He was not yet married. That was a nice way of saying it. He didn't really have any prospects of marriage. His father had all but disowned him, even before this war had begun, so there had been no one to arrange a marriage or even to make proper introductions to nice families, in the more modern way of doing things. He had met some girls at the university, and afterwards in connection with his work. One he had loved. He had thought his position might impress her, but during the Taraki regime she had publicly humiliated him by calling him a "godless minion of the Russian imperialists."

He had protected her because he had loved her. He had contrived to have the order sending her to Pul-e-Charkhi countermanded. Her whole family had disappeared from Kabul shortly afterwards, and he had later heard that they had gone to Germany. Despite his anger at her insult, he had grudgingly admired her courage.

Ayub had not found a wife among the Communist girls who would be acceptable mates in the eyes of the party. He found most of them brash and aggressive, and many were enamored of the Russians come to "advise" them. These girls had long since cut their traditional family ties, and were free to follow their impulses. None had led to Ayub. He hadn't had a girlfriend since Moscow. There the Russian girls had been charmed by his polite foreign manner, once they found out he wasn't a Soviet Tajik or a Tatar. An affair with an Afghan had been an enjoyable way to rebel against the strictures of Soviet society. He had had several pleasant flings, including the one with Sonia that he had recently and unsuccessfully tried to rekindle, but he had always intended to marry an Afghan girl.

He was terribly lonely now. His life had cut him off from his father, his brother, even his mother. He didn't blame himself. He felt that life just happened to him with no consent of his own. The fact that this view flatly contradicted the Soviet materialist view that men could be masters of their own fates if they could just wrest the means of production from the hands of the few and deliver it into the hands of the many, did not bother him in the least. It never occurred to him that his view of fate was far more traditionally Muslim than that of his brother, or even of their father. He didn't blame God per se, as he wasn't sure he believed in a god. How could a compassionate god have allowed this war, or the Vietnam War, or famine in Africa? On the other hand, he wasn't sure he didn't believe in God. All he knew was that things just seemed to happen to him.

Like this bombing raid on Badel. He hadn't ordered it, hadn't wanted it. But it had taken place. He had intended to deal honorably with the Mujahedeen, to test if *they* could deal honorably. If so, he had reasoned, the way could be paved for a truce, possibly even a U.N.-negotiated cease-fire. But the Soviets had made him appear a dishonorable liar. Lermontov had engineered it. Ayub knew he, not Lermontov, was supposed to be in control, but he was beginning to suspect the limits of his, or any Afghan's, power.

He sipped his tea. The house was silent. There was no music that would fit the contents of this report. He read on.

"It is not known with certainty whether the commander, Rahimullah Khan, was in one of the bombed structures, but it is thought that he and his men escaped. It is suspected that a number of people were killed outright, and others seriously wounded, some of whom may have since died. We have no information as to numbers, but have reason to believe they were all civilians. Though this is regrettable collateral damage, the probable effect of this operation should be to demoralize the rebels and elements of the population who up to now have supported them. We expect to have more specific information as to casualties and the morale of the rebels in a few days. End. FILE TOP SECRET.

So much capsulized in so few succinct words, carefully typed, right to left, in the graceful script of a language more suited to poetry. The report was wedged in between Dunahi, Asmar, Pashad, and Barikot. There was also a line about possible cholera in Deh Wagal. A man called Abdul Sharif sent to Peshawar. Advice that he be allowed to proceed, as there would be danger to all personnel if cholera began spreading through Kunar.

That too worried him. Yusuf was there. Cholera was a horrible death. Though no worse than a slow death from painful wounds, it did have the dubious virtue of not being caused by a fellow human being. Unless the Russians were using biological warfare too. But Ayub thought that would entail far too much risk to friendly parties. He never doubted that the Russians would hide it from their Afghan allies if they were using biological warfare. They had never mentioned chemical warfare either, but everyone who was in a position to know knew it had been used upon occasion.

He was glad Lermontov hadn't been here to observe his reaction to the report. He looked nervously around the room. He wouldn't put it past his "Russian uncle" to have installed a secret camera, or at least a microphone. Or to have put Mousa, or someone else, in his pay. There were plenty of poor men like Najeeb who were willing to sell their principles for a price. Ayub now wondered if he himself had ever really had any principles to sell. He had given himself away, without thought, his soul and his country at a bargain price.

His thoughts returned to the U.N. talks in Geneva. He listened to the BBC and the Voice of America every night, discreetly, as he did everything else in his life. He suspected a good 95% of Afghanistan did the same. There were the usual rumors of progress, of secret deals between the Russians, the Pakistanis, and some faction or other of the Mujahedeen. From what Ayub had seen of the miserable, demoralized, disease-ridden Soviet troops, he thought they would be overjoyed to see the backside of Afghanistan and face the familiar discomforts of a Russian winter.

Ayub had to admire the Mujahedeen, with the same grudging admiration he had reserved for the girl who had humiliated him. They were fighting the world's largest army, and one of the most modern. The Russians had air power and could easily punish the villages that aided the rebels. But they usually couldn't find the rebels themselves, unless some inexperienced fellow was foolish enough and undisciplined enough to start shooting at a helicopter gun ship. And a bad enough shot to miss.

Ayub didn't think he himself had the bravery of either the Mujahedeen or the ordinary Russian soldiers, who had no choice but to be brave. The Afghan government troops were worse than useless, tending to desert or surrender at the slightest opportunity even when threatening fire was directed at them from the rear. Ayub thought he might do the same if he were in their position. He supposed his own life was at risk too. It was not uncommon to be awakened at night by automatic rifle fire, and on two occasions guards had been killed outside his house.

He hoped Lermontov would be satisfied now, and would keep off his back about his father and brother. He had been relieved to read that it was thought Commander Rahim had escaped, but he knew he could not afford to show mercy to his own family if they stood in the way of the revolution. Perhaps his father would perceive the futility of carrying on a rebellion in this starving region. And the awkwardness of his own son's position, who was, he thought petulantly, his own flesh and blood and dreams. Perhaps his father would back off in order to keep Russian vengeance from the civilian population. And perhaps those damn peace talks would succeed soon.

Yusuf must have gone to the scene of the bombing. Perhaps the American journalist was there as well. She would probably write about the great humanitarian deeds of the Afghan doctor, and make things more dangerous for Yusuf and more awkward for Ayub. The Russians tended to ignore uncomplimentary things written about them in the world press, but this story could be embarrassing.

Perhaps she could be stopped. None of the foreign journalists sneaking into Afghanistan had yet been caught. Her capture would be a feather in his cap, a demonstration that he could produce results. And it might distract Lermontov from the problem of Yusuf and their father, and buy some valuable time.

Ayub smiled in self-satisfaction. This was the idea he had been looking for, the chance to strike back without actually hurting either his brother or his father. Now, how to accomplish this? She would be much easier to capture in the Kunar Valley on her way back to Pakistan, and it was unlikely that either Yusuf or their father would accompany her there. Yes, Najeeb Khan was due that evening. He would ask Najeeb to find out when this woman would be passing through the valley, and in what village she would stay.

Ayub began to whistle Beethoven's "Ode to Joy" through his teeth, and glanced at his watch. Twelve hours till the BBC would come on, with news of today's Geneva sessions.

CHAPTER 21
ELIZABETH

Leaving Badel

The day after the bombing, within the twenty-four hours prescribed by Muslim law, the dead of the village were buried in the new Martyrs Cemetery. Over the next days the village slowly assessed its losses and repaired its scars, though the villagers remained as stunned as the land itself.

Yusuf was ready to leave on the morning of the third day. All his patients had been stabilized, and he had already sent Malolai back to Amrau Tangay, accompanied by a small escort of Mujahedeen, so that the clinic would not be left unattended for too long. Elizabeth was also eager to leave, but Commander Rahim had insisted that they stay for lunch, arguing that the villagers had already procured a chicken for their honored guests.

Elizabeth had been watching Commander Rahim closely over the past days, and she knew he had likewise been observing her. She was impressed, even charmed by him. The old man seemed to add another dimension to his son, and indeed Yusuf was unusually subdued in the presence of his father.

Rahim spoke excellent English and, she gathered, Russian as well. He spoke with his son in Farsi, and with the others in Pashtu. He was exceedingly polite, combining British formality with Afghan grace and courtesy. When he drank tea with a circle of men sitting on a carpet, it became a ritual that transcended time and place, as if they were a party of nineteenth-century Mujahedeen fighting the British, or a band of warriors defending their homeland against Genghis Khan. Rahim was a commander of men, but he was also humble and hospitable, and it was he who poured the tea and conveyed the choicest bits of food to the large platter of flat bread that served Elizabeth as a plate.

Elizabeth wanted to interview Commander Rahim, but even more, to understand him. He fascinated her. Why would a man of such status, who could have easily obtained political asylum in a Western country, choose to become the trainer of a specially picked and highly secret commando group? What kind of an effect must he have on his sons? And how did he feel about the Communist son who had become Governor of Kunar?

But she sensed that this was not the time for a lengthy interview. It seemed unwise to give too much publicity to Rahim's sensitive operation, but she had quickly learned that one of the major weaknesses of the Afghan Resistance was a hunger for publicity. They would tell almost anybody anything, and would arrange trips "inside" for almost anyone, without checking backgrounds or even credentials.

Yusuf, however, couldn't care less about publicity. He simply did his work. He never posed, and seemed indifferent as to whether he had shaved that morning or several days before. But he did ask her to take pictures of the atrocities. Gingerly, respectfully, she had taken pictures of the woman's funeral, and of the small bundled body of the infant being lowered into a freshly dug grave. She had photographed the wounded, carried out onto the rooftops to get a little sun, and had shot pictures of the doctor examining his patients. Over and over, she had asked Malolai or Yusuf to apologize and to ask permission. The villagers had been more than obliging, and had smiled spontaneously, heart-wrenchingly, as she clicked the shutter.

And now, as Elizabeth and Yusuf prepared to leave, the villagers gathered on their rooftops, thanking both of them profusely and calling down infinite blessings upon them. Commander Rahim accompanied them up the hill, out of sight of the village. Along the way Yusuf completed his last-minute instructions for use of the medicines, salves, and bandages he had left behind.

Commander Rahim halted. "This is as far as I go today. Miss Elizabeth, I am honored to have met you." He extended his hand.

The incongruity of formal English farewells in the mountains of Afghanistan struck her, but she grasped his hand in both of hers. "The honor is all mine."

He smiled quizzically, a crooked smile that gave him charm. "I admire you. You are not like most other Americans I have met. You have courage, and you have a feeling for our people." He took her hand and kissed it, in a gesture far more Asian than European.

"I do hope to meet with you again, under better circumstances. *Inshallah*," she said earnestly.

He rewarded her with an ingenuous smile, then turned to Yusuf and embraced him. Still holding his son, he spoke at length in Persian, then said in English, "Go now. The weather may turn. Yusuf, you know where to go if it gets too bad. Or you are welcome to stay here."

Yusuf shook his head quickly. "We must get back. I must see if any more cases of cholera have developed."

"As you wish. Be careful. Go with God. *Ba'amana khoda. Inshallah*, I will come to see you after some days, and have a talk with the young lady."

Elizabeth followed Yusuf along the path, which led steeply up towards the crown of the mountains. The thoughts of days, mixed with lines of poetry, spun dizzily through her head.

They had been walking for perhaps an hour when it began to rain. At first it was only a few large drops spattering in the dust, and then it turned into an earnest downpour. Stoically, Elizabeth said nothing. Yusuf sighed and muttered something in Farsi, then called back to her, "We should reach a cave soon. We can rest there. Can you make it?"

"Why not?" It was more a statement than a question.

He laughed. "That's a very Afghan phrase. Elizabeth, how is your ankle? I'm sorry, I haven't thought to ask."

"You would have heard if it was bothering me. Thank God, whatever you did to it seems to have cured it."

"No more excuses to touch your ankle." He wasn't looking at her when he said that, but straight ahead, through the sheets of rain. At last he spied what he was looking for and quickened his pace. They soon came to a cave in the mountain wall, more like a deep crack, and rather like the *sangar* in which they had begun their acquaintance. Its entrance was wide and high, and though the floor didn't extend very far, the roof overhung nicely.

Yusuf climbed easily up to the cave by placing his hands and feet in convenient cracks in the rock. Elizabeth had more trouble, as her legs were not as long as his, and he finally grasped her under her arms and heaved her into the cave.

"Let me carry you across my threshold," he said, laughing.

"I thought cave dwellers were supposed to drag their mates and victims in by the hair," she joked back. "But I wouldn't try it if I were you."

"Which do you think you are?"

"What?"

"Never mind." He shook out his blanket and spread it out on the rough floor. "Get up so that I can put this down underneath you."

"There isn't much room to move."

"Sorry it's not centrally heated."

"I don't mind a little rain."

"Our Afghan rains can sometimes be floods."

"When you Afghans do anything, it seems to be extreme."

"How perceptive of you. You have grasped our national character in a matter of days."

She was abashed. "I'm sorry. I didn't mean…"

"I'm serious. It's something the Russians haven't figured out, and I doubt the Americans or the Chinese have either. Everyone refuses to learn from history. The British might have an inkling, but it took three rather brutal wars for them to figure it out. Perhaps it's something in all our characters. Maybe that's why my wife never understood."

The mention of a wife made Elizabeth uncomfortable. Yusuf stared out into the rain, which now came down in blankets. She wished the downpour would stop soon. His nearness made her uneasy in a way she could not explain to herself.

She mentally traced his profile against the gray light filtering into the cave's entrance. With its Roman nose, prominent chin, and high forehead, his face could have been that of an Arab, a Jew, or a Persian prince. But the man wore the soft rolled cap and bandoleer of the twentieth-century Afghan *mujaheed*. Beads of moisture had caught on the camel-colored wool of his cap, and black curls shot with silver hung damply from under it. Today he looked much as he had the first day she had seen him, a heavy growth of mostly dark beard struggling to catch up with a luxuriant moustache, and the lines around his eyes deepened by exhaustion.

Again she wondered what he had looked like in America. Closely shaven, she guessed, with carefully styled hair. Probably very neat. But the eyes would have been the same. They were of an intensity peculiar to this land, which Elizabeth now knew could be intensely hot, cold, snowbound, rainy, or clear. Afghanistan, like its people, did everything to extremes. Others might label this intensity fanaticism, but to Elizabeth it was the outstanding characteristic of both Afghanistan and this man who now sat so near her.

She was seated farther back in the cave than Yusuf, her legs extended rather stiffly. He crouched with the ease of a man born to the mountains, arms hugging his updrawn legs. He rested his chin on his knees and rubbed his temples with his hands. Elizabeth had noticed this gesture in Commander Rahim and wondered if father and son were prone to headaches. She wanted to touch Yusuf, to massage his forehead. If he'd been an American man, she would have. But Yusuf was, well, not Western. With surprise, she realized that she really didn't know whether to view him as a Western man, an Afghan, or a cultural hybrid. She had an easy familiarity with him, which she didn't have with

Ebrahim but did to some extent with Sharif. Perhaps the strict social mores of village Afghanistan had begun to infect her, she thought in some amusement. Yusuf was after all born an Afghan, and for all of his Western education and his marriage to an American, perhaps remained a stern and judgmental Muslim where women were concerned.

"Elizabeth, have you ever been married?" he asked suddenly. He turned a frank gaze upon her and she was again struck by the dark beauty of his eyes.

"No," she said quickly, then looked away. "But I have been in love."

He also looked away, back at the rain. "Then you are lucky. I have been married, but now I don't think I was truly in love."

"That's where you're wrong," she said without thinking. "Just because something is over doesn't mean there never was any love. I had to learn that too."

"Now you sound like my wife."

"I'm sorry."

He looked at her again, faintly amused. "Janet was not unperceptive at times, even though she was a psychologist."

"You seem to have a low opinion of psychologists."

"Only of those who judge others. You don't."

"But I'm not a psychologist."

"Perhaps you should be. You are perceptive." Before she realized it, he had taken her hand.

She felt like a teen-ager afraid of her Dad walking in. But she did not pull away. She answered instinctively with gentle pressure, and let her hand rest comfortably in his.

"I admire you greatly," she said guardedly. "I told you that before."

"And I told you I am no hero."

"All Afghans are heroes these days."

He looked at her quickly, then his glance veered away. "Not all. Some are collaborators. And sooner or later, all of us are fratricides."

She knew no answer that would comfort him, so remained silent, her throat knotted.

"'The war at the center of the world,'" he quoted softly.

She stiffened and tried to withdraw her hand, but he squeezed it more tightly.

"You're a good poet, Elizabeth. Not just a journalist."

She yanked away her hand and inched toward the back of the cave. She felt violated, though his words were sweet. "Damn you! You have a lot of nerve reading someone's journal."

He was unperturbed. "I didn't read it on purpose, Elizabeth *jan*. Your journal had fallen off the bed. When I bent to pick it up, a piece of paper fell out. I read it without thinking, then felt ashamed. Do you forgive me?" He did not try to touch her, but looked into her eyes with a contrite gaze.

"I'm embarrassed," she said confusedly. "It's not a very good poem. It's only a first draft. I never publish poetry anyway. And I only show poems to a few people, a few chosen people."

"I did apologize, and apologize again if it makes any difference. I wouldn't want anyone reading my poetry either unless I chose to show it to them."

She was caught off guard. "You write poetry too? In English or in Persian?"

"As a boy, in Persian. Now sometimes in English, more often in Persian. My father is a published poet. That was quite a lot for a son to live up to."

Somehow the son's writing poetry surprised her more.

"Is it that much of a shock?" he asked.

"Well, I just always thought you were more scientifically inclined."

"Why? Because I'm a doctor?"

"I've never known a doctor before who was also a poet."

"That is the mistake of Western society. You divide life so inexorably. You are a journalist, yet you are also a poet."

"An unpublished poet. I make my living doing journalism, not poetry."

"You survive on journalism. I think one lives and thrives on poetry. One's soul, at any rate. It takes a poet to know a poet."

Silence dropped between them again, and in that silence the roar of the rain sounded like a river in spate.

"Why did you come back to Afghanistan?" Elizabeth asked.

"When I was a child, my father always used to tell Ayub and me, and my sister as well, to serve the people. I never did. I enjoyed America too much. I thought as long as I was helping people there it was enough. And I'd met Janet. We knew each other for three years before we were married, then were married for five years. So you see, Janet took up a good part of the past eighteen years I spent in America. The divorce was final about eight months ago. Irreconcilable differences. So irreconcilable I haven't seen her since. I didn't argue about the house in Marin, or about the dog. It was a nice house. The dog wasn't that nice."

Elizabeth laughed. "I prefer cats myself."

"So do I. Cats are so sublimely independent."

"Like Afghans."

He laughed. "Muslims tend to prefer cats. Dogs are unfortunately considered dirty by many people, but there is a Muslim tradition that says that Prophet Mohammed liked cats so much that he once cut off the sleeve of his robe so he would not disturb the sleep of a feline friend."

Elizabeth smiled. "That's a charming story. Is it true?"

"You Americans always doubt the truth of everything. Many stories have value as metaphor rather than as reality. Whether they are true or not doesn't matter as much as whether people accept them as true."

She reflected. He spoke strangely for a doctor. "Sometimes life itself seems symbolic," she said cautiously.

"Exactly. Spoken like the poet that you are. I like your image of jets 'needling the silken sky of Central Asia, and embroidering the earth with death.'"

"Thank you. It's such a sad image though."

"I'd like a copy someday. Written in your own hand."

"Inscribed to you? *Inshallah.*"

He laughed again. "You may become a Muslim someday. Many people do here."

"So I've heard."

"Islam is a tremendously poetic religion."

"I know very little about it. We don't know much in the West."

"Neither do we in Afghanistan," he said, "nor anywhere else in the Muslim world, though we all think we have a monopoly on righteousness. We don't know, or choose to ignore, the spirit of the Koran, which is equality for all humans, men and women, and all races, and tolerance for other beliefs. The Koran repeatedly commands mercy, and reminds us that 'Allah is merciful, forgiving.' The first line of every chapter of the Koran is 'In the name of Allah, the Compassionate, the Merciful.'"

"Really? I didn't know that."

"Not many Westerners do. And we Afghans, and other Muslims, forget it. But one thing I have learned about our people, and that is why I have hope: we have faith. We have faith in the wrong things sometimes, but we also have faith in the unseen, and that translates to faith in the future. Why do you think we fight Russia?"

"I have seen this faith," she conceded.

"It is because of Islam that I can be a doctor and a poet both. The American anthropologist Dr. Louis Dupree once wrote that 'Afghanistan is fundamentally a nation of poets.' That and our extremism are the most fundamental truths about us. Islam allows me to be a scientist, to look at life precisely, to measure, to analyze cause and effect, and to diagnose and offer a prognosis. But God is the First Cause, the Reason for Creation. And so, Islam thus also allows me to be a mystic. And what else is a poet but a mystic?"

His words rang true, and were strangely appropriate for this rough cave and rough-looking companion in a furious rainstorm in a war-wracked land.

"What religion are you, Elizabeth?"

The question always made her feel uncomfortable. "I was raised Roman Catholic."

"And now?"

How to describe the years of disillusionment with organized religion, the unconvinced, armchair agnosticism mixed with a stubborn awareness of other, unseen worlds? She just couldn't view God as an old man surrounded by blond and sexless creatures with gossamer wings dressed in white silk. "Now...I believe in a God, a force. I believe in trying to be good, trying not to hurt other people. 'One planet, one people.' Maybe the Bahais have got it right. Or the Buddhists. What was it that the Dalai Lama said? 'My religion is to be kind.'"

"Maybe everybody who follows a religion truly has got it right. As long as they are tolerant of all others."

"You sound like a saint."

"I'm no more a saint than I am a hero. Just a poor doctor, and a man trying to be a poet. A man sitting here in a cave with a beautiful woman, an intelligent woman, a woman trying to be a poet and to save the world in the process."

"I'm not..." But all words choked in her throat when he looked at her. It made no sense, but he was kissing her, or she was kissing him. His lips were warm and soft, with a touch like the hands that had healed her. His moustache was soft, his unshaven cheek rough, but she loved that touch as his tongue made slow circles in a sensual dance with hers.

"I'm not sure I understand this," she whispered between kisses.

He leaned back and looked at her. "Do you need to understand it? Are you trying to make me crazy?" He kissed her again, with tender passion, and she felt his hands slip from her shoulders. One drew her closer to him, and the other slipped onto one of her breasts with a touch like instant fire.

She kissed him back fiercely, feeling herself melt into him, keenly aware of the dampness of their clothes and the thickness of the air around them. A wave of pure emotion, more profound than desire but containing desire, washed over her, and she nearly succumbed to its seduction, but pulled back at the last minute, catching her breath.

"Yusuf. Yusuf *jan*. This is crazy. Remember where we are."

"Elizabeth *jan*. I know exactly where we are. I am with you, and we are alone. No one will come in the storm."

She reluctantly but firmly extricated herself from his arms, having made her decision. "The storm is letting up. We should go soon." She could not look at him. "Lest we forget, we are in the middle of a Holy War."

"Meaning what?" He looked at her fiercely.

She glanced at him, then back at the ground, where her hands twisted the blue and red border of his blanket. "This is not America. Giving in to our feelings could make things awkward."

He stared out at the rain, which was indeed lessening. "I'm sorry," he said between clenched teeth.

Sorrow seized her so that she could not move. "Yusuf, say some of your poetry, please," she begged. "Quickly."

He was silent. She knew she had hurt him, in protecting herself, or perhaps both of them. "Oh Yusuf, you know so little about me. We can't think this way."

"I will recite one of my poems for you. In English." He seemed to be speaking more to the land outside the cave than to her. "I wrote it not long after I came to Afghanistan. It's called 'We Laugh No More.' I hope you don't find it too oppressively Afghan." He paused, breathed deeply twice, and began to speak:

"Fire surrounds us, lives within
      Burns fueled by our tears
         Which ignite fresh flames of hope and anger.

We have grown old, our heads crowned with snow
      like distant and imposing mountains,
Our faces lined and scarred as the desert hills.
Streams of laughter have dried up
      waiting for a kinder season
        on another earth.
For now is the time of tears and fire

the time of blood and flame
the time of silence.

With patience hard and bitter as pure spice
we wait for the time of sweet ripeness
When fire shall melt the snows of sorrow and age
and flood our lives with laughter."

Elizabeth wept. All the tears for the last days now poured out of her. She cried for the woman she had seen die, for the baby Yusuf had injected with a deadly sedative, and for the Mujahedeen who fought with scant weapons against the awesome power of possession of the skies. She wept, and finally sobbed in deep, wracking sobs. For a long time Yusuf did not move. Then he took her in his arms and rocked her back and forth. Dimly, she was aware that he too wept, but silently.

"It's a hard world, Elizabeth. Now you've seen it. I'd never seen it before either. My divorce was the first thing that had gone wrong for me. I think you had some similar experience. Now we've really seen the harshness of the world here. Maybe the same things brought us here, maybe we just wanted to escape from something, but we are here now, and we see, I see, that those things no longer matter." She remained with her head cradled on his shoulder, burrowed into his neck. She could hear his words, could feel the vibrations of each sound in his throat, and in her terror this comforted her.

"I'm afraid, Yusuf. I'm afraid of this world."

"Of what?" he asked gently. "God? Death?"

"Not death, dying. And pain. Not only my own, but that of others. And injustice that we can't make right."

He stroked the strands of her hair that had come loose from her braid and were frizzed in the dampness. "And love?" he asked thoughtfully. "We're all afraid," he went on, as if to himself. "You need time. I need time. The whole damn world needs time. I only hope we've got it, before we blow ourselves up, individually and collectively."

"You're not very comforting." She laughed shakily and felt his hand still stroking her hair, barely touching her head.

"Neither is the world. All we've got is faith. And maybe love? Forgive me for being Afghan." He kissed her quickly, once, on the lips, and then embraced her fervently. Then he moved to the mouth of the cave. "Look, the rain's almost stopped. Come on." He held out a hand.

Cautiously she edged forward and took his hand. The sky was clearing, but a light rain fell from a gray smudge of cloud directly above them. The cave faced east, and the land rolled and dropped away in great, glistening folds until it flattened into the moss-green of the Kunar Valley, and folded again into the blue range of hills that separated Afghanistan from Pakistan. The sun was behind their mountain, but its rays reached across the vast river valley, and gilded the distant mountains. The range was now soft violet and gold, the color of a flower at sunrise. A magnificent full rainbow shimmered, arcing high and brilliant into a fresh, pale blue sky that had not yet deepened to the indigo of evening. Like children swept into an awesome sky, filled with wonder, they watched, holding on to each other for balance as if they were perched on the edge of the world. In that moment Elizabeth found it incomprehensible that these same skies could hold such promise and such terror.

They remained for a long time locked into the spectacle, part of a moment never to come again. The rainbow faded, the sky deepened. The first star, brilliant as the dust of a butterfly's wing, shone in the western sky. It would be a dazzling night.

"Now I know what it means to be breathless," she whispered.

He squeezed her and sighed. "Elizabeth *jan*. I would love to sleep the night with you here, in this cave." His dark gaze burned into her very being. "What I mean is, I would love to make love to you here, tonight. But you are right." He looked away again, at the stars. "This is neither the time nor the place. We must wait for time, and see where the winds of destiny will blow us. In this world, we don't even know where we will be tomorrow. Know only that I love you." He kissed her forehead and moved to leave the cave.

"Oh, Yusuf…" His eyes captured hers from below. She could see his eyes clearly, even in the swiftly gathering dusk. But she could not say the words.

She saw disappointment in his face, sorrow and hurt that she could not answer in kind. But it was all so crazy. She needed time to think. She turned around to climb down to the path and allowed him to catch her. Near the path was a single wild rose, pink and brash. He bent and plucked it, then turned and twined it into her thick hair, behind her right ear.

"Now you look like an Afghan girl," he said, and kissed the rose by her ear. He faced her directly. "Elizabeth, I will never force you. I respect you and your spirit. But I want you to do one thing for me."

She looked at him expectantly.

"Tell me why you cried at my poem. No one has ever cried at my poetry before."

"Perhaps you have never written poetry like that before."

He stared at her intensely, trying to read her. "I see enough answer in your eyes. Think of it, and maybe it will come in words. Come, my beloved poet, we have far to go and much to do."

CHAPTER 22
ELIZABETH

Amrau Tangay

The skies were unstable, changing from hour to hour above the villages that clung tenaciously to the sides of friable hills. Elizabeth found Yusuf equally unpredictable during the days following his declaration of love. Confused by his oscillation from undying romantic love to cold distance and glib offhandedness, she dismissed the whole incident as war strain. People sometimes felt extraordinary feelings in extraordinary situations, but as soon as they returned to some semblance of normalcy the basis for the relationship collapsed and left those involved floundering in a flood of daily exigencies.

Calmly, logically, she told herself that this is what had happened between her and Yusuf. They had been thrown together by circumstances. They had worked together, and respected each other. And they were both lonely, on the rebound from broken relationships. What more romantic and dramatic spot than a mountain cave in the rain in the middle of a war?

Now Yusuf was reacting like a typical American male. Closeness followed by far more than arm's length distance. Yusuf had never touched her again, and had returned to his former mocking banter. She wanted to scream at him sometimes, to shake him, to make him look at her. A veil seemed to have fallen over his soul, and his eyes looked at her as if he only half saw her.

She didn't know if Yusuf was angry at her because she hadn't made love to him or because she'd let him kiss her in the first place. She was now glad that she hadn't let herself drift into making love with him there in the cave, as easy as it would have been. But if he reacted this strongly to a few kisses, he probably never would have spoken to her again if she'd made love to him. And if anyone had discovered them fornicating in the middle of the *jehad*, neither one of them, certainly not the woman in question, would have lived long enough to get dressed. No use kidding herself about Afghan morality.

Yusuf had spoken little during the rest of their night walk, though he had been quietly solicitous. Ismail had been there when they arrived, and had given them the good news that he had indeed found Sharif at Babur Tangay, with about an hour to spare. Ismail had unconsciously acted as a buffer between Yusuf and Elizabeth, snoring as peacefully as a cat in the little one-room hut while Elizabeth lay for hours with eyes wide open, staring into the darkness and listening to Yusuf's measured breathing. Eventually she would fall into a restless sleep, haunted by images of the baby without a face and the horrifically wounded woman. Twice she had awakened in the night, sure that she was whimpering and that it was the brush of Yusuf's comforting hand over her cheek that had awakened her. She had held her breath, afraid to open her eyes, but could only hear Yusuf's regular breathing and Ismail's snores. At last she had opened her eyes, but had seen only darkness and had drifted back into sleep.

Elizabeth was anxious to finisher her story so she could leave as soon as Sharif arrived and the cholera had been contained. She busied herself with taking pictures, and occasionally helped Yusuf and Malolai with medical procedures. Whenever she worked with Yusuf he was matter of fact and professional. He was the kind of doctor who would never allow personal strain to intrude on the care he felt he owed his patients.

Michel had left with Ebrahim on the day after Elizabeth's return to rejoin Commander Rahim in Badel. Their departure left her feeling isolated, as she watched the clouds drift over the sky's bright face and the changes drift over a face she had grown unaccountably fond of.

By the third day Elizabeth was thoroughly depressed. Pearly gray clouds bunched in the eastern sky, but behind, in the west, the low sun cast out golden rays to taunt her. Yusuf was busy in the dispensary with Ismail and Malolai, and Elizabeth sat on the *charpoy* in the courtyard, sighing occasionally, her open journal on her lap. She stared moodily out across the valley, which seemed to have narrowed in the past days.

A sense of expectancy, or perhaps foreboding, haunted them all. The sky had closed in on them, had isolated them from all news. Time seemed unsettled. At least the helicopters didn't fly when the weather was overcast, but in her gloom Elizabeth wondered if perhaps one day they would wake up to the crescendo of approaching MiGs, and Amrau Tangay would become a red dot on the wall map of some strategy room in Kabul or Moscow. Boom, no more clinic, no more doctor, no more journalist. Elizabeth wondered morbidly if Yusuf's brother knew of Yusuf's exact whereabouts. Would he protect his brother, or would he seek an angry revenge for his brother's betrayal?

She sighed again. Her right hand, pen poised, rested on her open notebook, but she hadn't written anything. Her left hand propped up her chin. She sat up straight, scratched, and turned to the poem Yusuf had read. It didn't have a title, perhaps never would. She reread it to herself, critically:

"*Jets screamed over Afghanistan*
     and on across the five-nation region
Needling the silken sky of Central Asia
     and embroidering the earth with death.
The war at the center of the world had begun.

Here at the center of the center
 is not the hurricane's placid eye
  but the tightening center of storm.
From here along the stony spine of these mountains
 synapses radiate –
The death of one is known to all others.

The skies spread wings of pale silk
 hiding our folly from the face of God.
The valleys are like raw emeralds
 set in rough brown-gray stone
  of Hindu Kush
Adorning earth.

At night the sky is a deep lapis arch
 its surface strewn with flecks of gold and silver,
But from skies of jewels and silk
 rains death
  upon field, forest, village.
I have seen mechanical death in these
 plateaux of skies
Have heard the dull thunder
 of life ending with distant thuds
Have seen its aftermath –
 obliterated faces and lives.

The skies have closed on us
 but hope grows even from the sharp earth-scent
  of freshly dug graves.
Hope grows from the cry of the living child."

Thunder rumbled vaguely, and a few large drops of rain fell. One splattered on the poem in Elizabeth's lap. She slammed the notebook shut. How dare Yusuf read anything without her permission! And how dare he ignore her.

She shivered and drew her blanket over her head, flinging one end over her left shoulder. Yusuf's blanket, his extra blanket, meticulously cleaned of course, but still bearing his scent. Damn, she did love him. But would she have loved him as a doctor in San Francisco? Or would he love her as a journalist in New York?

"Lizbet!"

She turned, startled, to see a grinning Sharif. He eased his heavy bundle off his back, set it gently on the ground, and eagerly shook Elizabeth's hand.

"*Staray mashay!*" she cried. She pointed to the blanket-wrapped bundle. "Peshawar? Vaccine?"

He nodded, and she could barely restrain herself from hugging him. She ran to the door of the dispensary. "Yusuf! Malolai! Sharif is back!"

Yusuf, Malolai, and Ismail rushed into the courtyard. Maololai's eyes were soft, yet sparkling, and she greeted Sharif shyly, then hurried to make tea. Elizabeth carried her notebook into the hut and sat on her bed. It was already dark inside, so she lit the sturdy German kerosene lamp. The three men entered the room, chattering in Pashtu. She looked closely at Sharif. He was obviously tired, though struggling to hide the fact. His skin was drawn tight over his cheekbones, and his eyes were dark and hollow. She calculated quickly. He had made it to Peshawar and back in six days.

Elizabeth helped Malolai serve the tea while everyone continued speaking excitedly in Pashtu. Finally Yusuf turned to her, his eyes shining in the soft light.

"Sharif came and went in six days," he said proudly. "There's something for you to write about."

"I know. This is what I mean about heroes."

"Just be sure you write about the right heroes. Don't be fooled by me." He looked at her in a way that cut her heart, then looked away.

The conversation continued in Pashtu, then Yusuf turned again to Elizabeth. She was unnerved by his sudden attention, and by the intensity of his stare. She had to concentrate on the meaning of his words.

"...made it to Peshawar without incident, though the storm was rough that first night. He went the next night to the border and reached Peshawar by nightfall. He went straight to Dr. Nasir's house. Dr. Nasir happened to have some people from the European Support Committee for Afghanistan over, and they had just shipped in some medicine, including cholera vaccine. Nasir left his guests and immediately went to the hospital to get the vaccine. Sharif waited for him, then went to Massoud Khan to give him a report. He spent the night in Massoud's house and left for Kunar early the next morning. He said he was sorry he didn't get here sooner but he didn't want to risk having the vaccine captured if he crossed the valley by day."

Elizabeth looked at Sharif, who was smiling at Malolai. "*Shabbash*," she said approvingly. She'd heard the word before and knew it meant "well done."

Sharif just laughed, showing his fine teeth, and then shrugged. He said something in Pashtu and Yusuf translated. "He says any *mujaheed* would have done it."

Elizabeth shook her head in disbelief. "If any *mujaheed* would do this, then I think you will win your war."

CHAPTER 23
ELIZABETH

Amrau Tangay

Word of the arrival of cholera vaccine spread quickly by means of that invisible village telephone that serves all societies that do not have electronic telephones. By sunrise people from all over Deh Wagal had already begun to gather around the clinic, waiting eagerly for their injections.

Sharif separated those who had come for the vaccine according to village, so that those from villages nearest the source of the cholera would be inoculated first. Elizabeth assisted Malolai in the courtyard while Ismail and Yusuf worked on the roof. Elizabeth kept her camera close, and whenever someone requested, she took pictures. These women did not seem either terribly shy or terribly fearful of their husbands. Some merely wanted a moment of their own to pose, to be flattered. Others insisted that Elizabeth write down their names and send a photo from America. Elizabeth dutifully wrote the names, guessing that if she sent the pictures to Massoud Khan they would eventually get here.

While she was photographing a strikingly beautiful woman being vaccinated by Malolai, a party of armed men led by the unmistakable, dominating figure of

Commander Rahim approached the clinic. Behind the commander marched a line of somber, disciplined men, and at the end walked Ebrahim and Michel.

"Good afternoon. Have we come at a bad time?" asked Commander Rahim. "You always seem to be hard at work when I see you."

Elizabeth extended her hand. "I'm glad to meet you again. You've come just in time to be vaccinated. Yusuf is up there."

He glanced up at the roof, then back at her. "I've come to talk to *you*."

His manner was unnervingly British. His accent, his gestures, everything. "Will you be staying for the night?" she asked. "We need to finish up here."

He nodded laconically. "There is time."

"Please sit down," she said to Rahim. She glanced around and called to Rahman, who came running from the corner where he had been sitting with other boys. "*Chai*?" she asked hesitantly. The boy smiled and nodded, then disappeared inside the house.

When the boy brought the tea, Elizabeth began serving with Commander Rahim. He indicated that she should serve Michel first, as he was a guest. "I think you are becoming Afghan, Miss Elizabeth," the commander remarked with a fatherly smile.

"It is a pleasure to be able to return your hospitality. Besides, you all look wonderful sitting there drinking tea in this afternoon light. If Malolai doesn't need me, I would like to take pictures of you."

The commander laughed, and spoke to Malolai, who said, "Elizabeth, there are not so many more ladies. Please talk to the Commmandant *Sahib*."

Elizabeth picked up her camera and began looking for angles. "Michel? Do you think you could move, please? I'm sorry, but, you know…"

Through the lens she saw his smile fade. "One picture of me, with Ebrahim?" he asked.

"Okay."

Ebrahim stared at her without expression, and Michel looked longing. The camera does not lie, she thought, it only freezes moments of truth and preserves them on celluloid to be the focus of future recrimination.

Michel graciously moved out of the frame and she concentrated on faces, familiar and unfamiliar. Young Karim was there, and so was Alam Shah. Again she was struck by the variation in these men's features, and she enjoyed the esthetic explosions of light playing on faces chiseled by mountain and sky, by peace and war.

By the time she had lost her light, the stream of patients had thinned to a trickle and Yusuf stood behind her, watching.

"May I join in?" he asked suavely.

"Of course. I can always use more pictures of the doctor with the bandoleer."

Yusuf embraced his father, but the embrace was more reserved and formal than those she had witnessed in Badel. She suspected this charade was for Ebrahim's benefit. She wondered if Ebrahim had given them any further reason to distrust him. She still had to reach Peshawar in Ebrahim's care, and felt uneasy at the thought. Was Commander Rahim keeping a careful enough watch on the young man?

When she finished taking pictures, she joined the men in the next round of tea. Malolai said good night and disappeared in the direction of the house where she stayed. Elizabeth smiled to herself when she saw her friend lingering on the path in the dusk, talking to Sharif. After tea, one of the men cried the *azan* and the Mujahedeen lined up to pray.

She sat beside Michel. They were the two outsiders. She was grateful that he did not speak and disturb the sense of communion, but she felt a strangeness in his attitude, a cynicism mixed with admiration and desire. He was like a beggar outside a lighted window. His eyes fixed on Ebrahim, watching him bend and straighten in the postures of prayer. Elizabeth suddenly felt the Frenchman's sublimated desire, and fought a choking intuition of disaster.

Yusuf had asked Rahman's father to kill a chicken, and now feasted the Mujahedeen. Elizabeth ate silently. She was getting tired of all the waste, of people outdoing each other in hospitality in a time of severe privation. And though Commander Rahim was this time the guest, he still picked out the best pieces for Elizabeth, despite her embarrassed protests.

At 8:45 p.m. they listened to the BBC Farsi language broadcast. Not all the Mujahedeen could understand it, but all strained to hear as the voice rose and fell on waves of static, reminding Elizabeth poignantly of their isolation, and the fragility of this invisible link with a kind of truth.

Elizabeth sat cross-legged on the carpet Yusuf had ordered brought out of the house, and Yusuf sat next to her. Still he had barely spoken to her. She was terribly aware of his nearness and again wanted to scream, to claw down whatever barrier had arisen between them.

Elizabeth knew the broadcast had ended when she heard the familiar signature music. Sharif took charge of the radio and began twiddling the knob, looking for Pakistan, or for Radio Free Kabul. The Mujahedeen talked among themselves excitedly, and Ebrahim gestured fiercely. Yusuf sat with his head in his hands, and Commander Rahim stared thoughtfully beyond the ring of lamplight as he puffed tobacco on the copper and carved-wood water pipe someone had passed him.

"More rumors of hope," said Yusuf. He glanced up at her.

"What do you mean?"

"The Geneva talks drag on, just like the talks during Vietnam. The Afghan Foreign Minister is interviewed, and implies there is progress. The Pakistani Foreign Minister is evasive, but implies the same. The Mujahedeen are not consulted at all. Who will decide our fate?

"The latest rumor is of a possible cease-fire, any time. If Pakistan decided to send back the refugees, where could we go? It will take years to rebuild the destruction you have seen. And likely there will be civil war. Maybe one day the Russians will do what the Americans did in Vietnam, just declare 'We've won. There is peace,' and pull out and let the government fall. Then there will be chaos, but they can blame it on the Afghans, and on American support of the Mujahedeen. Chances are we Afghans will be at each other's throats for the next twenty-five years, so perhaps America and Russia are gambling that no government based on Islamic values can come to power and threaten to influence the fifty million Muslims across the Soviet border, or the oil fields of the Middle East."

"You sound as if you don't want a cease-fire."

"We all do. On our terms."

"But is it possible?"

"Anything is possible if Allah wills it," interrupted Commander Rahim.

"I take your point, but do you have any realistic hopes?"

"Hope is all we have, young lady."

She disliked being patronized, even by someone she admired. She turned the tables. "Do you have time to be interviewed now, or are you too tired?"

He considered. "When are you leaving?"

"As soon as possible. My work is done here for the present." Behind her, she felt Yusuf get up abruptly.

The old man nodded. "Then now is a good time."

She glanced at Ebrahim and Michel, sitting within earshot. "Is it possible to go somewhere more private?"

He nodded again and spoke to one of the men, who moved an empty *charpoy* and a lantern to a corner of the courtyard away from the group. The commander got up and Elizabeth followed.

Sharif brought over two glasses of tea and her camera bag. She got out the black notebook, the one she'd reserved for "fact," as opposed to the green notebook in which she kept her journal of "feeling."

"Okay," she began, "what do you think of the Geneva talks?"

"Much as Yusuf said."

"But in your own words."

"The Mujahedeen have said over and over again that there can be no true peace without Mujahedeen representatives at the negotiating table. The present Kabul government is not a recognized one. Whatever decisions they, or the Pakistan government, make on our behalf cannot be accepted by us. If they replace Babrak Karmal with another Communist, we will fight him as well. It is not one man we hate, but a whole system."

She scribbled quickly. "What are your chances of military success?"

"None, in the long run. We are confined to harassment operations, and every time we do anything, the Soviets attack us with air power. They bomb innocent villages for sheltering us. We have no chance unless the Americans give us proper arms, not just a few smuggled Kalashnikovs, but effective weapons, surface to air missiles capable of shooting down a helicopter gun ship. And these weapons must not fall into the wrong hands. They must go to the honorable and trustworthy parties, those who believe in democracy and human rights, not the Wahabi fundamentalists who loathe democracy and despise human rights, and would institute an ignorant and imported version of Islamic law based on an interpretation of the Holy Koran as strange and twisted as your most fundamentalist Christians' interpretation of the Holy Bible. But I'm sure Massoud Khan and Mohammed Akbar and so many others have said all this often enough," he finished wearily.

She looked up, troubled by his revelations, and changed the subject. "Are the people behind you?"

"You have seen. Right now perhaps 90% of the countryside is free. Kandahar, Herat, even Mazar-i-Sharif have been in our hands from time to time. So have most of the regional capitals. Only Kabul is a problem, and even there we have our Mujahedeen, even in high positions. No Russian, and no collaborator, is safe. We can attack the power supply, and we can assassinate collaborators, even in broad daylight."

"But whose side is time on?"

"That, my dear, only God knows. The people grow tired. How long can they be bombed and starved for sheltering us before they give up? Maybe they won't be hostile to us, but they will stop feeding us, hide food from us, and then our own Mujahedeen may start to steal food. That would prove the Russians correct. Or maybe they will all just give up and go to Pakistan."

She felt a chill. "You seem very pessimistic."

"No, realistic. This is without taking into account the factor of faith. Civilizations have risen and kingdoms and tyrants have fallen because of the faith of a people. We are not fanatics, at least most of us. You have seen us pray, have seen us fight, and have seen us suffer. But there are men like Yusuf who have come back from the West. He is the prodigal son, and I am proud."

She looked at him sharply, but said nothing.

"I think you know our little secret. Please guard it carefully."

"Of course."

"Do you also know of my other son, the Governor of Kunar?"

"Yusuf told me. Not in great detail."

"That must be even more secret. You see what they have done to us? They have destroyed the spirit of our nation by turning brother against brother, son against father. We are truly the descendants of Cain."

"But in all societies, at some time, there has been civil war," she protested. "It's a terrible thing, but we had it in America too. My father's grandfather fought in the Civil War, on the Union side."

"There was a moral issue in that war. Slavery."

"Maybe. And also an economic issue. But there is a moral issue here too."

He looked at her squarely. "Elizabeth, we have a tradition. So do the Christians and the Jews. Adam had two sons, Cain and Abel. We call them Qabil and Abil. Qabil was jealous of his own brother Abil and murdered him. Your Bible says he went 'east of Eden' to dwell 'in the land of Nod.' Our tradition says Kabul was the land where Qabil dwelt after he murdered his brother. A mark was set upon him, you say. Perhaps that spiritual mark was also set upon us, his descendants."

"But you're fighting a foreign power more than each other."

"Yes," he agreed. "For now. But the real tragedy is that we are also fighting amongst ourselves. Ask Massoud Khan. Ask about the fights in the refugee camps that the newspapers don't report. And I'm sure you've heard about the Mujahedeen of one party attacking those of another party from the rear, even during battle with the Soviets."

"I've heard the stories. How true are they?"

"Less true than the Russians want the world to believe, more true than they should be."

Unity, the unobtainable garland that had cursed Afghans for centuries. "Any chance of unity?"

"Not that I see. All of this is off the record, of course. Write my opinions, my desire for unity, write of my work in training commandos. Nothing of my background. I can arrange for you to see the camp where we train, in Pakistan's Tribal Areas, if you are interested."

"Yes, of course I'm interested."

"Good. You can report to the world that we are not being trained by Americans or Chinese, but by Afghans."

She wrote, and in her heart felt a sudden and deep sympathy for this torn man.

"But there is always hope," he said. "Say that. Say that unity inside the country is improving, and parties have joint operations in some areas, and independent alliances. Say that we have hope for the success of the Geneva talks, for a ceasefire, for reconciliation of all Mujahedeen parties, and for rebuilding. We hope for continuing diplomatic pressure by the free world, by the Third World, by the Islamic Foreign Ministers Conference, and the Non-aligned Movement. We will keep fighting. By keeping pressure on both fronts, military and diplomatic, we may yet win our freedom."

"*Inshallah*."

"*Inshallah*."

"What are your immediate plans?" she asked.

He laughed. "That is not for anyone to know. Ears may be listening." He lowered his voice. "I operate only with picked men who have sworn an oath of loyalty and an oath of secrecy on the Holy Koran. We do not take even other Mujahedeen with us, with rare exceptions. The Frenchman was not a problem at first, as it was good to have a journalist along on our first few operations, our on-the-job training operations, so to speak. But he must leave before we can begin our serious work. Perhaps he will go with you when you leave."

Elizabeth tried to cover her dismay. "Isn't there another group he can go with? It is difficult to work with another photographer there."

Commander Rahim tugged at his beard. "We will see what we can do. Perhaps he can go with you as far as Babur Tangay, and stay there while you go on. Will you go back to Peshawar?"

"I am in no hurry. But my work here is finished."

He looked thoughtful. "Pity. Will you come back to Afghanistan?"

"Yes." She had spoken without consideration, from her heart.

He smiled. "One falls in love with my country, though it has become a place of mourning and tears. You are most welcome. You are different from most of the journalists. You really care. But write the truth. Do not trust any of us too much."

He looked up at the sky where the near-full moon rode high. "I think it is grown late, and we must sleep." He stood up and towered over her as he towered over his followers. He shook her hand, then kissed it.

"Good night, Elizabeth. I respect you very much, and thank you for what you have done. Both for the nursing, and the writing." He turned towards the group of Mujahedeen, most of whom were already sleeping in the open, their blankets wrapped around them. He turned back towards her suddenly, his hawk-like face formed by the lantern's fluttering flame. "By the way, my son admires you greatly." Without waiting for comment, he strode towards his commandos.

CHAPTER 24

ELIZABETH

En route to the

Pakistani border

When Elizabeth woke up just past dawn, Commander Rahim and his men were already gone. Yusuf had been up for some time and now bustled about impatiently, with occasional uncharacteristically sharp words for Malolai and Ismail. Elizabeth watched him wordlessly, searching in vain for some sign that Yusuf, as his father had said, admired her.

She sat alone on a *charpoy*, gloomily sipping her tea and slowly chewing on a piece of dry *nan*. She knew it was time to leave, but felt trepidation at the thought of the difficult journey back to the border.

Yusuf joined her on the *charpoy*. "Maybe I'll come with you as far as Babur Tangay," he said casually.

"Yes, if you like, that would be nice," she answered.

He got up just as suddenly as he had sat down. "No, I really shouldn't. I have too much work to do here."

She had obviously given the wrong response. "Oh well, it doesn't matter."

"What doesn't matter?"

"Whether you come with us or not. Your work here is more important."

"I'm glad you realize that." He walked away from her without another word.

Elizabeth did not want to leave Yusuf on bad terms, not after the closeness that had been between them. She lingered behind as her escort of Mujahedeen started off down the path to the valley floor, hoping she could think of the right words to say. She sadly embraced her friend Malolai. "I will miss you."

Malolai's eyes were bright with tears. "And I you. I hope you come back some day. It will be very lonely for me here."

"Don't worry too much. *Inshallah…*" *Inshallah*, what? "You're doing such good work for your people. Only be careful, Malolai. And do take care of Dr. Yusuf." She was trying to keep her tone light, but the words fell with the weight of lead.

"And you of Sharif."

The two women embraced again, and kissed each other's cheeks three times in the Afghan manner, right, left, right.

Yusuf had been watching, waiting. Now he took both her hands and sighed. He looked at her, looked down at their joined hands, and then returned his eyes to her face.

"I'm very glad to have met you, Elizabeth. Thank you for all of your help, and thank you for writing about Afghanistan."

Her heart felt as if someone was squeezing her unconscious. "Thank you for *your* help," she said unsteadily. "I will write the best article I can, and I'll send you a copy when it's published. Where should I send it? Through the Medical Association?"

He nodded. "I'm sorry if anyone here has done anything to make you unhappy."

That sentence seemed to sum up the whole experience for him. An apology for feeling. "Oh no, it's not like that. Everyone has been very good with me." She quickly dropped his hands and turned away.

"Maybe I'll see you in Peshawar," he said.

She couldn't look at him. "Maybe. When are you coming?"

"*Inshallah*, after two or three weeks. Just for a bit of a rest. Another doctor is due to replace me for one month, and then I will come back here. Will you still be in Peshawar?"

"*Inshallah*." She had learned that the word was sometimes a way of avoiding commitment.

"*Ba'amana khoda*," he said quietly.

She knew it was Dari for "Go with God." "*Ba'amana khoda*," she echoed, and resolutely strode down the path to the waiting Mujahedeen.

Her forward motion, away from the clinic, made her feel emotionally dismembered, as if she had forgotten a crucial part of herself back at the clinic. She knew she had dreamed of Yusuf last night. All day long, fleeting and insubstantial images floated just beneath the surface of her consciousness. Something about a white horse? A symbol of animal passion, she supposed, though she was annoyed at her subconscious mind's lack of originality. A spring of water gushing from the base of a tree trunk? Yusuf teaching her how to shoot a bow and arrow? Could that symbolize primitive, basic knowledge?

She half wished that Yusuf had come to Babur Tangay. But why prolong the agony? She doubted she would see him in Peshawar. Once she reached Pakistan, she would be busy writing, and then she should start thinking of going back to America and picking up a new life there, a life of freedom and personal choice, without Tom or any other man.

It was still a long way to Peshawar, but in her mind she was already there. Her work was finished, and she just wanted to get out of Afghanistan quickly. If they hurried, they could reach Babur Tangay before dusk, rest briefly, and set off on the long night march to Dunahi. In two days she could be in Massoud Khan's house, resting, writing, and talking to Salima.

Sharif hovered protectively at her elbow, seeming to sense her sadness. She appreciated his attentiveness to both her mood and her safety. It was not every man who would have carried her across rivers on his back. She wondered if Yusuf would. Maybe. Underneath the brittleness he was a very compassionate man.

They halted in a meadow under the shade of some olive trees. Tiny flowers dotted the green grass with blue, yellow, and white. Sharif dreamily picked some of the fragile blooms and pressed a handful on Elizabeth. He smiled at her, but she knew he was seeing Malolai. For a long time he held a sprig of *shin gul*, stroking the petals of ultramarine. His large brown hands dwarfed the delicate flowers, but Elizabeth was struck by his gentleness, by these hands of a man who could kill Russians, caress flowers, heal by massage, and probably make passionate love to a woman.

Malolai would be lucky if she married Sharif, Elizabeth thought. Sharif was the epitome of the Afghan paradox, macho sensitivity. It had its attractive side, though much of the gentleness seemed to be reserved for male comrades. Perhaps educated women like Malolai could tame the arrogance without taming the wildness, and draw the sensitivity towards women as well as towards men, flowers, and the poetry of battle. As long as the women didn't try to become more male than the men, they might succeed. Afghan women had an earthy heartiness, an indomitable fecundity, a natural sense of nurturing that recalled prehistoric mother cults. These women were even stronger than their men, and in the end it would be they who would prevail and free themselves, on their own terms.

That night, to Elizabeth's surprise, they halted not at Babur Tangay but at a small hamlet on a ridge, set among fruit trees covered with shell-pink blossoms. They were taking a different route back, not directly down the valley toward Babur Tangay but along the ridge separating Badel from Deh Wagal. As they approached the tiny village just before sunset, Ebrahim spoke to her in a low voice. "I didn't want the people to think we were going to Babur Tangay, so I headed for Badel instead. Too many eyes are watching, and we don't know which are spies."

She wondered how much Ebrahim was posturing for effect, and how much was real worry. She had decided that Ebrahim couldn't possibly be a spy, as he was far too quick-tempered, brash, and careless to make a good spy.

She sat on a rooftop in the warm dusk, feeling forlorn as she wrote her journal by lantern light. She watched the moths bat noisily at the lantern's glass, and sat for a long time with her green notebook open, chewing on the cap of her pen and wondering what to write about her feelings for Yusuf and for Afghanistan.

"You are like a baby chewing on a pacifier," said Michel as he joined her.

She laughed and quickly closed her notebook. "This is all rather difficult to describe. Don't you agree."

"Yes, of course, *trés difficile.*"

"What will you write?"

He shrugged. "Many things. Many things."

"I suppose you'll write about the prisoner exchange. I missed that."

"Yes, of course," he said absently. "And where will you go from here, Elizabet?"

"Tomorrow to Babur Tangay, and in the night to Dunahi. I guess we'll cross the border the next night."

"You are definitely leaving tomorrow?"

"Yes, why not? There's no reason to stay. How about you?"

"I go another direction tomorrow. Ebrahim will ask some Mujahedeen to go with me, maybe his friend Najeeb Khan."

"But where will go you? And do any of them speak English?"

"English, that doesn't matter. I will go here and there, wherever they will take me, for awhile at least. You know I don't want to go back."

"You have to, some day."

"Yes, yes, but not too soon. Maybe here in Afghanistan I will find something."

Everyone came to Afghanistan to find something by teasing death. Perhaps love, the gem in the dung heap, snatched at great peril and held most briefly. Or self, a treasure still more rare, the pearl in the dust of a mountainside that was once a seabed.

"Elizabet, I must talk with you."

She put away her notebook, resigned. "What about?"

"What do you think of Ebrahim?"

Was he about to tell her Ebrahim was a spy? "He has been very good with me," she said guardedly. "Massoud Khan trusts him, and he has taken good care of me."

"Yes, he is trustworthy," Michel said thoughtfully. "He has been very good with me also." He paused and looked toward the group of men on a nearby rooftop, where Ebrahim sat on a *charpoy* with one arm around Sharif, the other around the man called Najeeb, the same man Ebrahim had mistaken for a spy that day at Babur Tangay. "How do you think he feels about me?"

"I'm sure he likes you. Why not?"

"That's not what I mean."

She didn't answer.

"Do you think he would be interested in me?"

She glanced at Ebrahim, who was laughing uproariously at someone's joke. "I can't tell you. Aren't you supposed to have a sense about that? My brother calls it 'gay-dar,' like radar.'"

He smiled faintly. "Yes, usually I can tell. But this time I don't know. I have enjoyed his company so much. And I find him very attractive. But do you think he likes Sharif, or this Najeeb?" Jealousy flickered across his features.

"Oh, I'm sure not. Men here are just openly affectionate with each other. Actually it's refreshing after being around a lot of repressed western men."

"But surely you know the reputation of the Pathans."

"Well, I've heard a few things. But I haven't seen much obvious homosexuality."

He smiled sardonically. "In a society where men and women are so separated and heterosexual urges are repressed, it seems natural that men would turn to men. Homosexuality is tolerated, even accepted."

"Maybe." But she really had no idea how Ebrahim would react to Michel's advances. He might be flattered, or he might get very angry. The thought of Ebrahim angry frightened her. "Just be careful. If he isn't inclined that way, or isn't attracted to you, he could react badly."

"Tonight is my last chance."

"Are you in love with him?"

"You mean am I in love or do I just want sex?"

"Yeah, I guess that's what I'm asking. Remember that we're in the middle of a Holy War, and a lot of things may not be so acceptable. What does Islam say about homosexuality anyway?"

"I don't know. What does Christianity say? It exists in both societies."

"All I'm saying is you can do what you want, but don't get yourself shot over someone. It's just not worth it."

She got up and walked toward the group of Mujahedeen, wondering what Michel could possibly see in Ebrahim. The source of human attraction, she reflected, remained an inexplicable and infinite mystery.

CHAPTER 25
YUSUF

Amrau Tangay

Yusuf's father had left, and this strange woman Yusuf loved had left the same day. It made no sense. How could he love someone he hardly knew? And another American. How did he know she wouldn't turn out just like Janet? He didn't. Love was all a gamble.

Why had he just let her go like that? He cursed himself for his stubbornness. But she had not responded, even after he had given her several chances. If she had given just one response he wouldn't have let her go. Typical of a woman to suddenly freeze up after a moment of closeness. How could he ever trust again? He had thought this time would be different. Janet had enthralled him with her energy; Elizabeth had a depth that Janet had lacked, and a compassion that salved all fears.

But once again he'd given away far too much of his feelings to a woman, and she had given nothing in return. Why were women so afraid to risk?

He thought of all the women he had known in America. He had dated a lot before he met Janet, and had been briefly involved with several women since the divorce. These last had all seemed shallow "transitional" relationships. He was sure the women had dated him only in hopes of marrying a doctor.

Perhaps he really didn't know women, or perhaps it had simply been too soon after the divorce.

Maybe he shouldn't rush this either. The divorce had really shattered his confidence in his judgment, at least in that area of life. But here he didn't have the luxury of letting a relationship develop slowly, naturally. He could marry her...but that was crazy, and she would laugh at such a hasty proposal. "Marry me and live in a war zone." He didn't think she'd much like living in Peshawar with his mother and sister either. Her in America and him in Afghanistan?

Maybe the war would end soon, maybe the rumored cease-fire would come to pass. And maybe then they could go to Kabul. He wondered if she would like Kabul. He had always loved the city of his birth, but that had been years ago, long before the war. How much of Kabul would be left when the Russians and the collaborators finished with it, let alone if civil war followed? It would take years to rebuild. Would even an adventurous journalist want to commit herself to the reconstruction of Afghanistan when she could have a comfortable life and successful career in New York?

And would she want to live so far from her family? He knew he could no longer go back to America, even for Elizabeth, and the thought caught him by surprise. He had crossed an invisible barrier in his life. He had cast off too much, and had left the debris along the way, beyond bridges which he hadn't even realized had been burnt. He had discovered his destiny late, but perhaps "things that come late come right," as his father was fond of saying. Maybe his real marriage, his real love, would also come late.

Elizabeth was no girl. She was nearly thirty. He assumed that she had lived with the man she'd been in love with. That didn't particularly bother him, though he was curious to know more about the relationship. He wondered how many boyfriends she had had. She didn't seem to get close easily.

Love was irrational, and he was usually a rational man. But he was also a poet. The power of love was about all they had left to build bridges across immense gulfs between one human being and another.

Someday they might even have to love and forgive their enemies, though at the moment he recoiled from the thought, remembering the baby with the obliterated face. The Russians had made him a murderer of his own people. *Maybe this violence is in all of us,* he thought cynically. *We've all become murderers. Would Ayub spare him and* Baba, *if given the chance? Would he spare Ayub if the Mujahedeen won?* Ayub must have known about the bombing, and about so many other bombings of innocent civilians. Even if he hadn't ordered the bombings himself, he was complicit in them. *Poor Ayub,* he thought. *Unless he has completely changed from the sensitive younger brother I knew, he must be tormented by guilt.*

Yusuf took off his hat and rubbed his forehead and temples. He had been sitting for a long time, record books open, pen in hand, thinking. Malolai seemed subject to similar fits. The usually efficient nurse would suddenly stop in mid-step, like a watch stopping for a moment, then continue on her way.

Yusuf knew Malolai must be in love, but these were not the kind of things a man asked a woman. Long as he had been away from his native land, he had not forgotten this about his culture.

Malolai now approached him shyly. "Doctor *Sahib*, would you like some tea?"

He looked up and sighed. "Thank you. Please join me."

They sat in the open, enjoying the last translucence of daylight. No patients had come for some time, and Ismail was down the valley checking on the condition of a sick child.

Malolai sat on the *charpoy*, well at the opposite end. He liked the young nurse. She was full of life, and bold enough to joke with him. Sometimes he needed that. That was one of the things that attracted him to Elizabeth. Malolai reminded him of his younger sister, and that was indeed the way he regarded his nurse. Perhaps he could be the go-between to Sharif's family, if she would accept him in that role, and if that were indeed what she wanted.

"Doctor *Sahib*, I have a terrible problem."

"It cannot be so terrible, can it?"

She blinked, and tears overflowed. "There is someone I want to marry?"

"Why do you act as if it is not possible?" Respectfully, he looked away from her tears.

"I don't know. I don't know."

"Then maybe it is not impossible. Has he said anything?"

"Who should he say anything to? He cannot to me, can he? He does not even know my family. My brother is in Kabul, how can he speak to him?"

"Malolai," said the doctor gently. "I will be your brother now. I will protect your honor, and I will do what is necessary to ensure your happiness. Let him come to me."

"But maybe it is too late now."

"He will be back."

"Do you know who it is?"

"I think I do."

"It is Sharif."

"Yes."

"What do you think of him?"

"He is a good Muslim, and a good *mujaheed*. He would make you a good husband."

"Maybe my brother would not think so. Sharif is not as educated as I am."

"Your brother does not know Sharif. I do. And I know his family. His father is dead, and his mother is living. It is a good family. They were land-owners before this war. Sharif would have been educated, had not hardship come to them. They had a great deal of land, but it is now in the hands of the Communists."

"Could I be happy with Sharif?"

"Can any of us be truly happy now, in these times? We have no country. We have only faith, and if we are lucky, we find a little love. It is true that in Kabul you would never have met Sharif. But now we can't say what kind of life any of us will live, or even if any of us will live very long. Could you have lived in Narang with Sharif? Maybe you could have. Could he have lived in Kabul?

Maybe, but his job would have been below yours, and it would have hurt his pride and made him bitter.

"Now none of us can live in Kabul. And many of us are getting our educations from life, and from war. But Malolai, women like you are the future of Afghanistan. We must believe we will win, and when we do, you and other women who have broken the old barriers in exceptional times must stand on the stones and make sure that the same old walls are not rebuilt along with the rest of the country, that these stones are used for more constructive purposes, for social change. The old Afghanistan is gone, for good or ill. The Afghanistan we rebuild cannot be turning ourselves backward."

Malolai listened intently, then sighed. "I do love Sharif, and I do want to marry him, even though I am afraid for our future."

"I'm not surprised. Sharif is an exceptional man, just as you are an exceptional woman. When he comes back, *inshallah*, I will try to discover his intentions and what he would expect from you if he were to marry you. Neither of you can expect a normal life. Perhaps as a nation we are all rushing to marry, to find love and stability, a sense that we will continue no matter how many of us are killed. If you and Sharif decide to marry, you must decide what you want from your life, according to what is possible. I think he loves you not for the usual reasons of beauty or family background or education, but because of who you are, and because of what you are doing for our country. For this reason I do not think he will ask you to stop working for Afghanistan.

"Don't worry, Malolai. Be patient, and see what is in your fate. My little sister, I hope you have found love. Everyone should marry, and love."

She smiled at him. "I hope you too have found love. It is not good to be lonely in war. We need someone to be everything to us."

"Yes, we do," he said quietly. But what to do when that someone is lost?

CHAPTER 26
ELIZABETH

En route to the

Pakistani border

Elizabeth was awakened by the sound of slightly off-key singing. Slowly she came to consciousness, unsure of where she was, or who was singing "Light My Fire" with an Afghan accent.

She blinked stupidly, then groaned. The Mujahedeen were stretching and yawning, working up to their inevitable chorus of throat-clearing and spitting. She stumbled outside, rubbing her eyes in the early morning light, to find Ebrahim squatting on the dusty roof, washing his face as he cheerfully impersonated an American rock star.

The young man rubbed his face vigorously, then smiled up at her and handed her the jug of water. She greeted him tiredly and half-heartedly splashed ice cold water on her face.

"You're in a good mood today," she remarked, wondering if Michel had indeed made and advance and been accepted.

Ebrahim laughed. "Yes, in two days we will be back in Peshawar, *inshallah*."

"And you will be rid of me."

"Oh, Lizbet, don't talk that way." He clapped her on the back. "We have been happy to have you along, you and Mr. Michel."

"Where is Michel?"

"He went down to the river, I think, to wash."

She stood up and shook the water off her hands, then shaded her eyes and looked down toward the small stream that ran by the hamlet. Through some bushes, she could just make out Michel's pale white body bathing in the chilly stream.

She shivered. "I think I'll wait to have a bath, but I guess Michel is staying for awhile."

"Yes, he is going with my dear friend Najeeb Khan and other Mujahedeen. I think they will go north to Asmar. There is good fighting there, good for the photos."

"I think I've seen enough for the moment."

He grinned. "But Lizbet, you haven't even seen a fight from close."

"That day at Babur Tangay was close enough for me!"

Michel was coming up the narrow path from the river. But by contrast to Ebrahim, he was definitely subdued.

"Good morning!" she called to him.

He looked at her with sad gray eyes and a meek smile. "Good morning, Elizabet. So, today we all say goodbye, all of us old friends."

"Yes, we have become good friends in a short time. It's strange, isn't it? I guess all travel is like that, but this experience sure is more intense than ordinary travel."

Michel's disarming, roguish smile was back. "It's too early in the morning to be the philosopher. Let us all eat breakfast first, and then go while the sun is still low and it is cool."

Ebrahim laughed and joked with the other Mujahedeen as they ate their meager breakfast. As Elizabeth watched him gesture wildly and pull faces, she knew he was imitating someone. She guiltily recalled her and Malolai's imitations of Ebrahim and Michel. It was so easy to make fun of people, harder to give them the respect due to them merely for being human.

Michel sat beside her on a *charpoy*, sipping his tea thoughtfully. A sadness clung to him, but underneath she sensed agitation, which she attributed to his unrequited and unexpressed love of a man he would inevitably have to let go.

"So, you're going to Asmar?" she asked.

"Yes, by way of Chagaserai."

"Well that sounds exciting, and dangerous. Isn't that where the Governor's House is?"

"Yes, that's right."

She elbowed him affectionately. "Cheer up! You're doing exactly what you want to do. How many people can say that?" She wanted him to cheer up so he didn't rub off her own thin veneer of cheer. "Will you try to get into Chagaserai itself?"

"What? Oh, no, Najeeb just has to stop there. It is his home village. He will go into the town and get some useful information from the bazaar, and then we will go north from there."

"Oh, Michel." She looked at him fondly, but he did not look at her. "I'm glad I met you. I really hope you find happiness some day."

"Oh God, I'm so confused," he said quietly, as if to himself. He covered his face with his hands and rubbed his eyes."

"Don't worry. One way or another something will work out for you."

Najeeb called out Michel's name, and the Frenchman stood up, throwing his blanket around his lanky frame.

"Time to go," said Ebrahim brightly. "Lizbet, are you ready?"

"No, not quite." She was always annoyed when he rushed her. "Give me a few minutes. Are we in any hurry?"

"No, no hurry, no problem."

She shook Michel's hand, unaccountably reluctant to say goodbye. "Well, it was nice knowing you. I guess I won't see you again. I'll probably be gone by the time you get back to Peshawar."

Michel squeezed her hand, then said distractedly, "No, we will probably never see each other again. Are you ready to go? Do you want to walk with us until our ways go separate?"

"No, it will take me a few minutes to get ready. You'd better go."

Michel looked up at the sky, already bleaching as the sun climbed from the horizon. "It's getting hot quickly. Go soon." He squeezed her hand again. "Goodbye and good luck."

She waved as he, Najeeb, and several other men set off down the path. She kept watching for a few minutes and laughed when they had to halt at a narrow bend to make way for three Mujahedeen and a young, bearded man riding a donkey.

"Mujahedeen from a rival party," said Ebrahim under his breath.

"What does that mean?"

"I don't know. Sometimes they cooperate, and sometimes not. The one on the donkey is a mullah, but not a good mullah. He is very fundamentalist and ignorant." Ebrahim pulled Elizabeth's *chadar* over her head. "Don't let him see you. Go into the house and finish your packing, and I will try to get rid of them."

So now the danger was from their own people, she thought in irritation as she rolled up her sleeping bag in the dark hut. Just like Rahim was saying. Ebrahim seemed to fear these people more than he feared Communist spies. She was tired of all this intrigue. She shoved her sleeping bag into her duffle and moved to an angle from where she could see out the door, but not be seen in the dim light.

The four new arrivals stood talking to Ebrahim while Sharif watched from the side, one hand resting on the open holster of his bandoleer. Casually, Sharif sauntered towards the door of the house and stood in front of it, blocking her from view. He glanced back and flashed her a brief and reassuring smile.

She could still see most of the rooftop. Ebrahim seemed to be arguing with the men. The mullah remained adamant, and his armed bodyguards, or whatever they were, stood close by, Kalashnikovs planted in the dust in front of them.

Ebrahim kept gesturing toward the house and finally shrugged and came to the door. His face was dark with anger, and a vein stood out in his forehead. "Lizbet, this mullah demands to see you. I told him it was wrong to demand to see a woman's face, but he insists and says, 'she is not Muslim and does not cover her face anyway,' and…well, the rest is not good. I think you must come out."

She clenched her teeth. "All right, if that's what he wants I'll come out. I don't see how it can do any harm."

"Be careful what you say, and how you act."

"Can he speak English?"

"Ha! These kind of people cannot speak their own language, let alone English."

"Then be careful how you translate." She adjusted her *chadar* and walked out onto the rooftop. "*Salaam aleikum*," she said, offering her hand, forgetting that orthodox Muslim men don't shake women's hands. The black-bearded mullah stared at her, stony faced. She dropped her hand and smiled. His expression remained hard and angry, marring the features of an otherwise handsome young man in his late twenties. He looked to be younger than she, and his arrogance incensed her, but gave her a corresponding strength. She refused to be intimidated by this man.

The mullah spoke in Pashtu and Ebrahim translated. "He says why do you dare come here, with your Western ways? He blames me and blames Massoud for allowing you to come."

"Tell him that I work for a very important newspaper and I am trying to tell the world about your *jehad*."

Ebrahim looked uncomfortable. "He says why doesn't your newspaper show the respect of sending a man to write about our *jehad*?"

She was exasperated. "Tell him in my country men and women are chosen for their ability to do a job well."

"He answers that you have no respect."

"No respect! Who does he respect? Tell him I have respected all your customs, I have worn this dress, I have covered my head, and I have not done anything an educated Afghan woman wouldn't do."

Ebrahim translated, but quickly, and she knew he had left something out. "I'm not Muslim!" she blurted out.

This he did not translate. The mullah started to say something further, then at a word from one of his men, looked at the sky behind him. Elizabeth's gaze followed his to where three helicopter gunships droned across the distant valley on a diagonal course. As they approached their noise grew louder and louder until it filled the sky.

Panic seized Elizabeth. "Ebrahim, what should we do?"

Sharif put his hand on her arm and Ebrahim looked around quickly. "Come, we will go to a house on the outside of the village. Come!"

Everyone was disappearing into houses now, scattering like a flock of crows startled by a shot. She scrambled after Ebrahim to a house apart from the others. He shoved her inside to where two dark-eyed women and several children stared out the door frame toward the sky. The smallest child whimpered quietly and clung to his mother's veil, which the woman modestly tried to keep over her face as she exchanged words with Ebrahim.

"Stay here!" said Ebrahim urgently.

"What? What if something happens to you or Sharif?"

Sharif entered the house, respectfully looking away from the women as he deposited Elizabeth's two bags on the floor.

"Here, you can take good pictures now," said Ebrahim. His eyes were bright with excitement, his face flushed.

"What's happening? Are they going to attack us?"

He shrugged. "I don't know. There is no reason. I think they are really looking for Commander Rahim." He held his Kalashnikov close to his body, like a baby, and cocked the heavy weapon.

Outside the three helicopters circled and droned above the hilltop hamlet. The noise was almost unbearable. Elizabeth's hands shook as she got out her camera. These helicopters were so close she wouldn't need a telephoto lens. She checked to see how much film was in the camera. Good, thirty more shots.

From their position just outside the village they had a good view of the helicopters as they tightened their circles around the village proper. Suddenly a fusillade of fire erupted from the cluster of buildings where Elizabeth had been. The helicopters immediately answered with rockets and machine guns. The concussions of the explosions shook the whole mountainside, and the house trembled.

The women behind Elizabeth crouched further into a corner, holding their children tightly. One of them asked a question, and Sharif answered with a laugh. He had only his pistol, but seemed oddly serene.

Another burst of fire from the village, and some shouting. Elizabeth heard men crying "*Allahu akbar!*" and she half-consciously began her own litany of "God is great" under her breath. The thunder of the rotors nearly drowned the sound of the chant, and she watched with horror as machine-gun fire raked the rooftop where she had just been and embedded itself in the door frame.

Ebrahim pushed her toward the door. "There, go, take a picture now!"

Sharif put himself between her and the open doorway. She crouched next to him and attempted to focus on one of the helicopters above them, trying to hide the camera in the folds of her *chadar*. She held her breath and shot off a few frames of the swiftly moving machines. Then yet another burst of fire cut the air and she aimed her camera toward the village, shooting blindly as rockets exploded rooftops into rubble and clouds of smoke, fire, and dust rolled up the mountainside.

They were engulfed in black smoke. In the midst of it sounded a huge boom, and the roof above them began to move. Elizabeth cursed aloud, then prayed "Oh God, dear Jesus, please don't let me die!" Thje women behind her wailed and the children screamed. Ebrahim and Sharif were shouting as stones and mud fell from the roof into the room. Another explosion, and one of the roof beams crashed into the house. Sharif pushed her into a corner under a *charpoy* as machine-gun fire spattered on the fallen beam.

"Lie still!" shouted Ebrahim. "We are covered by the quilts. I don't think they can see us." He looked toward the women and children huddled under the two other beds. They were unharmed but terrified. One woman cried out, "*Ya Allah, ya Allah*," over and over, sobbing. When Ebrahim turned back towards Elizabeth, there were two lines of tears down his dust-stained face.

She closed her eyes and prayed, muttering, "Oh dear God, please make it stop, please make it stop..." And finally it did. There was one final loud explosion, and then the implacable roar receded as quickly as it had come.

Elizabeth breathed in short, sobbing breaths. For a moment she could think of nothing, could not move from her curled-up position under the bed. Then she crawled out through the dust, cutting her hands on newly fallen stones. She brushed some dust off of her camera and turned to the two women and the children, who were still under their beds. She knelt and extended her hand, helping them drag themselves out. No one was wounded, she saw with relief, and the two women hugged and kissed her repeatedly.

There was a lot of shouting in the village. Men came out onto the rooftops, brandishing weapons with cries of triumph. Ebrahim called out, and they answered him with a shout of victory.

"It is a miracle! No one has been seriously injured, and they have shot down a helicopter! Allah is with us!"

"What?"

"They've shot down one of the servants of *sheitan*! That's why they went away. They should have known better than to have come so near the Mujahedeen."

"Where is it?"

Ebrahim took her hand and led her to the edge of the roof. From the ravine below the village rose a curling pillar of black, oily smoke.

"No survivors," he said with satisfaction.

The mullah and the three other men scrambled up the hill to join them, clucking their tongues at the damage that had been done to this and several other houses. This time they all embraced Ebrahim and Sharif, ignoring Elizabeth and the women, who covered their faces and turned away. Finally the mullah pointed to Elizabeth.

"He says you must take pictures," said Ebrahim.

Elizabeth had gone numb, and there were tears in her eyes. How many human lives had gone up in that black smoke? She had no idea how many men rode in the gunships. She hated the helicopters, she'd wanted them shot down, she'd wanted all of them destroyed at that moment as they rained fire and stone on her head. She'd been so angry and so scared that she would have shot at them herself if she'd had a gun.

But the reality of death was something else. Down in that ravine were dead bodies of Soviet soldiers, charred bodies whose smell now wafted on the air of this column of smoke and ashes. But maybe this was a terrible truth that the world needed to know.

"All right," she said calmly. "Let's go. You want pictures, let's go now! Go ahead and pose on the wreckage, pose in front of the smoke."

She started off toward the ravine, slipping on the steep path and nearly losing her balance. The others followed, speaking rapidly in Pashtu.

"The mullah says why are you angry?" said Ebrahim.

She stopped and turned. "Aren't you? How can they just attack us like this? And how can there really be dead human beings in there?"

They had reached the bottom of the ravine. The helicopter had broken into many pieces from the force of its impact against the mountainside, but the main body of the wreckage was licked by flames.

"Lizbet, aren't you happy that we shot down this helicopter?" asked Ebrahim.

"Happy? Happy? How can you say such a thing? Oh shit, I just want all this to be over. I can't be happy that you've killed someone. I'm just glad they didn't kill any of us."

Ebrahim said nothing, and the mullah asked him a question, which he answered shortly.

She threw down her camera bag, sat on a rock, and dusted off her lens. She waved angrily at the men. "Go ahead," she said harshly, "pose. You love to pose so much, all of you, now pose in front of your work."

The men rushed down like eager boys, crowding each other out of the frame. Only Sharif retained a modicum of dignity, though he too posed with a proud expression. The mullah looked as if he had been the one to fire the shot that had brought down the helicopter. She looked into his arrogant eyes and saw something far colder than fanaticism.

She finished the roll sullenly. She hardly knew what she was doing anymore, but simply focused, checked the exposure, and shot. Years of training made the motions automatic.

She sat back down on her rock to put in a new roll of film, and suddenly began to cry. She immediately wiped her face off with her *chadar*, but her tears had been noted by hostile eyes. The mullah spoke to Ebrahim, who walked slowly towards her.

"Why are you crying for Russians?" he asked angrily.

"I'm crying for everyone," she shouted at him. "There are human beings in there."

"Humans? You call them human?" His voice teetered on the edge of hysteria. "You have seen what they did, what they almost did to us, and you call them human? They are animals, dogs, pigs, and they deserve to be killed. Those women could have been my mother! And you cry for these dead animals?"

She was in shock, and merely shook her head. "You don't understand. I don't understand."

"The mullah says that you should not shout the way you did."

"Tell him I am sorry. I was angry."

"He says women should not behave this way, and it is shame that you should behave this way in front of our women."

A cold fury lashed at her, but she controlled it. "Tell him I am sorry," she repeated. "That is all you need to say."

Ebrahim spoke at some length, then turned back to her uncertainly. "He thinks you are KGB, because you cry for the Russian dead."

She jerked her head up, her eyes wide. Suddenly the danger of her situation struck her with force. "Ebrahim, you know I am not KGB." She looked him straight in the eye, and he looked away.

"He wants to know how you knew of the raid."

"What?!"

"He says you planned to go today, and he kept you."

"That's the most ridiculous thing I've ever heard. If I were KGB and knew there was going to be a bombing raid, I sure as hell wouldn't have risked being so near the place. Would anyone in their right mind put themselves through that voluntarily?" She swallowed hard to keep her growing hysteria under control.

She watched Ebrahim closely as he translated. Was he a spy after all? Was he trying to set her up? No, he would never have been here during a raid either. Unless the mullah's appearance and argument really had delayed them unexpectedly. She scrutinized his closed face, but could read nothing.

He turned toward her impassively. "He says you must be KBG or CIA."

"That is even more absurd. I thought you liked the CIA anyway. Aren't they supposed to be giving you arms?"

"He says the West is as corrupt as the Russians, and only a corrupt power would send a woman here to do their dirty work."

Elizabeth was stunned. She looked at Sharif, who was watching intently, his dark eyes blazing defiance at the mullah. She looked back at Ebrahim. "Ebrahim, do you really think I am either KGB or CIA? Don't you know me by now?"

The young man stared at her, his lower lip trembling. Finally he shook his head. "Lisbet, I am scared of them. I am acting."

She sighed with relief. Somehow she would get out of this. Sharif began talking quietly to the other men, reassuring them, cajoling them.

Finally she began laughing. She could not stop, and gasped for breath, making the sounds that cross the border between laughter and sobs. The mullah and his men just stared at her, but some instinct told her it was time to move. She stood up, picked up her camera bag, and turned her back to her accuser. "Let's go, Ebrahim, we have a long way to go."

Ebrahim hesitated for a moment, then followed her. Sharif took up her laughter and called back cheery goodbyes to the men, who remained in the ravine, talking excitedly among themselves. Elizabeth waited for shouts, warning shots, footsteps in pursuit, but none came, and she knew they had won. She would cry later.

CHAPTER 27

ELIZABETH

On the way to Dunahi

Elizabeth chafed at the delay. They were already a day behind, and all she wanted was to get back across the border and to the safety of Massoud's house. Her brittle nerves were near a breaking point, and she didn't know how much longer she could stay calm.

In the faintly purple light of dusk, she could just make out the sentries ahead among a cluster of rocks. She heard their exchange of high-pitched cries as they flitted like birds from shelter to shelter. Behind them was Babur Tangay, and beyond lay the floor of the Kunar Valley and the white ribbon of road, dusty and potholed, scarred from recent bombings and from the Mujahedeen's mines. Somewhere on this road loomed skeletons of their successes, rusty hulks that spoke of fire and silence.

The sentries signaled and scurried toward the road. "Hurry!" Ebrahim whispered. She trotted quickly after him, fear welling up from her solar plexus to her shaking hands. She glanced anxiously at the sky, clear as a spring, white as a reflection. The light was fading, but if a late helicopter happened to fly over they would surely be seen.

As she stepped out onto the road her feet sank in the white dust. East, from Pakistan, the moon rose fat and white as a tropical fruit. The land was silver and pale blue, like watered silk. If only she could ignore the obvious signs of war, the rusted bits of metal among the wildflowers, or the cans carelessly tossed by the roadside, Russian words still visible on torn labels. Elizabeth looked nervously up and down the road, north and south. Nothing moved, and the only sounds were birdsong and the distant might of the river.

"That way is all Parchami and Khalqi," Ebrahim whispered, waving south. "A Russian base is there. And that way," he waved north, "is Chagaserai and Asmar. We have to pass near Khalqi villages, so we must go very quietly."

They soon came to the remnants of a destroyed tank. The men raced each other to pose on top of the hollow burnt shell, as if they had destroyed the vehicle that very day. Elizabeth thought of the men who had died in the tank, but this time kept her thoughts to herself. Without protest she took the pictures she knew would most please her companions.

Sharif held a single rocket launcher, which someone had just brought from Peshawar. To Elizabeth's annoyance, Ebrahim seized it and posed on the highest pinnacle of the tank, stern expression on his hard face, rocket launcher pointed toward the sky.

"Ebrahim," she asked when the Mujahedeen had clambered down, "do you know how to use a rocket launcher?"

"Me? Of course."

"Have you ever used one in battle?"

"No, but I know how to use one. It's easy, just aim and fire. We don't have enough. You must ask Massoud Khan for some when we get to Peshawar."

She didn't think her opinion would make much difference in Cold War geopolitical games. "What about Sharif? Has he ever used one?"

"Sharif knows a rocket launcher very well. He once shot down a helicopter near Chagaserai. The ruins are still there. Do you want to see them?"

"Maybe some other time."

While the men stopped for prayer Elizabeth sat on a rock watching the full moon rise. In the dust near her feet was a can of Red Army rations, its bottom spotted with rust. She examined it, imagining some strapping blond soldier, or more likely a Muslim conscript from Soviet Central Asia who looked much like the Afghans he was sent to fight, eating from the can, probably complaining about the food and then casually littering an alien land. She dropped the can and kicked it angrily. It bounced on the stones, clattering to a stop below the road.

Her fear subsided with the fading light. Most of the Mujahedeen returned to Babur Tangay, leaving Elizabeth in the company of her original escort. As the stars faded into being, the small party trudged on through the dust, each falling into a personal rhythm. They skirted the shell of a school, which Ebrahim said the Mujahedeen had burned the year before. "They were teaching propaganda," he said by way of explanation. "They also kept ammunition in the school, so what kind of school is that? The Russians say the Mujahedeen are against education. Write that it is not true."

When they reached the river the moon was high overhead, flooding the valley with light. They had to wade through several rivulets to reach the main current of the river. Elizabeth stoically removed shoes and socks, rolled up her loose trousers, and slogged into the cold water. The mud squished between her toes, then gave way to stones. She tried to grip them with her bare feet, but the stones were slippery and she stumbled and almost fell in the strong current. She was grateful that Sharif, as always, was there to steady her.

At last they reached the center stream, where a tall figure grasping an even taller pole loomed in silhouette in the sharp moonlight. Elizabeth slid down the muddy bank into the lapping water at the river's edge. Unseen hands helped her climb onto the bobbing cowskin raft. The river was noticeably higher and faster than it had been two weeks before. Warm weather and rain had melted snows high up in the Hindu Kush mountains, which straddled the Afghan-Pakistani border all the way to Chitral and beyond to their rendezvous with the Pamir and Karakoram ranges far to the north.

When the party was balanced precariously on the raft the ferryman poled out into the current, breaking the patterns of moonlight upon the still waters near the shore. When they reached the center, the raft skipped on the water and spray churned into her face. She didn't dare move, even though her tingling feet were almost numb. Four shots rang out, echoing in the valley. She drew in her breath sharply. "How near?"

"Not near," said Ebrahim. "But we must go silently on the other side."

Though the ferryman strained his pole against the swift current they landed much farther down the river than they had hoped. The men helped the ferryman drag the raft into a field, where they covered it with straw to hide it from the Russians.

The ferryman led them to the same village they had halted at before, the village where one of Elizabeth's escort had shot a dog. Then it had been pitch black, but now the village was lit by stark moonlight. Elizabeth gasped at the destruction. A wall rose beside their path, and a tower beyond that. The moon shone through jagged gaps in the tower walls.

"Is this new?" whispered Elizabeth.

"Yes," Ebrahim said tersely. "There has been much fighting since we came this way."

The house where they had had tea was still standing. Alam Shah, who knew the family well, scratched for a long time on the door. At last a light appeared and the door creaked open. The same old man greeted them and led them up the open, dried mud stairs to the upper room, then disappeared back downstairs. From below an old woman shouted and berated in a harsh voice.

"She is not happy that we have come," said Ebrahim. "She is complaining that we take too much food."

"Tell them we will only have tea. I don't need anything else."

Their host returned and protested for form's sake, but Sharif spoke quietly and convincingly to the old man. When everyone's honor was satisfied the man left the room and much later brought tea and *gur*.

Elizabeth was exhausted. She had hardly slept since the day of the bombing, and could not afford to doze off now. If they left this safe haven they had to reach Dunahi before daybreak, and with the food problem they certainly could not stay here.

The tea revived her slightly. She was not thinking of Yusuf now, or even of Peshawar. All she could think of was making it to Dunahi before dawn.

They left the house and plodded on through the adjoining fields. The bright moonlight lit their way, though beneath the trees the path sank into inky blackness. Silently Sharif encouraged Elizabeth, while Ebrahim went on ahead, occasionally turning to warn her to walk more quietly, pointing to a village about a kilometer away across the river plain.

She was glad when they reached the path that led across the meadows behind the rocky hills. Here the walking was easier, though she stumbled with exhaustion and was mindful of Ebrahim's warnings not to stray off the well-used path because of the danger of mines.

She fell behind, but Sharif stayed with her, a silent reassurance in the night. The others were resting in a meadow when they caught up. The moon silvered the stones, the grass, and the carpet of wildflowers that would be golden in sunlight. Tiredly she threw herself down beside the men. Sharif spread his blanket and beckoned for her to sit on it. She dragged herself onto it and collapsed in a heap. The other men were similarly sprawled on their blankets. Only Ebrahim crouched, alert as a predator.

Ebrahim snarled something at Sharif, who replied cheerfully. Ebrahim grew angrier and spat out harsh-sounding words. The other men sat up, watching. A few voices protested.

"He has disgraced your honor," said Ebrahim angrily.

"What?"

"He thinks we don't see what is happening, that he is always touching you for no reason and that he stays behind with you all the time."

"What are you talking about? Sharif has been a great help to me. He has never touched me except to help me when I'm falling."

"You don't know Afghan men," said Ebrahim darkly. He began shouting again in Pashtu. Sharif too grew angry. He took off his cap, threw it down in disgust, and turned to walk back in the direction from which they had come. At the same moment Ebrahim snatched his Kalashnikov from the ground and pointed it at his friend.

Elizabeth shrieked. "You're all crazy! I'm here with madmen! God help me!" She burst into tears and sobs, and as she had intended everyone turned toward her in surprise, and Ebrahim lowered his weapon.

Elizabeth was blindly furious. "I can't believe you people. We almost get killed together and then you fight over something that's all in your imagination. I can't take it anymore. I'm going on alone, and to hell with all of you." Without a blanket, without her bags, she stumbled off into the meadow.

"Don't go!" shouted Ebrahim. "Don't you know this place maybe be mined? How can you go alone?"

She stopped and turned. "I'll follow the path. I don't want to see any of you ever again."

Ebrahim lunged after her, still clutching the Kalashnikov. The others watched silently. He gripped her wrist and she struggled, surprised at his strength. "Let me go!" she hissed. His grip hurt her. She looked back at Sharif and heard him speak in a calm, quiet voice. Ebrahim relaxed his grip slightly and said simply, "Don't go into the mountains. It's not safe." She stopped struggling and they remained in tableau.

A cry split the darkness and echoed in the hills. For a moment all was a chaos of bolts sliding, voices shouting, and guns pointed toward the hills. Elizabeth swore in English, sure they were about to be massacred, a fitting punishment for this absurd argument. Then she started laughing hysterically. Before any of them, she realized the sound had only been the cry of a night bird. The high-pitched call shattered the expectant silence once again, and this time the men laughed with her.

"Okay," she said with more calmness than she felt. "We're all tired. I think we need to go on. Ebrahim, I will vouch for Sharif's respect and honor. If you think it's improper for us to fall behind then you have to go slow, because I cannot keep up. Is that agreed?"

Ebrahim's jaw was set, like that of a chastised child who knew he was in the wrong. His uncontrollable temper frightened her, and she wondered what sense of self-destruction propelled Michel toward this unstable man.

The party again strung itself out along the skirts of the hills. Ebrahim let Alam Shah lead and fell behind to keep an eye on Sharif and Elizabeth. Sharif appeared remarkably unperturbed. He marched ahead of Elizabeth, falling in next to Ebrahim whenever the path permitted, chatting easily. Elizabeth admired the way Sharif handled the friend who would have murdered him in cold blood. It had been either very clever or instinctive of Sharif to turn away at the last minute rather than going for his own gun.

Sharif stopped to pick wildflowers. He showed them to Ebrahim, who also stopped and sniffed them. The two waited for Elizabeth to catch up, then Ebrahim handed her a sprig. She knew it was what Sharif had intended, and glanced at him quickly and gratefully.

Ebrahim looked around sorrowfully and sighed. "If we could come by day you would see the whole meadow, from mountain to mountain, covered with gold."

"What are these flowers called?"

"I don't know. It doesn't matter. Maybe *zargul*, 'yellow flower' in Pashtu."

"No, it doesn't matter. They are beautiful."

The three walked on, Elizabeth behind. The two men held hands, and Elizabeth chuckled into her *chadar*, which she held up to her face to conceal her smile. In Afghanistan, emotions seemed to change like the weather.

Gradually her exhaustion shifted her into an altered state of mind. She plodded on, feet tripping on rocks, but she felt in a trance of timelessness, like the Tibetan messengers who were said to walk on the winds. She felt she could walk forever as the moon reached out to touch the western horizon, its light shedding a quality of unreality over the land. New York, Pennsylvania, Peshawar, all receded behind a veil of pure present. Improbably, she felt someone walking just behind her, heard soft steps, and turned her head quickly. Yusuf? Only the wind. Nothing living moved in the silent crystal landscape behind her.

It was very late when they reached the outskirts of Dunahi. Sharif picked two clusters of hanging blossoms off of a willow-like tree and handed one to her and one to Ebrahim. He gestured to her to smell, and said, "*Sansilla.*" The air was touched with an indefinable fragrance, and when she sniffed the blooms the scent assailed her senses and made her dizzy. She was sure such intense sweetness existed nowhere else on earth.

She clutched the branch as they made their way along the narrow dike leading to Sharif's uncle's house. She sniffed it again and again, each time taking new strength from its heady pungent smell. The village was unusually silent and peaceful. Even the pariah dogs seemed to be sleeping.

Sharif scratched on the door. No answer, no sound from within. He called out softly in Pashtu. They waited. Sharif tried the door of the guest house. Locked. He turned helplessly and called out again, more loudly. From inside the courtyard they could hear the quiet pad of steps. One person's steps.

The door opened a crack, then more widely. Sharif's aunt's face had lost its staunch cheer and her eyes were puffy. She handed Sharif a key on a black iron ring and gestured to Elizabeth to follow her. She embraced Elizabeth tightly, muttering, "*Al-hamdulillah!*" over and over.

Sharif entered the courtyard, followed by Ebrahim. Sharif's aunt spoke rapidly, hoarsely, tears coursing down her face, as she led them into the room where most of the family usually slept.

In the flickering light of the small clay oil lamp that Sharif's aunt held in her hand, Elizabeth could see that Sharif's uncle wasn't there. Nor were any of the boys. What had happened?

Elizabeth sat of the edge of a *charpoy*, suddenly alert. Sharif comforted his aunt, kneeling next to her on the floor, an arm around her shoulder, his face serious, his black brows lowered. Ebrahim's fists were clenched, his jaw set.

After some minutes of frantic conversation, Ebrahim turned to Elizabeth and said bluntly, "This morning the Russians were here. They came in the night and surrounded the village. In the morning they came into the houses. Sharif's uncle has been taken prisoner. One of his cousins was taken for the army. The other escaped from the tower on a rope."

Panic gripped Elizabeth's throat. "Then we must go, now. I am a danger to Sharif's aunt and to the women and children left here. Do you think they could have been looking for me?"

Ebrahim shrugged. "It is impossible to know. How could they know about you unless one among us is a spy? You have been seen by many people, but we have been careful."

"But don't you think they might come back? If they were looking for me they might try again, and the consequences would be terrible for Sharif's family."

"The consequences of just being an Afghan are terrible. They were lucky there were no arms in the house, and no Mujahedeen."

"And no journalists."

He nodded.

"What do you think we should do? Can we make the hills?"

"I don't know," said Ebrahim doubtfully. "But we have no choice, we have to try."

"Okay, then let's go now."

Ebrahim conferred briefly with Sharif. "Okay, I will go alone with you to a place in the hills. The others will stay here with Sharif. If the Russians come they will fight."

Elizabeth was horrified. "But there are only six of them, against how many Russians?"

Ebrahim shrugged. "We must protect our homes. What else can we do? Look what has happened here. If the Russians do not come today then the Mujahedeen will attack Chagaserai in the night."

"But…"

"Lizbet, you ask too many questions," said Ebrahim harshly. "Let's go, now! Put on your *chadari*. It is almost light, but if they see us maybe they will think you are a village woman. Take nothing with you that you can't hide under your *chadari*. And you must leave your shoes, and wear Sharif's aunt's sandals."

"What about my camera bag? That's all my work, that's the reason for the whole trip."

"Someone will bring your things, *inshallah*. Now come, don't you realize how much danger you are in?"

She didn't answer, but with shaking hands she dug her borrowed *chadari* and two small notebooks out of her bag. She fumbled as she unlaced her hiking boots and forced her swollen feet into the worn leather sandals she was given. She put the *chadari* over her head, leaving the face veil up, and held out her notebooks to Ebrahim. "Can you take them?"

He shook his head.

"Why not?"

"If we are seen, I will be searched. You may not be."

Sharif understood the problem and spoke to his aunt, who produced a faded square of red cotton and tied it around Elizabeth's waist under the *chadari*, tucking her notebooks safely inside. The old woman kissed Elizabeth quickly on both cheeks, firmly pulled the veil down in front of her eyes, and gave her a push toward the door.

The eastern horizon was already paling as Elizabeth followed Ebrahim out the creaking gate and along the irrigation channel. Again she smelled the *sansilla*, but now it seemed to her the sweet, cloying smell of imminent death. She clutched the pleated *chadari* close in front of her, as she had seen other women do, and hoped she was walking like a Pashtun woman.

Elizabeth could hardly see through the tiny openings of the crocheted grillwork that covered her eyes and nose, but as they neared the road that barred their way to the relative safety of the hills she clearly heard the roar of heavy vehicles approaching. Involuntarily, she stopped, but Ebrahim grabbed her elbow and pinched it. "Keep walking!"

"But…"

"Quiet! Do as I tell you."

She hated him at that moment, but not as much as she hated the men in the olive drab jeeps a hundred yards up the road toward Chagaserai, rumbling toward them, stirring up clouds of white dust which the newly rising sun tinted yellow gold.

She kept walking, stumbling occasionally. Ebrahim walked ahead of her, appearing indifferent, and she wanted to kill him. She hurried on through the last corridor between high mudbrick walls, which led to the road beyond.

She was sure the jeeps would be upon them as soon as they reached the road, and that something about her walk would give her away. She prayed frantically and silently, and went on walking.

The first car in the line of jeeps was only twenty yards away when she stepped into the dust of the road. Look unconcerned, don't hurry.

They reached the field on the other side of the road, and a sense of hopeful exhilaration propelled her aching legs onward. They had made it!

A challenge rang through the morning air. Ebrahim ignored it and kept walking. He started singing in Pashtu. Another challenge, and he stopped suddenly. Elizabeth collided with him and tripped. He took her roughly by the shoulder and pulled her up. "Say nothing!" he said desperately. "Go to the field and hide your face."

She stumbled off into the middle of the low rows of corn, one hand gripping her *chadari* so as to cover as much of her awkward body as possible, the other clutching the cloth tied at her waist. If they were looking for her, this was it. She couldn't bluff her way out of this one.

She could not see what was happening behind her. She heard footsteps, she heard the motors stop, and then she heard Ebrahim speaking cheerfully to some soldiers. Would he betray her now, after all this? Would he betray her now to save his skin?

She squatted in the field, face turned away from the men, body hunched up in fear. She listened for the sound of soldiers coming to get her.

A voice shouted an order in a language that was neither Pashtu nor Farsi. It sounded like Russian. Another voice replied, and two men engaged in a discussion for some time. Elizabeth stared down through the grillwork of her *chadari* to a pool of water in the field, which reflected a face with no identity.

More voices, followed by the slamming of car doors. Engines started, tires ground. She did not dare move. Footsteps crunched behind her, and the corn rustled as someone approached. A rough hand grabbed her. She gasped and turned, but it was only Ebrahim, with a warning look on his face. He again grasped her shoulder and yanked her to her feet, then turned and walked back toward the path. Behind them, on the road, the convoy passed, jeep after jeep. Ebrahim was again ahead of her, and she was furious at being left behind while there was still danger.

At last their path bent behind a hill and they were out of sight of the convoy.

Ebrahim turned to her. "Raise the veil of your *chadari*. Put it down whenever I tell you."

She flung the face veil over her head and stared at Ebrahim's impassive face. "Did you have to hurt me?"

"We're not out of danger yet. They would have hurt you much more. Come."

He led her not along the path to the border, but straight up the mountainside, up a bleached rock incline.

"Where are we going?"

"To a small place I know, where they will not look for us."

"What happened back there?"

He smiled grimly. "They wanted to search me. I let them."

"What else?"

"They asked if I had seen any *farangi* woman. I said no."

She heaved herself up a boulder and caught her *chadari* on its rough edge. She cursed and untangled the torn hem. "Was that it?"

"No. There were two officers there, one Afghan officer, a Parchami pig, and one straw-headed Russian. They spoke in Russian. I don't know what they said, but they looked at you in the field. I think the Russian wanted to search you."

Elizabeth shuddered. "Why didn't they then?"

"The Afghan officer began to ask me questions about you. I said you were my wife and a good woman. Then I got angry and said, 'How dare you ask questions about my wife!' I challenged him," said Ebrahim cockily.

"You what?"

"I challenged him as a Pashtun. In our culture it is very rude, inexcusable to ask about another man's wife. Men have been killed for less."

"What did he do?"

"He became ashamed. And he argued with his officer. His officer looked like he was thinking at first, then decided not to bother. The Russian must have been here in Afghanistan for some time. I think he knew that searching a woman will always make Afghans angry. He said some words in Russian, and I recognized a few because I studied Russian at university. He said, I think, 'She is a dirty peasant, not what we are looking for.' And then they left."

Elizabeth sat down right where she was and started laughing and crying. Ebrahim looked down at her with concern and squatted next to her. In pure relief, she embraced him, still sobbing.

CHAPTER 28

ELIZABETH

Near the Pakistani border

They spent the day in an isolated hut, crouched on the edge of a cliff with a spectacular view of the Kunar Valley. Elizabeth slept most of the day until she was awakened by Sharif's arrival sometime in the late afternoon. He and Karim had come together, bringing her camera bag and duffle.

She was overjoyed to see them, and full of questions. Ebrahim struggled to keep up with her as she fired question after question at him. The Mujahedeen, he told her soberly, had stored their weapons in a secret place in the wall of the overgrown, untended orchard attached to Sharif's uncle's house, then had dispersed into different villages.

Yes, in the morning the soldiers had searched the house again, though not as thoroughly as the day before. They had gone through all the houses in the village but had found nothing, no young men of draft age, no weapons or ammunition, and no journalists. Sharif himself had wrapped Elizabeth's possessions in a burlap bundle and loped off across the fields just before the soldiers had entered the village.

"They have come to say goodbye," said Ebrahim soberly.

"Aren't they coming back to Pakistan with us?"

"No. Tonight they go to meet other Mujahedeen, and they will attack Chagaserai."

"Chagaserai!"

Sharif nodded eagerly and smiled. He raised his gun and pointed it at an imaginary target.

"But they can't take that garrison. It's huge because of the Governor's House."

"No, but they can make trouble for the Parchamis and Khalqis. The anniversary of the cursed coup that brought these dogs to power is after two days. Tonight and tomorrow night we will attack."

"Are you also going?"

"No, I must come with you. *Inshallah*, tonight we will cross the border."

The moon was truly full that night, gold fading to silver as it navigated among continents of cloud. It hung on the high horizon of mountains just above them, indifferent to hurried and whispered farewells. Against all convention, Elizabeth hugged both Sharif and Karim. She looked at Sharif, whose dark eyes were bright in the moonlight, and wished she had the words in his language to tell him how she felt. She was immensely grateful to him. And she was terrified. She didn't want him to die, wanted to tell him to live for Malolai's sake. Sharif seemed to understand her thoughts, but just squeezed her hand, nodded, and was gone into the deepening night.

Elizabeth followed Ebrahim down the steep path to the stream that marked the floor of the narrow defile. When they reached it, their way turned back towards the hills that rose towards the border. They were already well into the hills when the fighting erupted behind them. When she heard the first volley of shots Elizabeth instinctively ducked, her heart pounding.

"They're far away now," said Ebrahim. "We can do nothing but pray for their success...Look!" he said suddenly.

She turned to see a macabre fireworks display of green and orange serpents tracing half-ellipses in the black sky. Serpents were followed by a deadly flock of fiery birds flying in formation. Loud reports followed seconds later.

"What is it?" she asked shakily.

"Fire. Of Kalashnikovs. There," he pointed, "the Mujahedeen. Now that, the government post." He laughed. "They are shooting into the darkness."

A ball of fire shot towards the zenith, white and glowing as a shooting star. For a moment huge areas of the land were lit up, then the ball faded to a dull red and burnt out before it returned to earth. "Flares," said Ebrahim. "So they can see the Mujahedeen."

"And us?"

"We are too far."

They watched the night fill with fire, followed by sound. The moon was high now, and lightning flickered indifferently at the western edge of the sky, throwing the dark range on the other side of the valley into stark relief.

"You want to take pictures?" asked Ebrahim.

"I don't know."

"Take pictures. There is time. We are safe here."

She unpacked her camera and tripod, which she hadn't used till now. She set up time exposures, and in half an hour had shot an entire roll of film. Some of these bullets were from the guns of her friends. Others might kill her friends. On celluloid they were all recorded as streaks of light, artistic patterns that might have come from manipulation in the darkroom, Kirlian photography of life and death.

When she was finished she walked on numbly, tiredly, praying for Sharif and the others, filling her steps with a repeated chant, "Please let them be all right, please let them be all right."

A light rain began to fall and the sounds of battle at last fell silent behind them. They walked in this chill rain all through the night. At dawn, when they neared the Durand Line, Elizabeth looked behind to the valley filled with curling mist and picked out Chagaserai. She wondered what had happened there, and how long it would be before she knew. As tiredness seized her she became convinced that all the Mujahedeen had died in the futile attempt to harass the Russians. Tank fire grumbled in the morning, reverberating off the mountains' walls as Afghanistan began another day of war.

On the crest that marked the border she hesitated, reluctant to leave Afghan soil. For the first time in the past two days she thought of Yusuf. She wondered if he would find out that the Russians had tried to find her. She tried to pick out the mouth of the narrow valley that led to his clinic, but in the jumbled land could not distinguish one closely folded ridge from another.

But all that was behind her now. She felt a sense of triumph stirring in her. The Russians had wanted her, and had failed. Now she would tell the world about what she had seen. An electric thrill ran through her body as she stretched in the morning breeze and let her *chadari* flap out behind her like huge silken wings. She stood like that for a moment, reveling in the sensation of freedom, then quickly followed Ebrahim's footsteps down the hillside and into Pakistan.

CHAPTER 29
AYUB

Chagaserai

Vivaldi's "Four Seasons" rang through the house. A light rain poured steadily from a pale gray sky. Ayub listened reflectively to the music as he stood at the window, hands clasped behind his back, watching the gentle rain falling on the roses in the garden of the Governor's House. Spring was indeed an unstable season.

Tomorrow would be the anniversary of the Saur Revolution that had brought the People's Democratic Party of Afghanistan to power. Ayub had known Taraki, the first Communist president, slightly. He had thought Taraki a personable enough fellow. An idealist, though he had allowed a cult of personality to form around him. Ayub smiled at the memory of the obligatory Noor Mohammed Taraki portraits that had adorned every public place. They hadn't been very good portraits. The president had looked rather like a nineteenth-century saint. Ayub wondered idly if that had been the artist's intention.

Taraki, however, hadn't lasted long. He had been killed by the treachery of his deputy Hafizullah Amin, who had supposedly "invited" in a hundred thousand Soviet troops to preserve Communist principles and power in

Afghanistan, and the party hadn't been united since. They had made so many mistakes, Ayub thought regretfully. Maybe if Taraki had been stronger and hadn't allowed Amin to imprison so many people and make so many enemies among the general populace, things might have been different.

And the clumsy way land reform had been carried out, sending out all those ill-informed and arrogant university students into villages they had never ever seen to tell mullahs and *maliks* how to change a system that had suited them for hundreds if not thousands of years. No wonder so many of the poor kids had been killed. Somewhere along the line those who proclaimed their intention to serve the people had lost touch with the people's wishes.

Ayub sighed and watched the beads of rain on the window. Small drops collected, ran into each other to form big drops, and of their own weight lost their fragile grip and slid into oblivion. Through the streaks of rain he could see splashes of roses, blurred as if in an Impressionist painting. He and his comrades had intended so much more for Afghanistan than this.

He hated these anniversaries, which had become not so much occasions for celebration as for tightening security while wondering what the Mujahedeen would do next. And afterwards there would always be the necessity for ugly reprisals. They'd called the first anniversary a "celebration" and throughout Kabul had erected triumphal arches covered with red bunting. They'd also put tanks in Shahr-i-Nau Park and closed off all traffic in and out of major cities for three days. The event had been uneventful and ill-attended, but had been billed a huge success.

He wondered what the rebels had planned for tonight. Last night's attack on Chagaserai had perhaps been a foretaste. It had been more violent than usual and had gone on into the early hours of the morning. Only after the onset of this rain had halted the fighting had he been able to get some decent sleep.

The rebels had become more brazen of late, he thought crossly. Ayub knew they had sympathizers at the very highest government levels. This knowledge tended to isolated officials from one another. Who could you trust? The

Mujahedeen had even blown up planes at Kabul Airport not too long ago. And they were stronger in the countryside, where security tended to be lax.

Despite last night's noisy attack, Ayub didn't feel in any personal danger. The only tangible result of the attack had been a few more bullet holes in the compound walls. But he was concerned that his troops might not be particularly loyal. Conscripts rarely were. Even with the threat of Russians at their backs, the Afghan Army soldiers often could not be prevented from surrendering en masse to the Mujahedeen, or simply refusing to fight them. The worst of it was that most of them took new Kalashnikovs and a supply of ammunition to the rebels when they surrendered.

The troops were at best unreliable and inept. Ayub was furious when he thought of how they had missed the American journalist. Even his usually reliable informant Najeeb Khan had let him down this time. Najeeb had dutifully given him the information that the woman was expected at Dunahi the day before yesterday, and Ayub had wasted no time in acting. But the troops had apparently gotten there either too early or too late and had only succeeded in drafting a few conscripts and arresting a doddering old man.

How could they possibly have missed her? The troops hadn't even found any clues as to her whereabouts. Now this troublesome woman had escaped and would write fine things about his brother Yusuf, which would put Ayub in a very awkward position. He wondered if she knew that he was Yusuf's brother and Commander Rahim was their father. He could see the headlines: "Father of Communist Governor Becomes Mujahedeen Commando Leader." More than mortifying. So much for his dreams of placating Lermontov with a journalist's head on a silver platter.

Lermontov had passed on today's intelligence report about the failed raid on Dunahi without comment. "For Your Information" had been scrawled across the top secret memo. Ayub knew the report was a mark of his own shame. Now he would be forced to take action against his father. As he brooded, obsessively playing over the sequence of events that had led to the escape of the journalist, he became more and more resentful of his father. How could his father shame his own son this way? How could he take up arms against his son when the son constituted the lawful authority of the land? If he had to join these ragtag rebels, why couldn't he at least operate out of his son's jurisdiction?

Ayub chafed as he looked out upon his grim, rain-drenched garden. It was some comfort that the raid on Dunahi had at least intimidated the villagers. Maybe now they wouldn't be so eager to shelter foreign journalists, and might even think twice about feeding the Mujahedeen. Lucky for this Abdul Sharif's family that the American woman had not been there or the troops would have killed all of them. The old man was now in prison in Chagaserai, though Ayub doubted that he knew any useful information. According to reports he seemed quite foolish and was too old to fight anyway.

Ayub silently tapped the pane of glass in rhythm to the Baroque music. A moth flying toward the light, or a cat tapping its nose against the window that divided it from its natural pursuits? Ayub suddenly felt terribly lonely. He hadn't realized how isolated he had become. He didn't enjoy anyone's company. The closest thing he had to a friend was the servant Mousa. Sometimes when no one else was around he would ask Mousa to sit with him. The old servant would bring in his *chillum* and smoke it while Ayub smoked imported tobacco in his Turkish meerschaum pipe. They would reminisce about Kabul, and usually Ayub would feel worse, thinking of the older brother he had so admired, the older brother who had abandoned him by staying in America and now betrayed him by choosing to oppose him.

But he had his music, and his books. He walked across the room to the rows of shelves that held neatly arranged volumes in English, French, Russian, and Persian. He ran his finger along the titles on the Persian shelf and picked out a slim volume, the *Rubaiyat of Omar Khayyam*. He sat in the overstuffed olive green velvet armchair, facing the rain-streaked window.

For a moment he paused, then looked around him surreptitiously. When he was satisfied no one was observing, he held the book between his palms, murmured the words, *"Bismillah ar-rahmani rahim,"* as his father had taught him and Yusuf to do when they were boys, and opened the book to find an omen, a sign, an answer to the many questions of his life.

The first poem his eye fell on was about a potter:

"One day I passed a potter's factory,
Where old man's hands shaped clay so patiently.
I saw a thing not seen by everyone,
My father's dust was turned to pottery."

Ayub felt a sudden, unspeakable chill at the thought of his own father's death. But it didn't really matter whether his father's death preceded his own, or his preceded his father's. They would both ultimately end up as dust, shaped by someone else in death as they had been shaped by something outside themselves in life. Here was the answer to his questions: a cold, wild wind blowing through life, sweeping all before it, clearing the sky of cloud and stars.

Yes, spring was an unstable season. But after spring came the hot, clear blue days of summer, the bold and ochre stability of autumn, and the white stillness of winter.

CHAPTER 30

ELIZABETH

Peshawar, Pakistan

lizabeth felt listless in the unbearably moist and heavy heat of Peshawar. She sat in the scant comfort of the shade of the verandah of Massoud's house, listening to bees droning in the roses. Even the light cotton fabric of the *shalwar kameez* that Salima had given her stuck to her skin in this heat. She fiddled with the long chiffon *dupata*, which flowed over her shoulders and down to her knees, and lazily fanned her perspiring face with one end. Sipping a cool glass of *doogh*, slippery with beads of moisture, she contemplated the letter she had just finished. If she couldn't make the experience of Afghanistan real to her own brother, how could she expect to translate it to the average American, who wasn't even particularly interested?

In the two days since her return to Peshawar she had worked with manic determination to write everything down before the intensity of the experiences began to fade. She had barely had time to enjoy the luxury of showers, a clean bed, and wholesome food, let alone the comfort of Salima's company and the reassurance of Massoud's quiet faith.

In just those two days of pounding away at the portable Olivetti manual typewriter she had lovingly carried from New York and left at Massoud's house for safekeeping, she had written a whole series of articles. She'd attempted to cover every angle of the story, from Yusuf's clinic to the position of women in Afghanistan to her incredibly narrow and lucky escape. This last was the most unbelievable, that such a simple ruse would actually work. She sighed, wondering if the editors would indeed believe her. Her dispatches and exposed film were all ready, waiting to be shipped by air from Islamabad tomorrow. She would go there herself to make sure they got on their way safely.

But would she get published? The thought nagged at her. She didn't exactly have an assignment, just a letter of interest from the *New York Times Sunday Magazine*. There were no guarantees that the editors would find her stories of compelling interest to a jaded public that, after an initial flurry of interest in Afghanistan when the Soviets invaded and Jimmy Carter boycotted the 1980 Moscow Olympics, seemed more interested in disco and Wall Street than the suffering of distant peoples.

She berated her exhausted spirit for having risked so much on what might bring no return. She hoped she had risked her life for a reason, but this heat precluded clear thought, and she sank into a pessimism as all-encompassing as the heat.

She sighed again and skimmed the letter to Mark. It didn't come near capturing her experiences, and in deference to likely censorship on the Pakistani end (and who knew, maybe on the American end as well now that Reagan was in office?), had left out details such as the complex relationship between Dr. Yusuf, Commander Rahim, and Governor Ayub of Kunar. But it would have to do for now. She frowned as she licked the flap of the envelope a third time, trying to get it to stick and once again pushing away the moral struggle of confidentiality of sources and their off-the-record statements versus her duty as a journalist to at least try to let the public know the truth.

The best story was the one she couldn't tell, or had made a conscious decision not to tell, she reflected. What drama! One brother a Communist official, the other a heroic doctor for the Mujahedeen. And the father choosing to be a top-secret commando leader and trainer operating in his own son's territory. Pure Hollywood. She could see the title: *War in the Land of Cain.*

And then she could see the danger to all the parties involved. No, she would stick to her decision. There were enough dramatic and effective and true stories without revealing the secrets she had come upon accidentally and perhaps had no right or reason to know.

She slammed her fist on the recalcitrant flap of the envelope just as Salima came out onto the verandah.

"Oh, there you are. I was wondering what had happened to you."

"I was writing to my brother in New York. I sent a telegram to my parents yesterday, but it's been a long time since my family has heard from me in detail."

She held out the unstickable envelope to Salima and the two women laughed. "Pakistani glue," said Salima. "I have some glue in the house that works. In Afghanistan, our glue was good, our weather was good, everything was good. Come into the house, it is too hot here."

Elizabeth followed Salima into the salon, where a fan cooled the air slightly. Salima produced a bottle of imported glue from a desk drawer.

"Really, we shouldn't complain about Pakistan as much as we do," said Salima. "We are lucky they have allowed us so much freedom to move. And they have taken on the burden of three million refugees. There is of course some corruption, but with so many refugees it is to be expected. Some Pakistanis are getting rich, but so are some Afghans. We fight this corruption wherever we can, and I think that at least the top levels of the Pakistan government do as well. You should see the refugee camps, Elizabeth. Do you have any plans to go?"

"Oh yes, I would like to. Can it be arranged?"

"More easily than Afghanistan."

Salima watched as Elizabeth meticulously glued her letter shut and capped the bottle. "How much longer do you plan to stay in Peshawar?"

"I'm not sure. I haven't made a reservation to leave yet."

Salima put her hand on Elizabeth's. Both had long fingers, though Salima's were larger than Elizabeth's and her nails were well-manicured and polished. "You are welcome to stay as long as you wish. Months, a year if you like. Don't ever go to a hotel again when you are in Peshawar. My home is your home."

Elizabeth was deeply honored, but also knew Salima's loneliness. "Thank you. I hope you will come to America someday."

"*Inshallah.* But only when Afghanistan is free. Massoud offered to borrow money to send me to my cousin during the hot season, but I refused. I hate the heat, really, but I want to be here, with Massoud, and near the country. Massoud is going to the front sometimes, and if I were in America and anything were to happen…"

"I know. You'd never forgive yourself."

"Massoud is everything to me. He is my husband, my lover, my brother, uncle, father, mother, friend, and child. I have no one else here."

Elizabeth looked at her with sympathy. "Where is your family?"

"In Kabul. I have not seen my parents since we went into exile. And they are old. I worry all the time."

Salima blinked hard and smiled. Her voice betrayed nothing. "But there are three million people in the same situation, separated from families. Many more are dead. By the grace of God, we have been lucky."

"How did you first come to Peshawar?"

"The usual way, dressed in a *chadari*, walking and sometimes on the back of a donkey. We said we were going to a wedding in Ghazni. Fortunately my husband had good connections with some families in Peshawar. They helped us a lot, though when we first came I was always angry and bitter, and missing my family. You see that now we are comfortable, and I know that in Peshawar some people speak against us, say that we are making money from the war.

"Elizabeth, look around you. By the grace of God, we are better off than almost anyone, but we are not rich. These things are all gifts from Pakistani friends. They offered to buy everything new for Massoud, but he refused. He finally accepted some things, only because of me, and because we often must entertain guests.

"This room has an air conditioner, but our bedroom does not. It is hard to sleep, you know, especially in the summer when the electricity goes out in the night. But I think of the refugees under the hot tents, and then I thank God and I sleep. We keep an air conditioner here for the guests, so the Mujahedeen can have a few moments of coolness when they come to see Massoud."

She got up and walked toward a low table next to the couch, and lifted its cloth. "Look. Rifle crates. You can see the words stamped on them. We have to be resourceful, not wasteful. Elizabeth, do you know how much we get each month from the party?"

Elizabeth shook her head.

"Fifteen hundred rupees. By Pakistani standards it is high. But the doctors at the Medical Association get more, twenty-five hundred, three thousand. And you see the number of the household we have to support, not just the two of us, but guards, servants, and guests. Every day people are coming. You have seen now how most days we eat simply. Now you are no longer a guest, but a part of the family. You are like my sister."

"I am honored, Salima. I don't have a real sister."

Salima kissed Elizabeth's cheek. "You do now. I have three sisters, but I am glad for another. I will miss you. Don't leave too soon."

"Not too soon. But I must leave when my work is done. I can't stay forever."

"Then do your work slowly. I will tell Massoud to arrange everything, but slowly. I will let you go only when the heat grows too much and it would be a crime to make you stay. Agreed?"

Elizabeth had nothing better to do, nowhere better to go. There was no man waiting for her, and her things were all in storage. And there was a lot of good material here. She wasn't ready to go back to New York yet. Maybe in June. "I won't hurry back," she promised.

"Good." Salima called to a servant to bring tea and biscuits, and popped a cassette into the stereo. The music was Afghan, an instrumental plucked on a string instrument.

Elizabeth closed her eyes and listened to the soothing sound. "What is it?"

"A *rebab*. Have you ever seen one?"

"No. How many strings?"

Salima laughed. "You must ask someone else, not me. Massoud says that Sharif, who went with you to Afghanistan, plays *rebab* beautifully, and that he also plays the flute. Maybe you will hear him sometime."

The quick notes reminded Elizabeth of a stream on rocks, or of the rain on the mountains of Kunar. It was the unmistakable sound of Central Asia, of mountains longing to touch the sky and people longing for wildness and independence.

"Let's sit on the floor," said Salima.

"Why not? I'm used to it by now."

Salima slid gracefully onto the soft Bukhara carpet, deep red with black geometric design. Elizabeth followed her example and absently ran her hand against the nap of the wool carpet in time to the music.

"You should have seen our carpets in Kabul," said Salima. "All over our house, the very best. Turkoman, Bukhara, Herati. This one is from Afghanistan, a Bukhara design. Most of the rest in the house are Pakistani Baluch. All of them are gifts from Pakistani friends."

"What happened to your house in Afghanistan?"

"My parents still live in my father's house, but Massoud's house was taken by the government as soon as we left. Some Parchami has been rewarded with that house. It was a beautiful house, traditional style with an open courtyard in the center, furnished in traditional Afghan style with carpets and pillows, but also with modern conveniences." She sighed. "All gone now. We'll never live like that again. Perhaps we never should have. We tried to make our lives always in beauty and contemplation. My father and Massoud's father were always generous, and every Friday we had guests. A lot of poor people came to see us as well, and these we also fed, much better than we can afford to serve our Mujahedeen now. But maybe we were wrong to live so well and so ostentatiously when so many were so poor. Now we, and our whole country, pay for it.

"I know what the poor people wanted," continued Salima. "And we didn't give it to them. A few of us cared, but most didn't. Most only wanted to go to the West for holidays and education. I don't think that a lot of the people who called themselves Communists, the Khalqis anyway, really wanted or even understood Communism. They were just reacting to the excesses of the ruling class and trying to bring about social justice and social responsibility. Many of them were very good Muslims. I think most of them are dead now, by the hands of their own comrades. But what I hate are those who willingly collaborate even now. They do so with their eyes open to what they have done to our country, and they will find flame in the end. What kind of people are they? I always wonder."

Elizabeth thought of Yusuf's brother and wondered what kind of person he must be. The two women sat and listened to the music in silence. A servant brought a tray of tea and unobtrusively poured it. As soon as he had gone, Salima took two embroidered cushions from the couch and put them on the floor for her and Elizabeth to recline on.

Elizabeth lay on her side propped up on one elbow, which rested on the rich pillow. The relaxed atmosphere reminded her oddly of Kunar, and she felt a sudden sharp stab of regret.

"Salima, I feel so sad thinking of Kunar. I feel guilty. Here I am in nice clean clothes, sleeping in a comfortable bed, and eating good food all the time. And there they are, all those people who I was with, still there. It's as if there are two different worlds with a border between them."

"Only two worlds?" Salima sighed. "What to do? You can't stay there. You had to come back here sometime to write. What you are doing will be of great help to those people. I understand how you feel, but please try not to worry, try not to think of them too much. It will only make you unhappy. Believe me, Elizabeth, I know this unhappiness every day of my life."

"I must go back to Afghanistan."

Salima's eyes widened. "After everything that happened to you there? Have you become crazy?"

Elizabeth laughed at her friend's shocked expression. "Yes, I know it's crazy. I can't even give a good reason why, except that, as you Afghans would say, my heart is telling me to go. I don't know, I feel I need to understand Afghanistan more. I just don't want to desert the people I left behind there. If I get published this time, I can publish more, maybe even write a book. Maybe I can help Afghanistan that way. It's important that the world does not forget what is happening in Afghanistan. There are so many wars in the world right now, but only in this one does it seem clear that innocent people are fighting against a superpower for their hearths and homes."

Salima looked at Elizabeth soberly. "On some days it is clear," she said ironically. "And others not. When do you want to go?"

"Autumn, I guess, when it's cooler. If I sell some articles and pictures now, I can go back to the States for summer and come back here in the fall."

"You are caught. Who has caught you?"

"Caught?" Elizabeth flushed.

Realization brightened Salima's face. "Oh! I was only joking. But I think you are caught. Who is it?"

"No, I…" said Elizabeth in confusion.

Salima sat up, eyes glittering. "I promise not to tell anyone."

"I am in love with Afghanistan," said Elizabeth, attempting to be off-handed.

"And who else?"

"No one. Really."

Salima frowned at her. "Am I not your sister? Don't you trust me? If you don't tell me, I am not your sister."

Elizabeth flushed a deeper shade of red and stared at her tea. "Oh Salima, it's stupid. I do admire someone, but I don't know him very well."

Salima's eyes were wide with expectation.

"Oh, it's nothing. Just that I really admired that doctor, Yusuf Hakim."

Salima's face was excited. "Really? I have heard he is a very dedicated and good man."

"Yes, that's why I admire him. Nothing else. Really."

"Did anything happen between you?" Salima's face leaned towards Elizabeth's.

"No!"

"Nothing?"

"One kiss. That's all. Don't tell anyone!"

Salima laughed. "One kiss is nothing. Even I kissed Massoud before we were married."

"I'm not going to marry him!"

"Only God knows the future."

Elizabeth was tired of all this talk of marriage. "Nearly thirty and not married? Why not married?" were standard second and third questions asked by strangers upon first meeting.

"Maybe you will marry an Afghan. We would have a wonderful wedding for you, even in these hard times."

"It would be better to have a wedding for Malolai and Sharif."

"What about them?"

"I didn't tell you before. Malolai and Sharif seem to be in love. There are some obstacles of course, as she is more educated than he is. But he seems to be from a good family, and he is certainly kind and brave. But…" she broke off, remembering the last time she had seen Sharif, fading off into the darkness. There had been no news yet.

A servant knocked softly and Salima called to him to enter. He spoke to her and Salima turned to Elizabeth triumphantly. "I think you say, 'speak of the devil.'"

"What?"

"Sharif and Ebrahim are here to see you. Out on the verandah."

Elizabeth sat up. "Really?"

"Go to them. Then come and tell me everything."

Without thinking, Elizabeth draped her *dupata* over her head as she had seen Salima do so many times, and hurried outside.

"*Salaam aleikum,*" she said excitedly. "And *staray mashay.*"

"*Staray mashay,*" replied Sharif.

Elizabeth looked at him sharply, but he didn't appear to be any worse for his fight. "What happened?" she burst out to Ebrahim.

"By the grace of God, Sharif's uncle is free. He was released after one week. He told them he was too old to fight and he acted foolish, and they believed him."

"But what about the attack on Chagaserai?"

Ebrahim looked down. "The Mujahedeen attacked Chagaserai for three nights. I think we killed a lot of Afghan government troops. But the day after the anniversary the Russians counterattacked. Jets, helicopters. Ten of the Mujahedeen of Babur Tangay were martyred. Karim was also martyred."

She gasped. "Karim? The young boy?"

Sharif nodded, understanding.

Tears started in Elizabeth's eyes.

"I think the doctor is busy," said Ebrahim nervously.

"Do you have any news of Dr. Yusuf?" she asked anxiously. "Or Malolai? Or Commander Rahim? Or Michel?"

"No bad news. So I think they are all well. We just wanted to tell you this news." Ebrahim shifted his weight to his other foot. Outside Afghanistan, their relations had become even more awkward.

But Elizabeth wept then, and bridged all gaps between them. "Tell Sharif," she sobbed, "I am glad to see him alive. But oh God, what an unjust world."

CHAPTER 31
ELIZABETH

Peshawar

"Elizabet!" A French accent cut through the frantic din of bus horns. Elizabeth turned and peered through the haze of motor exhaust, shading her eyes against the glare.

Michel caught up with her, his lanky form hurrying across the dirty platform of the bus station. He was not in cap and *shalwar kameez*, but in khaki-colored cotton trousers and safari shirt. It took her a moment to recognize him.

"Michel!" she cried. "What are you doing in Peshawar so soon? Are you on your way to Islamabad?"

He shook her hand warmly, flashing her a charming, boyish smile. "I've just come from there. And you?"

"I've also just come back. No space on the plane, so I took a minibus back. It was pretty hot through."

He laughed, and looked her up and down. "I see you have continued to adopt the native dress." Elizabeth was wearing a white *shalwar kameez* printed with small turquoise flowers, set off by a brilliant turquoise *dupata*. "It suits you."

"Thank you. It's comfortable in this heat, and it covers me well enough. I think some people think I am a Pathan woman. They start to speak to me in Pashtu, and then when I look blank they speak English."

"You make a beautiful Pathan."

Elizabeth had forgotten how charming Michel could be. Too bad he was gay. "Let's have some *chai*, or a cold drink," she suggested. "That old man there seems to be serving green tea to people who are waiting."

Michel looked at the old man with the white beard and the sweet, open face, wearing a pillbox hat embroidered with golden thread. He chuckled. "That old *baba* is from the Special Branch of the police. He sits and watches for foreigners and other suspicious people. He gave me two pots of tea yesterday while I was waiting for enough passengers to fill the minibus. I waited nearly two hours. Then he sat next to me and very politely said, "Passport please, I am from police.""

Elizabeth smirked as Michel waved at the man, who smiled back broadly. "If they only knew where we've been! Michel, how was the rest of your trip? Did you see Commander Rahim again, or the doctor? I didn't expect you to be back so soon."

He started walking toward the street, and Elizabeth followed, dodging smoking buses and small boys selling chewing gum. "No, I didn't see any of them again. I went north with the Mujahedeen toward Asmar, on the western side of the river. I saw them attack Asmar a few nights ago. And then Najeeb, Ebrahim's so-called friend, was discovered as a Parchami spy."

She stopped. "What? What happened to him?"

He shook his head. "It was very bad. There was a summary trial, and he was executed. I don't know exactly how he was discovered, because no one was there to speak English to me. But I shot the pictures."

"You shot pictures of the execution?"

"Yes, wouldn't you? That is our job, and that is how people win the Pulitzers."

She shuddered. "I don't know if I could shoot that. I had enough trouble shooting pictures of Mujahedeen posing in front of a helicopter they had just shot down."

"Perhaps as a female you just don't have the stomach," he said off-handedly. "But a helicopter shot down! That's marvelous. How did it happen?"

She ignored the implication of his first remark. "You don't know how lucky you are that you left when you did. The village was attacked by gunships within an hour after you left. Didn't you hear about it?"

He shook his head. "You forget, no one could speak to me in English or French." He lowered his voice. "Elizabet, do you think perhaps this spy Najeeb knew the village was going to be bombed and that's why he left?"

She sucked in her breath. "Then he must be the one who also informed them about me!"

"What?"

She smiled ruefully. "I was hounded to the border by Afghan troops and Russian officers. They'd sent someone to look for me in Dunahi, but I guess it was a lucky quirk of fate that the mullah delayed us."

"What mullah?"

"You remember the bearded man on the donkey that you had to let pass? He turned out to be a fanatical mullah who didn't believe women journalists should be covering the *jehad*. He argued with Ebrahim for awhile, and that's why we were delayed, or we would have missed the bombing too. That delayed us even more, but it turned out to be a good thing because we didn't get to Dunahi until a day later than planned, and somehow the troops had come early and missed me." She shook her head as if to clear it. "I've only been back a week, but already it seems like a bad dream."

They had reached the street, which was clogged with evening rush hour traffic. The sun glowed persimmon hot through the curtain of city smoke as it lowered toward the horizon. Michel hailed a rickshaw and the driver puttered up beside them. "Where are you going?" Michel asked Elizabeth.

"Home. I just got in."

"Home?"

"Massoud Khan's house. I'm staying with them now."

Michel raised his eyebrows. "Good. University Town?"

"Yes. Why don't you come for tea? I'm sure Massoud would like to talk to you."

Michel considered while the driver, a dark man with a thin face and pointed beard, looked at them impatiently. "University Town?" he urged.

"Yes, one minute," said Elizabeth. "Come with me, Michel. It's so nice to see someone from Afghanistan. It makes me feel closer to the people who are still there."

He hesitated. "I wanted to invite you to dinner tonight. At the Intercontinental."

"That sounds wonderful. But I should go home first. I don't want to come late or they worry."

Michel got into the rickshaw. "How much, *baba*?"

"Twenty rupees."

"What!" exclaimed Elizabeth. "It should be ten from here, at the most twelve." She started to get out.

"Okay, fifteen."

"Just because we're foreigners, they think we don't know," she stormed.

"Okay, okay, twelve rupees good. Get in."

Michel was laughing behind his hand. Elizabeth got back into the rickshaw and they sped off. "You are habituated to this country I think," said Michel.

"What? Bargaining? I spent some time in Mexico a few years ago."

"Do you like this part of the world?"

"Peshawar? Yes and no. A wonderful romantic city, full of history and intrigue. Also a pain. Too much noise, too many people, and now the heat. Afghanistan I loved, despite its obvious drawbacks. I wish I could have seen it before the war."

They were caught in a traffic jam near the old fort. Their driver tooted his horn frantically and shouted abuse at another driver trying to cut in on his right. "It has a certain charm, you must admit," Elizabeth remarked dryly. She glanced to their left toward the fiery sky that silhouetted the massive fort. "Did you ever see Afghanistan before the war?"

"I told you my story."

"Yes. But I thought you might have traveled before."

"Not before this, not so much. Are you staying in Peshawar long?" he asked abruptly.

"Oh, I don't know. No reason to hurry back. I just air freighted my stories and film to New York, so we'll see what happens."

"Now what will you do?"

"Cover the refugees. Maybe political stories, some cultural background. And I'm learning a little Farsi and Pashtu."

"You are a clever lady," he said admiringly. "I have little talent for languages. I once tried to learn Russian, and my little English."

"Your English is very good. Your only problem is your accent."

"Is it so bad?" His face looked hurt.

She laughed. "Most people think a French accent is charming, so you may be lucky. Why did you study Russian?"

He looked out at the traffic. "I like the literature."

"It might come in handy in Afghanistan if you were ever captured."

He looked at her sharply.

"Sorry. Bad joke. Especially after what nearly happened to me."

He looked at her, gray eyes wide with interest. "What did happen?"

"I started to tell you. When I got to Dunahi, the soldiers had already been there. They'd taken Sharif's uncle prisoner and conscripted his cousin. But there were really looking for me, and probably for you too. We had to leave immediately, but Ebrahim and I got caught in the open when the sun was coming up, and the soldiers were right there on the road."

"Ebrahim was with you?"

"Who else? I was so afraid he would desert me, or betray me, because they questioned him so much. But he probably would have been killed if they'd discovered me. I was stuck huddled in a corn field, praying. Ebrahim saved me. He was brilliant. He kept cool and told the Afghan officer that he was insulting him by daring to ask about his wife. Somehow we got out of it. I don't even like to talk about it much. I just wrote it in one of my stories and now I want to forget it."

"How is Ebrahim? Is he all right?"

"He's fine. I saw him and Sharif a few days ago. Sharif had stayed behind to attack Chagaserai and I was so worried about him. But they had bad news too. Do you remember Karim?"

"The small man, the boy with the beard like this." He stroked his chin.

"Yes. He was only eighteen. He was martyred."

Michel shook his head. "I'm sorry to hear it."

"Ten Mujahedeen from Babur Tangay were martyred. I don't know their names." She sighed, the sadness of these deaths tugging at her composure.

Michel seemed strangely unmoved. Perhaps all he cared about was that Ebrahim was well. "So, will you go back to Afghanistan sometime?"

"I think so, though I must be crazy. I'll be more careful next time. One spy is gone, but there are always more. It all depends on how my stories and pictures sell. If they sell I'll probably go again after the hot season. What about you?"

He shrugged. "My work is finished for now. I will ask instructions from France. Maybe I go to Bolivia next, or Lebanon, or Chad."

"Don't you get tired of war photography?"

"Death is the essence of life. Wars, poverty, riots, and rebellions are all reality."

"There are whole other sides to life."

"But those are only passing."

No wonder he had trouble keeping lovers. "So you've had enough of Afghanistan?"

"Oh, no, no. I like very much Afghanistan. But I must go where the work is. Maybe I also can return during the autumn. *Ouf,* it is too hot now. I think it is better to go to South America somewhere. Argentina, Bolivia."

"Oh well, I suppose Bolivia can be guaranteed to have a coup while you're there."

They were on Old Jamrud Road, the main road that led out past some of the largest refugee camps toward the Khyber Pass and the Afghan border. Traffic had thinned out. Near the water tower Elizabeth directed the driver to turn left, and guided him through the maze of streets that led to Massoud Khan's secluded home.

The driver berated them. "*Memsahib,* you say University Town, but this is very far."

"It's University Town," she said in exasperation. "What else can I call it?"

"But there is near University Town and far University Town. This is far, and should be fifteen rupees."

Michel intervened by handing the driver three five-rupee notes. "*Bas?*" he asked. The driver looked down at his palm sorrowfully. "Eh, *baba,* it is good," said Michel.

Elizabeth's anger evaporated and she felt sympathy for the man. The rickshaw drivers worked hard, and had to cope with both the high cost of fuel and increasing competition from Afghan refugees in search of a livelihood.

"*Da khodai pah aman,*" she said. The driver smiled at the Pashtu farewell and waved as his passengers turned toward Massoud Khan's gate.

The tall Pathan guard opened the gate and greeted Elizabeth warmly, but looked suspiciously at Michel. "Massoud Khan in garden," he said. "You come." And to Michel, "You wait."

The guard took Elizabeth's bag and she entered the garden where Massoud and Salima sat. Massoud stood up and shook her hand, and Salima greeted her happily.

"Guess who I've brought with me?" said Elizabeth.

Massoud looked at her questioningly.

"Michel Dubois, the French journalist."

"Ah, yes, I had heard he was back. Where is he? Show him in. Is he by the gate?" Massoud called to his guard, who escorted Michel to the garden. "You are most welcome," said Massoud. "I am glad you are safely returned. Please sit down. But first, meet my wife, Salima."

Salima shook Michel's hand warmly, but her eyes observed the Frenchman with keen curiosity.

"So, I hope you have had a fruitful trip," said Massoud. "Did you find our Mujahedeen helpful to you in all ways?"

"Yes, very much so. I saw lots of good fighting and took many good pictures."

Elizabeth let her mind drift as they discussed in detail the execution of the spy Najeeb. It was too strange to be speaking of the brutality of war in such a civilized place, in a quiet garden that might have existed for hundreds of years. A servant appeared out of the darkness holding a candle. The electricity was out again. Thunder rumbled in the dark and sultry sky, but it was not yet the season for rain. Another servant brought out a tray of tea and retired at a signal from Salima.

Elizabeth stood up and set glasses of tea before Michel and Massoud as Salima poured them. Massoud smiled at her and said to Michel, "Elizabeth is no longer our guest. She is a daughter of the house."

A tall, silver-haired figure in a light gray *shalwar kameez* entered their circle. "Dr. Nasir!" cried Elizabeth. "How nice to see you again. *Salaam aleikum*. How are you? *Chetour asti?*"

"Elizabeth? Have you become an Afghan?" asked the doctor in surprise.

"Salima is my teacher."

The doctor greeted Massoud and Salima, then was introduced to Michel. Dr. Nasir had a firm handshake and exuded vitality. The last month in Peshawar had done him good, Elizabeth noted, though she was sure he was as busy as ever with the Medical Association and the two Mujahedeen hospitals with which he was associated.

A servant brought another glass, and Salima served Dr. Nasir. "So, Elizabeth, I'm relying on you to give us the latest reports on the clinic of Dr. Yusuf."

"Haven't you had any news since I came back?"

"Oh, forgive me, I knew that you were back. But I was very busy and could not come."

"That's all right. I'll tell you what I can. I just thought maybe some more news had come since I arrived."

Dr. Nasir looked at her expectantly. "How is the clinic functioning? And how is the new nurse working out?"

"Very well on both counts. I think Malolai and the doctor work well together. They are both so dedicated."

"And the cholera?"

"At the time I left there had been a few more deaths but no new cases. It was lucky that Sharif was able to bring vaccine so quickly."

"Sharif is a good man," said Dr. Nasir.

"I don't think anyone else could have made the journey so fast," said Elizabeth. "And thank you, Dr. Nasir, for getting the vaccine to him immediately."

"For me it was not such a problem. Sharif was the one who left back to Kunar without proper rest. Is he well now?"

"Yes," answered Massoud for her. "He will go back to the front soon."

"Can you give us a copy of what you have written about the clinic?" asked Dr. Nasir. "And you, Mr. Dubois, did you also write something?"

"I am more a photographer. But I can send you some pictures perhaps."

"Anything either of you can give us will be most appreciated. I am so glad to hear our clinic is doing good work. What is this affair of the health assistant being traded for a Khalqi woman and her children, and the village being bombed in revenge?"

Elizabeth's face darkened. "Yes, it's true. I saw the results of the bombing."

"I heard you did more than just see the result," interrupted Massoud.

Elizabeth colored. "Who told you that?"

"Sharif and Ebrahim both spoke highly of you."

"But they weren't even in Badel then."

Massoud smiled behind his glass of tea. "Then someone else must have told them."

Dr. Nasir looked at her questioningly.

"Elizabeth helped the doctor and nurse care for the victims of the bombing," said Massoud.

"Anyone would have done the same," she said quickly. "I didn't want to be a paparazzi and just take pictures."

"Thank you," said Dr. Nasir, "for all you have done. I'm sure Dr. Yusuf is most grateful for your help as well."

"He already thanked me," she murmured, pretending to study a small tea leaf at the bottom of her glass.

"Dr. Yusuf is adjusting well?"

"Yes, I think so. He is liked and trusted. Don't you think, Michel?"

"Very much, of course."

"I was worried," confided Dr. Nasir. "When we Afghans have lived such a long time in the West it is often difficult to adjust to Afghanistan again, particularly to village life, which most of us never even knew before, and now to this life in a time of war. I know," he said ruefully. "Don't forget, I studied in France for some years, and my wife is French. You must meet her sometime, Elizabeth. Come for dinner one night. She will be glad to have someone to talk to her. It has been far harder for her here than for me. In Kabul we had our own life and house. After 1978 we went for awhile to France. It is she who insisted we return here, but it has been most difficult for her."

"I would love to meet her," said Elizabeth.

"You and Salima come for tea any time. And you must all be my guests soon. You too, Monsieur Dubois."

"Thank you very much, but I am leaving Peshawar quite soon."

"If there is time then."

Michel cleared his throat. He glanced at his watch and stood up. "Excuse me, Mr. Massoud Khan, and Dr. Nasir, but I should like to take the lady Elizabet to dinner tonight."

"But you must stay here for dinner," said Salima. "You must be our guest tonight."

Michel held up a graceful hand. "Thank you so kindly, but I already asked Elizabet if I might take her to dinner at the Intercon, and she agreed."

"Please, go then and enjoy yourself," said Massoud. "But please do not be late, as the security situation is uncertain these days. Michel, will you convey her back here safely?"

"Of course, of course."

Massoud insisted that they take his car and driver, as there were no rickshaws on the dark, quiet street. Michel spoke little on the way to the hotel, and Elizabeth watched the dark buildings pass. Lights flickered, then the electricity returned to Peshawar.

They sent Massoud's car home and went upstairs to the Permit Room where non-Muslim foreigners were allowed to drink alcohol out of public view. Elizabeth felt out of place in the utterly Western surroundings of the plush bar with its bottle-lined walls. They ordered *coq au vin* and Michel ordered champagne to celebrate their safe return.

When the bottle came, Michel told the waiter to stay and watch. "This is the way we do it in France," he said, "for very special occasions." He took a table knife and set it to the neck of the chilled bottle. With a flourish he severed the glass neck from the bottle just below the cork. He smoothly poured the bubbling liquid into their glasses and handed the open-mouthed waiter the cork, still in the glass bottleneck.

"Can I have it?" asked Elizabeth. "As a souvenir?"

"Madam, may I show this to my friends?" asked the waiter.

"Of course."

"I will bring it after. *Bon appetit.*"

The food was delicious, though according to Michel not up to the standards of cuisine in France. He grew slightly tipsy and made jokes about the cooking.

Elizabeth smiled, but felt sorry for the chefs called upon to cook an alien cuisine.

A phone call for Michel interrupted their meal. He got up excitedly. "That will be the call I booked to Paris!"

He rushed to the phone near the bar. He kept his face turned away from her, but she had seen his unmistakable excitement. Who could it be? Family? The long lost lover?

She concentrated on her chicken. She seemed to have lost all tolerance for alcohol. The champagne had made her giddy and she had laughed at Michel's jokes, even when she didn't think they were funny. Then she had gone melancholy and romantic. She stared at the candle flame and thought of Yusuf's face rim-lighted by the gold glow of lantern light in the mountains of Kunar.

Michel's face was flushed when he rejoined her. "Good news?" she asked.

"A good friend. Yes, good news. I must leave tomorrow."

"Where are you going?"

"Bolivia first, then after, Lebanon. After six months maybe I think of coming here."

"Your agent?"

"Agent?" his fork was poised in mid-air.

"Your photo agent."

He relaxed and delicately cut a piece of chicken from the bone. "A friend. With news from my agent."

He had decided to be evasive, so she let herself revel in fantasies of Yusuf, and hoped she would recover herself before she got back to Massoud's house. At least here she could indulge in real black coffee.

Michel poured the rest of the bottle of champagne into her glass. "In France we have a saying. He, or she, who finishes a bottle of wine will marry or hang before the end of the year."

"What a choice! What if I don't want either?"

He shrugged.

"I'm more likely to hang than marry."

"So am I. *À votre santé.*"

She raised her glass. "To life, and to freedom for Afghanistan." She drank, ignoring the inappropriateness of an alcoholic toast to a Muslim Holy War. But out of superstition, just in case, she left a swallow of champagne in the bottom of her glass and purposely spilled it. Now who had finished the bottle?

She was slightly drunk when they knocked again at Massoud's gate. Michel shook her hand solemnly and wished her luck. She smiled radiantly at the Pathan guard and walked lightly into the house. Salima was sitting in the salon alone, listening to a tape of *rebab* music.

"Elizabeth, where were you? It's late and I was worried."

"I'm sorry. The time passed quickly, and we started out late."

"Did you have a nice time?"

"Very nice. Excellent food. But he's a bit of a bore."

Salima laughed. "Have you been drinking?"

Elizabeth was embarrassed, remembering the cork in the bottleneck stashed in her purse. "Don't tell Massoud. It wasn't much, and was only champagne."

Salima sat next to her on the couch. "Was it nice?"

"Yes, it was. Have you ever had champagne?"

"Once or twice, when I was young, at weddings, but just a sip. We Afghans never considered champagne really alcohol, you know. Of course things are different now. Are you feeling good?"

"Yes," she said dreamily. "I think of romantic things when I am a little drunk."

Salima suppressed a smile. "You missed someone tonight. You should have stayed home."

Elizabeth raised her head from the pillow where she'd laid it. Her head spun slightly, but not unpleasantly. "Who?"

"Dr. Yusuf. He's back from Kunar."

CHAPTER 32
YUSUF

Peshawar

Yusuf thanked Massoud Khan's driver and turned toward the small house. He rapped on the iron gate and waited. After a few moments his cousin Rashid opened the gate.

"*Asalaamu aleikum*," the young man cried, embracing the doctor. "*Khala* will be happy to see you. For so long we have had no news. And what of *Kaka*? Is he still in Kunar?"

"He was well when I last saw him," said Yusuf. "How is my mother's health? Are you taking care of her? And how are you? How is your health? And my sister?"

"By the grace of God, *Khala* and everyone else is well. How are you? Is your health well? We heard there was cholera in Kunar and that there has been much fighting lately. Will you be resting here for some time? Come into the house, let me take your bag. You travel with almost nothing."

"Inside Afghanistan we get used to having nothing. I carry only my medical bag, a razor, and sometimes a change of clothes as a luxury. You can see I have just arrived in Peshawar." He ran a hand over his rough chin.

"When did you arrive?"

"Just now," lied Yusuf. Never mind about the visit to Massoud's house.

"Is anyone with you?"

"I came with a party of Massoud Khan's Mujahedeen, and also my nurse Malolai. She is staying with her cousin."

"*Khala jan* is in the salon. Come."

Yusuf entered one of the rooms that led off the small courtyard. There his mother, Bibi Hafizah, sat on the floor on a thin mattress, talking to his sister Maryam. The two women rose, faces full of surprised joy, and there was a flurry as first Bibi Hafizah and then Maryam hugged Yusuf.

Bibi Hafizah resoundingly kissed her son three times on his cheeks. Yusuf felt smothered, but tolerated his mother's display of affection. He put an arm around her thin shoulders as she started to cry.

"Now, Mother, don't cry. I am here and *Baba* was safe when I saw him three days ago. God protects us."

The woman smiled bravely and quickly wiped away her tears with her thin, laced-edged white veil.

"Stop crying, Mother. Let me see your face. You are are looking well. And you too, Maryam *jan*."

"It is because we are happy to see you that we look well. I am so proud of you for the work you are doing." Bibi Hafizah guided her son to the most comfortable mattress in the room and made him sit beside her. Maryam propped a thick pillow behind his back, despite his protests.

"You must be tired from the journey," said his sister.

"Or maybe from age." Maryam was twelve years younger than he. She laughed and slapped him lightly on the arm.

"How is your father?" asked Bibi Hafizah.

"He is well."

"Tell me everything," she said calmly. "Leave nothing out. Your father is a brave Mujaheed. I worry, but…" She spread her hands. "What can I do? I can only pray for both of you. I wish I could be there with him, and you, but I am too old now."

"You made the journey from Kabul with Maryam and Rashid," he reminded her. "Never say 'too old.' You are only fifty-one."

"And no grandchildren yet."

She didn't know how lucky it was that he and Janet hadn't had children. He kissed her cheek. "Maryam is twenty-three. She will marry soon, *inshallah*, and have children for you. Maryam, is there anyone you like?"

The pretty young woman blushed. She had honey-bronze skin, high cheekbones, dark, expressive almond eyes, and a sharply defined profile. Yusuf knew lots of men were interested in her as a possible mate. She had been popular at the university and had led demonstrations against the Russian occupation. She had been in Pul-e-Charkhi prison for six months. It was when she was released, two years ago, that his father had immediately sent her and her mother to Peshawar with cousin Rashid as their escort.

Maryam did not answer his question, but busied herself with pouring tea. Bibi Hafizah watched both of them. Yusuf was sure his mother could always divine his exact thoughts, and this discomfited him.

He should have come home sooner. Janet had been right about that at least. How she had berated him for not immediately rushing to the aid of his family after the 1978 coup and then the Soviet invasion of December of '79. He had argued that he couldn't leave just then, that he was, after all, sending his family money every month as his father had requested. But now the arguments rang hollow.

"Tell me about your father," insisted his mother.

"All right. You know about the commando group? He came with a number of picked men, and he brought my new nurse with them, as well as a French journalist. You know it is all a secret. He now calls himself Commander Rahim, Rahimullah Khan. His men love him. I think they would follow him anywhere.

"Their first operation was to release my health assistant, Ismail. *Baba* and his men captured a Khalqi woman and her children as hostages and offered them in exchange."

"*Afarin!*" Bibi Hafizah exclaimed. "He knows just what to do."

Yusuf put his hand on his mother's. "Yes, they were successful in making a trade. But one of the villages in Badel was bombed the day after, apparently in revenge."

"*Tobah!*"

"Repentance doesn't change anything, Mother," he said bitterly. "I had to rush there to treat the victims who survived."

"How many people were martyred?"

"Fifteen people. It was a small village. We saved a few people's lives, I think."

She sighed. "And your father?"

"He was tortured by guilt. But it was not his fault. Ismail thought it was *his* fault and that it would have been better to have left him to die at the hands of the Russians."

She paused in thought. "It is bad there then."

"The Russians have the power of the air. But Father's men are well-trained, and they will make special raids, on Asmar and Chagaserai, and later maybe on Kabul itself. If they attack the Russians in their own positions they won't know who to punish."

"God protect him. God protect all of them."

"What about Ayub?" asked Maryam. "Do you have news of him?"

"*Chup!*" cried their mother, hushing her daughter violently. "Don't ask. He is not my son anymore."

Yusuf put down his glass and looked squarely at his mother. "He is still our brother, and still your son. We must pray for him." He glanced at Maryam, who was crouching as tensely as a lioness about to spring. As a child Ayub had spoiled her, and she had always been much closer to her middle brother than to her eldest. "No news," he said. "I'm sorry. We only know he is still the Governor. And that he hasn't ordered the bombing of our clinic yet."

"*Tobah!*" cried his mother again.

"I'd like to think that he never will. As far as we know, no one knows the true identity of Commander Rahim. I don't know if that would make Ayub more angry or more careful. He was always headstrong."

Grief tightened Bibi Hafizah's face, and she looked momentarily old again.

"We can't know what is in his mind," said Yusuf softly.

Maryam blinked back her tears. "I think it was Ayub who finally got me released," she said.

"He should release the whole country," snapped Yusuf. "It is his kind who let the Russians into Afghanistan in the first place." And my kind who were too busy or lazy to stop them.

"We all made mistakes," said their mother. "Let's not make them any worse. You are right. We can only pray for Ayub."

Yusuf changed the subject. "What are you doing nowadays, Maryam?"

"I work a little for the Mujahedeen."

"She is writing articles in both Farsi and Pashtu," boasted their mother. "Rashid is also working in the office, as he knows typing. Maryam has also written some poems about the *jehad*."

"Really?" Yusuf's eyes glowed with pride for his little sister, who had grown up while he was away in America. He felt sympathy for his mother, who had only borne three children, and that with such difficulty. His own birth, when she was sixteen, had been hard on her. If better medical care had been available in Afghanistan, she might have had more children, as she had wanted, and easier pregnancies. Maryam's birth had just about killed her, even though she had been sent to England for the final months. He'd been twelve then, and that was when he'd decided to become a doctor.

Rashid searched through a pile of newspapers in a wooden cupboard and found one of Maryam's poems.

"It's not very good," she said. "But I wanted to give people something to sing."

He read the poem while Maryam cleared the tea. When she returned to the room, Yusuf said, "It's excellent. You have a gift."

His sister blushed. "If I do, it is a gift from God."

"She will be a gift to someone," he joked to their mother. Then, to his sister, "Hasn't she arranged a marriage for you yet?" He caught a faint glance from Rashid and suddenly understood his mistake. His mother, despite years of living in England and Russia, wished to arrange a traditional marriage for Maryam with her cousin Rashid, who had cared for them and led them to safety. Maryam, however, obviously didn't want to marry her cousin out of gratitude. He wondered if she had someone else in mind. He felt a protective urge, and resolved to help her follow her heart.

"I don't wish to get married," she said, an edge to her voice. "Not until Afghanistan is free again. I am married to the *jehad*."

Yusuf could see that poor Rashid admired Maryam all the more for her dedication. Rashid was a nice boy, very dedicated to the cause as well, but only a year older than Maryam and lacking his sister's depth. Rashid was of a different generation than himself, and hadn't had the same opportunities the slightly older generation had had. For an educated young man, he was strangely traditional. This war had broken down traditions in some and strengthened them in others, for whom tradition was the only stick of wood in a turbulent sea.

"You should not speak this way," their mother reproved Maryam.

"Why not?" said Yusuf. "I admire her for her devotion."

"So do I," cut in Rashid. "And they say that there may be a cease-fire within the year. Then we can all go back to Kabul and think of other things."

"It's not so simple," said Maryam.

"Our lives don't have to stop," said Rashid angrily. "We all must fall in love and marry and have children."

"And die," added Yusuf. Rashid glared at him and Bibi Hafizah looked shocked.

"Yusuf's right," said Maryam. "There is no point in having children who will only be refugees and live in poverty and not have education, or will only die in Afghanistan."

"We need another generation to fight the *jehad*," said Rashid.

"Afghanistan won't survive another generation," said Yusuf. "If we don't win in this generation it will be too late."

"Afghans will fight till the last drop of blood, till every last man, woman, and child is dead!" cried Rashid, obviously quoting from a Mujahedeen publication.

Yusuf nodded, and spoke softly. "But that may not be so long. Cousin, come to Afghanistan with me and I will show you. Even my father acknowledges that the people are getting tired. We can't all become refugees, and we can't all fight all the time. So some become collaborators."

"Like your brother."

Everyone in the room looked at Rashid angrily, and the young man looked down, ashamed. It was this gesture of humility that kept Yusuf from slapping his cousin.

"Like many villagers who started out on the side of the Mujahedeen," said Yusuf. He shrugged. "We must keep fighting, and provide food, clothing, and medical care. And we must keep the pressure on diplomatically. That is our only real hope."

"Correct," said Maryam vehemently. "We must not think of ourselves, but of our country. When our country is free, there will be time for love, marriage, and children."

Yusuf wanted to tell her that there was always a time for love. But that was something she must find out for herself. He examined her eyes. Perhaps she already had. Her harshness seemed an act, a desperate gamble to discourage Rashid without hurting or insulting him.

"It is late," said their mother. "Yusuf *jan*, I think you must be very tired, and you will want to wash. You must be hungry. I'm sure it is a long time since you had any good food."

"You are right. But I ate at Massoud Khan's house tonight."

His mother's eyes went dark with hurt. "You ate at Massoud Khan's house before you came here?"

"I had business," he said quickly.

"You lived in America too long. You have forgotten our ways. I am surprised Massoud did not send you directly to your mother."

"He didn't know I hadn't been here yet." Thirty-five years old, and his mother telling him what to do. What would Janet have thought? And what might Elizabeth think?

"Mother, all the Mujahedeen have to give reports as soon as they come back," interjected Maryam. "They come to the office all the time, unshaven, in dirty clothes. That is the only way we get news from the front."

Their mother was slightly mollified. "Still, they should come home if they have homes to go to."

Maryam hugged her. "He came as soon as he could. At least be happy that he is home safe."

"Well, I only hope he will be here for a time and not run off to Afghanistan after one week. He needs rest." The mother grasped her son's hand firmly. "Welcome home, Yusuf *jan*. I missed you. Now you wash, then you sleep long and deeply. Tomorrow we will talk."

CHAPTER 33

ELIZABETH

Peshawar

Elizabeth sat with Salima in the stifling salon. She watched the candle flame gutter in the light breeze that seemed to move no air but nonetheless blew out the candle, while lightning flickered outside and intermittently shone through the blinds.

Before the electricity went out they had been listening to music while waiting for Massoud to get home. Elizabeth was secretly hoping Yusuf might come by as well. Damn him. His visit had probably been a courtesy call. Or just business with Massoud. Salima said he had asked about her, but he had not said anything else when Salima had told him that Elizabeth was out with Michel.

Salima frowned and fanned herself with the Mujahedeen newspaper she had been reading before the electricity had gone out. "Massoud is very late tonight. And it's so hot. I'm sorry, no fan, no light."

"It's hardly your fault!"

Salima was agitated, and Elizabeth herself felt slightly panicky. Perhaps it was the oppressive weather. Salima sat up straight, listening like a cat, alert. "There's the jeep," she said with relief.

Elizabeth heard the jeep's motor, and the metal gate creaking open. Then a fusillade of close-range gunfire cracked the air.

Salima screamed, Elizabeth gasped, and the candle fell over as Elizabeth grabbed for Salima and hit the floor.

Spurts of automatic weapon-fire continued, mixed with shouting. Elizabeth cursed and struggled with Salima, who was screaming Massoud's name. "He'll be all right, he'll be all right!" shouted Elizabeth. "Oh Jesus Christ help us, dear God, Jesus, oh shit!" She grasped Salima's flailing hands and the two women, now lying under the coffee table, stared into each other's eyes, wide mirrors of horror.

The sharp concussions stopped. Running feet, a stifled moan. Voices. Elizabeth strained to make them out.

Salima whispered something in Farsi, then said excitedly. "He's alive! I hear his voice. But who is groaning?"

"Thank God he's alive! Don't move yet Salima."

The two women clutched at each other, shaking. Footsteps. The door to the salon opened. "Salima! Salima!" Massoud's voice.

Salima scrambled out from under the table and flew to her husband, sobbing. There was still no light. Elizabeth crawled out from under the table.

"Where's Elizabeth?" asked Massoud urgently, in English.

"Here. What happened?"

"You're bleeding!" gasped Salima.

"It's not serious," said Massoud brusquely. "Are you two all right?"

"Yes. What happened?" repeated Elizabeth.

"You must get to a doctor," said Salima. Then she said something in Farsi.

"One of the guards is dead," said Massoud. "And Ghulam Mohammed is badly wounded. I must get him to hospital, but I don't want to leave you here alone."

"We'll all come," said Salima.

"No, I don't want you in the open. Not until we find out who did this, and if they are really gone or just waiting for us to come out."

"What should we do?" asked Elizabeth. "The wounded man needs a doctor, and so do you. Have you called the police?"

Massoud went to the phone in the corner, clicked the line, then shouted into it. "Dead."

The lights came on, flickered, and came on again. In the bright light Elizabeth saw that Massoud's white *kameez* was stained scarlet with blood. Salima's hand flew to her lips, then she rushed to her husband, who still held his pistol in his right hand.

"Don't touch!" he warned. "It's only the shoulder."

Massoud's white face was even paler than usual. "You're losing a lot of blood," Elizabeth said in a calm tone calculated not to alarm. "You should lie down."

Massoud tensed at the sound of a rickshaw puttering outside. It stopped. He shut out the lights and hissed, "Get down and stay down."

Elizabeth grasped Salima again. She could feel the other woman's heart beating and her own pulse pounding. The two crouched under the table and looked out the window towards the verandah. A flash of lightning momentarily backlit two bullet holes in the glass.

Shouted challenges, exchanged words. The voice. Elizabeth recognized it. Yusuf! Dear God, don't shoot!

Quick footsteps. Massoud returned and turned on the light. Yusuf followed. Elizabeth and Salima quickly rose.

"Sorry we're always meeting at bad times," said Yusuf.

"What can we do to help?" asked Elizabeth quickly.

"You can stop Massoud's bleeding. Salima can boil water and tear up some sheets. Clean sheets. We'll need a lot for the one outside."

Yusuf caught Massoud as he started to faint. Salima rushed to her husband. The doctor spoke reassuringly and helped her lay him on the couch. "He'll be all right. But Elizabeth, you'd better get this bleeding stopped. And someone should phone the police. We've got a few dead bodies outside and no live ones to tell what happened."

"Phone's out," said Elizabeth.

"Shit. Who can go?"

"The cook," said Salima.

"Where is he?"

"In the back? I don't know."

"I'll look. You start tearing up sheets."

Elizabeth rushed to her room to find sanitary pads. She'd learned in First Aid that they were one of the best things for stopping bleeding. As she hurried back she heard voices outside. Massoud was still unconscious, but his breathing was regular. Salima was frantically ripping a clean sheet into long strips. Elizabeth gently unbuttoned Massoud's shirt and pulled the sleeve off his left shoulder. The wound was steadily oozing blood, but it looked clean. No artery had been hit, or the blood would be spurting. She pressed a pad hard on the wound and watched it grow red.

Yusuf came back into the room. "The cook's gone to get the police. On foot. He didn't want to go, poor man. Let's see Massoud." He came closer. "Good job. One more should do it." He grabbed a few strips of Salima's torn sheet and most of the sanitary pads. "I may need these outside. Don't come out unless you're sure you've got the bleeding stopped."

Elizabeth was glad Massoud was still unconscious. Another pad stained red and she put on a third. The bleeding slowed, and finally stopped. She took a long strip of sheet and bound the pad to the wound.

Salima brought in a bowl of steaming water. "Take it outside to Yusuf," said Elizabeth. "Tell him I've got the bleeding stopped but I'm afraid to try to clean the wound. It might start the bleeding again. But don't worry!"

While Salima took the pan outside Elizabeth checked for signs of shock. Massoud's skin was pale and a little clammy, his pulse was fast, but not too irregular. The regularity of his breathing relieved some of her anxiety. He looked so frail lying on the worn couch, bloody shirt pulled away from his wound.

Some of her own emotional shock began to wear off, and anger set in.

Who could have done this? The KGB? Rival Mujahedeen groups? Disaffected members of Massoud's own party?

Salima came back in and took her husband's hand. Elizabeth sensed that Salima wanted to be alone. "I will make tea," she murmured. "He will need it when he wakes up." She put her hand on Salima's shoulder. "Don't worry." Salima looked up at her, fear in her dark eyes.

"I was always afraid this would happen."

"It will be all right," said Elizabeth firmly. "He's not going to die." She went to the kitchen. The iron kettle was still hot. She poked through a shelf until she found a tin of black tea, and shook some into the kettle, trying to judge the amount. She lit the gas ring and waited.

She realized she was trembling. She had been calm while she stopped Massoud's bleeding and dressed the wound. Now the emergency was over, but she was still tense, unconsciously waiting for...what? Another attack? Help?

The house was quiet except for the low murmur of voices outside. The whole night was quiet. Even the thunder had stopped. A faint sound, outside the edges of consciousness. The rise and fall of a siren?

The kettle boiled furiously in the silence. She strained to hear. A siren, getting closer. More than one. Now loud, stopping in front of the house. The sound of voices, lots of voices. Now that the police were here, it sounded like all the frightened neighbors had come out. The scrape of metal on concrete as the gate opened. Arguing, in Pashtu she thought.

She turned off the gas ring, hurriedly stacked several glasses, tucked the bottle of cardamom under her arm, and made her way to the salon.

Massoud had regained consciousness and was talking quietly with Salima. The two were locked in a gaze of love, and Elizabeth's heart contracted at the sight. Salima was stroking Massoud's hair and brow. Massoud's gaze traveled to Elizabeth and he smiled. "Thank you," he said. "I would be worse off if you hadn't been here. Salima studied literature, not nursing."

Elizabeth set the kettle and glasses on the table. "Thank God you're all right. Would you like some tea?"

He smiled faintly, with apparent effort. His eyes were clouded with pain. "Thank you."

"We've got to get you some pain-killer," said Elizabeth as she sprinkled cardamom into the kettle. "And we've got to get you to a hospital to have that bullet removed."

Comprehension filtered into his eyes. "Ghulam Mohammed! How is he?"

"Dr. Yusuf is with him. I haven't gone out."

An engine started up outside and a heavy vehicle pulled into the drive. Blue lights flashed through the window. Massoud sat up.

"Be careful," Elizabeth warned. "Don't start the bleeding again."

"I have to talk to the police." He was up and out of the room before either woman could stop him. Salima crouched on the couch and peered through the chintz curtains.

"Who's out there?" whispered Elizabeth.

"An ambulance. Three policemen. One an officer I think. They are putting Ghulam Mohammed onto a stretcher, and Dr. Yusuf is standing there. Massoud is talking to the officer."

Elizabeth absently poured tea into a glass, sniffed it, and poured it back into the teapot, as she had often seen Salima do.

"Dr. Yusuf is coming in," said Salima, quickly settling into a dignified sitting position.

The doctor entered. He was wearing a stylish new light blue *shalwar kameez*, Elizabeth noted. It was stained with blood.

"I think the guard will be all right," he said shortly. "So will Massoud. Thanks again, Elizabeth. I guess we're in this together."

Salima spoke to him in Farsi.

"We won't know for awhile," he answered in English. "An ambulance has come. The police want to talk to Massoud, but I told them he has to go to the hospital first. I want to get that bullet out tonight and give him a dose of antibiotics and some pain-killer. And I want an x-ray. With luck, he can recover at home."

Massoud stood in the doorway. "Salima, Elizabeth, go to another room. The police want to search this room. Elizabeth, I don't want you involved in this at all. No one knows you're here."

"He's right," said Yusuf. "Go with Salima."

"Will you go to the hospital?" asked Salima.

"I don't want to leave you alone," Massoud said.

"They won't be alone," said Yusuf. "The boy brought Mujahedeen from the office. In fact, Sharif and Ebrahim are here. I'm your doctor, and I'm ordering you to the hospital in this ambulance. The police can come in for five minutes. You give them a brief statement and we're leaving. They can talk to you tomorrow."

Massoud nodded, then gestured with his head for Salima and Elizabeth to leave. Elizabeth followed Salima to her bedroom, where Salima sat on the edge of the bed and broke down into sobs. Elizabeth hugged her, rocked her. Only the need to keep Salima from hysteria prevented Elizabeth from crying as well.

When Salima's sobs subsided Elizabeth glanced at the clock on the bedside table. Only 10:30. It would be a long night. She could hear sounds in the salon, voices, doors opening and closing. The front door was on a spring, and sounded like a shot every time it closed.

Elizabeth heard the ambulance pull out, and the gate close quickly behind it. Someone came into the house and the footsteps came across the terrazzo hallway to their door. A quiet knock.

"*Bia*," Salima called out.

Yusuf closed the door behind him. "He's off to the hospital. I'm going in the police car. Don't be afraid, we've got several reliable and well-armed guards outside. Sharif and Ebrahim and three others will stay the night. There are also police guards outside the gates."

He put a hand on Salima's shoulder and spoke to her quietly in Farsi. She looked up at him seriously, nodding from time to time. "He may even be home tonight," he finished in English. "If I can I'll deliver him personally."

He stepped toward the door. "I'm sorry, Elizabeth. I had expected a pleasant evening of relaxed conversation."

"I hope to see you under better circumstances sometime," she said earnestly.

"For Afghans, there are no better circumstances anymore. Try to get some sleep."

CHAPTER 34
YUSUF

Peshawar

As Yusuf swabbed the ugly wound his thoughts went back to the night he had removed the bullet from Massoud's shoulder. It was hard to work on a friend, a lot harder than working at this clinic where streams of refugees and Mujahedeen, nearly all of them strangers, came for removal of old bullets and new pieces of shrapnel, for treatment of infected wounds, and lancing of simple abscesses.

He hadn't been back to the house since he had delivered Massoud at 4 a.m. the morning after the shooting. He'd had a quick cup of tea and had left with one of the Mujahedeen to escort him. Two nervous-looking Pakistani policemen had been standing guard outside the gate. The bodies of the dead guard and two assailants had been removed.

What a lucky fate it had been that he had been so eager to see Elizabeth. And luckier still that he had arrived exactly when he did.

Timing, he thought, it's all timing. Fate? Maybe. He hadn't thought this way in years. He'd always prided himself on being a rationalist, but war brought out the fatalism in a person.

Grimly, he took the tongs that Malolai proffered and firmly gripped the chunk of metal embedded in the forearm of the man who lay before him. He pulled, and the metal gave, followed by a little blood. The man gritted his teeth and inhaled with a sharp hiss, then let his breath out slowly, without a sound. Malolai stanched the flow of blood and Yusuf began suturing with a practiced hand.

Back to that night…luckily he hadn't arrived in the middle of the incident. As it was a guard had nearly shot him. Massoud would have been a lot worse off if Elizabeth hadn't been there, that was certain. And the guard, Ghulam Mohammed, probably would have died without the prompt medical care he'd been able to provide.

What was fate? He wrestled with the problem, as philosophers and ordinary men and women had for centuries. Massoud had told him of Elizabeth's narrow escape in Kunar. Strange the chain of circumstances. If any single factor had been left out, the equation would not have added up the way it had. His heart contracted. The fact that Elizabeth had faced death and danger not once, but three times now, made her ever more precious to him.

He'd planned a very different evening. A pleasant conversation, a chance to discern something of Elizabeth's attitude toward him. She'd stayed in Peshawar longer than planned. Had this been to wait for him? He needed to be alone with her, to speak to her again. He had wanted to ask her out. A nice elegant dinner at the Intercon. That snake Michel had gotten to her first. A cold jealousy stiffened him. He finished the last stitch closing the wound and snipped the black thread with a sharp, final sound.

"You'll be fine now," he said with more brusqueness than usual to a patient. The man sat up, looking at his arm with wonder. Malolai secured a fresh dressing over the sutured wound.

"Injection?" asked the man hopefully.

"No injection today," answered the doctor by rote. "You take these tablets, they'll do you good. Come back here after two days."

The man left and another replaced him on the table. This one had a dirty cloth wrapped around an infected leg. He'd just arrived from Afghanistan, and his clothes were in tatters. His dark eyes were sunken in a face made sharp by hunger. Malolai unwrapped the bandage and Yusuf went to work.

Yusuf couldn't afford to think too much about what he was doing. The anger and indignation would make effective action impossible. This professional numbness was better. Some might consider him lacking in bedside manner at times, but he knew he was a damn good doctor. Nasir was good of course, and a few of the others. Some who had done all their training in Kabul were top doctors, in his opinion, though not always up on the latest techniques. He thought of his own life, of the opportunity his father and his fortunate birth had given him to study medicine in America. He had been lucky in his life. Too lucky.

In the few days he had been back in Peshawar he had immersed himself in the work of the Afghan Medical Association's clinic in the Cantonment. Nasir had chided him, reminding him that he was supposed to be here for a rest. His mother had fretted. But he had asked Nasir to let him work afternoons in the Mujahedeen hospital as well.

He glanced at his assistant. Malolai's future was another problem on his mind. She too had insisted on working, and he had agreed because they made a good team. He knew she hadn't seen Sharif since they reached Peshawar, and he hadn't asked any questions. He would have to ascertain if she would indeed accept a marriage proposal from Sharif, and if so, then have a man-to-man talk with Sharif. If Sharif really wanted to marry Malolai, he would act as Sharif's go-between to Malolai's cousin, her closest relative outside Afghanistan. Malolai was a headstrong woman and would make her own decision, but it would help to have her cousin's consent. Yusuf was confident he could persuade the cousin of the wisdom of the match.

In one way, Yusuf was glad he had so much on his mind. It prevented him from dwelling too much on Elizabeth. His sister Maryam worried him as well. Rashid had the sanction of their mother, and could be quite insistent. He wondered if their father knew. He had said nothing to Yusuf about the situation, and Yusuf suspected that it had been hidden from his father. Yusuf loved his mother, but knew she could be manipulative. Most of his elder female relatives could be that way. He supposed it grew out of the Afghan matriarch's sheltered life. Confined to the home realm for much of her adult life, she learned to carve out an unassailable niche by whatever methods best suited her personality.

Not so for the younger women. Women like Maryam and Malolai had had their characters forged in the seventies, when the West had had an impact on Kabul, and honed in the fires of the war of the eighties. Their wits were sharp, their thoughts sure, and they were quite capable of simultaneously defying convention and remaining devoutly Muslim.

Even the village women had been affected. Before the war, their concerns had been home, children, family, religion, maybe crops and the village prosperity, and of course local gossip. But never the state of the nation. Ironically, the Russians might yet succeed in their stated goal of freeing Afghan women, just not quite in the way they had planned.

Yusuf would stand up for his sister, he'd decided, even against their mother. Bibi Hafizah was strong-willed, but Maryam's will could be stronger, even quite inflexible. He smiled at the memory of the determined little girl learning to ride a horse. Maryam had been only five when he'd left for America, but already she was feisty and tenacious. She'd loved their trips into the mountains for hunting expeditions, and their father had always called her a "daughter of the mountains." No wonder she'd grown into a courageous young woman.

He wondered how she would react to Elizabeth. They might get along, despite the age difference and the gap in experience. They had a spark of spirit in common, vitality and idealism. Both of them were far more free than he could ever be.

He felt in awe of the women in his life. Bibi Hafizah had been a big influence on him, though in more subtle ways than his father's harangues on the importance of discipline, achievement, and service. His mother had a steely courage underneath the roses that he had only appreciated as an adult.

His parents hadn't approved of his marriage to Janet. That was one reason he had never brought his wife to Afghanistan. Janet would probably have reacted badly. She hadn't been close to her own family, staunch Presbyterians from Omaha, Nebraska, so they had married in a simple civil ceremony in San Francisco, attended by a few mutual friends. She'd been twenty-five, he twenty-nine, and it seemed silly to make a fuss. So they'd been the seventies couple and had had the intimate casual party at home, hardly a reception, with California wine and cheese, sushi, champagne, and marijuana. What would his mother have thought?

Janet had never converted to Islam. She'd never even changed her last name. She had said it was her feminist statement, but for all her talk he thought she'd proved pretty dependent in practice. She had moved straight out of their house and in with her lawyer boyfriend after giving Yusuf what he thought was a sincere speech about her need to be independent, to "find herself without a man." He suspected there had been some overlap between marriage and affair. In any case, the little redwood house in Mill Valley had gone up for sale almost as soon as the divorce decree had been signed, and she and her dog had moved into the plush home that the lawyer had managed to salvage from his own divorce.

Perhaps at heart he was an Afghan hillbilly, thought Yusuf with some amusement. He just couldn't keep up with life in the fast lane of California. He hadn't met any American women like Elizabeth. Maybe it had been the fault of his profession, which had kept him busy and confined his social life to narrow circles. Or maybe she really was unique. Maybe facing war and danger had brought out the best in her. She was down to earth, capable, independent. She also had a sense of humor, an asset in a war zone. She was intelligent, perceptive, and he suspected, intuitive. She had compassion, and a poet's soul. And she was certainly attractive.

She looked like an Afghan girl, he thought, remembering the flash of her dark almond eyes, the curve of her cheek, the delicate point of her chin. He smiled inwardly. He was quite smitten.

He wondered if somewhere deep in his unconscious mind he was really looking for an Afghan mother figure. When he'd first gone to America he'd decided he couldn't find what he wanted in an Afghan woman, and had spurned all his parents' attempts to put him in contact with beautiful, educated young Afghan women living in America. He'd put an end to their efforts by marrying blonde, cool, successful, fun-loving Janet.

Yusuf washed his hands in alcohol and dried them on a towel. The long morning was almost over. He would take lunch and then work the afternoon in the hospital. And maybe tonight he would go see Massoud and invite Elizabeth to dinner. He didn't really know his own intentions. He just knew that he needed to see her.

He sighed. To the problem at hand. "Malolai, can you have lunch with me here, in the office? I'll send a boy out for *nan* and kebab."

Malolai's brows arched in surprise. "I don't know," she said uncertainly.

He laughed. "Have you ever seen *Casablanca*?"

She looked suspicious. "The American film, with Humphrey Bogart?"

"Right."

"Once, at the American Center in Kabul."

"To paraphrase a classic line..." He switched to English and screwed his face into what he thought was a Bogey imitation. "If you don't eat lunch with me today, it's something you're going to regret for the rest of your life."

CHAPTER 35
ELIZABETH AND YUSUF

Peshawar

Elizabeth sat alone in the salon, listening to a tape of Afghan popular music. She couldn't understand the words, but the singer, Ahmed Zaher, had a rich, mellow voice. She enjoyed the tunes, which had some of the sweet melancholy of French torch songs.

She twisted her white chiffon *dupata* nervously and looked at her watch for the umpteenth time. Typical of Yusuf to be late. Afghan time.

Elizabeth ran her fingers through her hair. Salima had curled the unruly, frizzy mass and had insisted that she wear her shoulder-length hair down. It felt strange, after weeks of wearing it in a braid or up to keep it out of her way.

She tapped her fingers on the wooden arm of her chair and closed her eyes, listening. Salima had translated this song for her. She couldn't remember the words, but knew it was a love song.

Another voice joined Ahmed Zaher's. She opened her eyes to see Yusuf standing in the doorway, spotless in a white *shalwar kameez*, a simply cut white cotton vest over the *kameez*.

She stood up hastily. "*Staray mashay.*"

He kept singing, his eyes warm and questioning. Her heart melted in his gaze, but she didn't want to let him know. From behind his back he produced a rose, which he offered her with solemn expression.

She smiled with delight. "Yusuf, thank you. Did you steal it from the garden?"

He just kept singing, a smile playing at his lips.

"Come on, talk to me. I can't understand the words anyway."

He glanced quickly through the open door that led into the hallway, then kissed her on the cheek. His eyes were glad, and she knew hers answered.

"Better circumstances?" she asked, sitting down. He sat next to her, but not too close. He put his right leg up on his left knee and leaned back.

"Much better. How is Massoud?"

"Not bad. They'll be here in a minute. They're praying."

He looked at her appraisingly. "White suits you."

"Thank you. I'm not really used to these clothes, but I do like them."

"You wear them well. Did you sell all your jeans?"

"Now, now. I figured out pretty quickly that they're inappropriate for Peshawar. They attract far too much attention. Why, do you prefer jeans? Shall I change?" She stood up.

He took her hand and pulled her down, a little closer than before. "You look beautiful just the way you are."

"You've never seen me in clean clothes before. Or with clean hair."

"You should wear it down more often."

She touched her thick hair. "I can't do anything with it. I think I should wear a veil all the time. It would be easier."

He glanced at the white wrap on the arm of the chair. "Don't tell me you've started wearing a *chadar*!"

"Only when convenient. It's part of my disguise. If I keep my mouth shut people think I'm an Afghan or a Pathan."

He ran a hand over his moustache. So many of his little gestures thrilled her, she realized, distracted for a moment.

"Wear the rose in your hair," he said. "It goes with the red roses on your *kameez.*"

"Has Salima been informing on me?" She twirled the rose in her hand.

He took the flower from her. "Here, this way." Gently he placed the rose in her hair, behind her right ear. His hand brushed her ear, lingered on her cheek, and returned to rest in his lap.

She felt the tingle of his touch, like a light static electricity. She drew in her breath quickly and swallowed hard. "How does it look?"

"I should quote from a Persian poem to begin to describe you, yet thou art more beautiful."

Massoud entered the room, followed by Salima. Massoud's left arm was in a sling, but he shook Yusuf's hand warmly and gestured to him to sit down. There were the usual extended Persian greetings, then conversation in English for Elizabeth's benefit, but she hardly heard a word.

At last Yusuf stood up, glancing at his watch. "I think we should go, Elizabeth."

Salima smiled secretly at Elizabeth and pinched her arm as she followed Yusuf out the door. Yusuf seemed to be disputing with Massoud, and finally said in English. "We will take the car only to the hotel, and send the driver back. You might need it."

Elizabeth got into the car and covered her head and shoulders with the white eyelet *chadar* she had borrowed from Salima. Yusuf looked at her strangely, but said nothing. He leaned forward to the driver and directed him to take them to the Intercontinental.

Elizabeth suddenly felt embarrassed. A sadness overtook her, and she wondered what she was doing here, so far from home, in strange clothes and with a strange man. She glanced sideways at Yusuf, who was looking out the window as they drove along Khyber Road. He looked so different from the first time she had seen him. That memory made her laugh, and brought her back full circle to reality as she suppressed a smile. This was a man she knew almost nothing about, but who she at the same time knew better than she knew almost anyone on earth.

They pulled into the long, flower-lined drive of the massive modern hotel. "Yusuf, let's go somewhere else."

"This is the best place in town. I wanted to take you out to a nice meal. I couldn't give you much hospitality in Deh Wagal."

"I want to go to the Old City. Do you know a place?"

He put his finger to his lips. "As long as you don't tell Massoud. We'll get down here." The driver let them out in front of the hotel's glass doors. Yusuf thanked him and led Elizabeth into the marble-floored lobby.

"After Kunar, I feel so out of place here," she said. "I love the old bazaar. There's so much more life there."

He glanced out the doors to where the taillights of Massoud's car were disappearing down the drive. "Okay, we'll go there. Are you sure you're okay with being the only woman not in a *chadari* or *burqa*?"

"I hadn't thought of that. I've been before."

"It's fine for you as a foreigner. You're exempt. But even someone as independent as Malolai or my sister could not safely go into the old bazaar without being harassed."

She looked dismayed and uncertain. "But I'm wearing a *chadar*. And no one has ever harassed me."

He laughed. "Okay, let's go. You Americans are crazy for the exotic."

"And you Afghans are crazy for the modern, Western, and plastic."

"Who's right?"

"Probably neither of us. The exotic is also often filthy, ignorant, and disease-ridden, while the modern is too often sterile, materialistic, and ugly. I learned a long time ago, when I spent some time in Mexico, that there is no beauty in poverty. But I'd already learned that there was none in sterile technology either, which is why I'd gone to the villages in Mexico."

"So what is your panacea?" he asked as he led her to the glass doors, held open for them by a doorman dressed as a Pathan tribesman.

"I don't know. Maybe a sense of balance?"

He nodded. "The Grand Synthesis of East and West. I used to believe in that."

"You don't anymore?"

"Where has it gotten us?" he asked with a trace of bitterness. It had started raining outside, a light, warm rain with the promise of a later cloudburst. "We'll take a taxi," he said shortly. "Rickshaws are no good in the rain."

His manner hurt her. "Would you rather not go? I don't want to force you."

He looked exasperated. "Elizabeth, I'd hug you if I could. This isn't San Francisco or New York. And I can't have a serious talk in the rain waiting for a taxi. Just relax, and don't be afraid of me."

She stopped, clutching her *chadar* around her chin. She hadn't realized she was afraid until he said it. "Are you afraid of me?" she asked.

"Terrified." A taxi pulled up and he opened the door for her. "Let's wait till we are sitting somewhere to talk of these things."

She suddenly laughed, and it was as if a blockage had dissolved. Why were human relations so difficult? Relaxing into the possibility of trust, Elizabeth became animated and talked excitedly as they drove through the night to Qissa Khani Bazaar.

The bazaar was crowded and frantic. Many shops were still open, and the streets were choked with cars, rickshaws, horse-drawn carts, bicycles, and pedestrians. Elizabeth wrapped her *chadar* around the lower half of her face, leaving only her eyes free, and stared out in fascination at the film unrolling outside. Music blared from cafes and *chai khanas*, horns tooted, bicycle bells jingled. In the traffic jam beggars stumbled up to their car in the rain, tapping on the windows, pleading. Yusuf rolled down the window and gave five-rupee notes to two beggars.

"In Islam, we're supposed to give alms," he explained. "But giving alms can justify ignoring long-term problems. Look out there, Elizabeth. It's beautiful, it's exotic. But do you see any women? They're all in the houses, in *purdah*. Did you know that a high percentage of them suffer from tuberculosis?"

"But these things have to change. And you can change them without giving up your culture and becoming carbon copies of the West," she insisted. "Islam has to come into the twentieth century, but it can still be Islam. I wouldn't have said this a month ago, but after seeing the Mujahedeen and meeting enlightened Muslims, I think it's possible."

He sighed. "Islam was very progressive back in the seventh century when Prophet Mohammed received his revelations. But now certain factions of fundamentalists are using it to hold people back, which just happens to keep them firmly entrenched in power. That's part of what set us up for Communism. It seemed to some, like my brother, to be a radical and quick solution for all the problems of Islam, an easy leap into a twentieth-century paradise for workers and peasants.

"But you're right. There is hope. There's actually nothing specifically about *purdah* in the Koran, and there are a lot of progressive scholars in the world who interpret the spirit of Islam rather than its letter."

"I suppose it's a lot like the fundamentalist Christians in the States," she said thoughtfully. "I'd hate to see them get into power either. They seem just as attached to literal interpretation of Scripture as the Muslims are."

"Islam has one more chance," said Yusuf. "If we can keep our faith, and remember that the spirit of the Koran, the spirit of Allah, is one of mercy and compassion, we could even have a Renaissance in the Islamic world. Do you know how many centuries Islam has existed?"

She thought. "The flight of Mohammed to Mecca, the Hejira, was 622 A.D. What's that, over 1300 years?"

"Fourteen hundred," he said proudly. "We count from the birth of the Prophet in 582 A.D., though our calendar dates from the Hejira. So it's just about time for a Renaissance, if we can combine spiritual wisdom, faith in the unseen world, and social compassion on the one hand with technology and progress for the good of humanity on the other. But maybe it's only a dream."

"Wait a minute. You're implying that all the West has to offer is technology, doing it bigger, better, richer, faster. We do have some other values, like a concept of human rights and of equality of women."

"Yes," he agreed. "But are these applied, or are they only wishful thinking?"

"Well, things were getting better till Reagan got in. But that's only a blip. Things are changing for women, and I believe America has strong values of support for human rights."

He looked at her admiringly. "Elizabeth, you may be the only truly independent woman I know. Besides my sister."

"I think that's a compliment?"

"It's intended as one."

"Wow, an Afghan who admires women's liberation. There can't be many like you."

"Maybe not. But things have to change when we rebuild the country. A lot of Afghan women will have learned from women like Malolai and my sister, and they won't just go back into *purdah*. They'll want an education, and some of them will want to work. With so many men being killed in the war, we'll need our women to participate in rebuilding."

Yusuf spoke to the driver, who stopped in front of a well-lit café. As Yusuf paid the driver Elizabeth sniffed the air, which was fresh from the rain. A hot scent of sizzling kebabs made her mouth water. Then she wrinkled her nose. Mixed with the aroma of kebabs was the stench of an open sewer.

They made their way into the café. The men inside all stared at Elizabeth. Thankfully, Yusuf knew several of them and introduced her as an American journalist, which broke the ice. Soon the tall, handsome men wearing huge striped turbans with one end draped elegantly in front of their left shoulders were smiling and greeting her enthusiastically, vying to be the first to serve her tea.

But Yusuf led her to a table at the back. "They'll leave us alone," he said. "They're mostly Afghans here, mostly Mujahedeen. And the cook is an Afghan. Is this enough local color for you?"

"I love it."

"Good. What do you want? *Kebab*? Nan? Salad? *Pilau*?

She suddenly felt too nervous to eat. "Whatever you like. I'm not that hungry."

He looked at her through narrowed eyes. "I told you not to be afraid of me. You'd better eat tonight. It's good Afghan food, and there are plenty of people in Kunar who would love to have the chance. Not to lay a guilt trip on you or anything." He turned to a teenage boy in a gray *shalwar kameez* and a gold cap and ordered. A minute later a chipped blue pot of tea was on the Formica table.

"Reminds me of Kunar," she said, smiling.

"Things are made fine by their company." He poured tea into their glasses. It was delicate and softly scented with cardamom. "To you." He raised his glass.

"And to you. And to freedom for Afghanistan." They sipped their tea, gazing at each other through the steam.

"I'm sorry I couldn't take you to the Intercon. But I couldn't have given you champagne anyway. I'm Muslim, you know."

"Champagne is not important."

"I think you've already been to the Intercon before anyway."

His slightly petulant look was somehow endearing. "With Michel? Great conversation. He told me whoever finished the bottle of wine would either marry or hang before the year was over."

"What?" His eyebrows raised.

"An old French saying. So he said."

"Who finished the bottle?"

"Technically it was champagne, not wine. He poured the last into my glass. I left a sip and purposely spilled it."

He laughed loudly. She noticed what a beautiful smile he had, all the more precious for its rare display. "You're wonderful!" he said.

"We both decided we were more likely to hang than marry in the next year."

"Oh, why?"

"Well, Michel's obviously not interested in…" She had started to say "women," but changed it to "marriage."

"And you?"

"Who would I marry?"

He looked at her piercingly and her heart faltered. "Don't you want to marry?"

"Oh, I don't know." She didn't want to talk about it. And she didn't know.

"So you never married the man you loved before?"

"What difference does it make? I'm not a Muslim."

"What did your parents think?"

"Look…" She slammed her glass down on the table. "How many years did you live in America?"

"Eighteen."

"In eighteen years you should have figured out we have different ideas about sex and marriage. Maybe they're right, maybe they're wrong, or maybe they're just right for us."

"I'm not attacking you, Elizabeth," he said softly. "I'm not judging you."

"You're not?"

"No. I don't judge people."

"How unusual." She was still angry. "Were you such a saint for eighteen years?"

He smiled wryly. "Only after I married. You wouldn't have liked me before I was married. I had lots of girlfriends. You would have called me a chauvinist pig. Though to be fair, I didn't go to bed with all of them."

"I didn't ask."

"I was completely faithful to my wife, for what it's worth. She had an affair with a lawyer who was a client of her psychology practice."

"Oh. I'm sorry."

"It's a bit late for that. Anyway it doesn't matter anymore. I just thought you should know."

Why? Was he warning her not to get too close? They postured warily, like two animals in a mating ritual. "It must have hurt you."

"Them's the breaks, kid. Now you know all about me."

"Is that why you came back to Afghanistan."

"Not entirely, but it was the original impetus. Why did you come?"

She considered, then looked directly at him. "Like you, I think originally I was running away when things weren't working out with Tom. And I thought it might help my career to do something a little risky. But that was before I came. Now I care."

"What were you running from?"

"Five years of being only half myself."

"Five years?"

"I lived for five years in New York with a man named Tom Dunne. You may have heard of him. He's a pretty famous photographer. He's had covers of *Time* and *Newsweek*. But Elizabeth Owen was always 'Tom's girlfriend.' A few people had heard of her as a writer, a few others as a photojournalist. But mostly she was Tom's agent, selling his pictures when he was in Tokyo or Beirut. Actually when he was out of town was probably the most peaceful time I had, but I was too stupid to realize it, so I always missed him when he was gone.

"You probably think I'm awful to talk that way. I sound bitter and callous. But the truth is I was madly in love with him." She laughed ironically. "'Madly' is the key word. I would have done anything for him. After all, that's the way Mom was with Dad. I was only too glad to be his agent."

"Are you sorry now?"

"What's the point? I just hope I won't make the same mistake again."

He stared down at the green, marble-patterned Formica surface.

"Do you regret the giving?"

She was surprised. "No, not at all. Only the inequality. When I am in love, I give all I can. It's my nature. I don't think it's Tom's. Or maybe he just wasn't in love."

His face was troubled, his lips pursed. "It's a terrible thing to realize, isn't it? I regretted the giving for a long time."

"And now?"

"Now?" He mused, then looked at her directly. "I think I'm ready to risk giving again."

"People shouldn't rush into things," she said quickly. "You know what they say, 'Marry in haste, repent in leisure.'"

"I wish I would have listened."

"So do I. You Afghans may think I was never married, and my parents may think I was never married, but I felt married, and I feel like I've gone through a divorce."

"I told you I don't judge people."

"That's refreshing. Other people do. Hardly anyone here knows that I lived with Tom."

"It's just as well. Our people are narrow-minded."

"But is that a good thing?"

"For us, yes, for now. But we do pay a price, as we do for everything. A repressed society has its own problems. We have a certain amount of homosexuality, and a number of unhappy marriages. If boys and girls grow up expecting an arranged marriage, it works out more often than not. But if they don't, it's a source of lasting unhappiness. Take my sister…" He stopped.

"You don't have to tell me."

"I find myself telling you all kinds of things, and I don't know why. You must meet Maryam. My mother wants her to marry my cousin Rashid, who is a year older than she is. Rashid is a nice boy. He works in the Mujahedeen office. But she doesn't love him."

"Is she in love with someone else?"

"I don't know."

The waiter brought a platter of kebabs, nesting on a mound of rice pilau mixed with raisins. Two large, fresh *nans* were deposited on the table, and a plate of raw onions, tomatoes, and cucumbers followed.

"I can't eat all this," gasped Elizabeth.

"The food is safe here. Try," he said kindly. "The secret is not to rush. We have plenty of time." He solicitously dished out portions onto her plate.

"It all comes down to consideration, doesn't it?" she asked.

"What?"

"Human relationships. Friendship, love, family, marriage. That's what Tom didn't have. He was awfully narcissistic. It sounds like your wife wasn't very considerate either. What was her name?"

"Janet. No, I suppose having an affair isn't very considerate."

"Were you always considerate of her?"

"I tried, I really did. Afghan men can be bastards until we're married, and some can be afterwards too. But we want to marry only once."

"Really? Aren't you allowed four wives?"

"Technically. But educated men of my generation only marry one. One is enough trouble and expense." He laughed at her dirty look. "No," he said soberly, "I'm afraid most of us have become romantics. I know I have."

Again he danced gracefully on the edge of unspoken truth. She sought refuge in her *pilau*, and found she had an appetite after all.

"So what will happen with your sister?" she asked.

"She says she doesn't want to marry until Afghanistan is free. I'm sure she's hoping Mother's intentions will blow over."

"What if she wants to marry someone else?"

"I'll stand up for her."

"Really?"

"Don't act so surprised. I don't want to see my sister's life ruined. See, I have picked up what you call values from the West."

"*Touché*. So we're back to consideration and respect."

"Elizabeth, I went to Berkeley in the late sixties. I went to peace rallies and marches for this and that. I was pro-women's lib. I smoked grass. I got older and decided a lot of things had started out with the right ideals and then gone too far."

"Well, I'm a little younger than you, but I went to rallies and marches too. But our generation made mistakes. It was always either/or. Women's liberation or black liberation or Chicano liberation, or free sex and free drugs. We forgot about human liberation, and free life. We got split up into too many separate groups instead of coming together. Then suddenly it was the seventies, the decade of the self. What do you think the eighties are turning out to be?"

"In some ways worse than the seventies, even more narcissistic and materialistic. But maybe we're searching a little deeper at the same time."

"In the West we got to be too shallow and impatient. We rushed into relationships, and at the first sign of trouble rushed right back out again."

"You're lucky, Elizabeth."

She arched her brows. "How so?"

"You've seen other cultures, and you know how to question. Not everyone does. But now you have some answers to your questions, something to compare."

"So do you."

"So we make a good pair. Oh, speaking of pairs, Malolai and Sharif are getting married."

"Really? That's wonderful! How did this come about?"

"I had a talk with Sharif. He said he wants to marry her, so I went with him to her cousin's house and he made a formal proposal. Malolai accepted and her cousin agreed."

"When will it be?"

"Soon. No use delaying during wartime. May 22nd."

"My birthday."

"Really?"

"Never mind."

"How old will you be?"

"Thirty. I'd rather not think about it. I don't know if I can trust myself. You know how we always used to say, 'Never trust anyone over thirty.'"

He laughed. "Will you still be in Peshawar? Malolai and Sharif will want you to come."

"I'll stay especially for it."

"Have you ever been to an Afghan wedding?"

"No. I've only been here two months."

"It won't be fancy. But it will be your friends."

"I'm so happy for them! Do you think they'll be happy?"

"Why not? They love each other."

She concentrated on her food, which she had been neglecting. Even with love, what kind of future did Malolai and Sharif really have? "Yusuf?"

"Yes, Elizabeth *jan*?"

"What will happen to Afghanistan?"

"That depends on if the Russians leave, and if so, who takes power."

"Will there be civil war if they leave?"

"You saw what happened to Massoud."

"But are they sure? Couldn't it have been the Russians, like Massoud told the press?"

"We have enough proof," he said sadly. "Massoud purposely told the press that the Russians had attacked him because he didn't want his own followers attacking the fundamentalists. Massoud is sometimes too honorable for his own good."

"Is there any hope then?"

"We're never without hope. Or we couldn't go on."

"But if the fundamentalists gain power…"

"Afghanistan won't be a very pleasant place to live in, though there are good men among the fundamentalists too. But it will be a terrible place for women like Malolai and my sister, who have, after all, fought in the *jehad*, each in her own way. My sister was in Pul-e-Charkhi for six months."

"What do you think the chances are of the fundamentalists getting into power?"

He made a hand gesture. "Fifty-fifty at this point. Afghans are not by nature fundamentalist, but look at which parties have the guns and the money. The CIA denies arming the Mujahedeen, but isn't it odd that the most fundamentalist parties somehow have the most arms?" He lowered his voice. "They say that the arms pipeline comes through the Saudis and the Muslim Brotherhood in Egypt, and that the Pakistani Inter-Services Intelligence agency decides who gets the arms and money, and the CIA allows them to do this."

"But why? Don't the Americans realize what will happen if the fundamentalists get into control? They hate democracy and western values, let alone women's rights."

He shrugged. "Perhaps it won't happen. Perhaps the Soviets will never leave, or perhaps, *inshallah*, there will be free elections and moderate Islamic democrats like Massoud Khan will come to power.

"In any case, we have a saying in Afghanistan. 'This too will pass.'"

"That isn't much comfort."

"It's all we have. And people like me have only ourselves to blame for the way things have turned out so far. We left. Afghanistan became polarized. The question became 'Are you Muslim or are you Communist?' 'Are you Muslim?' has started to mean 'Are you a fanatic?' at least to some. It's never quite that simple in reality."

Elizabeth watched as the waiter cleared the table and placed plates of sticky baklava in front of them. The boy poured fresh glasses of tea. She sighed. Afghanistan was a country that challenged you and forced you to care. You couldn't be neutral, yet there really wasn't a side to take.

"How much longer will you stay here?" he asked her.

"Now that you've told me Malolai and Sharif are getting married, at least till the wedding."

"Then?"

"I guess I'll go home and start a new life."

"'Home is in the heart or it is nowhere,'" he said cryptically. "Hermann Hesse said something like that."

"I'll go home for the summer. But I'll come back, *inshallah*."

"You'll come back?" He was genuinely surprised. "Why? You were very nearly killed in a bombing raid, nearly got captured by the Russians, and could have been killed when Massoud was attacked. And you don't even know whether you're getting anything published. Has it been worth it?"

"Yes, it has. Even if I never get anything published, to me personally it's been more than worth it."

He shook his head. "You'd be crazy to go back."

"But you'll go back, won't you?"

"It's my country. You've done your work and you've helped us, and that's enough. You have no reason to risk your life going back into that fire."

"Do I have to have a reason? I have fallen in love…" She paused, trying to gauge his response. "With your country."

"Did you get what you came for?"

"More than I bargained for. I owe you some thanks."

He looked hurt. "Never mind."

He changed moods like the wind. "Yusuf, I've learned a lot from you. I mean it."

He softened. "Eat your baklava. I should get you home early so Massoud won't worry."

She ate, but hardly tasted the sweet pastry. She waited at the table while he paid the waiter and sent a boy for a rickshaw. It was still wet out, though the rain had stopped, and it was chilly in the open rickshaw. "I'm sorry I don't have a blanket for you," said Yusuf. But they were close together, and she felt heat from the proximity of his aura. A long horizontal mirror surrounded by gaudy gold tape stared back at them, and Elizabeth was shocked to see her own reflection. To herself she looked like someone else. Her eyes shifted right and met Yusuf's eyes in the dark world of the mirror.

"In olden times," he said quietly, "Afghan brides and grooms never saw each other until the day they were married. They caught their first glimpse of each other in a mirror."

She couldn't raise her eyes to look directly at him, and she couldn't look away from his eyes in the mirror. In the darkness, his hand lay close to hers on the space of the seat between them. He did not touch her, but his gaze and his nearness were far more erotic than the most passionate caress.

CHAPTER 36

YUSUF

Peshawar

A large white envelope waited for Yusuf in the Afghan Medical
Association's administration office. He picked it up carelessly, then
recognized Elizabeth's handwriting.

"Who brought this?" he demanded.

A doctor glanced up. "Massoud Khan's driver."

"Oh. Thank you." Why hadn't she come herself? Crossly, he opened the
unsealed envelope. It was a copy of the first section of the *New York Times*.
No letter. His annoyance increased. He glanced at the headlines. Israel. Arms
limitation talks. Then his eyes froze on bold black print. "Inside Afghanistan,"
and bolder underneath, "Former Columbia Med Student Returns to War-torn
Homeland." The byline was Elizabeth Owen. In italics were the words, "First in
a series of three reports special to the *New York Times*."

Yusuf read through the article quickly. It was a dramatic narrative of the
bombing raid in Badel and how he had walked through the night to give
medical aid. There was the story of Sharif walking for six days to bring the
cholera vaccine in time, and a lot about how hard Malolai worked each day
and how important her presence was to the village women. All was told in a

vivid yet scrupulously factual manner, though he was relieved that she'd left out mention of his brother and his father.

There was a long quote from him: "We educated people made mistakes, and now the whole country is paying for them. It is time we give back some of what we took, and stop relying on the privileges conferred by the accident of birth. I think you would do the same thing if America were suddenly attacked."

Yusuf impatiently flipped the paper open to read the rest of the article. A blush crept up from his neck to the roots of his hair. On page nine was a picture of him examining an old man. He was shocked at his appearance. Did he really let himself go like that when he was in Kunar? Several days growth of beard, sunken eyes. It was not a picture he would have chosen for a mass circulation newspaper.

His colleagues crowded around him, talking excitedly, but he didn't respond. He was proud, but at the same time extremely embarrassed.

He read on, skimming the words quickly.

Elizabeth had accurately described the problems the clinic in Kunar faced every day, as well as the mission of the Afghan Medical Association. He smiled. She hadn't left out his poignant plea for "his adopted country, the United States, to take a greater leadership role in providing urgently needed humanitarian aid while diplomacy is taking its course."

He read the last paragraph over twice:

"This war will be won only through sacrifice," states Hakim, "sacrifice on every level. We pray daily for the success of the (U.N.-sponsored) Geneva talks, but we know that we must keep fighting to let the Soviets know that we are not yet tired." Hakim himself leased out his comfortable renovated Victorian home in San Francisco and left the security of his job at the University of California at San Francisco Medical Center for the uncertainty of practicing frontline medicine at a simple, poorly-equipped clinic in the rugged mountains of Kunar province, where he is the only doctor for an estimated 120,000 people at war. Perhaps that is what he means by sacrifice.

Yusuf closed the paper and covered his face with his right hand. Why did she have to center the article on him? He was glad Janet wouldn't see it. She didn't read the *New York Times*. Unless one of her New York friends happened to send her the article about her ex-husband.

He became aware that Malolai had entered the room, and that his colleagues were talking excitedly. Malolai crouched beside his chair and quietly asked if she might see the article.

"There's a lot about you in it," he said, smiling. "It's a good article."

She jabbed his knee. "Why aren't you happy? You must be proud."

"Not for myself."

"For Afghanistan then. This is the *New York Times*!"

He felt strangely hollow. "Yes. Elizabeth has been doing good work."

"But not for her own sake. You know that." Malolai's green eyes peered at him.

"I'm just feeling embarrassed," he whispered.

"I'm not. I'm proud. For all of us. Let me see the paper."

She stood up, paper in hand, while doctors and nurses crowded around her, peering over her shoulder. "I'll read it out loud," she said. "Sit down." Her melodious voice slowly read the English words, stumbling over a word occasionally, giggling when her own name was mentioned. Then she translated the entire piece for the benefit of those who didn't understand English.

Yusuf felt self-conscious as his friends and colleagues looked at him, murmuring "*Shabbash!*" and "*Afarin!*" as the story unfolded. He tugged nervously at his moustache, which was far better trimmed than in that damned picture.

Dr. Nasir entered the office, causing the small knot of people to scatter respectfully. He looked curiously from Yusuf to Malolai, who was still standing with the newspaper open to page nine.

"There is an article on the clinic," said Yusuf offhandedly, "in the *New York Times*."

"The *New York Times!*" Dr. Nasir beamed. "That is excellent publicity. From Elizabeth?"

Yusuf nodded as Malolai thrust the paper in front of Dr. Nasir, pointing to the picture.

"You look like a *mujaheed!*" said Dr. Nasir. "I didn't know our doctors wore bandoleers all the time."

"Oh, it's some idiot editor's idea of a guerrilla doctor."

"I think it's a wonderful picture."

"I don't."

Dr. Nasir sat down at his desk and nodded with satisfaction as he skimmed the first few paragraphs. He looked up to find the entire office watching him. "All right, we'll put it up on the bulletin board later. But we've got two hundred people waiting outside, so we should open up the clinic now."

The doctors and nurses filed out. Yusuf got up to join them, but Dr. Nasir asked him to stay for a minute. Yusuf stared down at his hands while his friend read the article. He had known Elizabeth would write something about him, but the reality was quite different from what he had expected. Did she have to praise him so much? It was Malolai, or Ismail, or the average *mujaheed*, or the village man or woman who supported the Mujahedeen, who deserved far more praise. The editor had hooked onto the "former Columbia student" and "U.S. citizen" angle he guessed.

He was further annoyed that she hadn't personally delivered the article. Not even a note. Dr. Nasir finished reading and closed the paper neatly. He handed it to Yusuf. "You'll want to take this home. See if you can get another copy, or make a photocopy for us."

"No picture?"

"No picture, if you don't want. It's not so bad. I never realize you were shy."

"Neither did I."

"She's a nice girl, and very perceptive," said Nasir thoughtfully. "You must have impressed her."

"Afghanistan impressed her."

"Maybe. You must bring her over for dinner sometime. Come with Massoud and his wife."

"*Inshallah.*" Yusuf glanced out the window at the growing crowd waiting for treatment. "I must go. It's not fair to leave all the work to the others."

Dr. Nasir nodded. "Don't forget the photocopy." He was already engrossed in the day's correspondence.

Yusuf made his way through the courtyard to the surgery room, stopping to shake hands with some of the men he knew. A low murmur echoed in the courtyard of the rundown, two-story building. A far cry from Columbia, indeed. We're not resourceful because we want to be, he thought, but because we have to be.

Malolai was waiting for him. Everything was meticulously prepared for the series of minor surgeries he would perform. He worked automatically, cleaning, swabbing, suturing. He was glad he had managed to arrange Malolai's and Sharif's upcoming marriage. Since the date had been set Malolai had been cheerful and light-hearted and never lost patience. He only wished he could arrange his own life half so well.

His thoughts turned again to his indomitable mother. He had long ago decided that most Afghan men were mother dominated, despite the patriarchal character of the society. He wondered if that was one of the subconscious reasons why he had stayed in America. Bibi Hafizah didn't write letters. All the letters had come from his father and Ayub, and though they had always contained references to his mother like, "Your mother is pining because you refuse to visit," they had been easy to ignore against the backdrop of a busy life filled with medical school, ski weekends, and friendly American nurses who appreciated his wit and humor.

Again, he came back to the question, should he introduce Elizabeth to his mother and sister?

Maryam would love Elizabeth, and Elizabeth would be sure to take Maryam's part in the question of her marriage choice. Elizabeth had so far been sensitive to the different customs of Afghans, but she might very well alienate his mother on this issue.

And what would his mother think of him bringing home an American girl, after the fiasco of his first marriage? First marriage? He mulled the words over in his mind as he examined the badly healed tibia of a middle-aged man. Did that mean he was considering a second marriage? What did he have to offer Elizabeth or anyone else? The same quick wit and shallow charm he'd offered the young nurses in the ski lodges of Vermont? He hoped he'd grown since then, but sometimes he wondered.

Bibi Hafizah might even be hostile to Elizabeth. No, she would be the soul of courtesy, even if she disapproved. She'd be proud of the article, he thought irrelevantly, then divined the connection. She'd also be proud of the woman who had written it. It was the perfect excuse to introduce Elizabeth to her. Elizabeth was not his girlfriend, or even his friend, but simply "the journalist who wrote the article in the *New York Times*."

CHAPTER 37
YUSUF AND ELIZABETH

Peshawar

"**S**o this is the girl," said Bibi Hafizah in heavily accented English. "You are most welcome." The handsome, raven-haired woman embraced and kissed Elizabeth with sincere welcome.

"*Khosh shudam,*" murmured Elizabeth. She had learned a few words from Salima for the occasion. It translated roughly as "pleased to meet you," and had the desired effect.

Bibi Hafizah smiled broadly as Maryam greeted Elizabeth, and the American woman gracefully and naturally went through all the proper motions. "She's just like an Afghan girl," said Bibi Hafizah approvingly.

"Thank you," said Elizabeth. "Coming from an Afghan, that is a great compliment."

"Please sit down," said Bibi Hafizah, gesturing toward a mattress on the floor. Yusuf solicitously placed a large, soft pillow behind Elizabeth's back. It was a little uncomfortable, but she smiled. Yusuf sat down across the room from her, not saying a word.

"Please excuse us," said Bibi Hafizah. "We are poor refugees, we cannot offer you more."

"Please, I am honored to be here. Yusuf has told me so much about you. Both of you." Yusuf glanced at her with amusement. She actually knew very little about his mother.

"I am very impressed by the generosity of the Afghan people everywhere I've gone," continued Elizabeth. "People who have nothing, in Kunar and in the refugee camps I have visited, always insist on making me their guest. I guess I've learned something from it."

"I am glad."

There were a few moments of silence. Maryam seemed very shy, and quickly left the room, saying something about *chai*. Elizabeth examined the room. One bed, three thin mattresses on the floor, a small red Bukhara carpet in the middle, a few flowered cotton pillows that didn't match anything else. On the wall, a motif of Arabic letters carved in wood, which Elizabeth had seen often enough to know that it said, "In the name of God, the Compassionate, the Merciful, there is no God but God, and Mohammed is His Messenger."

"Something else just arrived today," said Yusuf to his mother. "Pictures in *Newsweek*." He produced the magazine from his medical bag.

Elizabeth watched apprehensively as Bibi Hafizah looked at the pictures long and without comment. Most were of the Mujahedeen. She turned the page and saw the picture of her son. A slow, proud smile lit her face.

"Better than the one in the *Times*," commented Yusuf.

"I'm sorry about that," said Elizabeth. "I just take the picture. It's the editor who chooses."

"And the camera doesn't lie?"

She merely smiled.

"These pictures are very good pictures," commented Bibi Hafizah. "I think you must be famous in America."

"Not at all. I make a living. And even that depends on luck and timing. They hadn't done their biannual article on Afghanistan yet, and it was cheaper and less risky to use my pictures than to send a staff photographer."

"You should be famous. My son also tells me you are a very brave girl."

She glanced at Yusuf, chagrined. "Been telling tales, eh? I don't think I did anything a lot of other people wouldn't have."

"You speak like my son. But humility is the essence of spirit."

Maryam brought in the tea. Elizabeth got up to help her serve, but Maryam protested. "You are a guest tonight. You sit, please."

"I feel useless!"

"A guest has only to be a guest," said Bibi Hafizah.

Elizabeth accepted a glass of tea, took a toffee, and turned the wrapped sweet over and over in her hands. She knew Bibi Hafizah was sizing her up, and it was an uncomfortable feeling. She decided on a direct, friendly offensive. "Where did you learn your English?" she asked sweetly.

"Oh, my English is not so good."

"No, really, I understand you very well."

"I lived in England for two years while my husband was training. I learned the language, but I was never able to be rid of this accent."

"Well, I understand everything you say."

"You have learnt some Persian?"

"Very little. But I am trying. Massoud's wife is my teacher. I'm also learning a little Pashtu."

"It is rare that anyone takes the trouble to learn," said Bibi Hafizah.

"After all, I am in your country. Or I was. We are foolish to expect the world to learn English."

"It's better than Russian," put in Maryam. They all laughed, and the awkwardness of new acquaintanceship vanished. When Maryam looked at her and winked, then rolled her eyes, Elizabeth knew they were going to be friends.

Elizabeth sipped her tea slowly, and smiled at Bibi Hafizah. "I must admit, you are younger than I expected," she said. "I know Yusuf is thirty-five, and I was sure his mother would have to be much older. You must have been very young when he was born."

Bibi Hafizah was visibly pleased. "Yusuf *jan*, where did you find such a charming girl!"

"She flatters everyone."

Elizabeth glared at him. "No, I…"

"I must apologize for my son's behavior. But after three weeks in Kunar, you must have come to know it well."

This time the laughter was at Yusuf's expense.

"How old are you?" asked Bibi Hafizah.

Here it comes. And not married. "Almost thirty, I'm afraid."

"You look younger, in your early twenties."

"Now look who is flattering!"

"Elizabeth was too smart to get married," said Yusuf.

Elizabeth felt her face burning, and flashed him a dirty look.

"I don't blame you," said Maryam. "There are many more important things to life."

Elizabeth had been warned. "But marriage too can be wonderful. I would love to get married, someday, to the right person." She looked frankly at Maryam, avoiding Yusuf's eyes. "It would have to be a very special person though. And someone very patient!"

"Do you want to get married soon?" asked Maryam.

"Oh, not too soon. I think I'll know when the time comes."

"You foreign people!" said Bibi Hafizah. "You wait too late. How will you have children when you leave it so late? I was married at fifteen, and Yusuf was born when I was sixteen. Now Maryam is already twenty-three, and I worry about her."

"You worry too much about everyone," cut in Yusuf quickly. "But that's the privilege of an Afghan mother. Many women in the West are marrying later these days, and having healthy babies right through their thirties."

She shook her head. "But when you get old you have much less energy to care for young children."

"You were twenty-eight when I was born, *Madar jan*," said Maryam. "So I still have five years."

"Maybe the war will be over by then," said Elizabeth. She had meant the remark hopefully, but it put an unintended damper on the conversation.

"Then the civil war will begin," said Maryam. "We will never accept the rule of the mullahs."

They all knew she had spoken a terrible truth. "But there has to be a middle way," said Elizabeth.

"Elizabeth is an optimist by nature," said Yusuf. "She doesn't know our people very well."

"Someone has to have hope," said his mother angrily. "And someone has to have the ideal not to harm his countrymen."

"Tell that to the people who tried to assassinate Massoud Khan," said Yusuf.

Bibi Hafizah stared at him in silence, her dark eyes burning.

"At least they will be Afghan problems," said Maryam softly. "The same ones we have always had. If we cannot unite in the face of a foreign aggressor, what will keep us united when we have vanquished the aggressor?"

"God will keep us united," said their mother. "We have a God, and the Russians do not."

"Our problem is interpreting that God," said Yusuf. "Do you, or Maryam, or Baba, agree with the interpretation of the Wahabis and the Muslim Brotherhood?"

"First our freedom, then we can discuss these things," cried Maryam.

"It seems," said Elizabeth deliberately, "that most of these problems can gradually be solved. Women like you, Maryam, and like Malolai, the nurse who works with Yusuf, will play an important part in changing your society once Afghanistan is free again. Surely the fundamentalists can't forget that women have sacrificed as much as men."

"You don't know our mullahs," said Yusuf. "Though to be fair, some are quite honest and a few even learned and broad-minded. The problem is really outside interference, radical interpretations of Islam foreign to Afghanistan seeping in with the arms and money."

"But if you really believe that the most right-wing fundamentalists will gain power, then aren't you fighting for nothing?"

"We have no choice," said Yusuf. "We play our part. And now you play yours as well."

"Are you talking about a fixed fate?"

"No, I think we do have choices, within reason. We're just happier when we make the morally right ones, even if they are hopeless choices."

"Do you feel hopeless?"

"I was in prison for six months," interrupted Maryam quietly. "Even there I was never hopeless."

Elizabeth was shocked, though Yusuf had mentioned his sister's imprisonment. "It must have been horrible."

The young woman nodded. "But I was not alone. I was doing it for God, for my family, and for my country. But not for the mullahs."

"Then all of your sacrifices must come to something, they must help bring about some change for the better."

"That is the way of human beings," said Bibi Hafizah, "to hope." She sighed deeply, and for a moment her face was lined. "But all my children, and my husband, are making sacrifices."

In the thick moment of tension in the room, Elizabeth realized Ayub was present in everyone's mind.

"*Ai, khoda mehrban ast,*" Bibi Hafizah murmured. She turned to Elizabeth. "God is great and kind, and knows all. Do you believe that?"

"I do believe in a compassionate God," she said carefully.

"What is your religion?"

Almost as bad as "Why not married?" "I don't really follow a specific religion. I believe all religions have some truth to them."

"So long as they are not practiced fanatically," said Maryam approvingly.

"Right."

"But what is the religion of your parents?" continued Bibi Hafizah.

"They are Roman Catholics."

"Are they religious?"

"My mother is. She is very active in church work and social work. My father…well, he's an honest man, but he doesn't feel the need to go to church much. Only on holidays."

"Do you go to church?"

"I pray in my heart, or in a church, or in the mountains, wherever I am."

"Do you know that Muslims, Christians, and Jews are all People of the Book?"

Elizabeth was surprised. "I had not heard this term before."

"They certainly don't act like it," scoffed Yusuf. "Especially in Palestine and Israel."

"If they read their Books, they might understand," said Bibi Hafizah severely. "We all believe in Allah, by different names, and we all have Books. Our Prophet, peace be upon him, has permitted our sons to marry the daughters of the Christians and the Jews."

Maryam laughed. "*Madar jan*, you are as literal as the mullahs! We should all marry whom we please."

Her mother looked at her sadly. Elizabeth recognized a familiar kind of emotional blackmail. She hoped she would get to know Maryam a little better, and that she could give her some emotional support, even if it meant crossing Bibi Hafizah, who did have a lovable side to her. Well, maybe not lovable. But she was admirable, an indomitable matriarch, a worthy mate to Commander Rahim. Their marriage had doubtless been arranged, and most likely she clung to its success as the justification for arranging a marriage for her only daughter, in firm denial that times and expectations had changed.

Bibi Hafizah appealed directly to Elizabeth. "See how my children have become? They have no respect for my opinions anymore. They have taken such terrible habits. This one has been in America for eighteen years, so what can I expect? But this girl, I don't know what to do with her."

"They love you very much," said Elizabeth reassuringly. "And they also respect you. But these are difficult times. I think you can be very proud of both your children." And broken-hearted and shamed by the third.

The older woman was slightly mollified. "You speak well. I hope you speak truly."

"As truly as I know how."

"Yusuf, she's a nice respectful girl. I wish you and Maryam could be more like her."

Elizabeth shot Maryam a glance and was relieved to see that Maryam didn't take the remark at all personally.

"If my opinion is of any value," said Elizabeth humbly, "I admire both Yusuf and Maryam. And you. You taught them their values."

Bibi Hafizah laughed delightedly. She was obviously a woman who loved flattery.

"Maryam," said Bibi Hafizah, "I think it is time to serve the dinner. We will sit and talk some more, as my son is never home, though he is now in Peshawar, and so he never has time to talk to his mother." She turned to her son. "Now, tell me how you arranged Malolai's wedding," she commanded him.

CHAPTER 38

ELIZABETH

Peshawar

The heavy gold-embroidered royal blue *dupata* kept slipping off Elizabeth's shoulders as she served the guests. The female portion of the wedding party was crowded into the salon of Massoud Khan's house, and the male portion was outside in the garden. The furniture had been removed to a servant's quarters in the back, and about forty women and children sat on the red Bukhara carpets, propped up by mirrored pillows.

As Elizabeth poured tea, she said a word of Farsi or Pashtu to each woman. What a colorful and varied group they made! There were modern women, like Salima and Maryam, dressed as she was in sleek, elegant silk *shalwar kameez*. Her own, the color of lapis lazuli, was newly made for the occasion. Salima had opted for turquoise and Maryam for white as a statement of mourning for those martyred in the *jehad*. A few other women, nurses and health workers from the Medical Association, were more simply attired in printed or solid cotton, but wore especially festive dupatas, brightly sequined or embroidered. The women of Sharif's family wore the traditional full-skirted tunic of Kunar over wide trousers made with yards of cloth. Glittery veils covered their heads but left their faces free to show their joy. Sharif's sisters wore heavy silver jewelry, while his mother wore gold bangles, earrings, necklace, and nose stud.

Sharif's mother reached for Elizabeth's arm as she passed, and tugged at her hand.

"*Staray mashay*," said Elizabeth. She tried to convey through gesture that she had lots of work to do, but the older woman cleared a space on the carpet beside her. Sharif's mother called to Maryam, who came across the room carrying a pot of tea.

Maryam smiled. "She says she is very glad to see you again, that you are a brave girl, and that her son has spoken well of you."

Sharif's mother went on at some length, laying a hand on Elizabeth's shoulder and gesturing emphatically. Elizabeth watched her as she spoke, marveling at the strength of character of these Afghan matriarchs.

"She says Sharif thinks of you as a sister, and therefore you are as a daughter to her," Maryam summarized.

Elizabeth was touched. "*Mehrbani*."

"She apologizes that you can't see a real Afghan wedding. She says you must understand we are refugees now, we have become poor. It is only by the grace of God that Massoud Khan and his father have been so kind as to offer Massoud's home for the wedding."

"Tell her that Sharif is one of Massoud's bravest Mujahedeen, and that Massoud really loves him and wanted to give the best gift he could for the wedding. Tell her she should never apologize for anything, for she and her family have given me generous hospitality in difficult times."

As Maryam translated, tears started in the old woman's eyes. Elizabeth was always amazed at how openly sentimental most Afghans were. Being prone to open displays of emotion herself, she felt at ease with them. Her friendship with Salima and her newfound friendship with Maryam had given her a feeling of sisterhood she had never known before, even with most of her American girlfriends. She loved the easy familiarity and natural physical affection of the

Afghan women. Traditionally there had been strength and encouragement in this support. It was all they had had.

"Tell her I am happy for her today," said Elizabeth, putting a hand on the woman's shoulder and rising. Sharif's mother kissed her hand and smiled, then spoke again.

"She says you are very beautiful in this dress, but your heart is more beautiful."

"*Mehrbani.*"

Elizabeth apologized, saying she must go and serve more tea and sweets. More women had arrived, and despite the air conditioner, the air in the room was growing heavy in the sultry late May heat. *Rebab* music played on the stereo, but barely rose over the buzz of conversation. Elizabeth went to the kitchen for another pot of tea and ran into Salima, who looked cool and unharassed even while supervising the whole operation.

"You must rest," Salima scolded. "You should not be doing so much work."

"I want to," protested Elizabeth. "For Malolai."

"Then go into my room and talk to her. She is very nervous. Maryam and I and the servants can serve the tea." Salima sighed. "I wish we could do more. In better times, we would have had musicians too. But because Sharif's mother and sisters are in *purdah* now, we can't have musicians."

"Salima, they won't expect Malolai to follow *purdah* now, will they?"

"That is Sharif's decision. But I think he and Malolai have already discussed it. How could she keep *purdah* when she is a nurse and the people need her?"

Elizabeth was relieved. "He won't go back on his word?"

"Sharif may not be educated, but he is open-minded. This war is changing the way of thinking of some, and making others more stubborn and rigid. Now go to Malolai, and I will try to come later."

Elizabeth walked through the hall, where a pile of *burqas* and *chadars* lay in a heap on the table, and knocked softly on the bedroom door. It opened a crack, and Bibi Hafizah peeped out, then welcomed her. Malolai sat on the bed, dressed in a full-skirted tunic of red velvet, red *shalwar*, and a red silk veil bordered with heavy gold embroidery.

Her slippers were likewise embroidered with gold thread, and her arms were weighted down with golden bangles and rings. Her hair, which was too short for the traditional braids, was tucked under the veil, with a few dark curls brought forward from under a skullcap, to which an antique silver ornament, studded with carnelian, was pinned.

Malolai giggled. "I feel so nervous! I am shy."

Elizabeth hugged her carefully. "Don't be. You look beautiful."

"So do you. That is a good color for you."

"Salima gave me the silk. She does too much for me."

"She does too much for everyone. I am so ashamed. My cousin has been able to do so little. Most of this is from Massoud Khan and Mohammed Akbar, and Yusuf's dear family."

"It is because they want to do it," Elizabeth reassured her. "Besides, your cousin has provided most of the food, and Sharif's family has given you clothes and jewelry."

Malolai bowed her head under the heavy veil, weeping softly. "I never thought it would be like this."

"No, be happy! You're marrying a wonderful man. These other things don't matter."

The young bride looked up, surprised. "No, not these surface things. But freedom. I miss my brother, my aunts and uncles and other cousins. And I miss my country."

Bibi Hafizah put a hand on Malolai's knee. "I will be her mother today. I am happy to be her mother."

Elizabeth sat next to Malolai on the bed. "Sharif is such a good man. This is what I dreamed of for you when I first saw that you two cared for each other. You're so lucky! Sharif is really handsome."

Malolai blushed and giggled nervously. "I hope I will be a good wife. I hope I will do all the right things today at the ceremony."

"And afterwards?" Elizabeth teased.

"It is simple," said Bibi Hafizah to Elizabeth. "She can't do wrong things."

"Would you like to be dressed like this at your wedding?" asked Malolai, mischievousness creeping into her eyes.

Elizabeth laughed. "It looks better on you. Do all Afghan girls dress this way?"

"Oh, no. This is a traditional Pashtun dress. Salima probably wore a white gown, like you do in America, and Massoud probably wore a suit. If I had been married in Kabul I would have worn a white gown also. But it is good to be traditional now, since we are not in our country and have lost so much."

A knock at the door; it was Salima's voice. Bibi Hafizah called to her to enter. Salima shut the door behind her. She looked radiant, as if it were her own wedding. "The food will be served soon," she said. "Elizabeth, will you eat in here with Malolai?"

"Of course."

"I don't think I can eat at all," said Malolai.

"Bibi Hafizah, please make her eat something, or she may faint!" said Salima.

The older woman nodded, looking fondly at the girl.

"Elizabeth, you don't mind? Maryam and I must help serve. Eat, and then come and wait for the bride and groom to come in."

A servant brought mounds of *pilau* with sweetened carrots, raisins, pine nuts, and slivers of almonds mixed in. Buried under the rice were tender, juicy chunks of lamb. There was a dish of eggplant and tomato in yogurt and garlic sauce, and *bolani*, a mixture of spices and chopped leeks stuffed in fried triangles of thin dough.

Bibi Hafizah coaxed Malolai to eat, but the young woman alternately laughed and refused, finally forcing down a little rice. Elizabeth realized that her friend must be anticipating, perhaps fearing, her first experience of sex as well as the radical change of married life. All the ritual had once been intended to help a girl become a woman and a boy become a man, to ease the passage to the full responsibilities of adulthood.

Elizabeth thought of her own first sexual experience at the University of Pennsylvania, with a boy she had thought she loved. She had been nineteen, he twenty. She'd lost her virginity relatively late for her era. And she'd had only her roommate to share the news with. No rituals, just a Chinese meal and an illicit glass of wine back at the dorm. She'd been happy then. But the relationship had soon fallen apart, and the boy had betrayed her. This first experience of lost love had outraged her liberalized but still Catholic sensibility. She certainly didn't believe in waiting until marriage, as long as you really cared about a person. That was hypocritical, frustrating, and nobody did that anymore. But she had expected a little commitment.

She'd fallen in love a few more times before she met Tom, and she'd been dumped a few more times. Tom had been the biggest con artist, she thought with a flash of anger. And she would have married him in a minute had he asked. She'd been faithful to him, with no great difficulty, for five years. And she'd been celibate since the breakup.

She looked at Malolai with a kind of envy. Malolai's decisions about sex had been made easy by lack of choice. She didn't have to decide if and when to sleep with someone. Maybe it was easier for Afghan men too. Some probably went with prostitutes, and others just sublimated their desires until marriage. The less choice, the simpler life becomes. But we've eaten of the tree, we've made our choice, or our surroundings have made it for us. No going back to the simple life.

The surrounding culture really did affect a person, thought Elizabeth. If she had met Yusuf in New York she almost certainly would have made love to him by now. Though she suddenly wondered if she would have been attracted to who he would have been in New York. But here, among morally conservative Afghans, she didn't feel free to respond so spontaneously. Maybe it was a good thing. It had kept her out of trouble. She'd been accepted by his sister, even his mother. Perhaps Yusuf would just end up as a dear friend, and all of the roses and longing would fade away.

They had eaten in silence. Elizabeth had enjoyed her food immensely. Now Maryam came to the door and summoned Elizabeth to the salon, where she found a place in a corner next to Salima. The children, who had been running around excitedly, now became hushed with expectancy.

There was a fusillade of shot. Elizabeth gasped and grabbed Salima's arm. "What was that?"

Salima laughed nervously. "Nothing. It startled me too. But it is our tradition to fire guns when the groom arrives."

More shots, at close range, and then the sound of voices coming into the hall. It seemed an interminable time until the door opened and Sharif and Malolai entered the room slowly, Korans wrapped in golden cloth held above their heads. Malolai looked downwards, shy, as befitted an Afghan bride, but allowed a glance to catch Elizabeth's eyes.

Massoud Khan was in the group, as was Yusuf, his mother, his sister, and Malolai's cousin. Bibi Hafizah, as promised, took the place of Malolai's mother in the rituals. For this part of the ceremony, the male guests crowded into the room, standing well separated from the women.

Sharif looked proud and spotless in a simple white *shalwar kameez* topped with a red velvet vest richly embroidered with gold. A white turban crowned his long black hair, the end hanging down in front of his left shoulder.

An elderly mullah with a gray beard and a powder blue turban accompanied them. He looked impressive in his long white robe, and his kindly face was wise and reassuring, completely opposite to the young fanatic who had accused Elizabeth of being a KGB agent.

The ceremony seemed chaotic to Elizabeth, not at all like the carefully choreographed rituals of the Catholic church. The mullah said some words to the couple and leaned toward each of them in turn. The Koran was passed over both of their heads. A dark mud was applied to the right little finger of both bride and groom, and small triangles of silver cloth tied fast over the mud. "Henna," whispered Salima. "For luck."

Sharif's younger brother produced a velvet box, and the couple exchanged rings, then sipped juice, one holding the glass while the other drank. "Sherbet," said Salima, then "*halwa*," as Sharif took a small scoop from a mound of sticky sweet paste on a silver plate and fed Malolai. Then the ceremony appeared to be over. Elizabeth couldn't really tell. People's attention seemed to be drifting, and people had started talking to each other. The bride and groom relaxed and sat in two chairs draped with red cloth, smiling at each other.

"Time for tea and *halwa*," said Salima, getting up. She pinched Elizabeth's arm. "Maybe you'll be the next."

Yusuf took the seat Salima had vacated. "So, what do you think of our weddings?"

"I'm not sure I know what's going on. But the food is delicious and I'm happy for Malolai and Sharif."

They gazed at the happy couple as people crowded around them with congratulations and Massoud took photographs of family and friends.

"Elizabeth," called Malolai. "You and Yusuf with us. Sharif"s request, and I also would like it."

Elizabeth protested, but Yusuf grabbed her hand and dragged her to stand behind the bride and groom. Elizabeth felt self-conscious and wouldn't look at Yusuf. She was glad to escape to an inconspicuous corner, where Yusuf again sat next to her.

"Embarrassed to be seen with me?" he asked casually.

"What? Of course not."

"Just wondering."

He stared at the bride and groom, a smile fixed on his face. He glanced at her sideways, looked back at Sharif and Malolai, and sighed in agitation.

"Elizabeth, would you like to get married this way?"

"I don't look good in red."

"Yes you do."

She realized he was looking at her and forced herself to look back. What she saw terrified her. "Is this a proposal?" she asked, laughing.

"Yes."

He looked at her steadily and she abruptly stopped laughing. "What do you mean?"

"You know what I mean. I love you and I want to marry you."

"You've got to be kidding." As soon as she said it, she knew she was not communicating well.

His face grew tight with hurt. "Forgive me. I see you don't feel the same way." He got up to go.

She pulled him back down beside her. "Wait a minute. I didn't say that. It's just…it's so sudden."

"It's not sudden. I realize now that I loved you the minute I saw you. I loved your courage and strength, and your compassion."

"Oh, Yusuf, there is so much I admire in you also. But how can we talk of marriage? We hardly know each other."

"Neither did Malolai and Sharif."

"But I'm not Afghan."

"And I am. Is that the final difference?"

She was confused, and was growing angry at him for having broached the subject now. "I won't be forced into a decision!"

"You won't be. I see you've already made up your mind."

"No, wait! You don't understand. I just don't want to rush into something that will change my whole life."

"If you wanted to, you wouldn't have hesitated. Please forgive me for having spoken out of turn. And don't tell anyone. It would be a disgrace for my family." He got up quickly.

"Yusuf, I do love you, if it makes any difference," she said to his back. It was the first time she had said it, and she didn't know whether he had heard or not.

PART II

AUTUMN, 1988

CHAPTER 39

YUSUF

September, 1988

Amrau Tangay

Yusuf pulled the crumpled air mail envelope from his pocket and held it in the beam of light that slanted through the doorway of his Amrau Tangay house. The postmark was smudged, but he could just make out the words, "Bethlehem, PA" and a date, "July 22."

The address was written in a flowing, artistic script, leaning markedly toward the right. "Dr. Yusuf Hakim, c/o Massoud Khan." Massoud's address, neatly written. And scrawled to the left of the address, "Massoud, please see that Yusuf gets this." After all these years he remembered the handwriting of the American journalist he had fallen in love with.

Massoud Khan had sent the letter by the hand of Sharif, who had just arrived back in Kunar this afternoon. Yusuf was busy at the time, and had stuffed the envelope in his pocket after a cursory glance. He knew very well who it was from, though he couldn't believe she would suddenly be contacting him after over four years. With some effort of will he had put the distracting thought out of his mind.

Now he sat heavily on the *charpoy* nearest the door, debating with himself. Should be tear up the letter right now, without ever opening it?

Curiosity was stronger than caution. Resolutely, he tore open the envelope, vowing to ignore the letter if it contained anything he didn't like.

The letter was handwritten in the same graceful script as the address, full of flourishes, but not without humor. He was glad it wasn't just typed and printed out on a computer. With a pang he realized that even her handwriting still reminded him of her. It was delicate and strong at the same time. He hesitated again, then plunged into the letter.

Bethlehem, Pennsylvania
July 20th, 1988

My Dearest Yusuf,

Forgive me if I call you that, and forgive me if it sounds strange to you after the months of silence that have somehow grown into years. You may not realize it, and maybe I didn't before either, but distance and time have made me aware that you are indeed dear to me, whether or not I ever see you again. In English they say, "absence makes the heart grow fonder," but then they also say "out of sight, out of mind." I don't know which is true for you, but in my case I have grown fonder of you since that last horrible day at dear Malolai's wedding. I have no idea how you feel. Perhaps you have long since forgotten me. I am distant, and perhaps therefore I no longer exist for you.

So much has happened in these years. I know only that you are still there in Kunar, helping your people. But perhaps we will soon have a chance to catch up in person. Surprise! I always told you I would come back to Afghanistan, and now I have definite plans to come back in September or October (inshallah). And I want to come back to Kunar, to Amrau Tangay if you'll have me.

If you'd rather I didn't come, I will ask you to get a message to me through Massoud Khan. I expect to reach Peshawar between September 15th and 20th. Since I have to make my travel plans through Massoud anyway, I can decide at that time whether to come to Kunar or to go somewhere else (I'm on a definite assignment this time). If I don't hear from you, I'll assume you don't object to my coming, and I'll go ahead and make plans.

Clever woman, he thought. She's trying to force me to answer. He smiled in spite of himself, and read on.

It's both harder and easier to speak to you in a letter. You can't answer back to me, and yet I miss seeing your responses and looking at your eyes. I know I behaved badly the last time I saw you. I didn't mean to act like I didn't take your proposal seriously, but you caught me off guard. I laughed because I didn't know what else to do, I was so shocked. But it really wasn't fair of you to expect an instant answer! I never did say no, by the way, I just didn't say yes.

So much has happened in these intervening years, and yet I have never forgotten you. Would you believe me if I told you I haven't been with anyone else since I met you? Sure I've dated, but everybody always seemed to fall short when I thought of you. It's silly, I suppose, but I have a real longing to see you again, to spend time with you, to get to know you and let you get to know me. I would like to know you, whether as a dear friend, or...???

His heart beat faster, with great confusion, a little anger, and more than a little love and desire. Clearly, though his days allowed little time for reminiscence during the years of war, he had not forgotten her either. He turned the thin blue page quickly.

It's the middle of summer here now, and very muggy. I've been based in Pennsylvania, near my parents, ever since I returned from Afghanistan. I came back to find my dad had been diagnosed with colon cancer and my brother Mark with AIDS. Mom and I have had our hands full. Dad went through chemo and is doing really well now. Mark, unfortunately, died of AIDS about a year ago.

Dad's illness and Mark's death have brought the remainder of our family closer together. I decided I didn't want to live in New York anymore. I just didn't fit in, and I wanted to be close to home when I wasn't traveling. My career, by the way, has gone well, and I've traveled a lot and done a lot of interesting stories, but had the freedom to stay home when Dad was so ill from the cancer treatment and later when Mark was dying.

All this resulted in a lot of thinking, and also a lot of poetry. I've published a small chat book called Those Who Walk the Line Between Life and Death. I will bring a copy for you when I come.

I have my own apartment, but I spend a lot of time at my folks' house, where I am right now. I enjoy the peace and quiet of the little frame house with the Colonial style furniture and the upright piano in the living room. I go up to the cabin in the Poconos with my folks and some friends most weekends, and Dad has let me stay up there on and off so I could work on some of my stories and poetry.

This year we had a great old traditional 4th of July, with hot dogs, Cokes, hamburgers, and fireworks. A couple of my old friends from school came up. They're all married now, a lot of them married to each other, and they're involved in raising children and "socially smoking" marijuana. An odd combination, but that's Bethlehem. I'm just about the only one who never married (I just say I never met the right man, but that's not quite true). They all think I'm crazy for going off to foreign wars and famines and going to South Africa to write about AIDS. But they tolerate me for old times' sake.

I doubt if most of them know where Afghanistan is, even now. A girl I've known since first grade asked if it was in Africa. Sometimes I feel that no one understands me. Mark did, but he's gone now. It was like losing a best friend as well as a brother. When I told him about you he told me to follow my heart, and quoted from The Little Prince, "It is only with the heart that one can see rightly; what is essential is invisible to the eye."

I had every intention of coming back to see you four years ago in the fall, but then life happened and it wasn't as planned. Dad got sick, Mark got diagnosed, and there never was a good time to go.

But Afghanistan was a life-changing experience, more than any other place I have been. Oh Yusuf, was it Afghanistan, or you, or both? Something changed me irrevocably. I was always perfectly happy living in the States before, though of course I always liked to travel. And I really used to love living in New York. But now so much has gone dead for me. Have I expanded my horizons too much?

You once told me that Hermann Hesse had said something like: "Home is in the heart, or it is nowhere." I think, after all this time, my heart may be in Afghanistan. But I'm not sure if I could live in Afghanistan, even a free Afghanistan. I've only seen it in time of war. You and Salima have told me what Kabul was like before, but it won't be like that again, ever. I'd love to explore all of Afghanistan, to see the deserts, the mountains, the lakes of Band-i-Amir, the giant Buddhas of Bamiyan, and the mosques at Mazar-i-Sharif and Herat, if any of these treasures survive this endless war. But could I live in Kabul during reconstruction? Maybe. Maybe a few months there, a few months here.

I never contacted you because I didn't want to complicate your life. I couldn't imagine either of us living in Bethlehem, or even New York or San Francisco. I just couldn't see how a marriage could work out between us.

It's been a long time, and maybe your heart is with someone else. Salima tells me only that you have not married, that you are married to the jehad. I wonder what you will do when it's over, if it will be over?

I hope this reaches you in time to allow you to answer, if you wish, one way or the other. Meanwhile, if it means anything to you at all now, know that you are always in my heart, and that a good part of my heart is there with you now. I'm sorry for hurting you. I think you have a pure and compassionate heart, and this makes you the rarest of gems.

I am waiting, hoping, for the chance to see you again. I hope at the very least we will be the best of friends. Till then, be careful.

It was signed, "Love, Elizabeth," but her signature appeared shaky and uncertain. The "E" was large and the rest of the name small, smaller even than her writing in the body of the letter. It was clear that sending this letter had been an act of faith.

He visualized her sitting outside a small frame house in Pennsylvania. Maybe a summer storm brewing, gray-black thunderheads gathering, a light breeze stirring leaves the full green of the season. She'd be sitting on the back porch, drinking lemonade, or maybe a can of diet soda. He realized he had no idea what she liked. And what were her parents like? What did they think of their daughter going to Afghanistan by herself, especially after they'd lost their only son to AIDS? What would they think if she did marry an Afghan, a Muslim?

Maybe she'd been right to hesitate. Maybe her parents were narrow-minded and would never approve. Janet's parents hadn't, but Janet hadn't particularly cared as she wasn't close to them. Elizabeth might be far more concerned for her parents' feelings, especially after all they'd gone through as a family. Clearly it had not been her fate to marry him when he'd asked four years ago. She was needed back home and would have been in terrible conflict if she'd committed herself to him then.

But if a few weeks in Afghanistan four years ago had made such an impression on her that she felt estranged from her childhood friends, what would those friends think if she showed up at a 4th of July picnic with an Afghan husband? But then Elizabeth must always have been different, or she never would have come to Afghanistan in the first place.

Yusuf shook his head. Where in the world was there a place for a woman like Elizabeth, or for a man like him? They had crossed a line that made them different from the society of their respective births, and yet neither could fully belong to any other culture.

A pang gripped his heart when he thought of the last time he'd seen her. Four years, but it felt like a moment ago. It had been her birthday. She hadn't given him a chance to say anything about that. He'd had a ring in his pocket, an engagement ring. He'd really expected her to accept his proposal, then and there. He'd made a fool out of himself. For her sake and his own, he was glad he hadn't told anyone of his intentions, especially his mother. The shame of rejection had been his alone.

Yet he felt guilty. He must have spoiled her birthday and spoiled Malolai's wedding for her when he had left so abruptly. He'd intended it all to be such a nice surprise, but in his self-concern had misread her responses.

His cheeks burned at the memory. It must have been awkward for her to explain to Massoud and Salima why Yusuf wasn't coming around any more. Knowing her, she'd handled it coolly. Her work had been finished by then and she had intended to fly home soon anyway. He'd heard that she left Peshawar three days later, just before the month of fasting began.

And he hadn't heard another word until this letter. So often he had thought of writing to her, but pride had stopped him, and then life got busy in the long years of war and hope and despair and hope again.

He remembered how, against his mother's strenuous objections, he had left that next morning for Kunar. He'd worked with only Ismail for a few weeks while Malolai and Sharif had gotten to know each other in the little house in Bajaur. One baking afternoon in the middle of June the two had walked up the path. They had set up housekeeping in the dispensary. Whenever Sharif was off with the Mujahedeen, Malolai resumed her arrangement with the village family.

Malolai was joyous when her husband was in Amrau Tangay, calm and stoic when he was at the front, busy at all times with their growing son, Hakim. Sharif had asked her if she wished to remain with his mother and sisters in the safety of Bajaur, but had not pressured her even after their child was born. She insisted that they had been safe at Amrau Tangay for all these years, and if they were not, it was the will of Allah.

Sharif was proud of his wife's work, proud of her courage and stubbornness. Her staying in the village to work as a nurse, and his granting her permission to do so, was a strong act of defiance of the mullahs, who seemed to be growing ever more powerful with the help and support of their foreign friends. Yusuf frowned, thinking of the so-called Mujahedeen from Saudi Arabia and Pakistan and other countries, long-bearded men with fanaticism in their eyes and disapproval in their expressions, not defending hearth, home, culture and love from alien invaders as the Afghans were, but holding on to some vision of a pan-Islamic state ruled by those who literally interpreted the *shariat* law.

And this was just as alien to Afghanistan as Soviet-style Communism, thought Yusuf. And like the old saying, it too would pass.

The Afghans were the ones who would stay here, fighting for their homes and their way of life. Sharif loved to have a real home to return to after time at the front. Yusuf would watch with well-concealed pangs of envy as Malolai would cook for her husband, wash his clothes, and massage his aching muscles. Maybe every Mujaheed needed this extra reason to fight.

But Malolai hadn't needed an extra reason. Our women are our real strength, thought Yusuf. We men are like little children sometimes, enjoying risk without thinking of possible consequences. Women had a much stronger sense of preservation of the species, continuation of the race. They were cannier, more careful, and in the end more firmly rooted than their menfolk. They were the nurturers who kept an ember alive in their breasts, in mountains, in *sangars*, in deserted villages, and in the camps in Pakistan. They were the guardians of hearth and heart, the last line of defense.

He was still staring down at the letter when a figure blocked the sunlight.

"Yusuf," said Malolai, "Come to us and eat. I have cooked."

He started guiltily and folded the letter quickly.

"From Elizabeth?" she asked.

He nodded brusquely, inwardly cursing women's intuition.

"We have not heard from her in years. I thought she had forgotten us."

"Apparently not."

"How is she?"

"Fine. Very well." Except for her terrible losses, but how could he presume to speak of those?

"What does she say?"

"She might come in September. Then you can ask her everything yourself."

"Here?" she cried excitedly.

"Yes, I think she will come. *Inshallah.*"

CHAPTER 40
AYUB

September, 1988

Chagaserai

Ayub was getting tired of conflicting reports. With the completion of the Soviet withdrawal scheduled for mid-February – *if* the Soviets abided by the Geneva Accords – the war continued to rage in a pattern of chaos and confusion. On the one hand, many of the villages in Kunar had grown quiescent. Of course there weren't very many people left in a lot of the villages. The number of Afghans on all sides who had lost their lives in nearly a decade of war did not bear thinking about.

On the other hand, there seemed to be constant harassment by small, well-armed commando groups. The riff-raff seemed to be better armed by the damned Americans and Pakistanis than ever before, which as far as Ayub was concerned violated the spirit of the Geneva Accords, and were shooting down a shocking number of gunships with newly supplied Stinger missiles. That in turn caused the Soviets to carpet bomb whole regions, turning the conflict more and more into a brutal war of attrition, not unlike the situation on the West Bank.

He read today's depressing batch of reports while sipping *doorgh* in his garden, sitting in the shade of a mulberry tree. The tree's fruit was ripe, and occasionally a sticky black mulberry dropped onto his table, even onto his sheaf of reports. The fruit was so ripe that it would splatter, leaving a dark, red-purple streak, rather like dried blood, before falling to the ground.

Much of the country's infrastructure had been destroyed, and would need to be rebuilt. But Ayub had his doubts that the People's Democratic Party of Afghanistan could hold on to power in the near vacuum that was likely to result, and shivered at the thought of the alternatives. Civil war or rule by fanatical mullahs and their foreign supporters? What was it they said in America, Tweedledee or Tweedledum? Perhaps the Scylla and Charybdis metaphor was at least more classical.

Lermontov seemed much more detached of late, and oddly cheerful for a representative of a country that was effectively losing a war and retreating, despite the good face they were trying to put on it. The Russian general spoke a great deal of home and family and plans for summers at his *dacha* outside Moscow, and less of politics and power. Everyone was weary. Perhaps this was a good thing, and those who had survived this far would be able to survive the new era of so-called peace and victory, and even reconcile with each other.

Contrary to Ayub's expectation or at least hope, the Geneva Accords had not slowed down the war. Perhaps emboldened by the fact that the Soviets were now actually negotiating with them, the rebels continued their relentless attacks with their ever more sophisticated CIA-provided arms. But there were serious food shortages in many areas, and fuel shortages threatened, especially in Kabul, as winter approached. Ayub thought cynically of the American dictum in Vietnam, "It was necessary to destroy the village in order to save it." He wondered if Lermontov and his cronies back in Moscow thought the same about the whole nation of Afghanistan. If it was "Brezhnev's war," as the new Gorbachev leadership seemed to be eager to characterize it, then why was it continuing after the peace agreement was signed?

He sighed and tapped his fingers impatiently on the reports. His personal information sources had dried up almost entirely. He'd never again had an informant as good as Najeeb Khan. He had tried over and over again to cultivate that kind of loyalty and efficiency in another man, and had spent a lot of both government and personal money in the attempt. But everyone he groomed seemed to be a double agent in the end, and in hindsight Ayub wondered if Najeeb had been too. After all, he'd provided wrong information in the affair of that American woman journalist that his brother was dallying with a few years ago.

Luckily, she'd never returned to Afghanistan and Yusuf had lain low, quietly serving the population from the same Amrau Tangay base. His father, on the other hand, had cleverly played cat and mouse with the Soviets. Sometimes Ayub had wondered if he'd taken his commando group to other provinces and was operating under other names. Then suddenly he'd hear something about the famous Kunari Commander Rahimullah Khan being back, and there would be an act of terrorism against a government post, or a helicopter would be shot down, or a loyalist would be kidnapped.

It was all so confusing. Lermontov, who on and off had appeared to have excellent sources of information about the rebels – with the sole exception of Commander Rahim's top-secret group – had delicately suggested that Ayub set up his own intelligence network as the Soviet friends of the revolution prepared to leave. Lermontov had also implied that the Afghan government would fall within weeks if the Soviet troops indeed pulled out in the next few months.

Ayub had bristled and loyally claimed that the Afghan Army was capable of handling its own affairs, from intelligence to security. But to himself he acknowledged that Lermontov was right. The Red Army would leave its loyal Afghan allies to the tender mercies of the rebels, as the Americans had left the South Vietnamese when they so ignominiously evacuated from the roof of the American Embassy in Saigon not that many years ago.

Once again, the Afghans were the pawns of the Great Powers, as they had been for centuries. Where was it all going to end? Would the Afghans be able to stop fighting and work together after all these years of war? Would America and Russia again start acting like ardent suitors, building a road here, a school or airport or dam there?

Ayub's thoughts turned once again to his brother. He must be busy, between rebel and civilian casualties, since carpet bombing had intensified with the prospect of Soviet military might abandoning the country. With no reliable spy, Ayub had had no news for a long time. He wondered how often his brother left the relative safety of the clinic. Perhaps he came down into the valley whenever there was a major bombardment.

After that fiasco of the big piece in the *New York Times* a few years ago, the media had been quiet about Yusuf. To his relief, Lermontov had dismissed the article as "typical capitalist propaganda" and had opined that the people of the Third World could see through a media controlled by multi-nationals and moneyed interests. Ayub wondered which was worse, a corporate-controlled media or one directly controlled by a totalitarian government.

Ayub had been relieved that the American woman hadn't written anything about the doctor's brother being Governor of Kunar. Strangely enough, no other journalist had written anything about Yusuf or his clinic, despite the rebels' overt hunger for publicity. The Western press seemed to be obsessing on other subjects, thought Ayub. He hadn't heard of much on Afghanistan at all except for that piece with Dan Rather dressed up in a turban. Despite himself he broke into a smile at the thought.

Ayub felt great resentment against his father for choosing the wrong side in this war, though it might ultimately be the winning side. He had secret fantasies of capturing his father. Sometimes at night, when he couldn't sleep, he thought out complicated strategies for tricking the old man into surrender, trapping him in a situation from which he could not escape. Ayub would achieve great status by removing the terrorist scourge from the Kunar Valley. This would put an impeccable seal on his loyalty, and ensure that he could get into any Ph.D. program he wished at a prestigious Soviet university.

Oh, ultimately he would show mercy to his own father, of course. Once he'd neutralized the commando unit, Lermontov and his cohorts would be so grateful that they would allow Ayub his one wish, as in a mythical tale: to spare the life of his father. He just had to come up with a way of capturing the old man alive.

He tilted his head back and looked up at the blazing sky. Belying the season, it was still the pale blue of summer bleached by a white and indifferent sun. Suddenly he missed his mother and sister terribly. No news for so long. He was alone in the world now. He'd pulled strings to get Maryam out of Pul-e-Charkhi, and she'd never even thanked him. She and their mother had disappeared immediately afterwards, as he'd known in his heart they would.

He supposed they must be in Pakistan. Or maybe Yusuf had gotten them an American visa. But knowing Bibi Hafizah and the steely strength she had imparted to her daughter, they were still in Peshawar. Bibi Hafizah wouldn't live halfway across the world from her husband. And Maryam was a real firebrand. But what did Islamic revolution have to offer a girl like Maryam? Obviously she thought it was a preferable alternative to…to what? To foreign rule? How had this foreign rule become part and parcel of the socialist revolution? It had been a national democratic revolution, he corrected himself, lacking a mass base. The Russians had to come in to defend us from feudal counter-revolutionaries. And if Afghanistan were ever to move forward, this revolution could not be allowed to be reversed.

At least that's what the Soviets had said. Ayub and many of his compatriots in the People's Democratic Party of Afghanistan had come to suspect other motives as what they had secretly begun referring to as "the occupation" had dragged on. There were now sophisticated Soviet air bases in Nimroz, in the south, within striking distance of Persian Gulf oilfields. Rumor, though notoriously unreliable in Afghanistan, had it that there were missile bases up in Wakhan, in the high mountain pastures bordering China.

Would the Soviets really keep their commitment to pull out? Ayub sighed as he finished his now-warm glass of yogurt drink. Maybe this damn war would finally end. He had hoped for a cease-fire during the summer as the endless peace talks dragged on. It was so hard on the men to fight in the heat, and he felt pity for them, especially for the Red Army boys. Other than the ferocious Spetznats, the equivalent of the American Special Forces, most of the soldiers were young conscripts, still teenagers or in their early twenties. Many were European Russians, unused to the dry oven that Central Asia became in summer.

Ayub knew that they'd taken more and more casualties, and that fearful stories of mutilations were passed around the barracks. On the BBC he'd heard that there was increasing unrest in the Soviet Union due to too many young men coming back in body bags or missing limbs. They were even starting to have problems with what used to be called shell shock and now had some fancy name like Post Traumatic Stress Disorder. American Vietnam veterans had even gone to meet with Soviet Afghan veterans in Moscow, discussing the horrors of fighting a guerrilla enemy.

And the condition of the Red Army bases was deplorable. Ayub wrinkled his nose distastefully at the memory of his visit to a Russian base, intended to boost morale by showing the friendship troops that the Afghan people were grateful for their support. It had been all he could do not to vomit at the stench of the latrines ripening in the heat. A good number of the men had been down with various diseases endemic to Central Asia, primarily some form of simple diarrhea, but he also knew that many had been sent home with debilitating cases of hepatitis. Perhaps these were the lucky ones.

Soviet Uzbeks and Tajiks were far more accustomed to the harsh conditions of Central Asia, but years ago it had been recognized that they had proved unreliable soldiers. Some traded ammunition for Korans in the bazaars. A few had even deserted to the rebels and taken up conservative forms of Islam.

It must be hell for those boys to fight against an enemy they can't see, thought Ayub. He knew the rugged mountains of his land, and knew that if a party of men were firing from the shelter of a ridge, it was close to impossible to neutralize their positions without collateral damage. Ayub wasn't surprised that a lot of the soldiers were smoking hashish, even getting hooked on opium and its derivatives. He was in a position to know that a certain percentage of the Russian troops regularly smoked an unrefined form of heroin. Ayub also knew that his countrymen were clever enough to capitalize on the occupying force's hunger for one of Afghanistan's oldest exports.

It was a stalemate, he thought angrily, and it had been ever since the Russians sent in their troops and overthrew Comrade Amin at the end of 1979. This was a chess game that could never be won. Fewer and fewer players remained on the board, and Ayub wondered if it would come down to two symbolic kings, the Soviet Union and the United States, facing each other off on the board of his country, devoid of the annoyance of an actual population.

He had already applied for that Ph.D. program in International Relations that he'd fantasized about, and hoped he'd have his acceptance letter and visa before the pullout was completed and all hell broke loose.

To whose hands would the blood stick when it was all over? An awful lot of blood had been spilled, and the survivors would be angry. There was an old Afghan tradition of blood revenge, and Ayub doubted the mullahs would counsel mercy. Suddenly the future loomed dark as the coming winter.

Ayub closed the report he had been staring at, but not reading. A sudden gust of cool breeze shook the boughs above his head, causing a fat mulberry to drop and splat on the cover of his file. He brushed it away in annoyance, but the stain remained.

CHAPTER 41
ELIZABETH

Arriving at Amrau Tangay

Elizabeth reveled in the gold coolness of the mountain autumn. Today, *inshallah*, they would reach Amrau Tangay and she would at last see Yusuf. He had not replied to her letter, and she had no idea of the reception she would get. She wondered if anyone had warned him of her impending arrival, or if she would surprise him.

She had come a different route this time, crossing the Durand Line in the north and passing through the foothills of Nuristan. The summer's scorching heat had dried the river into a few shallow, muddy rivulets, which they had easily waded across before making their way south through the myriad side valleys west of the river. Given the intense fighting on the floor of the Kunar Valley, this route was also the safest way.

Unbelievably, she was again traveling with Ebrahim and Michel. It was like Old Home Week, she thought, but so much had happened in everyone's lives, and the war had taken a toll on everyone. She was happy that Ebrahim had survived several more years of war, as irrepressible and blustery as ever, at least on the outside. She noticed that he was sometimes given to sudden bouts of intense silence, and wondered what he'd seen in the years she'd been gone.

She was glad to see Michel too. He had sympathized with her, of course, about her brother's untimely death, and had told her quietly of his own mother's passing. He had suddenly been called back from one of his periodic forays inside Afghanistan, and had been able to be at her bedside when she'd gone.

It was an amazing coincidence that he'd arrived in Peshawar just as she had. How often do you run into someone you know at obscure Third World airports? Surprisingly often, she reflected, at least in a certain circle.

So far, their trip inside Afghanistan had been blessedly uneventful. The land was waiting, expectant, as if it knew that a great change was about to take place. What had been green in that long ago spring had turned to the warm yellow of golden topaz, and the fields had spread themselves out under the embrace of sky. At home they would have called it Indian summer. Here she thought of it as the summer's last dance. The mountains were swathed in ripe shades of gold, orange, and pomegranate. In a few isolated villages tucked far into the mountains' skirts, there had finally been a harvest, and life had been somewhat eased. The rooftops were covered with drying grapes and other fruits, and occasionally Elizabeth and her companions were offered honey to eat with their *nan* and yogurt.

As in that spring so many years before, a deceptive peace cloaked the land. Muffled explosions could be imagined to be the shots of deerhunters in Pennsylvania woods. But the illusion faded when Elizabeth observed the land more closely. The debris of war was everywhere, rusting in fallen oak leaves, blooming on barren land. From a distance a village would appear to be a village; when they drew close, Elizabeth would see that it was only a shell of stone, and that its fields were not ripe with wheat, but choked with long dry grass and parched weeds, through which the autumn breeze spoke in hushed tones of a season of hunger.

She was shocked at the change in Kunar. Many of the small villages she had seen before were now deserted. Much of the Kunar Valley was now considered "free," but crops had been meager, as the occupying force once again cut off the flow of river water to fields in areas controlled by the Mujahedeen.

The day was warm and painfully transparent as Elizabeth followed Ebrahim and Michel up the valley that led to Amrau Tangay. The sky had the clear beauty of newborn eyes, or eyes that have accepted death with courage, she thought, remembering her brother's final passage. Afghanistan in this autumn of crisis seemed a land blazing in clarity before fading away into a forgotten century.

Elizabeth saw Yusuf long before he saw her. From the valley floor she made out the familiar cluster of houses that formed the hamlet of Amrau Tangay. Several small figures stood on one rooftop, but on the adjoining roof stood a solitary figure that she recognized instantly. He gazed out over the valley, towards the dusky sky opposite the sunset, then returned to his chair. Still hard at work, she thought. Has he even given me a thought in all this time? She began to doubt the wisdom of her coming here, but resigned her heart, all at once heavy with doubt, to whatever was meant to be.

By the time they had reached the clinic the sky had deepened to the color of bruised plums, and Yusuf was at his prayers. Ismail greeted the tired travelers, and Elizabeth sat down on a *charpoy*, watching Yusuf silhouetted on the dark roof as he spoke to his God, alone.

Ebrahim was telling her a story, but she was not listening, only nodding at what she hoped were appropriate times. She watched as Yusuf picked up his blanket, put his shoes on, and turned to see who had entered his courtyard.

She could not make out his features in the dark, but somehow their eyes found each other. The others were talking amongst themselves, but Elizabeth sat still, face upturned, staring at the figure on the roof's edge, who remained motionless. Abruptly he turned towards the mud stairs, and in a moment was hurrying across the dusty court and grasping her hand in both of his.

She knew her hand was trembling, but she only stood and half smiled, half bit her lips. The muscles of Yusuf's throat worked, and a small sob escaped him. Then he took a deep breath.

"Glad you made it," he said casually. "I didn't realize Afghanistan was such a tourist attraction now that the war might be winding down."

She squeezed his hand, then dropped it. "Why you scoundrel," she drawled in her best Scarlett accent, "you haven't changed a bit."

He bowed slightly, then turned to greet the others. She observed him closely, trying to solve the puzzle of his face.

"Where are Sharif and Malolai?" she asked abruptly.

"They will come," said Yusuf. "Soon." He surveyed her in the light of the lantern Ismail had brought. "You still look like an Afghan girl."

"Not quite so elegant as I did the last time I saw you…" She faltered. "And a lot older."

"To me you look just the same. You were in blue silk."

"And now in shabby flowered cotton. How fortunes change."

They sheltered awkwardly in cardhouses of words. Yusuf turned and spoke to the others in Pashtu, then said to her, "The nights are cold now. Come inside. We light fires at this time of year."

She followed him, heart stretched tight, and sat where he indicated on the woven carpet placed near the square hearth in the center of the room. She stared as Ismail built a fire and the blue-orange flames crackled and licked hungrily at the air.

"Are you tired?" asked Yusuf softly. "Hungry?"

"Yes to both."

In the dim firelight, she felt a hand on her shoulder. "Something will be ready soon."

What had she expected? Suddenly she felt incredibly foolish, to have come all this way thinking that this man would have kept his love for her alive through years of no contact. And yet, against all her expectations, sense, and will, she knew her love for him remained alive, burning as brightly as the hearth fire.

It must have been her writer's imagination, but she'd fantasized warm embraces, passion, apologies on both sides. Instead, Yusuf was the kind, professional doctor, caring for her as he would have for a somewhat distant friend. She wanted to cry, to put out the flames burning her heart, but all her tears were caught in her tight throat.

Two figures entered the room, and in the heavy smoke she recognized Malolai and Sharif. She sprang to her feet and embraced her old friend, kissing her and letting the tears flow for everything.

Malolai too wept, and Sharif smiled as the two women hugged each other over and over again and time dissolved. Elizabeth finally turned to Sharif and grasped both his hands, laughing with the sheer joy of seeing an old friend.

"Marriage is good for both of you," said Elizabeth. "You both look happy and healthy, *nam-e-khoda.*"

Behind her, Yusuf laughed. "*Nam-e-khoda.* You have learned some Farsi."

"Also some Pashtu," she said shyly. "But more Farsi. I have a teach-yourself book on modern Persian."

He wrinkled his nose. "That's Iranian Farsi. Dari Persian is the real Persian, in its pure and ancient form."

"You can see that our Yusuf has not changed," said Malolai.

Elizabeth forced a laugh, hating the shallow jokes that obstructed true communication.

"Malolai, sit with me now," said Elizabeth. "We need to catch up."

Malolai spoke to Sharif, who nodded and left the room. The two women sat down close to each other, hugging and laughing.

"How are you doing?" asked Elizabeth. "Are you really okay here?"

"Very well. And I have a surprise for you."

Elizabeth looked at her questioningly, but Malolai merely smiled.

"How is it for you as a woman here in the village?"

"Sharif has encouraged me to keep working, but the mullahs don't like that women are working as nurses or doctors. Sometimes Yusuf says that I and Hakim should go to Pakistan, but..."

"Hakim?"

Sharif entered the room holding the hand of a small boy, who immediately ran to Malolai and hugged her.

"Our son." Malolai and Sharif beamed. The child buried his head in his mother's lap and giggled.

"*Salaam*," said Elizabeth sweetly. "*Salaam*, Hakim."

The boy looked up, surprised, and replied a quick, "*Salaam*," before pulling his mother's *chadar* over his face.

"How old is he?" asked Elizabeth.

"He is in his fourth year. We were blessed soon after we were married."

Sharif picked up his son and put him on his shoulders, playing pony as the boy shouted and laughed.

"How is your family?" asked Malolai.

How to answer? "Well, now. Actually my dad had colon cancer, but he went through treatment and it's been three years, so the prognosis is good. I've gotten really close to him and mom now."

"And your brother, Mark?"

She looked away, unable to meet her friend's eyes. "Mark passed away about a year ago. It was an unexpected illness." She didn't know if Malolai, isolated in an Afghan village dealing with war, knew about the growing AIDS epidemic, and the implication of a young man dying of AIDS.

Malolai's face showed the greatest sympathy. "Oh, Elizabeth *jan*, I am so so sorry. It must be so hard for you and your parents."

"Life is hard for so many people these days, all over the world. In some ways I think America under Reagan has become a Third World country, with huge gaps between rich and poor. When I went back to America after being in Afghanistan, I felt like I didn't fit in. We seem to have so much wealth, and to use it so badly."

"But it's your home," said Malolai.

"Yes and no. Maybe the whole world is my home now."

"I still would like to live in New York," cut in Ebrahim. "I know I would like it there."

"You might also like Paris," said Michel softly.

"First bring freedom to Afghanistan, then think of where to go afterwards," said Elizabeth shortly. "By the way, how is Commander Rahim?"

"He is well," said Yusuf from across the smoky room. "You will see him soon, *inshallah*. He knows you are coming."

"Did you know?"

"Yes, he told me. I didn't know when you would arrive."

Ismail brought in tea and Malolai helped him serve everyone. Conversation sputtered in various languages. Little Hakim grew sleepy sitting on his mother's lap near the fire, and Malolai tucked a loose quilt around him.

Elizabeth wrapped her own blanket more closely about her and stared into the fire, wondering why she was here. A disembodied voice to her left said, "I don't think you're very happy to see me." Yusuf squatted down beside her, holding a glass of tea in one hand.

"What! I thought you weren't happy to see me."

"Don't be silly. We will talk later." He got up and disappeared into the smoke.

Elizabeth turned back to Malolai. "How are things now, with the war and with the political situation?"

"We have many of the same problems here we've had all during the war, and would have had without the war. Malaria. We have not enough prophylactic tablets, and too many mosquitoes."

"What about the war?" Elizabeth insisted.

Malolai looked into the fire. "We have both won and lost. By the grace of God, my husband is well and my son is well."

"Has there been lots of fighting here?"

The young woman sighed and adjusted her veil. "We are isolated here. But all over Kunar, too much fighting. All over Afghanistan, the same. It seems worse since the Geneva Accords, not better. You see what the bombardment has done."

"It was a shock."

"We have been hungry sometimes, but not as hungry as the villagers. I think the Russians are trying to choke us before they leave. Before, we could get our medicines and carrot juice and baby food from Peshawar. Now it seems only arms come across," she said bitterly, "and Wahabi Arabs who are supposedly supporting our *jehad* but are instead telling us what to do. Anyway, now the river is low and I think it may be possible to get our supplies again, if they can cross the valley in the night."

Yusuf brought in a clean cloth and spread it on the floor in front of his guests. Malolai distributed *nan* and Ismail set a large platter of steaming white rice, upon which nested a whole roast chicken, in the center of the cloth. Yusuf poured broth into wooden bowls and set one between every two people. In keeping with tradition, the two women shared. Another large bowl, roughly carved, held yogurt. Yusuf ladled out a portion for Elizabeth and Malolai to share.

"Malolai," whispered Elizabeth, "why did he have to kill a chicken? Chickens lay eggs."

The nurse put her hand on Elizabeth's arm. "Don't worry. You are our guest. And this is an excuse for us to eat chicken as well, and for me to be able to eat with everyone. Usually I must eat alone with Hakim. Most of the Mujahedeen nearby belong to Massoud Khan's party and are not fundamentalist, but we must be very careful these days."

When the meal was finished, another round of tea was brought. Sharif left the room carrying his sleepy son, and after a while returned cradling a large stringed instrument in his arms. It was a type of lute, its face made of stretched animal skin and its carved wooden body inlaid with mother of pearl.

"What's that?" asked Elizabeth.

"*Rebab*," said Malolai. "An Afghan folk instrument."

"Ahh, so that's what it looks like. I used to listen to cassettes with Salima."

She watched, fascinated, as Sharif tuned the instrument, adjusting pegs and plucking the strings with his small wooden plectrum. He picked out a few notes and waited for the room to fall silent. A few more tentative notes, a strum across all the strings, and then a run of notes, which continued like rain, grew faster and faster, formed a pattern, repeated it, varied it. Someone picked up an aluminum pot, turned it over, and softly tapped out the rhythm that would be filled by a *tabla*. With a flourish, Sharif eased into another tune. It built slowly, in the uncountable rhythms of Central Asia, as Sharif's graceful fingers raced along the slender neck of the instrument.

Sharif's eyes were closed, and whenever he opened them it was to look into his wife's eyes. He held the instrument like a child, caressed it like a woman, begged it, cajoled it. Someone began snapping his fingers in rhythm, and others soon took it up. Ebrahim and the other Mujahedeen snapped their fingers in a curious manner, fingers of one hand against knuckles of the other. Elizabeth tried and fumbled. Malolai giggled, took Elizabeth's hands, and positioned them. Elizabeth tried again, but finally gave up and surrendered to the spell of the music.

The lively tune faded to a slow, longing mode, each note distinct and exquisite. It grew faster again, and reached a crescendo of frenzy. Sharif bent over his instrument, head bobbing. His cap fell off, unnoticed, and when he finished with one last glissando, there were whistles and shouts.

After the shortest of dramatic pauses, Sharif rushed into a tune that evoked images of covered bazaars and mosques with tall minarets and blue-tiled domes, of caravans across empty steppes, and of twisting, precipitous mountain paths. Elizabeth closed her eyes and dreamed of all the things in Afghanistan she had never known, might never know, but longed to see and understand.

A sound to her left, in the darkness, a soft sound as a man sat cross-legged beside her. Quiet breathing, a sense of someone moving in rhythm to the music, a hand brushing her knee, then taking her own two hands, which rested in her lap, as she swayed her shoulders and head to the sensuous music. She opened her eyes and looked into Yusuf's eyes, which glittered in the firelight like embers of spirit. Without speaking, he positioned her hands for the Afghan finger-snap, and then let them go.

Her heart was now beating even faster than the tempo of the music. Over and over, she tried to snap her fingers, and at last produced a sound. Satisfied, she rested her hands in her lap and watched as Sharif and his instrument were transformed by darkness and smoke, and by the magic of the spell he conjured with his fingers. The firelight glowed dull orange and haloed the magician in shadow and light.

Late in the night, Sharif put down his instrument and humbly bowed his head. He flashed them all a smile as they whistled and clapped and cried, "*Shabbash!*" and "*Afarin!*" to show their appreciation.

"This is what we are fighting for," said the voice to her left. She looked at him quickly, but he had already moved to the other side of the room. He pulled out a carved wooden box and a *chillum*, loaded the bowl of the water pipe with tobacco from the box, and offered the pipe to Sharif.

Sharif fished an ember from the fire with his bare hands and lit the pipe. He drew once or twice on the long wooden tube that led to the carved body of the *chillum*. As he puffed, clouds of smoke rose and swirled around him. Elizabeth was entranced. Here was a scene that could have taken place a thousand years ago. Beside Sharif was his wife, her head respectfully covered, her indomitable features etched by firelight. These two in that moment epitomized all that was worth fighting for, not only in Afghanistan but in Vietnam, Africa, Central America. They were the strong and simple people, huddled round a hearth for light, warmth, and companionship.

Elizabeth looked around the room and was seized by the terror, the sense of the brevity of life, and the impermanence of feeling and manifestation. Any one of them could die tomorrow, here or in the illusory safety of New York.

"This too will pass, Elizabeth *jan*," said Yusuf softly, as if in answer to thoughts he had read. "Omar Khayyam once said:

In circle without end we come and go,
Where soul begins or ends we cannot know.
Not one who's taken breath on earth can say,
From what source we were born, or where we flow."

He was gone before she could reply. Malolai and Sharif said goodnight and left for their home across the courtyard. The others settled into their beds, with some talk, a little laughter, a cough here and there. Elizabeth continued to sit, arms hugged around her knees, staring at the fire.

Finally she rose, stretched, sighed, and walked to the door, which was still open to the star-frosted night.

"Where are you going?" asked Yusuf sharply.

"To the bathroom."

"I'd better come with you."

"I don't need an escort to the bathroom!"

"If you go after dark in Afghanistan, someone had better come with you."

She watched as he took his bandoleer off the wall peg and strapped on his pistol. "Is it really that dangerous?"

"Maybe not. But anybody could be around at night. And as it gets colder, wolves start coming down. Come on."

She followed him out into the moonless night. She could barely see him as he led her down a familiar path and stood aside while she made her way between boulders lit only by starlight. When she returned to the path he was still facing away from her.

"Okay, thank you. Let's go." She took a few steps, but he didn't move. When she turned back towards him, he was staring at her. She didn't know who took the next step first, but they were hugging each other like leaves clinging to a tree, refusing the entreaties of frost and wind. It was not passion, not desperation, but a joyous embrace of two people who had long ago come to know and trust each other, without ever knowing when it happened.

For a long time neither moved, neither spoke. They did not kiss, but stood motionless, breathing in the scent of their closeness in the autumn night.

He released her. There were tears in his eyes. "Who left whom?"

She shook her head. "I don't know. Maybe it had to happen."

He caressed her hair, which hung loose to her shoulders. "I'm glad you came back."

"I had to. Not only for you."

His eyes questioned her.

"For Afghanistan. I need to learn more, to understand more, to tell this story of the Soviets pulling out when the rest of the world never thought they would."

"And I never thought I would see you again. Forgive me for my boorish behavior."

She laughed. "I thought you might write and say you never wanted to see me again."

"Your letter was a clever way of forcing me to write if I didn't."

"You figured that out?"

"I think we know each other. Maybe we're two of a kind."

He hugged her again. Then they kissed, at first tentatively, and then more passionately, tongues exploring unspoken feelings. She leaned back in his arms and gazed at the sky as he kissed her neck. She felt as if they were falling into stars and void. Then suddenly she remembered they were in Afghanistan.

He went on kissing her neck as she disentangled herself, against his gentle resistance.

"We're still in the middle of a Holy War," she whispered fiercely.

"What?"

"We've got to go back to a room where there are five Mujahedeen with very orthodox morals."

"But if we're going to marry…"

"Wait a minute. I didn't come here to marry you."

He looked stricken.

"Yusuf, I haven't said no. But I can't say yes. We really don't know each other, and it's been years. I just wanted to see you again, needed to see you again, to see how we both feel."

"I thought you knew that."

"My heart says yes, my body certainly says yes, but my head says go slow, be careful, and my spirit…just doesn't know yet."

He stiffened and stepped away from her. "I have again acted out of turn."

She tried to touch him, but he pulled away. "Yusuf, please understand."

"I'm not sure if it's possible to understand. I didn't think you were like all the others. I didn't think you were the kind of person to play games."

What others, she wondered briefly. "I'm not playing games. I'm telling you the truth, and you don't like it. You think I should fall all over you and commit my whole life just because you're who you are. Who are you anyway? Plenty of other people are just as heroic."

She knew she'd hurt him, and she'd meant to. Now she hated herself.

"I have nothing to offer you anyway, I know," he said with quiet resignation.

"No, no, of course you do. Damn it, I'm terrified and you're terrified. Why the hell is it so hard to love? It seems easier for people to kill than to love."

He sighed. "Yes. Hard to love, hard to heal, hard to build."

"I want to leave here tomorrow, to go meet Commander Rahim."

"I see."

"No you don't. I just need time to think. I want to come back, and I want to help you. If I go now, we'll both have time to think."

"I have already thought, for over four years. But as you wish."

She was frustrated by this sudden ice wall. "I love you, damn it!"

His face softened. "Really?"

"I don't lie."

"I love you too. You know that. And this time I will wait. Forgive my forwardness." He took her hand lightly. "Come, let's go sleep now."

CHAPTER 42

ELIZABETH

Traveling with Commander Rahim

Elizabeth slowly climbed the steep path that led up towards a chill, veiled October sky. As she walked a stiff breeze licked the sweat from her body and sent her *chadar* flapping behind her.

She had fallen behind everyone else, partly because she wished to be alone to think. She looked up to see Commander Rahim and the others already resting on top of the sharp ridge, and wearily plodded on.

The parting with Yusuf that morning had not been particularly pleasant. He had been polite of course, but cold and distant as a sacred mountain. She felt angry, but also felt a dull pain in her heart. How could he possibly have interpreted her letter to mean that she was coming here to marry him? Was it the difference between men and women, or between East and West?

She smiled briefly when she joined the others on the ridge, then sat down in the dirt, panting. She sat away from everyone else, hands clasped around her knees, starting out at the rugged, uneven ridges below them.

Sharif brought her blanket, which was in the bag he was carrying, and her water bottle. She thanked him gratefully. Sharif knew she was always thirsty at their rest halts. And he was also sensitive enough to know when she preferred to be alone.

As Sharif withdrew, Ebrahim sat down beside her. "How are your feet?" he asked.

"Fine, thank you."

"What about your legs? Do you need a massage?"

"No, thank you."

"It's harder for you now than it was when you were younger a few years ago."

"Not really. I had a sprained ankle then, and I've kept fit."

"These mountains are higher."

She looked around in exasperation. Commander Rahim, who had met them on the way, was now standing, pointing out something to Michel. Sharif was in conversation with several other men, but he looked up, and seeing her face, immediately understood. He called to Ebrahim, who excused himself, much to Elizabeth's relief, and joined the other group.

Perhaps it was the weather that made her feel so melancholy. Or perhaps it was the war. Every now and then, a sense of the terrible waste of war, even the most righteous war, would creep up on her consciousness, and she would despair. All these young men, and old men, and women and children. Had there not been a war, some might have gone to the university, some would have been farmers, others merchants or teachers. All would have married, had children, and seen their children grow up, marry and give them grandchildren. And then, their purpose in life accomplished, they would have died peacefully. Now they skipped most of the living part, or at best rushed to marry and bring a new generation into the world in the fear that the those in the current one might die before their time.

Yusuf had never mentioned whether or not he wanted children. And that was one of those practical things men and women were supposed to talk about before they decided on marriage. She'd seen a lot of relationships break up over just that issue. The ambitious man who didn't want children to clutter up his lifestyle, or the career woman who agreed without question at twenty-five that she didn't particularly want children. By thirty, the woman was usually hearing the loud, inexorable ticking of the biological clock, and reconsidering.

Elizabeth had turned thirty-four and still wasn't sure if she wanted children. She'd never considered it with Tom, given his single-minded twin obsessions with himself and his career, and after meeting Yusuf had never met another man that had seriously interested her. This surprised her, and sometimes she wondered if there was something wrong with her. Of course between her career and her care-taking of first her dad and then Mark, there hadn't been a lot of time for dating in the past few years.

She wondered if a conflict over children had contributed to the breakup of Yusuf's marriage. He seemed the kind of man who would want children, but did she really know him?

Elizabeth kicked a pebble and watched it bounce down the hill. How could Yusuf expect her to give him an answer when they hadn't even discussed the most fundamental questions? It was a miracle that they still seemed to have feelings for each other after four years, but they hadn't ever discussed where they would live, what they would do. And there was still the matter of her family. Elizabeth's mom was pretty intuitive, and may have guessed a lot when she first got back from Afghanistan, but had never said anything. But her dad, even after facing his own mortality, still let an occasional racial slur slip out, and might not take well to an Afghan son-in-law. And they wouldn't be thrilled about her living overseas, especially if Afghanistan didn't settle down.

And what if I have to become a Muslim to marry him? They hadn't discussed that either. The idea of conversion didn't much bother Elizabeth, who had a free-floating idea of God and believed S/He understood every language and ritual that came from a sincere heart. But her devoutly Catholic mother might draw the line at accepting her daughter's conversion to a heathen faith.

"Lizbet! Let's go!" shouted Ebrahim. "I called you three times."

She looked up. "Oh, sorry. How much farther today?"

"One more hour."

Commander Rahim gave him a reproving look. "We can stop somewhere sooner, but our *sangar* is still some hours away. We will not reach there until well after dark."

Resigned, she fell in behind the group, which filed along the ridge, then down a steep path into Badel valley. She balanced carefully on the rocky path, which twisted steeply. Occasionally she would dislodge a stone, almost losing her footing. Sharif, as always before, stayed near her.

Malolai was very lucky. Sharif was kind and generous, open-minded, intelligent, and brave. Not to mention good-looking. Elizabeth actually preferred Sharif's looks to Yusuf's. Yusuf's face was too angular, his nose was too large, and he sometimes looked pasty and sallow. Sharif was robust and healthy, with a taut face that easily broke into a smile. Yusuf never seemed to smile much, though he did laugh at times. Though even his laughter was sometimes mirthless and sarcastic.

She smiled to herself. Odd how paragons of virtue turn a bit ugly when one is angry or hurt. One could find flaws in Michelangelo's David if one looked. In truth, she thought Yusuf was incredibly, dangerously, magnetically attractive. She loved his hair and his eyes most. She now knew the soft feel of his hair, and thought again of running her fingers through its thickness. And she thought of his eyes, deeply set in his strong-boned face, eyes which were by turns warm, intense, and arresting.

"You are so quiet these days," came Michel's voice from behind her. They had reached a part of the path that continued flat along the edge of the cliff for some way, and Michel had fallen in after her. "I am worried about you." Michel's gray eyes were soft with concern.

"I'll be all right."

"I think you do not want to talk."

She sighed. "I'm not sure if talking would do any good." But Michel was a European, and might understand. "How are you doing? Don't mention names," she added quickly, signaling with her eyes toward Sharif, who was close behind.

Michel shifted his eyes ahead, toward Ebrahim. "Not so well. I think I am wrong, and my feelings are unrequited. I have waited years."

"And you've never said anything?"

"I did not want to jeopardize my mission if I am wrong."

"Well, I finally learned that if the feelings aren't returned, it's better to move on. They say there are plenty of fish in the sea, right? It's better not to make a fool of yourself. The universe makes big enough fools of us."

Michel laughed hollowly. "But feelings do not go away just because you tell them to."

She looked at him sharply. "Why did you come back this time?"

"I like Afghanistan. And it's good for my career. It's expected of me now."

"Really? Nothing else?"

"*Ouf*, I was stupid to keep hoping."

She glanced at his aquiline profile. Not a weak face, yet his personality was oddly dependent.

"Why did *you* come back?" countered Michel.

"I like Afghanistan."

"And?"

She debated with herself briefly. "And I like an Afghan."

Michel raised his well-shaped brows. "Who?"

"No name."

"Ahh. Is he a doctor?"

"Yes."

"Like, or love?"

"Like. Maybe love. I don't know."

"Does he want to marry you?"

She jerked her head toward him. "What makes you think that?"

"He is an Afghan. If he wanted only to sleep with you, he already would have. If he respects you, he will want to marry you."

"You sound like an expert."

"Has he asked you?"

"Twice."

"What did you reply?"

"I said I can't give him an answer yet."

"That is reasonable."

"To us. Not to him."

Michel laughed loudly, and Ebrahim turned around to look back at them.

"I'm sorry. I think you should be patient and see what happens. It is very romantic," said Michel."

"Too romantic. What about reality?"

"He will not make you wear a *chadari* or live in *purdah*."

Men, even gay men, never understood the obvious. "I know that. But where would we live, how would we live, what would we do? And does he want children?"

"People in love are not supposed to think that way."

"Maybe that's why so many marriages don't work out," she said sourly. "Maybe people should think of these things before they commit."

Michel seemed suddenly sad, and said nothing for a few moments. "I would like to get married someday. I want to have children."

It didn't surprise her. Mark had said something similar when he was young, before he knew he was HIV-positive.

Michel looked thoughtful. "To the right woman, who would understand. I do not much go with women, but I am able to. For children I could."

"I think most women want more than that in a relationship."

"Maybe I can give it. If I try."

Love was so difficult, betrayal so easy. "Who knows? Maybe you can. And maybe I will marry Y...my friend."

"And leave me to hang?"

"What?"

"It was an old joke."

"Oh, I remember, about the bottle of wine. That was four years ago. I think the statute of limitations has expired."

Michel put an arm around Elizabeth's shoulders. "If you don't marry that other person, I would marry you," he said affectionately. "I hope I meet a woman like you some day. You understand so much, and do not judge."

She felt a surge of fondness for Michel, and squeezed the hand that rested on her shoulder. "God help both of us."

At the next rest halt, Commander Rahim spread his blanket next to hers. "I hope you are not too tired?" he solicited.

"Oh no, I think I can make it."

"It is far. We will reach the mouth of the valley by dusk, continue up the road, and then into the next valley. I'm sorry for the trouble."

"Don't apologize." At least he was honest. "Do you think we'll get any food before we get there? Not that it's important, but…"

"Of course we will, in the village near the mouth of the valley. Even we cannot go so far without any food. My son is correct, you are very brave and strong."

"Yusuf said that?"

"Yes. You are surprised. I told you before, he admires you very much."

"That was a long time ago. I admire him as well. And you."

"Don't waste admiration on an old man."

"But you are such a charming old man."

To her surprise, Commander Rahim blushed. Just as quickly, he controlled it. "You Americans have sweet tongues. You in particular have the gift of words."

"Thank you."

"Thank *you*, for all you have done to tell the story of our *jehad*, and of the suffering of the Afghan people. Your previous stories garnered a great deal of attention at a crucial time, and the publicity helped us both with our diplomacy and with the humanitarian donations we so sorely needed.

"And thank you for being here again, for risking your life so that the world will not forget us. Sometimes I think they have. Maybe the Western powers think that the Soviets will withdraw and then the country will be back to normal. They forget how much help we will need in rebuilding after a decade of war."

She was embarrassed by his gratitude when she felt she had done so little, and for partly selfish reasons. Looking away from the commander's riveting eyes, she changed the subject. "Do you think they will keep to their agreement?"

"Some agreements have been kept. Others have been broken. That is the way of nations."

"And after they go, will there be peace? Can all the different factions of the Mujahedeen work together?"

The old man stroked his white beard, then turned to her. "God knows. But man hopes."

CHAPTER 43
YUSUF

Amrau Tangay

Yusuf knew he was being foul-tempered and snappish, but he could not seem to restrain himself. Malolai was at first tolerant, but as the day went on she lost no opportunity to make a joke at his expense. By the end of the day, both she and Ismail were laughing, and he felt ashamed of his behavior. How could he possibly have allowed Elizabeth to make him this angry?

Late in the day he was in the dispensary, ostensibly taking inventory. Why wasn't anything ever in order? If they ever needed anything in an emergency they would never be able to find it. Ismail had no concept of order. None one of them had a concept of order.

And these bottles of carrot juice. It was amazing that they didn't break, the way they were stored. And they looked as if they had been buried for years. Torn labels, dirt clinging to them. Hadn't anyone thought of cleaning them so they didn't look so disgusting? They looked like greater disease-carriers than an unwashed cup.

Yusuf aimed a savage kick at the box of bottles. He heard the sharp, satisfying clink of breaking glass, and in the dim light saw a stream of orange running out from under the box. He cursed in English. A laugh behind him startled him in his guilt, and he whirled around to see Malolai standing in the doorway.

"Bad mood?" she asked, feigned innocence in her green eyes.

He stood facing her, fists clenched at his sides, teeth gritted. "What would make you think that?"

Her eyes traveled down to his fists, then back up to his face. "Is there anything I can do? Are you angry at me, or at Ismail?"

He unclenched his fists in sudden shame and looked at his nurse, abashed. "No, no. I accidentally broke a bottle of carrot juice."

"Accidentally?"

"Well, no. I kicked it in a fit of anger. Now I am ashamed. We should never waste food. Now a child will not have this bottle of juice to drink."

Malolai knelt down next to the box. The earthen floor had already absorbed the juice, and only a trace of dampness remained. "Only one bottle," she announced, holding up the shards. "It is not so bad."

Yusuf sat down heavily on the nearest *charpoy* and cradled his head in his hands. What would his father think if he had witnessed the last scene?

"Would you like some tea?" asked Malolai. "I will make some before I go to the village."

He nodded gratefully. "Thank you. And please sit here with me and drink tea before you go."

Malolai left Yusuf to meditate on his shame. He was glad to be in the dark, the corner where anger and selfishness came to live.

And yet he did not understand his own anger. Elizabeth had not refused him. She'd even said she loved him. But he resented being teased this way. If he could be sure of his feelings, why couldn't she? And if she didn't really care, then why was she leading him on? Why had she come back now? Was it just for a career opportunity, or did she really care about Afghanistan, and him?

He felt better now that he had had his tantrum. He was sobered by his destructive act, thankful that it hadn't been worse. He remembered some of the times in America, when he'd had too much to drink and then Janet had said something he had taken as an insult. More than a few glasses had gone, a door had been damaged, and one spectacular evening a large art deco window had ceased to filter the light.

Maybe Elizabeth saw his faults too clearly. Maybe she recognized his pride and ego, his temper, and his simultaneous insecurity. Pride and insecurity always seem to go hand in hand. One feels too good for one's situation in life, and feels misunderstood and unappreciated even while fearing that the unappreciative world is right after all.

Malolai entered, setting the teapot on a low wooden table. She poured out two glasses, then sat on the *charpoy* opposite Yusuf's and sipped her tea, waiting for him to speak.

"I'm sorry," said Yusuf. "You and Ismail work so hard, and I have been very rude to you without reason."

"It doesn't matter. We are just worried about you when you are like this."

He looked up, shame-faced. "But it does matter. We are not supposed to treat friends so badly. This is not the way I was taught. I have shamed my family."

"No, no, no," said Malolai comfortingly. "Just please tell me what is wrong. Can I help you in any way?"

"Nothing is wrong. I am just in a bad mood today."

"Are you angry at Elizabeth?"

He hesitated.

"I am a woman, and I understand things. I am her friend, and yours. You can tell me."

He looked down at his glass and sighed. "All right. I'm not angry *at* her, but because of her."

"I am like your sister because you arranged my marriage. Tell me, do you want to marry Elizabeth?"

"I think it would be foolish to marry an American now, when we are so uncertain of our country's future."

"But did you ask her to marry you?"

He looked at her soberly, tiredly. "Yes, twice."

Malolai frowned. "She refused?"

"Yes. I mean no, not really. She said neither yes nor no. The first time I asked was at your wedding. I even had a ring. She just laughed at me."

"Elizabeth laughed? That is strange. But there must be some reason."

"I don't know. When I received that letter from her after all these years, I thought she had reconsidered and was coming here to marry me. I am a fool!"

"No, not a fool. I think she loves you."

His face was hopeful. "Has she spoken with you about me?"

"No."

His face fell.

"But she is my friend, and I can tell. Hasn't she said anything to you?"

"She did say she loved me…"

Malolai laughed at his tragic expression. "There it is! It is just a matter of time."

"I don't know if we have time."

"If it is in your *naseeb*, then there is time. Women need time."

He sighed. "It is hard to have faith."

"But faith is the cause of all miracles. What were her reasons for not saying yes?"

"I don't know."

"You say, 'I don't know' a lot. You feel you have no power."

He smiled wryly. "I don't. And I don't like it."

"All Afghan men are spoiled."

"You are perceptive."

"Just realistic. Are you angry with Elizabeth because you cannot be with her right away?"

"Yes. But I know it's not fair. She wants more time. She wants to know me better."

"That is fair."

"But you married Sharif soon after you met him."

"I am Afghan. We are brought up to marry as early and as quickly as possible. I did the right thing. For Elizabeth this would not be right."

"My first wife was a psychologist."

"Then your second will not be."

He laughed unexpectedly. "You should have been!"

"Have you asked Elizabeth what she wants in a husband, or have you told her what you want in a wife?"

The idea somehow shocked him. "No...but where would you get such ideas?"

"I have seen many American films in Kabul, so I have some idea how Western women think. She may wonder, for example, if you want children."

This question had never occurred to him. "I suppose it would concern her."

"I once saw a film, I think a French one, about two women. One wanted children but her husband didn't. The other did not want children but her husband did."

"What happened?"

"The two couples divorced and each married the spouse of the other."

He didn't know why this should strike him as funny, but he laughed.

"So you must discuss these things with her. And where to live, and what to do."

"If the Russians really leave in a few months, we could go to Kabul."

"*Inshallah*. But Kabul will be unsettled for a long time, even if there is not full-scale civil war. Do you think she would want to go with you? Would her parents want her to go to such a dangerous place to live when she is their only remaining child?"

"I don't know."

"Then you must talk to her when she comes back here. She is the only one who can answer you."

He sipped his tea, now grown cold. Malolai refreshed his glass and pressed two lumps of *gur* on him.

"How does an Afghan woman come to understand an American woman so well?"

"Women are women, men are men, in every country, in city and village."

"But I think Afghan women are different. More faithful."

Malolai's eyes sparked angrily. "You may mean that as a compliment to the women of Afghanistan, but it is an insult to Elizabeth. She has been faithful to you for years without even a promise between you, I can tell. And she would never be unfaithful to anyone. And some Afghan girls would be unfaithful, in heart if not in deed. Did your wife hurt you so badly that you judge all American women so harshly?"

He looked at her uncertainly. "Can I trust you, Malolai? I have never spoken so much to a woman."

"By the Holy Koran, you know you can trust me as your own sister."

"My wife did hurt me badly. She had an affair with a client of hers, a young lawyer. Younger than me. Younger than her, actually. I was never for a moment unfaithful to her, and I do not understand why it happened."

"*Naseeb.*"

"What do you mean?"

"If it is in your fate to marry Elizabeth, then the first marriage could not work out. May I see the omens in your hand?"

He extended his hand, feeling foolish. "I don't believe in this. I'm a doctor."

"And I'm a nurse. It does not harm." She gazed at both his palms for a long time, comparing, running fingers over each hand, bending his hands backwards and forwards, and making small clucking sounds.

He grew impatient. "What do you see?"

She looked up at him with a sly smile. "As I thought. Two marriages."

"Fortune-tellers always see what they want."

"No, look here." She pointed to a spot below his little finger. "These are marriage lines. Two of them. On both hands, a little separate, the second stronger."

"I wouldn't know whether you are making this up or not."

"I read what I see," she said in an injured tone. "I do not lie."

"Where did you learn this?"

"From my mother's eldest sister."

Curiosity was winning over rationalism. "What else do you see?"

"I can see you are nervous, always thinking too much. I don't have to look at your hand to tell you that. And you have an excellent mind. Look, the head line is long, straight, and unbroken. Your heart line contains sadness though, but you are happier later in life. There is one great sadness in your life, a loss that will be with you for many years. And your life line…"

He laughed and snatched his hand away. "I don't believe in this anyway."

"Do you believe in *qismet*?"

"I believe the moment of birth and the moment of death are fixed. All else is our responsibility."

"And our marriages?"

"I had not thought about it. They say, "trust in God, but tie your camel first."

"It's true. God gave us the gift of intelligence in order to set us apart from the animals. Some say the lines in the hand can change from time to time, by our choice, and by prayers to God."

"Maybe."

"If even a few things, such as birth and death, are fixed, then why could they not be reflected in the hand?"

"Hands, stars, cards. Even if they are, what is the sense of knowing? Will knowing change anything?"

"Knowing might make us able to change some things. She locked him in her gaze. "If Elizabeth is truly in your fate, and you in hers, then nothing you do will alter that, and you will act in a manner to bring her to you."

"But it is her decision."

"And yours. And ultimately God's. But it will do you no good to break bottles!"

CHAPTER 44

ELIZABETH

With Rahim's commandos

"Elizabeth," said Commander Rahim sternly. "I want you to stay here until we send someone for you. Mr. Michel, you stay as well. At the mouth of this valley is a government garrison, and beyond that Chagaserai, where there is a large Soviet garrison and the Governor's House. We will not attack until nightfall, but we will get into position now. Ebrahim will stay with you, and I will send someone to fetch you when it is safe. You may come close enough to see. I would rather that neither of you be close enough to be hit."

"How long will we have to wait?" asked Elizabeth.

"My dear, this isn't a well-planned war. Please be patient."

"Of course. I'm sorry." Elizabeth was nervous. She had wanted to see Commander Rahim's famous commandos in action, but the reality was frightening. She could feel the tension in the men like that in the spine of an animal ready to spring on its prey. The group had had phenomenal success in combating both government and Soviet forces with a minimum of casualties to themselves. But their success had not been without a price, and each man knew he could be the next martyr.

"Okay. *Ba'amana khoda*. We'll be waiting," said Elizabeth. She stood on the cliff outside the cave that served as a *sangar*, taking pictures of the commandos as they filed down the narrow valley, off to battle.

Michel just watched, and Elizabeth wondered what was in his mind. "Why aren't you taking any pictures?"

"You are taking pictures."

"So? We deal with different markets. By the way, where on earth have you managed to keep getting published all these years?"

"Oh, as I told you before, *Paris-Match*, *Der Speigel*, other European magazines. They've always been far more interested in Afghanistan than the American press."

"Tell me about it." She felt annoyed at the sense of old rivalries rekindled. Michel never had been very forthcoming. She felt as if he didn't trust her for some reason, or thought she would try to undercut him, and this hurt coming from someone she considered a friend.

Ebrahim, who had accompanied the party of commandos partway down the valley, climbed up to rejoin them. "It will be a good attack," he grinned.

She wondered if Ebrahim was jealous of Sharif, who had been accepted as a full commando and had gone through the rigorous training at Rahim's secret camp in Pakistan a few years ago. On the other hand, Ebrahim had carved out his own secure niche with the Mujahedeen by guiding foreign journalists. And it was a lucrative niche. Ebrahim had boasted to her about all the gifts his newfound friends had sent from their home countries. She herself had sent him pop cassettes and a Swiss Army knife, and had brought jeans and a Polaroid camera when she came this time.

Poor Ebrahim. His family was in Kabul, and he was alone except for his friend Sharif, who was now married. Afghan men generally didn't allow marriage to get in the way of their male friendships, but Sharif seemed to enjoy spending as much time with his wife as possible. Elizabeth watched Ebrahim, a compact, wiry man standing guard outside their cave, like a small boy watching wistfully as the army marched away and he was left behind with the women and children.

The night was cold, and Ebrahim wore a sweater over his *shalwar kameez* and a blanket wrapped around him. His white skullcap of warmer seasons had been replaced by a camel wool cap, and the beard he had grown made him look older and more serious. Elizabeth wondered why he hadn't yet married. Perhaps he didn't have enough money to support a wife, or maybe he just didn't have the inclination, being at the front so much. He reminded her of a puppy-dog at times, the way he gazed sad-eyed at women. He had looked at her that way during her first trip, but now seemed to have accepted her as a sister. Although his personality often grated on her nerves, she felt a fondness for him, born of all they had lived through together.

She felt for Michel too, as he turned his own hopeless puppy-dog glances toward Ebrahim. In the soft dusk she felt a surge of fondness for both of the men with her in this tiny cave.

Yusuf suddenly flashed into her mind with the clarity of a photograph. The vision was so strong it startled her. She had left him, what, a week ago? She had felt a sense of calm since her conversation with Michel, a feeling that, left to themselves, things would work out. But suddenly she regretted their parting. She could die, he could die, and neither of them would never know how the other really felt. Now she understood the hastiness of wartime marriage. Her parents had been married during World War II while her father was home on leave. She suspected they had hoped a baby might come soon, in case her father died in the Pacific, but Mark had disappointed them until well after demobilization. Her mother had worked in the Steel during the war and was probably lucky no children had come until after. But Catholics never saw it that way.

Even if there wasn't a war, there were always plenty of ways to die suddenly, she thought morbidly. Car crashes, plane crashes, a beam falling off a building. The stuff of women's magazines at supermarket checkout counters. "It was 3 a.m. before Maggie realized her husband John might not be coming home. But still she clung to hope, though it not like John to stay out late without calling. John had always been the perfect husband…" All those perfect husbands and perfect wives about to be snuffed out suddenly. Sometimes it was hard to believe in a personal and compassionate God.

A sharp concussion resonated through the valley in the dusk, and Elizabeth gasped. "What was that?"

Michel did not react. "Tank fire," said Ebrahim, scanning the valley floor anxiously.

The echoes were swallowed by silence. Elizabeth crouched alertly, her camera resting in her lap. Then she heard shouts, followed by the spatter of automatic rifle fire. Why were they firing? They couldn't have reached the main valley yet.

Ebrahim's face turned toward her in the dark. "They have run into trouble."

"Should we go after them?"

"It is against orders. We can't endanger ourselves."

There were more shouts, this time a little closer. More rifle fire, and the hoarse boom of tank fire. Elizabeth now stood by Ebrahim, peering into the dusk. Suddenly the sky was lit up by a white-green flare, which faded to a dull red. Even this far up the valley their faces glowed faintly.

"Get down!" ordered Ebrahim, pushing her to the ground.

She lay there, heart pounding, trying to flatten herself. Ebrahim shouted a challenge, and she strained to recognize some words of the shouted exchange.

"Sharif's been hurt," said Ebrahim. "He and some others stepped on a mine." His voice was dead cold.

"What! How badly are they hurt?"

"I don't know."

"We have to do something. What about the others?"

"Some others killed. Others wounded."

"What about Commander Rahim?"

"He is alive."

"I'm going."

Ebrahim came to life, and grabbed her arm. "You cannot. Commander Rahim's orders. It is too dangerous."

Gunfire punctuated his comments. Elizabeth twisted away from his grasp. "I know first aid," she said in a commanding voice. "Rahim would want me there. I am the only person who can help."

"It is dangerous!"

"It's dangerous here too. I am the only one who can help Sharif. Do you want him to die?"

It was the opening she had gambled on. "I'll tell Rahim you didn't see me go. Just tell him I ran in the confusion."

Ebrahim looked at Michel. "You will not say?"

"It won't matter once we help the wounded," said Elizabeth. "*Inshallah,*" she added under her breath.

Michel nodded. "You have my word of honor."

"Then go, quickly," said Ebrahim. "What do you need?"

She rummaged through her bag till she found a box of sanitary pads and two boxes of stretch gauze. She threw the supplies into a nylon shoulder bag and scrambled off down the path.

Ebrahim shouted something to the two men who had come with the message, and then shouted after her, "Go with God! And come back."

One of the two men's faces was covered with blood, but she couldn't tell how badly wounded he was. If he had made it this far he was probably okay. She would see to him later. She started to ask a question and then realized with a start that no one but Rahim and Ebrahim spoke English.

Another flare lit up the sky, and one of the Mujahedeen pulled her beneath the shelter of a bush until the glow faded. When it was safe they went on, as booms resounded throughout the valley.

From a ridge above and ahead of them the fiery orange hyphens of tracer bullets streaked out toward the valley. An answering stream was directed at the ridge, and occasionally a fireball sailed into the sky and landed on the mountain far above them.

She forced herself to go on, though her whole body shook and she was short of breath. Malolai, Malolai, was all she could think. Malolai would save Yusuf. I must try and save Sharif. Dear Sharif, please God let him be all right, let me get there in time. Oh please God, I must not be afraid, I must be calm.

The panting of her companions in the icy night and the dry leaves crackling underneath her stumbling feet sounded as loud as explosions. At every step she expected the explosion of a mine to blow her back towards the *sangar*. The two men walked ahead of her and she rationalized, step by agonizing step, that this path could not be mined, that too many men had already walked over it. The mine the men hit must have been newly laid. Maybe even right then, in the dusk. How had Rahim failed to consider that possibility? She knew the old man would blame himself, and felt sorry for him. God, please let us get there soon.

Ahead, figures were silhouetted for a moment in the frozen light of a flare. Her two escorts raised their Kalashnikovs and tensed, waiting. They held their fire until the figures got closer, and they saw that four of their own men were carrying two wounded men. One of the wounded was Sharif, who was barely conscious. She looked down his body, arms, trunk, legs. Blood was dripping from somewhere. Please, not the stomach or the trunk, please. Then, in the momentary light of a flare, she made out his mangled right leg, twisted and bleeding.

She glanced quickly at the other man. One bloody trouser leg, and one arm of his shirt, on the same side, covered with dark, spreading blood.

"Here!" she cried in a hoarse whisper. They all looked at her uncertainly. "Doctor, doctor," she said urgently, gesturing frantically for the men to lay down their burdens.

At last they understood, and gently laid the wounded men down on the bare earth of the path. "Others?" she asked. What was the Farsi word? "*Digar*?"

They shook their heads. The firing continued unabated behind them, and she hoped this would be a safe place to stop the worst of the bleeding. She glanced at the two prone figures. Who was more seriously wounded, who was younger, who had lost the most blood? Sharif was half-unconscious from pain, but appeared to have only the one wound. The other man, a youth really, was unconscious and bleeding in several places.

She knelt beside the youth and felt the pulse in his right wrist. For one panicked moment she couldn't find it.

Good, the pulse was surprisingly strong. She leaned over the man, putting her ear near his lips and listening. His breath was quick and shallow. She knew he'd lost a lot of blood. She found her small flashlight and shined it first into one eye, then the other. Both responded to the light. At least the poor fellow didn't appear to have a concussion.

Be calm, she told herself. Let your training take over. What next? "*Bismillah*," she murmured, hoping that the beginning word of the Muslim prayer would somehow comfort the spirit of the unconscious man.

Carefully she removed the shirt from the man's left arm. He had caught a piece of shrapnel in the upper arm and a vein steadily oozed dark red blood. But wait, the leg wound might be more serious. It seemed to be in the thigh, or the groin. Without thinking she pulled down the man's trousers. There, in the fleshy part of the upper thigh, was another wound. "Thank God it didn't break the femur," she muttered.

She applied direct pressure to the arm wound, which appeared to be deeper and was bleeding faster. She gestured to one of the other men to do the same to the leg wound, and also pointed toward Sharif. One man picked up a pad and examined it curiously, but another understood and took the pad from the first and pressed it hard on the wounded youth's leg. She looked up impatiently and again gestured toward Sharif. The man pressing on the youth's leg said something, and the first man moved to Sharif and pressed a pad onto the jagged open wound in Sharif's lower leg.

The youth's bleeding would not stop, and she began to panic. She elevated the arm and continued pressure. Still no success. She threw away another pad and gestured to the man working on the leg to press on the arm wound and keep the limb raised while she pressed hard on the pressure point in the armpit.

Slowly the flow of blood was stanched. She said a quick prayer of thanks and checked the leg wound, and then Sharif's leg. All had clotted at last.

Now she could bandage. The wounds might start bleeding again when the men were moved, but hopefully not as seriously now that they had clotted.

Suddenly she remembered the man whose face had been covered with blood. She looked around wildly, then realized that he was the man who had stopped Sharif's bleeding. He had washed the blood from his face and when she examined him she found no more than a superficial scalp wound.

Sharif moaned softly, and she squeezed his hand. His dark eyes flickered, and he called in a low voice to Malolai. Elizabeth kept praying. She seemed to come into focus for him, and he smiled slightly, then squeezed her hand in answer. "Thank you, Lizbet," he said in English. Sharif's lips were hot and dry, and he could hardly speak. She felt his forehead. Feverish. What was the Pashtu word for water? *Aaba*?

One of the Mujahedeen scrambled off to the bank of the stream and returned with his wool hat turned upside down, dripping water. Sharif lifted his head and sipped slowly. The man with the hat then dripped some water onto the unconscious man's face and made another trip to the stream. Sharif drank again, and then the cool hat was placed on his feverish head.

The night was growing colder, and two men gave their blankets to cover the wounded men, tucking them in as they might have tucked in their own children. The youth was lucky, as he remained unconscious to the pain. But she worried about Sharif, who she knew had to be in great pain. Occasionally a moan would escape him, but no more. She wished he would cry out, as moaning seemed to release some of the terrible pain.

The firing had slackened and now there was only an occasional burst of fire from the ridge, answered from below. An ominous silence descended on the night. The rush of the river was so constant that it too seemed like silence. For a few horrible moments Elizabeth was sure that all the rest had died. Commander Rahim would not come back, and she, Ebrahim, and Michel would be forced to carry Sharif and the other wounded man to Amrau Tangay, traveling by night, hounded by helicopters by day.

Suddenly the Mujahedeen slid the bolts of their rifles. Elizabeth peered wildly into the blackness, but could see nothing.

She heard a staccato exchange in Pashtu, and then made out Commander Rahim's solid figure approaching her.

"I asked you not to come, Miss Elizabeth."

"Please don't be angry. Ebrahim didn't see me go and couldn't leave Michel to get me back. I knew I could help the wounded. Are there any more wounded?"

He shook his head curtly. "Not seriously. But six men were martyred."

"Oh God…"

"And you! You could have been killed. Don't you have any idea of obeying orders? You people are a danger to us, and a danger to yourselves. Didn't you realize they were shelling this area? Don't you realize you are my responsibility?"

"I'm my own responsibility. I take my own risks to come here. I'm sorry. I admit I didn't think, I just acted."

"You acted well, and bravely." His manner softened. "I think your spirit is Afghan." He turned toward his men and spoke in Pashtu, then turned back to her. "Now, we have to transport these men to Amrau Tangay, and we have to leave now. We must be out of this area by sunrise, and hide by day. They may send helicopters out to look for us. Can these men walk?"

"One is unconscious. Sharif's leg is badly wounded and he can't walk. Both of them are weak from loss of blood, and there is a big danger from infection. I haven't even cleaned the wounds yet. I will do that when we can halt tomorrow. How many days do you think it will take us?"

The commander thought. "We will try to reach Amrau Tangay in two days. Tomorrow we rest. After that we will walk day and night until we reach my son. What is your opinion of the chances for saving Sharif's leg, and of the other man's wounds?"

"If we get to the clinic soon enough, the wounds won't get infected. Then I think Yusuf can save Sharif's foot."

Rahim looked full of doubt, and in the dark night he seemed to have shrunk in size. "How shall we carry them?"

Elizabeth explained in detail how the wounded men could be carried flat, one man at the head, one at the feet, and two on each side locking arms beneath the body. After much awkward handling of the wounded men, they started on their way.

Commander Rahim looked worried. Elizabeth fell behind with him. "How long must we carry them like this?" he asked. "It is hard on the men, and we can't go very fast."

"Just tonight, I think. If we find boards or strong sticks we can make stretchers out of blankets."

"We will do what we must."

Elizabeth wanted to ask him what had happened, and why. What had gone so drastically wrong? But the commander himself seemed at a loss in the aftermath of the ambush.

"*Commandant sahib*?" she asked.

He looked round at her.

"What about the dead?"

He looked straight ahead. "God must take care of them. We put a handful of earth on each man's face and covered them with their blankets. We had to take their weapons and what was left of their ammunition. I do not like to think of anything else. They were my friends, my men, each of them like a son to me. And Almighty Allah granted that they died a martyr's death."

She knew that those who fought the *jehad* believed that if they died fighting for Islam they would go directly to Paradise. Many of the Mujahedeen took this quite literally, and were not afraid of death. But wasn't it better to live to rebuild their country, so near to being freed from foreign occupation?

The attack had been a bitter setback. These men had lost their lives in what might be the last days of the war, the proverbial eleventh hour. To Elizabeth it suddenly seemed a shocking waste.

But the Soviets had clearly not stopped fighting, and the Mujahedeen had no choice but to keep fighting back. She watched the back of the strong commander ahead of her, hunched with sorrow and weariness. How had this carefully planned attack, using only the most trusted men, gone awry? Somehow the Soviets had to have known the commandos' plans. She caught her breath, realizing the implications? Who was the spy among the Mujahedeen? Was it Ebrahim, as she had thought? Had he contrived to stay behind in the safety of the *sangar* with her and Michel and then deliver them into the hands of the Russians? No, it didn't make sense. If he was a spy he wouldn't have saved me before, that time near Dunahi.

But who then? Rightly or wrongly, she just couldn't bring herself to trust Ebrahim after this.

CHAPTER 45

ELIZABETH

With Rahim's commandos

"Stop it!" Elizabeth screamed as Ebrahim again hit Michel hard on the side of the face. Michel cowered as Ebrahim brandished a revolver at him. "What are you doing? What happened?" She screamed again with shrill panic as Ebrahim viciously cuffed Michel's bruised face with the butt of the revolver.

Ebrahim's face was dark and ugly, his narrow eyes sharp and beady with hatred as he dragged Michel onto the roof, pressing the gun to the Frenchman's head. The worm has turned at last, thought Elizabeth in terror.

Others came running. Ebrahim remained standing, trembling with anger and still pointing the gun at the Frenchman's temple. Ebrahim shouted something in Pashtu to the men, and suddenly other guns were pointing at Michel. Elizabeth looked to Commander Rahim for help, but Rahim's eyes were fixed on Michel, who was bleeding from the nose and the corner of the mouth.

"What is happening? Would someone please tell me?"

Rahim turned to her slowly. "Get your camera. I want you to take a picture of the spy."

"Spy!"

Ebrahim took something out of his pocket and threw it to her. She fumbled and missed, and the small object fell to the hard ground at her feet. She picked it up gingerly and looked at it curiously, turning the oblong metal box around in her hands.

"What is it?" she asked, mystified.

A look of relief crossed Commander Rahim's face. "I am glad you don't know. I didn't think you were working with him, but I needed to see your reaction, and the men needed to see it for themselves. This object, my dear, is a transmitter."

"I caught him making a report," said Ebrahim harshly. "He was speaking in Russian into this transmitter." He spat at the cowed Frenchman's face. "Because of him, how many of my good friends have been martyred over the years? Show the KGB dog no mercy."

Michel stared at the ground, contradicting nothing. His sandy hair was disheveled and matted with blood, which dripped from time to time into the dust. Elizabeth looked at the transmitter in her hand in disbelief, unable to grasp the full implications.

Commander Rahim shouted to one of his men, who entered the hut in which they had rested for a few hours the night before. The man brought out Michel's two bags and unceremoniously dumped the contents into the dust. He probed the Frenchman's empty camera bag and found a concealed flap in the zip-over top. Elizabeth winced at the sharp rip of velcro as with a flourish the man produced several pieces of paper that had been hidden under the flap. Several of the Mujahedeen started forward, but Rahim halted them all with a gesture. The man brought the papers to the commander, who leafed through them.

"Detailed maps," he commented. "Finely drawn, very accurate. All the places we have been." He flicked his eyes toward Elizabeth's horror-stricken face.

She'd been wrong, terribly wrong. All of Michel's strange glances, silences, and evasions flooded into consciousness, and her brain suddenly made the connection. She had been suspicious of poor, honest Ebrahim and had trusted a spy, blithely telling him everything about her personal life.

"Please get your camera," said Commander Rahim.

Though he had said please, it was a direct order and she dared not disobey. But she felt sick when asked to photograph Ebrahim standing over the fallen Michel like a hunter proud of his kill, then Commander Rahim with Michel, and finally the entire group posing soberly with the unmasked spy.

"He's made his last transmission," hissed Ebrahim. He kicked at the bloodied man on the ground, who doubled over gasping for breath. Ebrahim looked up at a sharp word from Commander Rahim, then looked at Elizabeth. "I let him finish so they wouldn't know we had discovered him. You write all that."

"We must have a trial," said Rahim calmly. "You also write that we give even spies a fair trial. We will take the prisoner and judge him."

"How will you judge him?"

"By the evidence, and by his deeds and admission. We want to know the truth before we decide what to do. God will have mercy on him."

"And you?"

"He was responsible for the deaths of six of my men yesterday. He's been in and out of the country probably twenty times in the past four years, with many different Mujahedeen groups. How many lives have been lost because of him?"

His gaze penetrated Elizabeth, but it was not without wisdom and compassion. "We will need that as evidence," he said, indicating the transmitter. "Normally a woman would not be present at this kind of trial, but if you wish you may witness the trial of Michel Dubois, accused of spying for the Soviet KGB."

She felt sick, confused, betrayed. The bastard had killed her friends as surely as if he had pulled the trigger or planted the mine. And thinking back to that terrifying morning in Dunahi four years ago, he had very nearly caused her to be captured or even killed. Yet even as her throat burned with rage and outrage, her background would not allow her to even consider dispensing with a trial and countenancing a summary execution. Perhaps her presence as an outside observer would ensure some semblance of fairness, though it was more likely that she would witness some version of the harsh eye-for-an-eye code of "Pashtunwali," the justice of mountain and desert unrefined by the niceties of walls and ceilings.

"Yes, I will come," she said shakily. "And with your permission, I will shoot pictures to document your justice.

A *charpoy* was brought for Commander Rahim, while the rest of the men squatted in a circle. Opposite Rahim was Michel, head still bowed. The Frenchman acquiesced meekly as Ebrahim took turbans from two men and bound his hands and feet. He bound them harshly, but at a word from the commander, loosened the bonds slightly.

Elizabeth stood apart, grimly taking pictures from all angles. The camera seemed to place a barrier between experience and the horrible, inexorable reality of what had happened and what was now taking place.

Commander Rahim cleared his throat. "Michel Dubois, if that is indeed your name, you stand accused of spying on behalf of the Soviet KGB. Do you plead guilty or not guilty?"

Michel looked up, and his gray eyes briefly flashed defiance directly at Commander Rahim. Elizabeth clicked the shutter at that precise moment.

"What does it matter what I plead? You have already judged me and executed me. I am proud to plead guilty."

Commander Rahim's face revealed nothing. With the objectivity of a court reporter, he translated the proceedings into Pashtu. There was an outcry of indignation from the assembled men, which Rahim stayed with a raised hand.

"Who sent you here?"

"An agent of the French Communist Party."

"Are you a member of the French Communist Party?"

"Yes."

"Are there KGB agents in the French Communist Party?"

Michel hesitated. "Not officially."

"Are you a KGB agent?"

"I have worked for the KGB and reported to their agents. I am not an agent."

"But you were sent here by them?"

"That is correct."

"Are you being paid by the KGB?"

"Yes. Why not?"

"How much? How much are my men's lives worth? How much for the lives of the civilians killed in the bombing raids you called down on the villages?"

The accused man did not answer. Elizabeth watched Michel's bruised and swollen face, unable to believe in the reality of anything she was witnessing. What if it were all a mistake? She remembered all too clearly the mullah who had accused her of being a KGB agent just because she had cried at the death of Russians. What if Michel had snapped and was just telling them whatever they wanted to hear?

"I was paid enough to cover my expenses, and then some. I did not get rich," replied the Frenchman at last.

Commander Rahim frowned, said a few words in Pashtu to his men, then commented, "The amount is not important. The point is that you were hired to spy upon the Mujahedeen of Afghanistan. We believed you were a journalist, as you said, and we trusted you. Too much. We have paid the terrible consequences. You have been discovered in an act of treachery toward those who believed they were your friends. Now you must pay the consequences of your actions."

Elizabeth watched as Michel's steady gaze met that of Commander Rahim. They were both men of principles, but Michel's choices repelled and frightened her. To be a sincere Communist was one thing, but to win people to friendship and then betray them was insidious.

"Who is your contact in Aghanistan?" Commander Rahim asked.

"There is no need to betray a friend. You are going to kill me anyway."

"You have already betrayed enough friends. But do not be so sure we will kill you. A live KGB agent might be useful in Peshawar with the talks going on between our representatives and Soviet diplomats."

"I told you I am not an agent."

"An employee of the KGB then." Commander Rahim waved the maps and transmitter. "But with or without you alive, this is all the proof we need. And we have an independent witness."

Elizabeth's heart flinched as Michel glanced at her. "Everyone has spies," said the Frenchman, "the KGB, the Chinese, the CIA…" He glanced again at Elizabeth, and her heart froze. Would he really try to cast suspicion on her to save his own neck?

"That is not the question here," said Rahim. "The question is what were you doing in Afghanistan?"

"I told you I was sent."

"To do what?"

"To discover the methods of operation of the rebel guerrillas, particularly the terrorist band under the command of Rahimullah Khan, father of the patriot Ayub Khan, Governor of Kunar Province."

Ebrahim's face betrayed nothing, and Elizabeth knew the others had not understood. Commander Rahim stared hard at the bound Frenchman. "How did you come by that information?"

"A spy must listen carefully, and remain alert," said Michel in a mocking tone. "Your son has known who you are for all these years, and he will do everything to destroy you."

Elizabeth watched the commander, but he gave no outward sign of turmoil.

"Whether Governor Ayub knows who Commander Rahim is or not is irrelevant," said the commander. "It is Governor Ayub's chosen duty to destroy Commander Rahim, and Commander Rahim's chosen duty to destroy Governor Ayub and all he stands for."

"You people are barbarians!" said Michel contemptuously. "Father against son, brother against brother. If you were not such fools, you would learn something from the West."

"From Northern Ireland?" asked Rahim ironically. "Or do you mean from Communism?"

"Yes. The idea of equality, equality of workers with everyone else, of women with men, of all races."

"Do you really believe that Communism will bring that?"

Hesitant eyes, then a flash. "Yes."

"Enough to die for it, I suppose."

"If need be."

"You must have known all along what the consequences would be if you were discovered. But tell me, how did you make such a mistake after being so careful for all these years? How did you come to let Ebrahim discover you?"

The Frenchman now lost his defiance and hung his head. For a moment Elizabeth thought he had fainted. Then Ebrahim began speaking in Pashtu, and the men began to murmur angrily. When he was finished, Rahim translated coldly, in third person. "The agent Michel Dubois had made repeated friendly overtures to Mohammed Ebrahim Khan, Mujaheed, who accepted them as simple friendship. When Dubois walked away from this village, ostensibly to perform his toilet, Ebrahim followed a few minutes behind, as he wished to ask Dubois' advice regarding a personal matter. Upon hearing Dubois' voice, Ebrahim hid himself, and heard a transmission in the Russian language. From the words that Ebrahim understood, names of persons, places, and so forth, he deduces that the transmission recounted the events of the past three days, including the number of dead and wounded. He also is nearly certain that the spy has informed the Russians of our probable destination.

"Ebrahim allowed the agent to complete his transmission, not wishing to alarm him and cause him to call for help. Upon completion of his transmission, Dubois looked up to see Ebrahim nearby. He did not seem certain whether or not he had been detected. Is that true, up to this point?"

Michel muttered, "It does not matter now."

Commander Rahim continued. "The agent then made a proposition of an improper nature to Ebrahim." Rahim cleared his throat and appeared embarrassed. "You have lived in America, Miss Elizabeth. I think I do not need to explain further."

She tried to say a word, but couldn't. Her throat was dry with sorrow.

"Ebrahim found this proposition offensive and struck the agent, Dubois. He struck him repeatedly, then brought him to us for judgment."

Elizabeth swallowed hard. Michel was so young to be a spy, so young for such an end. Why couldn't he have been content in the gay scene in Paris?

"I loved Ebrahim," said Michel hoarsely.

"So much that you arranged to have his friends killed," said Rahim. He sighed and broke off his interrogation to translate to the men. Their faces were cold and stern, and their expressions frightened Elizabeth. She had never before seen hatred so naked.

Rahim turned again to Michel and spoke in English. "Did you draw these maps?"

"Yes."

"They are fine and accurate. They will be useful to us. They would have been more useful to our enemies."

Michel glared at him.

"Are you a professional cartographer?"

"Among other things."

"The KGB trains its men well. But not well enough. How old are you?"

"Twenty-six."

"Young to die. But many of those you have killed were younger. So, you were a brilliant student, just out of university when you were approached. Prime recruiting material for any spy or mercenary service. My men would like to know, in your own words, why you wanted to come to Afghanistan, and why you want the Communists to be in power in Afghanistan when the people do not want them."

Michel looked straight at the commander. "I knew that Afghanistan was a backward country, with the majority of people ignorant and uneducated, and the female half of the population enslaved. You people are slaves to an outmoded religion. Communism can offer the promise of a better society, of education and medical care, of an equal society, with no more landlord and tenant, and no more poverty. Sooner or later the people will see what Communism has to offer."

"Islam also preaches equality, and so does Western democracy. You talk of equality, education, medical care. You people always talk of self-determination. Why don't you respect the wishes of a people and let them change in their own way, at their own speed? I know the position of women in Afghanistan must change. My elder son knows, Ebrahim knows. Maybe a lot of our Mujahedeen don't see it yet, but we will show them in time, through example.

"We are an Islamic nation. There are many ways to interpret Islam, but nothing in the Koran that inherently prevents equality or progress. *Inshallah*, when our country is at last freed from foreign domination, we can make our society anew and slowly educate more women, more villages, more of our ethnic minorities.

"You talk of economic planning and economic aid. But the Russians have taken the natural gas from our fields in the north. For years they paid us less than it cost to produce it. Now they just take it from us. Is that economic aid to a friend?

"You have seen with your own eyes the results of this war, the bombed villages, the starving children, the dead women. You have seen the millions of refugees in Pakistan. Is that the result of a friendly nation helping a weak friend? No, my friend, I am sorry. Maybe you think that America is evil, and maybe America is also cynical and manipulative, maybe all powerful nations become a little bit cynical. But your beloved Soviet Union is not a worker's paradise, and it is not a savior to the benighted Muslim peasant of Afghanistan.

"I have seen the Soviet Union. I trained there for two years. We lived in the diplomatic compound of Moscow, and were followed every time we left it. No," he shook his head emphatically. "Soviet Communism is not for us. Whatever evolves after this war is finished, at least it will be Afghan."

Elizabeth watched Rahim, whose face was sober and decided, then turned her gaze back to Michel, whose face had gone blank. She knew she should be taking pictures, but had neither the heart nor the nerve.

The commander translated his conversation with Michel at great length. The men remained silent, nodding somberly from time to time. Elizabeth realized she was holding her breath, and let it out slowly, measuredly. She prayed they wouldn't execute Michel right there in front of her.

Rahim rose, and the others rose with him. "We are going out of the village to deliberate and judge among ourselves," he said. "Talk to this man and see if he will tell you anything. We will send for him."

Elizabeth shot a few pictures of the line of men filing off the rooftop and out of the tiny village. It was nearing dusk now, and in that light the men looked like a procession of Medieval executioners.

She sat down in Commander Rahim's place on the *charpoy* and laboriously cleaned her lens, even though it didn't need it. There was a lump in her throat. She was startled by the sound of a strangled sob, and looked up to see that Michel was weeping. But he seemed like a hologram, unreal, unreachable.

"I thought I was doing the right thing," he sobbed. "Ever since I was a little boy, I only wanted to always do the right thing. That's why I went along with the priest, because I thought it was the right thing."

"What are you talking about?" Cold anger flashed in her heart. "You think betraying people is the right thing?"

"I did everything wrong, and now I'm going to die. Elizabeth, please, I have something I must tell you."

What did it matter now?

"Remember I told you that I became gay because my headmaster molested me? It was not just the headmaster, it was the village priest."

She reeled, her consciousness drowning in yet another wave of shock and disbelief. "A priest?! But you said..."

"Yes, I did love him. I was a young boy, I wanted to do everything to please him. And people did come to know. That part I told you before. He had to leave, I had to leave. But everyone blamed me, saying that I had seduced a man of God. So then I went to Paris to the university, and I realized that I loved men."

Was this tortured man capable of loving anyone, she wondered?

"It was because of love that I became a Communist, and because of broken love that I came here."

She just looked at him, expressionlessly, and waited for him to continue.

"It was because of my political science instructor. You see, I did tell you the truth."

"Everything but the most important parts," she said angrily. "You let me think you were my friend."

"I was. I am."

She wanted to spit at him at that moment. "Sharif is my friend. And Sharif may lose his leg because of your reports. Not to mention all the men who have died. You arranged to have us ambushed, didn't you?"

"I knew you would not be there. I knew Commander Rahim would make you wait behind until it was safe."

"You gambled that, with *my* life. But it never was safe. How did you plan it so carefully?"

"They knew the plan before, and came at the last minute to ambush."

"And the mine Sharif stepped on?"

"We gambled that Rahim would be over-confident and not check at the last minute. It was his reconnaissance party that stepped on the mine."

"We!"

"Elizabet, I tried to protect you."

"Some protection. What about Yusuf? And others I love?"

"Marry him quickly and take him away from this insanity. Afghanistan is doomed, whether the Mujahedeen or the Communists win. Don't you see? It will be no life for you."

"I'll decide that, thank you. I can't believe any of this is happening. It was you who set me up in Dunahi four years ago, wasn't it?"

"I tried to protect you. You weren't supposed to stay in that village when it was bombed. I did not know that the mullah would come and delay you."

"That was what saved me from being captured. Thanks a lot. You tried to protect me from being bombed so I could be captured. That's a great choice.

"And now I don't even know if we will reach Yusuf's clinic, or if we will be bombed on the way, or if the clinic will be bombed. And you call yourself my friend!"

"I advised against bombing the clinic," he said quietly. "They only want Rahim. If he'd turn himself in it would stop." He tried to catch her gaze, but she coldly scrutinized his face: the gray eyes that had seemed so sincere, the fashionably cut hair, now streaked with dirt and blood, the bruised and swollen cheekbones, and the aristocratic nose, dried blood congealed beneath the nostrils.

She cursed and searched through her bag for toilet paper. She wet the paper with water from her bottle and advanced slowly toward Michel. Even a spy should be allowed to die in dignity.

He smiled faintly. "My hands are tied."

"And they will stay tied." She sponged the blood off his face and neck, and shook some water on his hair. "Does that feel better?"

"It doesn't matter now. It's too late I think."

"Too late for all of us?"

"Can you save me?"

"You have a lot of nerve to ask, after what you tried to do to me and the way you lied to me," she said in disbelief. "But I feel sorry for you. I don't know what kind of person you must be to make people think you are their friend and then betray them. If it's any comfort to you, I don't want you to die. I hope they decided to take you to Peshawar."

"Will they listen to you?"

"No. It's not my decision."

"I see." He was quiet for a minute. "Please believe that I meant well."

"We can only see what you did, not what you meant. Because of your actions I could have been in a Russian prison for the rest of my life, and we all could have been killed yesterday. Rahim said it all better than I can."

The Frenchman sighed. "Thank you for your compassion. You do allow me dignity. Perhaps it's more than I deserve."

She looked at him, and could no longer feel anger towards this pitiful man. Now that the threat had been removed, it was easy to be merciful. "We're all human. And we all act inhuman from time to time."

"Do you forgive me?"

"I don't know. If it makes it any easier for you, yes, I will try. But forgiveness can't bring back the dead."

"Do one thing. Send a messenger to the doctor right away. Tell them all to leave Amrau Tangay. It may be bombed, despite my advice, because of my information that Commander Rahim would be going there. Make the doctor come here, to your friends. Then maybe Sharif won't lose his leg."

She stared at him. He'd been responsible for the deaths of countless people, and now he was worried about Sharif's leg.

"It's all I can do. It's my last gift."

Elizabeth heard voices as Commander Rahim and Ebrahim climbed onto the roof. "You go with Ebrahim," said Commander Rahim to the Frenchman.

Michel smiled. "Will he carry me? My feet are tied."

"Untie his feet," said Rahim. "Completely."

The Frenchman stumbled when he stood up, and shook his feet. "No circulation," he said. "Sitting in that position is not good for the circulation." He straightened up at last, towering over Elizabeth, who stood near him. He took a deep breath, set his face in a brave smile, and followed Ebrahim. At the roof's edge he paused and looked back at Elizabeth. "Goodbye, Elizabet. If I am to hang, then perhaps you will marry soon. God bless you." He turned and did not look back again as he followed Ebrahim to his judgment.

Elizabeth's breath caught in a sob, and she blinked hard. Why should she cry for a spy? "He said God bless." She looked at Commander Rahim for a reaction.

"It is good he remembers God now. It is not too late."

"Will they kill him?"

"I left the decision up to them."

"What do you think they will decide?"

He shrugged and shook his head. "He has been responsible for the deaths of many Mujahedeen. When we discovered and executed the spy Najeeb Khan a few years ago, I thought we had solved the worst problem. Oh God, too many spies." Commander Rahim sat down heavily on the *charpoy*, removed his turban, and rubbed his temples. "I am a soldier by training, but all this killing is a nasty business. Maybe I am getting old, and close to God."

"He said one thing to me," said Elizabeth. "He said to send a messenger to Yusuf right away and tell them all to leave Amrau Tangay, in case it is bombed. For what it's worth, he recommended against it. But he said Yusuf should come to us here, and that all the Russians really want is Rahim."

Commander Rahim replaced his turban and thought a moment. "Yusuf should not come to us here. It could be another trick. If they want me, we are not safe here. They won't know that their spy is no longer serving them, so they may hesitate and wait for his next message. For now, we must keep moving, but in another direction. I will send a message to Yusuf to meet us at another place."

"I think Michel was trying to make up for the terrible things he has done by warning us."

"Then may God have mercy on his soul."

A single shot sounded, and Elizabeth gasped. Her eyes met Commander Rahim's. He passed his right hand over his face and murmured, "*Bismillah.*"

She tried to control her trembling as she crouched on the roof, watching the returning party of men led by Ebrahim.

Ebrahim's face was hard and chiseled. "Before he died," he reported, "he said, 'Tell the woman I'm sorry. And tell the doctor to be careful.'"

Elizabeth stared at Ebrahim. "Did he say anything else?"

"'God have mercy on us all.'"

CHAPTER 46

AYUB

Chagaserai

Ayub zipped up his leather jacket against the chill breeze that whisked dead leaves through his garden. The papers in the file on his lap fluttered in the breeze, and he held them down in some annoyance, scanning the reports line by torturous line. From time to time a fat drop of rain spattered on the paper, which he would brush off quickly, smearing the printed ink.

It was cold outside, but some grim part of him didn't want to go in, not yet. Some part of him remembered October days in Kabul, short autumn afternoons when he would hurry home from school, or from the bazaar. Sometimes he used to buy the *nan* for the evening meal, and would run back with the flat oblongs of warm bread folded under his arm, trying to reach the house before they got cold.

And in October, on Fridays there had been hunting with his father and Yusuf, in the mountains near Paghman, outside Kabul city. The days had been just like this, and sometimes they'd gotten wet and gone into a headman's house and had *chai* and *nan*, and often *pilau*, dried fruit, and nuts as well.

And now his own father had tried to attack him, and he had fought back. He had in fact insisted on masterminding the plan to ambush the rebels himself, gambling that the troops might take his father alive. He glanced down at the report. The rebels had taken heavy casualties, but had fought back fiercely, directing their fire consistently and with surprising discipline, and the government and Soviet troops had also taken considerable casualties. The Soviet ambush on Rahim's commandos had been carefully planned, he thought, but they had not counted on the commander's quick-minded responses, or the degree of training the men had.

He guessed it was a credit to his father, but he cringed inwardly. It had been demoralizing, in fact shameful, to have once more failed to capture the famous commander.

He turned the page. Lermontov's mole, whoever he was, was thorough and analytical. There was even information that his brother Yusuf seemed to be in love with that American woman journalist, who after all these years had turned up like a bad penny. Supposedly Yusuf had even asked her to marry him, though how a spy could know that Ayub couldn't imagine. He felt a sudden stab of jealousy, followed by an equally strong stab of sentiment. So Yusuf was in love. The woman must be in love with him too, or she would never have returned to Afghanistan at a time when the war had become so much more dangerous for journalists. A number of journalists had been killed in action, and several more captured and held indefinitely. After having come so near to being captured herself, why else would she come back unless she was in love or insane?

He smiled at the comparison, despite himself. It was a long time since he had been *majnoon*, or "crazed with love" for a woman or anything else. Well if Yusuf had any sense he would talk this woman into marrying him and they would get themselves out of Afghanistan and back to America as soon as possible.

Ayub looked around his garden fondly. He lifted his head to look at the starkly etched trees silhouetted against a soft gray sky. He couldn't escape the nagging thought that his days were numbered, or at least his days here. He somehow doubted that he would see another spring and summer here.

He imagined the graceful garden under the control of the Mujahedeen. Or would several factions fight over the Governor's House, and the Governor's power, if they took over Asadabad, as Chagaserai was now called?

He looked back at his reports for some clue as to the future. Curiously, the detailed reports broke off two days ago. Perhaps Lermontov hadn't yet transcribed the latest batch, though that would be unlike him.

As if his thoughts had summoned the Russian, Ayub became aware of a car outside his gate. He heard a challenge, the familiar creak of the gate, and then the roar of a powerful motor. Ayub pretended not to notice until the hard tread of a heavy man approached him from behind.

"One could easily be surprised, being so unaware."

Ayub rose and turned. "My dear Lermontov. What brings you here? By the way, I am quite confident in my security arrangements."

"A smart man does not allow himself to be lulled into complacency. Especially with the Red Army troops being recalled to Kabul so soon."

"A good point. How soon?"

"Except for a small detachment, within a week."

"I see." Should he invite Lermontov to sit in the garden, in the cold? He thought better of it, as the man still might be of help to him in getting a visa to study in the Soviet Union, and gathered up his papers. "Please, come into the salon and have some tea."

Lermontov forced a smile, which ill-suited him. Ayub wondered momentarily if Lermontov loved his wife and had children that he loved and missed. Ayub had once thought that he knew Lermontov well, but now he thought that men like him always seemed to exist in a vacuum.

Ayub showed Lermontov into the salon and rang a bell for Mousa, who appeared discreetly and quietly took his master's orders. Lermontov scanned the room, looking for signs of treason, thought Ayub cynically. The Russian's pale blue eyes settled on the matched carpets that hung on the wall, woven portraits of Lenin and Marx on a red background. Their heads appeared to be materializing out of flame and cloud. They were the ugliest things Ayub had ever seen.

Lermontov's eyes lit with pleasure. Surely it was more at the demonstration of loyalty than with esthetic appreciation, thought Ayub. Lermontov was one of the true believers in Communism, who had risen to prominence under Brezhnev, and Ayub wondered how he'd do under Gorbachev's new regime.

"Where did you get these?" asked the Russian, gesturing to the rugs on the wall.

"In Kabul, when I was last on leave. There is a small factory where they are made using traditional methods." He didn't add that they were custom made. There wasn't an overwhelming demand for such carpets in Afghanistan, and most of the factory's products were exported to the Soviet Union.

Lermontov thoughtfully pulled out two Havana cigars and offered one to Ayub. The two men sat and smoked as they waited for Mousa to bring the tea. Ayub determined not to make small talk. He knew Lermontov never came without a reason.

Mousa served the tea silently, courteously. The Russians think most of us are barbarians, but they could learn something from the Afghans, thought Ayub in a surge of nationalism.

When the servant had gone, Lermontov spoke. "Something disturbing has happened."

What now? "Oh?" Ayub frowned with concern.

"We have not received reports for two days. We think something untoward may have befallen our informant."

Ayub, who knew absolutely nothing about Lermontov's informant, said optimistically, "Perhaps he simply has found it awkward to make reports."

Lermontov shook his large head vehemently. "He was very reliable."

"What could have happened?"

"We think he may have been discovered. Our reconnaissance flights report no activity at either Amrau Tangay or at the village where the rebels were last reported. The doctor and his friends have fled, and so, once again, has the elusive Commander Rahim. Even with two severely wounded men they have disappeared into the hills. Do you have any idea where they might have gone?"

"I don't know those mountains any better than you do," Ayub said angrily. "There are hundreds of places where people can hide, and villages we don't even know about."

"A pity our informant is dead," said Lermontov. "He was a fine cartographer, and had detailed maps for us. Now they will fall into the enemy's hands."

"But perhaps he is not dead."

"There are two indications. First, his record of reliability, and secondly, someone appears to have warned the doctor to leave his clinic."

Ayub felt relieved. At least he would still not be forced into direct action against Yusuf. "What are our choices?"

"Right now, we wait. If our informant has been murdered, we will be forced to punish the responsible parties. If the responsible parties cannot be found, we will punish their sympathizers as we have done before.

"With the Afghan government due to take over security in the next few months, it would be useful for you to consolidate your control over your area of jurisdiction, would it not? It would be useful to capture the terrorist commander and exhibit his deeds before the world, especially the U.N. And need I add that the Soviet Union will be most grateful to those who have served us efficiently?"

I thought we were serving our own nation and the workers of the world. "You have a valid point," observed Ayub noncommittally.

Lermontov slurped his tea. "It's very hot." He set the glass down. "Perhaps the greatest brotherhood between Russians and Afghans is that we both prefer to drink tea out of a glass."

"Traditionally we drank our tea from shallow, handleless cups."

"But now we have become as brothers," Lermontov said with a slight smile. "Yes, brothers in many ways. I hear there will be some good positions open for Afghan doctoral students in Moscow. They will need excellent recommendations, of course."

"It sounds attractive. I had neglected to mention to you that I had actually submitted an application to the International Studies Program at Moscow University."

Lermontov looked at the Governor ironically, making it clear that few of Ayub's actions escaped detection.

"So the next step, I suppose, is a letter of recommendation."

"I suppose. May I call upon you when the time comes?"

"The time is coming soon." Lermontov gulped down the rest of his tea, still scalding hot, and rose, clapping his protégé on the shoulder. "Do your best, and you'll be rewarded."

Ayub rose with him, debated with himself for a moment, then said decisively, "I think we should bomb the clinic."

Lermontov's eyes narrowed. "What purpose would it serve? The doctor, your brother," he emphasized, "is not there."

"Intimidation," Ayub said briskly. "We need to show the bastards we can maintain control after the Soviet troops leave."

The general laughed. "Your training in Moscow serves you well. We studied the American methods in Vietnam and learned from their mistakes. Very well, we will consider your suggestion an order from the Governor."

Ayub saw the Russian to his car and returned to his salon, disturbed. Was the price for safe-conduct to Moscow to be producing his own father's head on a silver platter? It made him uneasy to hear Lermontov talk this way.

But Ayub had made his choice. He would do whatever was necessary to acquire a visa to Moscow, as even Lermontov seemed to take it for granted that the present government would not long survive the Soviet withdrawal. He wondered how many student visas to Moscow were being held out as carrots to keep loyal officials loyal. They would be permanent visas, he reminded himself. He contemplated a future of spending the rest of his life in Moscow. At least he hoped he would be given a coveted Moscow residency permit, and wouldn't be transferred somewhere like Bratsk, several hundred kilometers north of Irkutsk in Siberia, or Magadan in the Soviet Far East.

He also wondered just how many loyal officials the Soviets might be willing to sacrifice to appease the Afghan populace. Just how far would the carrot lead him before it was either given to him or snatched away?

Rain had begun to spatter the windows, and thunder growled low in the throat of the sky. Half consciously he remembered a spring day, over four years ago. The years seemed like centuries of suffering, he reflected. But without thinking of what he was doing, he walked over to his bookshelf and took down the same slim volume of Omar Khayyam that he had consulted on that distant spring day when hope seemed so much closer.

He hesitated, then sat in his armchair. He looked at the rain, closed his eyes, whispered, "*Bismillah ar-rahman ar-rahim*," and opened the book, letting his eyes fall upon a quatrain. Its lines struck him with force:

"*All my life my soul God's knowledge sought,*
Few secrets had I failed to unknot,
These seventy years I thought both night and day,
But now I come to know that I know naught."

CHAPTER 47
ELIZABETH AND YUSUF

Badel Valley

Elizabeth was shaken by Michel's execution, but more so by the aftertaste of his betrayal. She sat outside the room where Yusuf was operating on Sharif and the other wounded man, waiting for news. Nervously she scanned the sky, which now and then reverberated to the sound of distant bombs, and then returned her gaze to the dark rectangle that led into the house.

At last Yusuf came out, shaking drops of water off of his dripping hands and wiping his face with a towel.

"Will they be all right?" she asked anxiously.

He sat down beside her and put a steady hand on her shoulder. "I think so. Largely because of your emergency care. You did a good job."

"Thank God! But what about Sharif's leg? And the young boy, Zahir?"

"Don't worry. They'll both be fine in time. Sharif will limp for awhile, but we saved his leg. As long as no infection sets in he should be as good as new in a couple of months. But I think it's a good idea for him to take Malolai and Hakim and go back to Peshawar as soon as he can walk. It's too dangerous here. Not only from the Communists, but from the Wahabis. Has Malolai told you about the death threats?"

"What! No! From whom?"

"We're not certain. But we have heard rumors that there are those who do not consider it proper for a married Afghan woman to be working as a nurse, or for an unmarried doctor to be working with her."

Elizabeth looked at him in shock. "After all she's done for your people for all these years?"

"I know. And most of the villagers and Mujahedeen appreciate it, and respect her and know she is a good Muslim. Life is not without risk."

"So what about the clinic? Will it still be there when we get back?"

He sighed heavily. "It's hard to say. Everyone in the near villages took food and went to the caves in the mountains."

He covered his eyes with his hands and rested his elbows on his knees. She put her hand on his arm. "Yusuf, you look so tired. Is there anything I can do?"

He laughed, and his face lost some of its haggardness. "I'm no more tired than Malolai or Ismail, or you for that matter. Poor dear Elizabeth, you have been through hell in the last few days."

"No kidding. I…Oh, Yusuf, I'm just so glad you're here now. After finding out that Michel was a spy, I don't even know who to trust anymore."

He put a hand on her shoulder. "I hope you trust me. Come on, you need to be on top of a mountain for a little while. Come and watch the sunset with me, and try to forget about the war. It too will pass."

His ingenuous face appealed to her. "I can't refuse a face like that," she said. "But aren't you tired? You walked half the night and then worked all day."

"Not too tired to walk with you, even to the ends of the Earth. Come on, bring your blanket. We'll be back before dark, but it gets cold long before that."

She followed him up the hill behind the village. They didn't speak as they climbed, but Elizabeth was slightly out of breath when they reached the top. From there they could see the sun sliding down toward a range of brown hills in the west. The air was autumn clear, the sky limitless and translucent. The opaque land wore intense and solid colors of gold, russet, and tamarind.

Yusuf stood beside her, breathing lightly. "Stay here while I pray. Then we will talk." He faced her and wrapped her blanket closely around her, tucking one corner under her chin.

A stiff breeze hurried across the mountains. Elizabeth hunched down in the cold, shivering slightly as she watched Yusuf prepare for his prayers. She had seen the motions so many times, yet he made them appear fresh and meaningful. The wind stung her eyes, and tears blurred her vision of Yusuf as he stood, prostrated, sat up, prostrated again, and again stood. And there in the chill twilight, shoulders hunched forward, arms clasped around her legs beneath her blanket, she too prayed. For once her prayers were not requests, but humble thanks. As an afterthought, she added a prayer for mercy on poor Michel's soul.

Yusuf shook out his blanket, wrapped it around himself with a flourish, and came to sit next to her. "Are you too cold here?" he asked.

"No. It's too beautiful and peaceful to move from here. Look at the colors."

He trailed his gaze to the horizon, where a few long, thin clouds glowed molten gold, shading to deep lilac in the shadow of the sun.

"Kabul is that way," he said, pointing.

"So near and yet so far."

"Maybe we'll be able to go back soon, *inshallah*. Would you like to see Kabul?"

"I'd love to see Kabul some day. But I suppose it will never be the city you remember."

"But we can rebuild it. And you can be part of it, if you want."

She looked at him with uncertainty. "Will you go back to Kabul when the war is over?"

"That is my plan. As soon as possible."

"What about the food shortages, and the blockade? And don't you think there will be civil war?"

"I've always dreamed of being present at the liberation of Kabul. I have responsibilities here, but the Medical Association can arrange for someone else to come. The people of Kabul will need doctors too. Too many of us have gone to the West, and too few will come back. Even fewer will be welcome, after they sat out the war in comfort. But once the fighting is over, the need will be for normal medical care, and for development of the infrastructure of a village health care program. My expertise will come in handy."

"But you didn't answer my question. Don't you think there will be civil war?"

He spread his hands. "God knows. Maybe it's all a dream. But it's my dream. Maybe we will have to wait longer, but *inshallah* one day soon Kabul will truly be free and peaceful, and I can be part of the rebuilding."

"Can I come with you?"

"If it is safe, you can come as my guest."

"Guest?"

"Or wife. The offer is still open." He caught her eyes and held them. In that dusk they were drawn together, but he waited, and did not touch her.

She was the first to look away, towards the deepening sky. "There is so much to think about before I can say yes."

"And so much to talk about. So we may as well start now. That's why I brought you here."

She looked at him with false indignation, hiding her laughter. "You sneak! You brought me here under false pretenses."

"Where else can I have a private talk with you? Not in the village, and not in the clinic. Now I understand something," he continued. "Before you can decide whether or not to marry me, you must think about what kind of life we'd have, where and how we would live, what I can offer you, if you want children, all those kinds of things."

"All of the sudden you have become terribly practical. Where did you get these ideas?"

He looked embarrassed. "I wish I could say I thought of them myself."

"All right, 'fess up. Where did you get them?"

"Malolai had a talk with me the day you left. I've thought of nothing else since. I was a mean bastard to everyone the day you left."

"I had hoped I'd have a better effect on you."

"You do have a wonderful effect on me. That's why I want to marry you and spend the rest of my life with you. Elizabeth, do you know how much I admire and respect you? And love you of course?"

"Yusuf, I feel the same toward you. But is that enough for a marriage?"

"What are you afraid of?" he asked, piqued.

"I'm not sure. I guess I'm afraid of what any other unmarried woman my age is afraid of: losing my freedom. That may sound cliché, but it's a very real fear for a woman."

"Especially a woman marrying a Muslim man?"

"It's true," she conceded. "I've seen too many marriages not work out."

"I lived in America for eighteen years."

"So did my friend Katherine's ex-husband. He was from Lebanon, a student at Penn. And I knew a woman in New York who married a Pakistani. She loved him so much, but then he changed on her. They're still together, but barely. They have children, so she doesn't want to leave him."

"What makes you think I would not be a good husband, and not give you your freedom?"

"It's hard enough for an American man. I finally left Tom because everything had to be around him. He expected me to write his query letters, contact his agents, print his pictures, and keep the house clean and gourmet food on the table. He said I was free to do anything I wanted, but who had the time? He expected me to be there whenever he wanted anything. Because I loved him so much, I wanted to make him happy, so I tried for years.

"And with you, Yusuf, I can't help being afraid. You say you love me and admire me. In your eyes I am free, independent, and successful. I go around the world doing my work and maybe it looks glamorous and romantic. It's not, but I do admit to enjoying my freedom.

"If I marry you, how long will it be before you start telling me to stay at home in Kabul, or in Kunar, or in your mother's house in Peshawar? How long before you tell me what to wear, or ask me why I'm talking to Sharif, or Massoud, or an American guy friend of mine?"

"I was married to Janet for five years," he said quietly. "During the last two years she was having her affair with the lawyer. I suspected it, then she eventually told me the truth. But I didn't ask for the divorce, even then. I didn't leave her till she left me."

"I'd never leave you," she said spontaneously.

"I don't think you would." He held her gaze, and for a moment looked very tired. "Strangely enough for an Afghan male, I'm not so jealous. But I was very hurt. And I was angry at myself for not having pleased her. My pride was injured of course. But I didn't see the point in jealousy. There's already too much pain in the world. And for a long time I thought that if I was patient she would come back to me." He half smiled. "So you see, Elizabeth *jan*, I won't be censoring your mail, or going into fits of jealousy if you talk to another man. And I won't put you in *purdah*, in Kabul or Kunar."

"You're a very unusual man."

"And you're a very unusual woman."

"What does that make us?"

"Two very unusual people in a relationship."

She laughed and just looked at him, letting the moment last, suspended in time.

"Don't forget, I've seen a lot of the world," he added.

"Yeah, well so have lots of other men who mistreat their wives and confine them in the name of religion."

"Then they learned nothing from the world. Don't insult me by putting me in the same category as them."

"I don't." She paused, and looked at his vulnerable face. "Yusuf *jan*, I am already faithful to you. I've never made love to you, but I realize now I've been faithful to you for four years. I've been waiting for you all along, as crazy as it seems. I can't even conceive of being unfaithful to you."

"Neither can I. Not from the first time I saw you in that cave."

Again, his transfixing gaze, which she broke with an effort. "So, you agree that I'm free to continue my career, and to travel when I need to, even if you can't or don't want to come?"

"Yes, of course. Though I will do all I can to make you want to be with me more than away from me."

"I'll hold you to all of this! But Yusuf, be practical, where could we possibly live?"

"As soon as Kabul is free, I will take you to Kabul. If you don't like Kabul, we can go anywhere else."

"I think I would like a free Kabul," she said thoughtfully. "But when the war is over, I could even stay here with you in Kunar for awhile, and help you in your work. I'll need to go to New York for business, of course, and I'll want to see Mom and Dad at least once a year."

"I still have friends in the States," he reminded her. "If you prefer to live there, we can."

"I don't think you could be happy there anymore. Not after having worked here for nearly five years. That's what I love about you, your crazy idealism and your commitment to your people. Remove that and you're just an ordinary intelligent, sensitive, good-looking doctor who also happens to be a poet. Nice enough, but no reason to marry someone. Here you are a hero."

"Not a hero. I've told you that before. But trying."

"That's more than most people ever dream of."

"But is it enough? And has it convinced you to marry me?"

"It has to be enough. And it has almost convinced me. Yusuf, you're not just trying. You succeed. You are rare." Impulsively, she reached out and grabbed his hand.

"Your hands are cold," he said in surprise. "Should we go?"

"No. Your hands are warm." She squeezed his hand and considered how to broach the next subject. "Yusuf, tell me, why did you and Janet never have children?"

"I am glad now. It was fate."

"Yes, but why?"

"Janet didn't want children. It seemed like a good idea at the time, as we enjoyed just being together. After two years I began to want children. We were better off financially by then, but she still didn't want a baby. Not too long afterwards, the affair started." He hesitated. "Just before I left the States, I heard that she was pregnant by the lawyer and they were getting married. Her child must be about four or five by now."

Elizabeth probed Yusuf's eyes, which had gone dark with hurt. "Yusuf, would you like to have children with me?"

"Yes," he said simply.

"And I think I would with you. I never wanted a baby with anyone before, but with you it's different. I don't want to get pregnant right away of course, but once we get settled. And I only want one child. If we decide we want more, I would rather adopt. We could adopt an Afghan orphan, and give him or her opportunities they wouldn't have otherwise."

He looked at her with awe and admiration. "You are so full of love. You will make a good mother." He hugged her impulsively and tightly, then kissed her on the lips three times before he pulled away. "Now, is there anything else to discuss?"

She felt happy, and oddly peaceful. She was following her intuition, and hoped to God it was right. She had nothing to go on but his words, though they were certainly the right ones. "Well, I can't think of anything else. I guess I can finally say yes."

"There is one more thing," he said. "Your parents have to agree."

"They'll agree. What about yours?"

"We'll tell my father tonight. I don't think he would go against the wishes of his eldest son. And my mother and sister will be happy that I'm marrying anyone again, as they'd given up on me.

"But I'm worried about your family. They've never met me, and we are so far away. What will they think?"

"My mom always told me I should follow my heart. My dad might be surprised at first, but he'll come around. We all got so much closer after he got sick, and when Mark died." Her voice caught, and Yusuf reached out to comfort her. She buried her head in his blanket and murmured, "I think Dad will just be glad I'm actually marrying somebody instead of living in sin."

Yusuf tilted her chin up to him. "But Elizabeth *jan*, I must have your parents' permission before we get married."

"What about *my* permission? Isn't that enough? I'm thirty-four years old."

He looked at her severely. "I am still enough Afghan that I must respect the wishes of the elders of your family."

"But what if my father is against it?"

"You would marry me anyway?"

"Of course."

"But I could not. I can't come into a family unwanted. I did that once, and it was a mistake."

She squeezed his hand. "I guarantee you he won't say no."

"Then write him and your mother a letter, tonight. We will find someone going to Peshawar. I'll send someone if I have to. As soon as we receive their answer, if it is favorable, we will marry, wherever we are, here or back in Amrau Tangay. Agreed?"

She could hardly take the bargain seriously, but put out her right hand and shook. "Agreed."

"It won't be a proper *arussi*, a wedding party, like I would like to give you. That we will do in Peshawar, *inshallah*, and again in Kabul one day. And we'll have a wedding in America with your family and friends. But I want to have a *nikah*, an exchange of vows with a mullah present, as soon as possible. Then we will be legally allowed to live as man and wife," he said, kissing her. "And that I don't want to wait for a day longer than necessary."

She luxuriated in the long-awaited kiss, then untangled herself from his grasp. "Wait a minute, one thing I forgot to ask, do I have to become a Muslim to marry you?"

"That's up to you. Islam is a good religion, a great religion. But you don't have to become Muslim if you don't want to."

"Do you want me to?"

"It's entirely up to you. I do want you to come to understand Islam, and to recognize the difference between custom and spirit."

"I think I see that already. But will you yell at me if I drink a glass of champagne?"

He laughed aloud, then kissed her again. "I will never yell at you for anything, unless you really piss me off of course. And I hope you'll show me the same consideration. I am not a dogmatist. I can see you are respectful of my culture, as I am of yours.

"You and I are a good match, we're both half and half. People like us are lucky, because we can draw on two cultures. Hopefully we will pick the best things from both, like choosing the ripest, sweetest strawberries from an endless field.

"Don't worry about your religion. As a Muslim I am allowed to marry the daughters of the Christians, and the Jews for that matter. And you are a believer, you have your own faith. If you ever come to Islam, you are welcome. If you don't, you are still part of me."

"Only God knows the future," she murmured, just before they kissed again. This time they kissed slowly, deeply, and for a long time, enjoying each other's warmth and the promise of passion.

It was Yusuf who broke away. "Let's go back now. You can write to your parents, and I will pray for a quick answer." He caressed her cheeks and kissed her forehead and her eyelids as she surrendered to the future.

The stars were out as they strolled down the hill, hand in hand, like two lovers in an enormous, borderless park. When they neared the village he squeezed her hand once and let it go. Then they walked into the village, side by side, as two friends.

CHAPTER 48
ELIZABETH AND YUSUF

Amrau Tangay

The days had gone gray and icy, the nights sharp and merciless as autumn deepened. Elizabeth sat outside Yusuf's house, which had miraculously survived the bombing that had leveled the dispensary and two nearby houses. Stoically, the villagers were rebuilding the houses of stone and earth. Elizabeth looked up from time to time and watched them putting the finishing touches on their work as she prepared a package of stories and film to be hand-delivered to Massoud by the messenger from Peshawar who was expected today.

A man Elizabeth had never seen before wandered into the courtyard and greeted her in Pashtu, then thrust a slim air mail letter into her hands. It was from her parents. She called to Malolai that the messenger had arrived and must be thirsty, then thanked the man quickly and disappeared inside Yusuf's house. Her heart was pounding and her throat dry as she clumsily tore open the envelope, tearing the letter in the process.

She held the pieces of the letter together. Mom's writing. She turned to the end of the second page. Signed by both, she saw with relief. "Love You and Miss You, Mom and Dad." She went back to the beginning and skimmed, her eye searching out key words and phrases. "We want you to be happy…" and "We're glad you've finally found someone who is responsible and respects you enough to marry you…"

Elizabeth's hands were shaking. She sat down on the edge of a *charpoy* and read the letter in the gray light that filtered through the door.

A shadow fell over the letter. "From your face it looks like tragedy," observed Yusuf cheerfully.

She smiled broadly. "You're getting to know me. It's only excitement. Yusuf, it's all right!"

"Can I see?"

"I'll read it aloud. Then you can read it and see if I'm telling the truth."

"Is it from your father?"

"Written by Mom, signed by both. He hates to write letters. Here, let me read it:

"Dear Elizabeth,

We really miss you and love you, and want you to be happy. Dad sends his love too, but you know how he hates to write letters. But this is from him too, don't worry. I'll make sure he signs it.

Your letter came as a surprise to Dad, but not to me. You're my daughter, and I've always known what's on your mind, even when you don't tell me. I always wondered about that doctor and why you never dated after you got home from Afghanistan. I know we've had a lot going on in the family, but still, there were plenty of nice and intelligent men that you met through your work.

I guess we would rather have had you marry a Catholic boy with a good job in Philly or New York, but we have to accept that a lot of things in the world have changed, and your generation is different. I was beginning to think you'd never get married, and you know how we worried about you when you were living with Tom.

We're glad that you've finally decided to get married. I talked to Dad, and he agrees that you should go ahead and get married as soon as possible, however they do it out there, as long as you are really sure of your feelings and this Yusuf treats you right. But we hope you'll be married in the Church as well, and that you'll both come home to visit as soon as you can.

I just hope you know what you are getting into, but you're a grown woman now, and I think you're going into things with your eyes open. Dad and I would love to have grandchildren!

I know that up in heaven Mark is really happy for you too.

You know we want you to be happy, and we're glad you've finally found someone who is responsible and respects you enough to marry you. We're looking forward to meeting him. So give him our love and blessings. Let us know when you're married, and let us know when you're coming home so we can make plans with your friends. Meanwhile, stay safe!

Love You and Miss You,
Mom and Dad"

Elizabeth looked up at Yusuf, grinning. "You look as if you've been hit by a football. There's still time to back out."

He hugged her head tightly against his chest, till she laughed and twisted away. "Hey! None of this kinky stuff. I can't breathe!"

He kissed her forehead. "I just can't believe my luck."

"I told you they'd be fine with it. I just hope I know what I'm doing. Sometimes I think I must be crazy. So, what do we do next?"

"What do Afghans do on any occasion? We have tea. Then we tell Malolai and Sharif, and we send a message to my father. We talk to the mullah and choose a date. Or we could go back to Peshawar now and marry there, and then go on to America to meet your family."

"Not so fast. You're needed here, so we should stay for awhile. Let's do the *nikah* here, and then we'll see what happens. Life has a way of working itself out."

"I can't wait till the wedding night," he whispered. "When can it be?"

"As soon as possible!"

"How about Friday? I wonder if we can get everything ready by then?"

"What everything?"

"Clothes. Kunari dress. A chicken or two. *Halwa*."

"We're still in the middle of a war."

"These are small luxuries. We'll have a real party in Peshawar, and in Pennsylvania, I promise you. And eventually in Kabul, *inshallah*. Money won't be a problem. I've got money invested in San Francisco, and I still own a house there, if we ever want to live there. I want to give you the best possible life, but I'm supremely grateful that you're willing to share this hard life for awhile longer."

"I never really thought I'd want to share so much of a life," she said thoughtfully.

He hugged her quickly. "I'll go and send for the mullah now."

"What mullah? Not the one who accused me of being a KGB agent I hope."

"I know a very kind old mullah from a village just up the valley. He is a truly holy man." He looked at her apprehensive face and laughed. "Don't worry, Elizabeth, we'll have another wedding in Pakistan, and another in America, but at least we'll be married here under Islamic law." He flashed her a grin. "By the time we're done we'll certainly be well married."

When word spread that the doctor was to marry the American journalist, the village women insisted on providing Elizabeth with proper clothes. One offered a red-flowered length of cloth for the low-waisted, full-skirted tunic. Another produced a long-treasured length of red cotton for trousers, and a third donated her own richly-embroidered wedding veil. A *mujaheed* who had been a tailor in Kabul brought a sewing machine from Badel on his back and cheerfully stitched Elizabeth's wedding clothes.

The day of the wedding, Malolai spent an hour braiding and rebraiding Elizabeth's thick and wayward shoulder-length hair. Finally she placed the veil on Elizabeth's head and stood back to survey her handiwork.

"You do look like a Pashtun bride! But no jewelry. I wish I had some of my own here."

Elizabeth felt awkward in her wedding clothes, particularly in the veil, as the heavy border weighted down her head. "I always thought I'd be married in a white dress. And probably in a church."

"Only God knows our fate. And you'll do that at home with your parents in a few months, *inshallah*. Come, look in the mirror."

Elizabeth stood up clumsily and walked over to the small, rusted rectangle that Yusuf used as a shaving mirror. When she saw her reflection, she restrained an impulse to look over her shoulder at the stranger who must be standing behind her.

"You need more *surmah*," said Malolai. "Sit down."

Elizabeth obediently sat down and let Malolai apply the black powder to her eyes. She winced as the stick poked the corner of one eye and a trace of powder got into her eye. She blinked and her eyes teared.

"Good. That spread it more evenly," said Malolai.

"But it hurts!"

"It will stop. Let's see your hands."

Elizabeth displayed her palms which, like the soles of her feet, were stained with henna to a deep, rusty orange. "I won't be going back to Peshawar for awhile," she said ruefully. "And certainly not to America. How long does it take to fade?"

"Only a few weeks, or a month."

"A month!"

"Everyone will know you were married. That is good."

"Do I have to go through this again in Peshawar?"

Malolai's face creased into a smile. "I think your wedding there will be like mine. And you will have a third in America. Lucky girl!"

Elizabeth carefully sat down on a *charpoy*. "I'm more nervous than I was under shell fire. When can we get this over with?"

"First, many women will come here. We will all drink tea and eat *gur* together. Some women have brought honey, and we will also have that with *nan*. Normally, the groom should feast everyone. But I think people here understand that he can't now. We will give what we can, but there is so little.

"After, the mullah will come and the Koran will be passed over your head, and you will be given things to eat and drink. You will have to say some words, but Yusuf will tell you what to say. Don't worry, you will do well."

"I'm not so sure."

"Are you sad?" asked Malolai, sitting down beside her and putting her arm around her. "Don't be sad. Why?"

Tears started and took Elizabeth by surprise. "I miss my family, just as you missed yours at your wedding. And I wish my brother were alive so he'd at least know that I'm getting married." Suddenly she knew what it must be like for a village girl on the day of her marriage, when she is snatched from the familiarity of her family into the arms and household of a stranger. There was a time in her life when she could never have imagined this place or this person. She looked down again at her hands and found them the hands of a stranger.

Malolai hugged her. "I know. I lost my parents when I was so small. I had to marry with no one from my family there, only my cousin, and you know how important it is for us to have family at every occasion. But I am your sister."

"I know," sobbed Elizabeth. "I just suddenly miss my mom and dad so much."

"Your *surmah* is smearing. Now I will have to do it again! We'd better hurry. The ladies are arriving soon."

Elizabeth dried her eyes. "I'll be all right. I am happy to be marrying Yusuf. This has happened quicker than I would ever have dreamed when I came back here, but somehow I feel it's right."

"He is an extraordinary man, and you are an extraordinary woman. Now sit and let me finish your *surmah*."

While Malolai was rimming Elizabeth's dark eyes, the first two women arrived. One was Halima, the matriarch of the house where Malolai and her son stayed when Sharif was away. Both women arrived bearing bright silver jewelry, which they offered to Elizabeth.

"Take it," Malolai whispered. "They want to give it. It would be an insult to refuse."

Elizabeth was touched, but at the same time guilty that these poor women would wish to give up their most precious possessions. She knew it was a measure of the esteem in which Yusuf was held by the people he served. Graciously murmuring, "*Mehrbani, mehrbani*," she accepted the necklaces, earrings, head ornaments, and a very old and heavy silver belt.

Malolai fastened two necklaces around Elizabeth's neck, and the belt around her waist. She pinned two hair ornaments to her veil, and Elizabeth felt the weight as they jingled down over her forehead. Elizabeth looked skeptically at the heavy earrings with their thick wires. Her ears were pierced, but she doubted the wires would go through. Malolai simply grabbed an earlobe between thumb and forefinger and deftly inserted an earring, which had a needle-sharp end. Elizabeth stifled a cry of pain as the earring went through, but before she could stop her Malolai had inserted the other. Elizabeth smiled to cover her discomfiture, but whispered, "They're killing me."

"You'll get used to them."

"They're heavy and they jingle too much."

"You're marrying a doctor. It won't do any damage that he can't repair."

"My ears will never be the same."

"Yes they will. Mine became normal again soon after my wedding."

More women arrived, young, old, middle-aged, women with babies, women with young children, and young girls who keenly watched the proceedings, aware that they too would probably be married in a short time. Elizabeth felt self-conscious as the women smiled at her and the young girls whispered in each other's ears behind their hands. Yet she felt a surge of affection for these people, who had brought the stranger silver and honey and cloth. She smiled inside. This was sure to be an event that would be talked about in Amrau Tangay long after the war had ended. The day the *Amrikai* married the doctor. Her heart contracted, and she suddenly wondered if Amrau Tangay would survive this war. She pushed the thoughts of war from her mind. Not today.

The small house was packed with women, and the level of conversation rose appreciably. Women paid their respects to the bride in twos and threes. Elizabeth smiled tolerantly, allowing herself to be touched and pawed as the women examined her hair and jewelry, and inspected her palms and the soles of her feet, assuring themselves that the doctor was marrying a proper Pashtun bride.

Elizabeth was beginning to wonder if the ceremony would ever take place when she and Malolai were summoned outside into the courtyard. There stood the mullah, a tall, thin old man with a long, wispy white beard. He looked stately standing under the leafless mulberry tree in the afternoon light, but when he caught sight of Elizabeth his stern face broke into a smile of delight. "*Shabbash,*" he said in satisfaction, and then continued speaking in Pashtu.

"He says you look like an Afghan girl," whispered Malolai, "and that you will make a fine wife for our doctor."

Elizabeth stood uncertainly, waiting for something to happen. Then she saw her groom approaching, followed by Sharif and Ebrahim. Sharif supported himself with a wooden stick, and held a somber and serious face until he caught Elizabeth's gaze and broke into a brief and joyous smile.

Yusuf looked as proud as a prince. He was dressed all in white, and his head was crowned by a white silk turban, which Massoud Khan had sent specially from Peshawar. In the soft, glimmering afternoon light, Yusuf's face was elegant and finely drawn, like a portrait in a classic Persian miniature.

Slowly Elizabeth walked forward to meet her husband. Malolai held one hand, Halima the other. Her heart was beating so fast she could barely concentrate, and she was hardly aware of the ceremony. Her mind focused on details: the sound of birdsong, the brilliant sapphire sky, the vein-like tracery of mulberry branches, the texture of the gold brocade cloth held over their heads, and the dreamy look in Yusuf's rich and expressive eyes.

She moved on instinct, spoke when she was told to speak, and repeated the unfamiliar words as best she could. A slight breeze sprang up, and she shivered in the draft. "It will soon be over," whispered Yusuf.

She began to feel faint with repressed excitement, and wished the ceremony would end. Halima passed her a glass of grape juice, which tasted sharp and slightly fermented. "Like life," whispered Yusuf, "both sweet and sour." Then handfuls of sweet *halwa* made from precious sugar, oil, and flour. As she ate, she could sense Yusuf close to her and could feel his soft breath warm on her cheeks.

At last the mullah gave them his blessing, and it was over. Elizabeth, conditioned to her own tradition, expected Yusuf to kiss her, and was surprised to be led back to join the women instead. "Patience," he said, squeezing her hand unobtrusively. "Soon I will come to you."

She was relieved to sit, and patiently smiled and thanked the women for blessings and congratulations as she watched them drink tea and eat *halwa*. Many of the guests discreetly left before the simple meal was served. There was a platter heaped with *pilau* cooked with raisins and nuts, which had become luxuries here in wartime, in the midst of which was chunks of lamb. In honor of the occasion there were dried grapes, ripe apples, and a bowl of wine-colored pomegranate seeds.

Elizabeth ate the tart, crunchy seeds a few at a time, dipping them in salt to sweeten them. She gazed at a handful of seeds, like polished garnets in her rust-dyed palm, and thought of the myth of Persephone, who had eaten six seeds given her by the King of the Underworld, condemning the Earth to six months of fall and winter while the Earth Goddess Demeter mourned her daughter's absence in the Underworld for half the year. She wondered what sort of legends Afghans attached to the autumn's richest fruit, and what fateful commitment she might be making at this, her wedding feast.

After the village women took their leave, Yusuf entered his house, grinning widely and followed by Commander Rahim, Ebrahim, Ismail, and Sharif, who was carrying a small wooden flute and leading his son by the hand. Yusuf reclined next to Elizabeth on a throne of plush red pillows, and Sharif sat to one side of the square hearth, now occupied by a wood-burning *bukhari* stove.

After another round of tea, the small group grew quiet with reverence as Sharif drew out the spirit of his simple homemade instrument, painting intoxicating dreams of love found, lost, and regained, and vivid images of the human struggle for freedom and the soul's yearning for God. As Sharif blew with pursed lips into the body of the flute, he seemed to be breathing life itself into the instrument, as he had before caused music to be born from the womb of the *rebab*. The voice of the flute was by turns cheerful and longing, vibrant and tragic. It teased, implored, and finally seduced its listeners into an enthralling spell, into the rapture of existence. In the darkness that descended outside, like a curtain slowly falling on an era, the voice became a defiant refrain of hope that could not be silenced. It was the music of breath itself, the spirit of the land, the spirit of a people, the spirit of resistance, and of healing, blown with a man's breath into a vessel that gave the spirit form.

Malolai danced for them, moving gracefully in the small space, turning in tight circles, gesturing eloquently with long-fingered hands. Yusuf sprang up beside her and pulled Elizabeth along with him, spinning her and urging her on. At first she tried to follow Malolai's steps, then she gave in to the flow of the music, as irresistible as the current of a river in spate. Twirling and weaving, oblivious to all, she glimpsed some hint of the ecstasy of the dervish.

Suddenly she realized that the music had stopped, that the other dancers had stopped, that only she moved to a silent song, while her husband stared at her, transfixed with desire. She faltered in midstep, and her veil settled behind her. Her hands, orange-dyed palms upturned, were extended in a gesture of supplication, and her feet were poised for flight. Sweat stood out on her face and trickled down her back. Her chest heaved with the effort of the dance.

Slowly she stepped toward her husband, who took her hand and led her to a *charpoy*. He looked at the others, who perceived his signal and got up, one by one, to take their leave. Each of the men respectfully shook Elizabeth's hand and embraced Yusuf. Malolai kissed Yusuf on both cheeks, then hugged Elizabeth, kissed her goodnight, and carried her sleeping child out into the night.

Yusuf shut the wooden door behind his guests. The kerosene lamp threw his shadow giant and dark upon the rough wall behind him as he stood looking at her. "They'll allow us privacy for a week," he said softly. "We may as well enjoy it."

"Yes, it was very kind of Malolai and Sharif to let the others share their room." She suddenly felt awkward and speechless.

Yusuf too seemed awkward. He dragged some wood out from under one of the beds and stoked the stove as she watched. He closed the stove and looked at his hands. "I can't touch you like this," he said embarrassedly. "I'll go wash." Before she could protest he was out the door. Uncertainly, she sat on the edge of the bed, as formally as a little girl whose feet barely touched the floor.

At last her husband entered the room and bolted the door behind him. Slowly, deliberately, he walked toward her, arms outstretched. She rose to meet him. He did not kiss her immediately, but held her tightly, running his hands over her body and rubbing his face against hers. Then they kissed, as if they had been doing so for lifetimes, tongue entwined with tongue in a playful and passionate dance. As she turned her face upwards to his, her bordered veil fell onto the floor, unnoticed.

Gently, he sat her down on the bed, where a soft new mattress had been laid, and clean new blankets were piled. He began to undress her, in between kisses, lingering over the process and laying each garment carefully on another bed.

"I've never kissed a man in a turban before," she said with a sly smile.

"Do you like it?" He leaned down towards her and kissed her again, nuzzling her cheeks and chin and neck with his moustache.

"Mmmnn."

"Should I leave it on?"

"You'd look ridiculous wearing only a turban."

She leaned back on the bed, waiting, as he unwound the turban, then removed his vest and pulled the long shirt over his head. With a thrill she realized she'd never seen him even half-naked before, and she liked what she saw. His chest was lithe and muscular, and had just the right amount of hair, just enough to be a little bit soft. She hugged him with abandon and laughed suddenly. "I never thought I would wait till I was married to make love to my husband."

"If I had met you in America, you wouldn't have. But one must concede to local customs. I'll bet you never thought you'd be spending your wedding night in a hut in Afghanistan."

"Hardly. And I never could have imagined this dress. Will you love me as much in jeans?"

"As much as I love you right now, in nothing. Will you love me in a business suit, or surgeons' scrubs?"

"As much as this minute."

He grinned and walked across the room to the lantern that hung from a wooden beam. He blew out the lamp, and in the dim glow of the wood stove she watched him approach her. He stood by the bed where she lay waiting, and she reached up to find the drawstring of his trousers.

The two huddled in the narrow bed together, holding each other and letting their desire grow naturally, as a river grows in strength and depth as it nears the sea.

She felt shy, as she had never felt shy with a man before, but she gathered up her courage, pressed herself more tightly against him and kissed him with all the generosity of her spirit.

CHAPTER 49
ELIZABETH AND YUSUF

Late autumn, 1988

Amrau Tangay

"We've been married for six days and you haven't been mean to me once," said Elizabeth sweetly.

They were sitting on the floor inside their house, drinking tea with Sharif, Ebrahim, and Commander Rahim. Malolai was restless as she worked on a piece of embroidery in the dim light, and Elizabeth could tell she was fretting about her son Hakim, who had been sent to Peshawar with Halima's family a few days ago.

"Give me a chance," Yusuf replied laconically. "Or give me a reason. By the way, where do you want to go on our honeymoon? Badel? Chagaserai? Nuristan?"

"Nuristan sounds nice."

"Or maybe Kabul? Anything is possible. The news should be on the BBC soon. What time is it?"

She looked at her watch, something she seldom did these days. "Eight-thirty."

Commander Rahim looked up from his book of Persian poetry. "BBC Farsi service is on in fifteen minutes."

Yusuf found the shortwave under a *charpoy* and fiddled with the dials, cutting through static. The sounds of trying to tune in an often-jammed broadcast always filled Elizabeth with longing and desolation, mixed with fragile hope. Hearing the sound of Big Ben's chimes made her feel as if she was at some distant outpost in time and space, with only the most tenuous links to the world outside this valley.

"If the Soviets really leave, maybe I can go to New York with you," said Ebrahim.

"What about Kabul?" asked Yusuf. "Don't you want to see your family?"

"Anyway, we're not going to New York," said Elizabeth. "Not for awhile. If the Russians pull out on schedule we'll go to Kabul first."

"Elizabeth is trying to get a reservation on the first convoy in to liberate Kabul," quipped Yusuf.

"Well can you imagine what that would be like?" she asked excitedly. "Do you think we might be able to pull it off?"

Yusuf looked at her with narrowed eyes. "*Inshallah*," he said enigmatically.

"Do you think America might give a visa to a veteran Mujaheed?" persisted Ebrahim.

"No more refugee visas," said Elizabeth a trifle gleefully, suddenly annoyed at Ebrahim's lust for the West. "In fact, they might even start sending people back to Afghanistan."

"Most of them won't want to go," said Yusuf.

Seeing the disappointment in Ebrahim's face, Elizabeth felt guilty for her unkind words. "Who knows? Maybe someday, *inshallah*, when things are better, we can sponsor you to come and visit America as a tourist."

Ebrahim's melancholy face brightened slightly. Elizabeth was about to add some affectionately teasing words when Commander Rahim silenced them with a word, and Yusuf turned up the radio.

Elizabeth sat quietly, watching the intense and serious faces of her companions as they listened to the waver and crackle of the fading voice. Yusuf, her husband now, she reminded herself, with his pale face hawk-like in its concentration; his father Rahim, whose dignified countenance might have been jolly under other circumstances, but retained serenity even in the face of brutal war; the dark and dashing wounded warrior Sharif; his brave wife Malolai with her frank green eyes that seemed to see into hearts, souls, and the future; and Ebrahim, whose sad black eyes always seemed to betray a hunger for things he could scarcely dream.

Her friends reacted to words she could not understand. Groans, sighs, nods, cautious approval all colored their faces as images of possible futures tumbled through Elizabeth's mind. She watched her husband's face become wet with tears. Dare she hope that she could actually accompany him on his return to Kabul? The city's name thrilled her. It spoke of ancient conquerors and wild nomads, hectic bazaars and tranquil, perfumed rose gardens. Would she at last see the city's ring of snow-mountains and come to know the high valley that had given birth to the man she had come to love?

Commander Rahim shut the radio off, and the Afghans engaged in an animated conversation.

"What happened?" asked Elizabeth impatiently.

"So many things going on all at once," said Rahim thoughtfully.

"What things? And how do they affect *us*?"

"So many questions," said her husband. "Free Elections coming in Pakistan in the next month. Benazir Bhutto is expected to win, but we don't know how she will be on the question of Afghanistan. Your elections happening in America at the same time, and we don't know how that will affect us either."

"And close to home, more fighting than ever," added Rahim. "And the parties still cannot work together, at the front or in Peshawar in the talks with the Soviet diplomats. I have heard that the fundamentalist parties are about to attack Chagaserai, but they have not contacted us to coordinate strategies."

"Do you think the Soviets will keep their promise?" asked Elizabeth.

"It was made under the auspices of the U.N.," said Yusuf.

"The U.N. has been ignored and defied many times before," pointed out Rahim. "In the cases of Israel and Palestine, India on the Kashmir question, South Africa and apartheid."

"What do you think will happen, Baba?" asked the son quietly.

The old man shook his head and spread his hands. "I truly want to believe this war will be over soon. No one is more weary of war and killing and blood than I am. I want to believe the Soviets will withdraw on schedule. I don't care if they declare it victory or defeat. But they had better take their Khalqi and Parchami henchmen with them if we are to have any peace."

Elizabeth knew in a flash that he was thinking of his son, her unknown brother-in-law Ayub, the Governor of Kunar. "So what's next?"

"My dear, I think you call it jockeying for position. It can only get worse before things get better, though I do believe they will get better some day. But I think it's time for you to leave, all of you."

There was a chorus of protest in various languages. Rahim raised his hand. "I won't hear it!"

The conversation continued at high volume. Sharif, Yusuf, and Ebrahim all seemed angry, Malolai uncertain.

"Would someone please tell me what this is about?" demanded Elizabeth finally. "I have a feeling it affects my life."

"The *commandant sahib* believes things will be more dangerous even here," said Malolai quietly. "He wants us all to go, but I don't see how we can leave that quickly, when the people need us so much."

"At least have the sense to go to your child in Pakistan! You are a mother first," shouted Rahim at her.

Elizabeth had never seen the old man so angry, not even after the murderous ambush that had killed and wounded so many of his men.

Again there was a torrent of Pashtu from all sides. Elizabeth gritted her teeth in an effort at patience.

Finally Yusuf spoke to her. "Dearest, it is decided. Malolai and Sharif will leave tomorrow. I would like you to go with them."

She was stunned, and bristled like an attacked cat. "What do you mean 'it is decided?' By whom? I didn't even get a say here."

"It's not safe anymore. There are too many threats against Malolai by the fundamentalists, and they may be the ones who take the provincial capital first, and even Kabul. If she is not safe, you, the American wife of an Afghan, are definitely not safe."

"I'm a journalist. My job is to report. I'll disguise myself as a boy Mujaheed if I have to."

"It's for your own good," said Yusuf shortly.

"No thank you. I prefer to stay."

"It's very touching that you don't wish to leave the side of your husband," said Yusuf, "but foolish. No, just plain stupid."

"You're calling me stupid?"

"Yes, actually."

Fury began to overtake her sanity. Dimly she realized that she was really drowning in fear, and anger seemed the only thing that would keep her afloat.

"You'll have to tie me up and drag me like a sack of potatoes."

"Fine, that can be arranged."

Yusuf got up, opened the door of the *bukhari* stove and started slamming wood into it, then slammed the door.

"Look, I just don't want to abandon Afghanistan at such a crucial time," she argued. "*You're* not going to."

He looked at her in exasperation. "Actually I plan to join you in a few days."

"How many journalists are in Afghanistan right now?" she asked.

"Very few. Most of them have more sense than you do."

"Thank you very much. Then it proves you need me as a witness. The world needs me."

Commander Rahim's white brows glowered. "We will see. I have made all the arrangements for you to leave tomorrow. It is up to you and your husband to decide."

Elizabeth looked intently at Yusuf. "Do you really want me to go?"

"Yes. And no, of course not. I don't want you to go away from me for a moment. But I want you to be safe."

"Do you really think it's all that dangerous?"

Yusuf sighed. "No one knows. God knows. Amrau Tangay has been attacked before. They say lightning doesn't strike twice in the same place, but how many villages have been bombed over and over? Unless my brother…"

"We can't count on Ayub's loyalty to his family any more than we could count on his loyalty to his faith and his people," interrupted Rahim. "He didn't stop the bombing of Amrau Tangay before. What makes you think he would stop it now?"

"One thing is in our favor," said Yusuf. "The spy is no longer with us."

"Yes," agreed Rahim. "But do you think there are not others? We too have a network of spies who give us useful information. How do you think I know that Ayub has always known that you have been based in this village, and soon after my arrival knew that I was Commander Rahim? I have known Ayub's servant Mousa since I was a boy myself. Mousa is a good Muslim and a loyal Afghan. He has been sending information to us ever since he accompanied Ayub to the Governor's House, and before that in Kabul."

Yusuf stared at his father. "You mean you set a spy on your own son?"

"To prevent worse things. And to protect him. But that is how I have come to know that he indeed ordered the bombing of Amrau Tangay. Don't fool yourself about this. Though to be fair, he waited until he knew we had been warned. He has shown a degree of civilization rare in this terrible and crazy war."

There was a moment of shocked silence. "So," continued Rahim, "Perhaps you are right, perhaps your brother will not bomb the clinic while you are here.

Or perhaps you are wrong. Do you want to gamble your life, and your wife's?"

Rahim rose, and the others filed out behind him with murmured good-nights. Elizabeth and Yusuf saw them to the door, then Yusuf bolted it behind them.

Yusuf stoked the fire as Elizabeth sat on the floor, watching, still angry, and at the root of her anger, terrified. Her husband finally sat beside her and lit a cigarette, something he seldom did unless he was under severe stress.

"Cigarettes can kill you," she said.

He blew several careful smoke rings, then looked at her. "And we could all die tomorrow. Let me have my vice."

She couldn't help smiling. She even loved him in his anger and pig-headedness.

He caressed her hair, and as she tried to turn away from him, pulled her chin toward him. "Elizabeth *jan*, I never want you to leave me, ever. But if you stayed here and something happened, how could I live with myself?"

"And if I go to Peshawar and something happens to you, how do you think I would feel?"

He stared at the flames through the partially open door of the *bukhari*. "*Jan-e-jan*, dearest of my heart. There is no answer for any of these questions. We could be standing beside one another and one of us be killed and the other have to go on living. That is the nature of this life."

"I just thought...I don't know. I've nearly been killed how many times now? But I didn't think anything would ever separate us." She started to cry in earnest, her eyes overflowing as the dam of sorrow and fear burst. She clung to him, suddenly fearing the worst.

"Shhh. Sssshhhhhh," he comforted her as he kissed the top of her head, her forehead, her eyelids, lightly, tenderly as a mother. "We'll see what tomorrow brings," he whispered in between tender kisses. "I think you are right. Nothing can ever separate us, even death. We are always together as long as either of us live."

She surrendered to the growing urgency of his kisses and her answering desire, and felt she was falling through time in a moment of endless, perfect peace.

CHAPTER 50
ELIZABETH

Leaving Amrau Tangay

The next day a heavy bombing raid in the Kunar Valley took the decision out of all of their hands. If indeed it had ever been in their hands, thought Elizabeth. It was impossible to go anywhere, just as the rightness of the decision to go became abundantly clear.

They all lived out of already-packed luggage, ready to go at a moment's notice. The bombing continued for three days, from dawn till dusk, dull explosions echoing from hill to hill up into their no longer so isolated valley.

Commander Rahim left immediately with his men, grimly implementing his contingency plan of raids on key government-held positions. Elizabeth was kept busy helping Yusuf and Malolai tend the endless stream of wounded Mujahedeen and villagers who had managed to flee to the tenuous safety of the mountains.

The morning of the fourth day dawned in a heavy veil of fog and cloud. Yusuf tried to prevail upon Elizabeth and the others to leave immediately, promising to follow them in a day or two. But the clinic was full of wounded men, and some women and children, and neither Elizabeth nor Malolai could bring themselves to leave the doctor alone until the situation was at least somewhat stabilized.

It was late afternoon when they were finally ready to leave. Commander Rahim had appeared with a few of his men early that morning and had slept most of the day. He insisted on accompanying Elizabeth and their party as far as Babur Tangay, but vowed to leave Afghanistan only upon direct orders from Mohammed Akbar.

Elizabeth nervously packed and repacked the few things she had with her, trying to get what she thought she might need in the easiest to reach places. But she knew nothing would ever satisfy her about this journey. She glanced out the door of the simple house in which she had known such happiness, once she allowed herself to be happy. Outside the dull sun dodged in and out of swiftly scudding clouds, stretching to reach the western horizon of the sullen sky.

Yusuf's figure blocked the door. "Are you ready? You should go soon."

"I guess so." She faced her husband, looking as stricken as a refugee. Yusuf took both her hands in his and looked at her seriously, then finally laughed at her. He slapped her lightly on the cheek. "Come on, it's not as bad as all that."

"I just wish you were coming now. Or that I wasn't going."

"Don't worry. I'll be along in a day or two, *inshallah*."

She looked at him with concern and a hint of distrust of his words. "Yusuf *jan*, are you really going to come?" she asked anxiously.

"*Inshallah*. But truly, *jan*, my intention is to come. Don't worry. We'll see each other in a day or two. I know how to travel by night, and I've walked these paths a thousand times in the past five years."

"I know. I just hate to leave you."

He smothered her protests with a kiss on the lips, then on the forehead, the cheeks, and again on the lips. "This will have to last us until Peshawar. Don't go to my mother's house yet. Go to Massoud Khan's and wait for me there. We'll have more privacy there."

He put his hand under her veil and felt the warmth of her neck, and then slid his hand down to her shoulder. She stared into his warm eyes, feeling weak at his touch, thinking of their lovemaking of the night before and desiring him again.

"Hey, you're making me want to leave less and less," she whispered seductively, running her hand slowly along his jaw. "Are you sure you want me to go now?"

"No, I'm sure I don't want you to go now. But you'd better." He hugged her impulsively, kissed her again, and stepped away briskly. He put his arm around her and walked her out into the courtyard where the others waited.

"You take care of yourself," he lectured. "The nights are unseasonably cold, and it may snow. I don't want to get to Peshawar to find my wife laid up with pneumonia. Now go. You've got an hour before dusk. The sun sets early this time of year. See you in Peshawar, *inshallah. Ba'amana khoda.*" Another quick kiss, as if he could not let her go, and then she was following Malolai, Sharif, and Commander Rahim up the path that led onto the ridge between Badel and Deh Wagal. The sharp wind stung her face and encouraged the already-formed tears in her eyes. When she turned to wave goodbye, the figures of Yusuf and Ebrahim were blurred.

CHAPTER 51

AYUB

Leaving Chagaserai

The day was gray and patchy, and Ayub spent it by himself, listening to Beethoven symphonies in his spacious salon, now heated by a *bukhari* stove. From time to time Mousa would come in and replenish the wood, or bring a fresh pot of tea. Ayub skipped his lunch. He just didn't have much of an appetite these days.

In December it would be nine years since the Soviet invasion. Friendly intervention, he corrected himself. But nothing had been particularly friendly. Now this era of Afghanistan's history was about to be over. The Soviets had all but abandoned this post, and the Mujahedeen seemed to be getting closer night by night. Every night there was fierce fighting, and a few more of his men died.

He would not be here for one more night of fighting, he was determined. Afghanistan was finished for him. Before tonight he would leave this Governor's House, this fortress with the chips and holes from recent mortar fire and the glass that had been replaced twice. He would go to Kabul and meet with Lermontov to make arrangements for his travel papers to Moscow. Although he had not heard anything definitive about his acceptance into the doctoral program, and the necessary scholarship to make life and studies possible, he was confident that all would be well. After all, he had proven his loyalty by ordering the bombing of Amrau Tangay.

Outside, the day did nothing. It neither rained nor snowed, and no one danced, celebrated, or even mourned. Ayub sat alone, watching the daylight hide intermittently behind a *chadar* of cloud, and then tease those below with brief revelation. He wished fervently that this was a winter day in his childhood, and he had never heard of Russia or America or China, of Khalq or Parcham or the Mujahedeen. He thought of the long winter afternoons in the family room by the *bukhari*, of Kabuli men in karakul caps and camel wool blankets, of ice in the air, horses' hooves muffled by snow, and always, the sting of smoke in the air. Then the smoke had not been that of destruction, but of wood giving its life for warmth, burning to cook food for sustenance and pleasure.

Regret is infinite, thought Ayub. He got up and looked at his garden once more. Brown and gray, like the sky. Hard black lines of trees, rose bushes cut back so they would bloom in spring for whomever might inhabit this house. The windows were smudged now with needle patterns of frost, and were smoky on the inside, despite the stovepipe that vented through the roof. Ayub ran his finger along the surface of the window and it came away black. Entranced, he traced the letters of the Persian word for freedom, *azadi*, on the window. Five Persian letters, right to left.

Now they would have their freedom, he thought abstractedly. Will they do any better with it than we did with ours? Or was it all just an illusion? Angrily he thumped the heel of his hand against the glass, which rattled in the pane, and fiercely wiped away all traces of his apostasy.

The governor went back to the couch where his open satchel sat. It was a large doctor's satchel, sent to him long ago by his older brother the doctor, but Ayub had only ever carried papers, books, and a few extra clothes in it. There didn't seem much point in taking many things where he was going now. He stared down into the open maw of the bag. Just then the electricity went out, and the gloom of the winter afternoon leaped palpably into the room. Ayub sighed. The music had stopped.

An extra shirt, a pair of jeans, socks, underwear, shaving kit. He was wearing a cashmere pullover and would put on his leather jacket and karakul cap when he left the house. He had clothes in the house in Kabul, Western-style suits and such things. He wouldn't need Afghan clothes in Moscow.

Ayub walked over to the bookshelf and debated. Marxist books he would find in Moscow. And history books. His hand rested on the thin Omar Khayyam. His finger tapped it twice, indecisively, and he removed it. Impulsively, he took a heavy volume of the poetry of Hafez as well. The rest could wait.

On the highest shelf was a Koran that had been his father's and was inscribed from his grandfather to his father, and from his father to him. He laid the two poetry books gently inside his satchel and reached for the Holy Book. Grasping it in both hands, he brought the heavy volume down to eye level, and then clasped it to his chest. He hated to abandon it. But he might be searched at customs going into the Soviet Union. Better not to start his new life under a cloud of suspicion. He kissed the Holy Book, held it to his forehead for a moment, then replaced it on the high shelf.

There was still a little room in the bag. He glanced through his small but select library of cassettes. He chose a couple of Mozart, Vivaldi's *Four Seasons*, the Third and Sixth Brandenburg Concertos, and Beethoven's Fifth and Ninth. His hand passed over Tchaikovsky. He could get that in Russia.

The electricity was still out. The afternoon was growing late and dim. If he were going to fly to Kabul today, he'd better leave soon.

Then Ayub did something he hadn't done in years. He went to the chill marble bathroom and washed his hands ritually, first the right three times, then the left. He took off his shoes and socks and washed his feet. He washed out his mouth and nose, his face, and behind the ears, then ran his wet hands over the back of his head. He looked into the mirror and thought how haggard he looked. He was only thirty-five. Yusuf was about to turn forty-one. Ayub wondered how well his brother had aged. He wondered where Yusuf was, and if he had ever married the American journalist. He would almost certainly never see Yusuf again, and this certainty contracted Ayub's throat and heart.

Ayub ran his fingers once more over his face, then dried it. He picked up his shoes and socks and hurried across the cold floor of the hall to the warmth of the salon. He looked around. There was no *ja-i-namaz* in this house, no proper prayer rug or mat, except maybe hidden in the servants' quarters. He looked at the carpet portraits of Lenin and Marx, and smiled at the irony of the thought. But he couldn't, not after all the blood that had been spilled in the clash of ideologies.

Nor could he bring himself to pray on the bare floor. The thought went against the grain of everything inculcated in him since childhood. Then he remembered the blanket in the other room. He'd seen enough pictures of Mujahedeen praying on blankets, in mountains and deserts. And he would take this blanket with him into exile, his one memory of his native land, all he could bear.

In the cold bedroom he also grabbed a soft rolled cap of white wool. It would do to cover his head for the prayers.

He shivered in the hall, through which a stubborn breeze found its way. In the salon again, he shook out the blanket. He had to think for a moment to remember the direction of Mecca, and again think to remember the beginning of the prayers. But from the first *"Allahu akbar"* to the last *"salaam,"* the prayers flowed unimpeded from the great unconscious treasure of his childhood.

When he finished he remained sitting on the blanket, thinking of nothing in particular. The electricity came back on, and it startled him. The somber measures of the second movement of Beethoven's Seventh honed the regret he already felt. He sprang to his feet and deftly removed the cassette. Time to go. He switched off the stereo, inserted the cassette into its plastic case, and snapped shut his leather satchel. The sum total of nearly five years as Governor of Kunar was now packed into a small leather bag.

He put on his leather jacket, zipped it up, and looked at the karakul hat doubtfully. He decided to wear the rolled woolen cap, though it was usually associated with the Mujahedeen. He reopened the bag, shoved in the karakul hat, folded his blanket as small as it would go, and forced the clasp shut. He straightened up and tied an English lambswool muffler around his neck. When he left the room, he glanced around once to make sure he'd turned off the stereo. He shut off the light behind him and closed the door.

As he had expected, no one questioned his orders to be taken to the heliport. He was still the Governor, and there were no longer senior Red Army officers to second guess him. At the heliport, he found that all the transport helicopters were already gone. Only a few gunships remained on the field. He ordered a pilot and a small tactical gunship. It was a non-regulation way to travel, but under the circumstances it seemed unlikely anyone would dispute his orders. The pilot was a Russian boy, one of the few Red Army soldiers left. He was young, courteous, and blond. He smiled and greeted the governor politely, asking where he wished to go. The boy assured Ayub that they would reach Kabul before nightfall, though if they wanted to do so they should leave immediately.

Ayub would say no goodbyes. He had told Mousa, the only person he cared for here, that he was going to Kabul for a few days to discuss further orders.

They were in the air, the machine's rotors cutting out all external noise and making conversation difficult. Ayub saw the ground fall away beneath him, vertically. It always gave him a slight feeling of vertigo, the way these machines maneuvered. So different from the smooth and quiet flight of a plane. Soon they were high over Chagaserai and all of its problems receded into remote unimportance. They ascended above the snow-dusted peaks that rose high and steeply from the dun valley floor. From up here one could see no scars. He loved this land and he loved these people. Tears came to his eyes, but he stifled them. Maybe as an old man he could come back.

"Where is Amrau Tangay?" he shouted on a sudden impulse.

"Ahead and to the right, sir. It is in the direction of Deh Wagal, isn't it?"

Ayub suppressed a smile at the boy's pronunciation of the Afghan names. "Is it out of our way?"

"Not too far, sir, but…do you wish to go there for some reason?"

"Yes, to take a look. Only to look."

"Yes, sir."

Expressionlessly, the boy maneuvered the helicopter up a side valley and over a ridge. They were still very high. Far, far below, the villages looked like small clay blocks perched on stone ridges.

"Is that it?" asked Ayub.

"Yes, sir. I think so, sir."

"Can you go closer?"

"I can circle again, sir."

The boy pilot guided the helicopter round in a wide arc, descending slightly. Still Ayub could not see his brother's home clearly, but he saw the scars of the bombing he had ordered and felt a wave of shame. He was seized by a desire to know whether his brother might still be there, and wondered if there were any sign at all by which he could tell. He knew it was foolish, but it was his only way of saying goodbye, from this detachment and distance.

"Can you get any lower?"

The boy gave him a doubtful sideways glance. "We fly high to avoid the danger of the enemy, sir."

"Go lower."

"You don't want me to land, sir?" the boy asked, horrified.

A moment's serious thought, then, "No. Only to go a little closer so I can see something."

The helicopter hovered in mid-air. The boy appeared undecided. "That is an order," said the governor firmly. "I will take full responsibility."

"Yes, sir. I will be prepared to take evasive action immediately if necessary."

The ship descended quickly, as if the boy were eager to make a pass over this unimposing village and get it over with. They were right in the crack of the narrow valley, below the rock walls that rose sheer to form sharp ridges. Ayub craned his neck to see if there were any figures on the rooftops. Was he mistaken, or did he see someone? Could it possibly be Yusuf?

For no particular reason his eyes traveled up toward the sun, now a dull red, like the rind of a blood orange. Then a second sun streaked by them, ten meters off to port side.

The boy put the helicopter into a sudden, rapid ascent and pressed a button. Two rockets streaked out from the wing-mounted rocket pods of the rising craft and sank home in the toy-houses directly below, which crumbled into earth, fire, dust, and black smoke.

"What have you done?" Ayub tried to scream in horror. "My brother was in there..." His voice failed to rise above the roar of the chopper's blades.

The boy continued to look straight ahead, concentrating on raising his machine out of danger, simultaneously shouting into his radio, calling for urgent reinforcements. The boy threw a quick accusatory glance at the governor. "They fired at us first, sir. I had to return fire."

Ayub covered his eyes. "God have mercy on us."

CHAPTER 52

ELIZABETH

Leaving Amrau Tangay

From the ridge above Amrau Tangay, Elizabeth heard the helicopter approach. In the hills, which had fallen silent in anticipation of the night, the sound was louder than a heartbeat in a lonely night of fear.

Commander Rahim found cover for them under a jutting rock protected by bushes. All four crouched and scanned the sky, wondering what the helicopter would do.

Elizabeth's heart beat in her throat as she watched the helicopter descend lower and lower. The beat of its rotors filled the valley until the sound overpowered the thud of her own heart.

A figure came out of Yusuf's house and stood on the roof. Ebrahim, brandishing a rocket launcher, she saw with horror. Where was Yusuf? A flash shot from the mouth of Ebrahim's weapon. With a resounding boom, the rocket sailed up towards the helicopter and went wide. Immediately afterwards, there were two more booms, and Elizabeth's scream rose above the roar of the helicopter as Yusuf's house crumbled into smoke and fire.

Hands restrained her, she didn't know or care whose. All she wanted was to run down to Yusuf, to pull him from the flames and stones, to dig with her bare hands through the dust until she found him, to breathe life into him. She couldn't hear herself shrieking, and didn't hear Commander Rahim fire the shoulder-fired Stinger missile he had been carrying to war. The heat-seeking missile went straight into the rising helicopter, which exploded suddenly into flame. The machine tumbled from the fire-tinted sky and crashed on the cliff below Amrau Tangay.

CHAPTER 53
ELIZABETH

Leaving Afghanistan, lost

In the aftermath of the crash a deadly silence descended on the land. Unnoticed, the sun slipped behind a dark rim of mountain.

Elizabeth ceased straining against the hands that held her. A numb shock took over her body and her brain, and the core of her being felt cold and brittle as ice.

Commander Rahim turned towards her. His face was white. "I have avenged the murder of my son," he said tonelessly. "Now the servants of *sheitan* will be as thick as flies over us. I cannot come with you. You must go with Sharif and Malolai, quickly."

She stared at him, uncomprehendingly. "What do you mean? I can't leave. I have to go find Yusuf." Her voice was cold, controlled.

"You are still my daughter-in-law," said Rahim vehemently. "I won't let you die. Go!" Seeing her stricken face, he embraced her tightly, his chest heaving with unshed tears. "Go!" he said fiercely.

She pulled away from him. "I won't go! Yusuf might be alive. What are we waiting for?" She scrambled down the hillside, reckless and out of breath, her *chadar* trailing behind her.

She was sobbing as she ran, praying, cursing, flailing her fists angrily in the air. If she could just reach the ruined village, she could force her way through that black, choking cloud of smoke and dust and dig him out. It was not possible for Yusuf to die, oh, please God, no, not Yusuf, not now when he was just about to leave, not now when the war might finally end in just a few weeks.

Commander Rahim and the others were shouting at her, but she couldn't hear them, and the adrenaline of anger and fear gave her the strength to keep her lead. And above the pounding of her running feet and her labored panting, she also did not hear the helicopters until they thundered over the ridge behind her, guns blazing. Still running, she looked straight up to see three monstrous choppers bearing down on the narrow valley. She screamed as a spatter of machine-gun fire kicked up dirt a few yards ahead of her, and at that moment lost her footing and fell hard onto the rocky path, skidding on her hands and knees.

Rahim was right behind her. He jerked her up and pushed her under a rock overhang. "You fool!" he shouted. "Why don't you ever listen? I told you they would be coming. Now get out of here while you still can!"

She looked down at the circling helicopters, now below them, methodically shooting rockets into every home in Amrau Tangay, those still standing and those already in ruins.

"Yusuf would never leave me. How can I leave him?" she asked hoarsely.

"Yusuf is dead!" he shouted at her.

His voice stunned her with its truth.

"He wouldn't want you to die too. Please, go now," the old man pleaded.

She met his gaze, wondering if she would ever see him again.

"Can you walk?" he asked.

She just nodded.

"Then go now. And go with God." Commander Rahim spoke rapidly in Pashtu to Sharif, who had joined them, and turned and embraced his daughter-in-law quickly. Then, tears in his eyes, he rushed off toward his own fate, an empty missile-launcher slung over his shoulder and a Kalashnikov in his hand.

Sharif urgently pulled Elizabeth away, dragging her until she started to stumble along by herself. She went on, weeping, heading for some chimera of safety that no longer held meaning for her. The roar of the helicopters haunted them until well after dark, when they saw the ships ascend high into the lightless sky and veer away from the scene of carnage, leaving it to the scavengers.

They marched through the blessed oblivion of the night. Flickering lightning and the rumble of nearby thunder only reminded Elizabeth of the horror she had witnessed, a tape her mind played over and over as she tried to change the ending.

By the time they reached Babur Tangay it was sleeting, though the cold wet snow did not stick. The sun did not come up that day. The sky merely grew lighter and stayed a dull gray all day long before fading again to black blankness. Elizabeth hunched by a fire in the cave, shivering and trembling, refusing all food and tea until the firm pressure of Sharif's hand warned her that he would tolerate no more of such behavior.

"He says you must eat, or you cannot walk," said Malolai. "He is limping and cannot carry you. If you are too slow you are a danger to us as well."

Her friend's concern cut through the fog in Elizabeth's brain, and she held out a hand for the bread Malolai offered her. She listlessly chewed the hard, flat, tasteless bread, slowly sipping a glass of hot, sugary, weak tea. She knew Malolai and Sharif had also loved Yusuf. But he had been her husband, the one man she had finally chosen to be with for all her life. A few days of marriage, and then nothingness. She shivered again, and did not resist or even react as Malolai covered her with a sleeping bag. She fell into a restless, uncertain sleep, from which she only awakened in the late afternoon. It had been twenty-four hours since the death of her husband. Still the sky spat at them and the ground was slick and muddy. But they would go on in the night, pressing hard to reach the safety of the border before dawn.

This night there were no flashes of fire, only forks and sheets of lightning that briefly flashed, but illuminated nothing. There were no explosions of destruction, only thunder, the beating of still living hearts, and the restless thump of footsteps desperately trying to outpace the inevitable.

Elizabeth walked dutifully, habitually. She did not fear or care for anything anymore, but something deep inside her held on to the illusions necessary for self-preservation. Strangely, surprisingly, it was easier to go on living once all hope had finally died and the torment of uncertainty was replaced by the calm numbness of resignation.

Again and again, before her eyes, like an endless TV news replay of some horrific disaster, she saw the walls crumble and burn, saw black, charring smoke mix with dust and engulf the ruins of her life. It was senseless that people kept dying in what were surely the last days of this war, when attrition had been made obsolete by its sheer meaninglessness. But it had happened to the man she loved, and would keep happening to others. Now all that was left was to, step by step, get herself and her two companions safely back to Peshawar. And then…but her mind refused to advance beyond the border.

It was so dark in that black void night that no stars reflected in the turgid stream that was the Kunar River in winter. Even in the open, the path was found mechanically by her feet, not her eyes. Sharif led, she followed, and Malolai came behind. Sometimes in the darkness a hand would find her, from behind or before, and the brief pressure would assure her that this was not a dream, as she begged God for it to be.

They did not stop except for the briefest of rest halts. No one lived in the village where they had once obtained a raft, in a long ago spring. No full moon lit ruins, which now huddled as sullen, hope-bereft shapes, crumbled as inexorably as the palaces of long-vanquished conquerors of long-vanished centuries. The night was undeniably dark, the thickest of cloud covers blotting up all light, covering the jeweled face of night more thoroughly than the heaviest *burqa*.

They passed through the field where golden wildflowers once grew in a spring that seemed to have bloomed on another planet. Here Sharif and Ebrahim had picked the flowers that had been a token of friendship reaffirmed.

With a sudden twist of her heart, Elizabeth remembered that Ebrahim too was dead. But why had Ebrahim fired at the helicopter? Maybe the helicopter would never have attacked if he hadn't fired. And why did he have to miss?

Now her tears for Yusuf, buried deep under layers of pain, began to flow as if hard ice had melted inside her. As she stumbled uncaring through the fields, a cold wind sucked the hot tears from her cheeks and carried them away to become again hard ice in the winter sky above her adopted land.

She wished for stars, for a tiny flame in the night, a lantern, a candle, for some proof that other than darkness still existed. This darkness had no character. It was not the darkness that comforts, or even the darkness that terrifies. It was only blackness, which held not even the catharsis of grief, but was only loss in its purest form. Being, then Not-being.

One step in front of another, feeling like a worm in a cave slipping through primeval mud. Not the simmering primordial soup that precedes and promises life, but the cold mud that will still exist when life has finally ceased and a lifeless cinder drifts in endless blackness.

In this field were mines once, she thought. Maybe still are. There, by that hill, we rested, and there Ebrahim almost killed his best friend. Now Ebrahim is dead. Dead, not even martyred, not really. It was too late for martyrdom, though they would still use the word and it might comfort Ebrahim's parents when word reached them in the newly liberated city of Kabul.

There, right there they had sat. She looked at Sharif in front of her, his head bowed, and wondered if he too remembered and grieved for his friend. She could just make out the jumbled outline of the rocky hill from which a bird had startled them from their folly. A bird, sometimes a symbol of freedom and striving, sometimes the sign of innocence and peace, reality synchronistically forming itself into omens for we poor humans to interpret. Or maybe we poor humans are just wedging random events into symbols and meanings in a desperate effort to order the chaos of existence, to impress pattern on the senseless.

She was more tired than she had thought possible. She wanted to stop, but remembered that Dunahi had been bombed into a place that was uninhabitable. The reality of the march dissolved into a dream of a dark night. Endless, endless, slow, steady plodding. When morning came it would bring no comfort or change. But they must be in the hills by then.

A miserable rain began and soon soaked them through. Elizabeth shivered violently, hoping to purge herself. She could not bear to think of Yusuf's face, voice, body. She had never suffered such intense loss before, not even when her brother had died. At least she had had months to prepare herself for the inevitability of that searing loss.

And now slowly, as she put one foot in front of another, now skirting where people had for generations inhabited a place called Dunahi, now slipping on river stones wet with spray and rain, a strange newborn feeling of thankfulness swelled in her jumbled thoughts. She had lost that which had become most precious to her, but Yusuf's beloved Afghanistan would soon be free. In some form Yusuf must live on. His consciousness, his vital life energy, could not just dissipate. It would take on some other form. Some part of his consciousness might even now linger and observe her, laughing at her poverty of spirit.

Dawn was near, and they had reached the foothills. The house where she had once sheltered with Ebrahim would be near here. Perhaps they would again shelter in an upper room. They would lie on *charpoys* between carved posts and painted walls, and dream.

People survived, she reminded herself, not only survived, but triumphed. She knew not what might come for Afghanistan after the Soviet withdrawal, but against all odds and hope, they had triumphed, through patience, faith, tenacity, and sacrifice. Her heart contracted at the thought of that word "sacrifice," which Yusuf had used so often. Now he had sacrificed, ultimately, and so had she.

She was grateful for the shock that continued to numb her heart. Someday soon, in Peshawar, reality would hit her and she would cry uncontrollably for days, crying out her anger at God and at the cruel, unjust, irrational world. And one day, who knew how long after, the pain would dull, pass, fade, and remain finally as a scar visible only under certain emotional lights, revealed willingly only to those closest to her heart.

It was dark and misty and still raining steadily when she hauled herself up the slippery slope to the small farmhouse where they would rest. In the wet, the straw and animal waste outside the house had become a damp, earthy muck that clung to their boots. Elizabeth waited, swaying slightly with exhaustion, as Sharif knocked on a wooden door. An old woman dressed in black, her gray hair in braids that peeked out from under her veil, let them in. Another woman, roused from her sleep, came to greet them. It was Sharif's aunt, who embraced first Sharif, then Malolai, with obvious relief. The two women then embraced Elizabeth and led them all up a steep stairway. In the upper chamber they took off their shoes, and Sharif and Malolai crouched by the brazier in the center of the room while Elizabeth hunched shivering on a bed, chin cupped in hands, elbows on knees. Sharif took her hand, looked at her with compassionate eyes, and wordlessly persuaded her to warm her hands over the coals.

Sharif's aunt entered the room carrying a scoop full of embers, which she dumped into the shallow brazier. Behind her came Sharif's uncle, stooped with rheumatism. Mechanically, Elizabeth rose with Malolai and Sharif and watched as Sharif embraced his uncle and wept.

More people crowded into the room, and Elizabeth recognized most of the relocated members of Sharif's family.

The warmth of so many bodies created heat, and thick, dry blankets were brought for the tired travelers. A thin gray light filtered in through windows covered with stretched animal skins. Elizabeth hunched over the brazier, blanket over her head, staring into the dying coals.

She dozed in that position, and had started to fall forward when Sharif caught her. Gently he helped her to a bed and tucked her in as he would a small child. She slept the sleep of the exhausted in spirit, descending into deep, healing sleep, then slowly ascending through layers of consciousness into a dream state, her eyes flickering open and shut. In between dreams she opened her eyes to a vision of Sharif's uncle seated cross-legged on the woven rug. A heap of grains of corn lie on a skin spread out in front of him. One by one, he counted out what seemed to be thousands, murmuring *Allahu akbar* as he numbered each grain in a litany of inexhaustible hope.

When she woke in the late morning she felt rested. For a brief moment she was disoriented, wondering where she was, and then the desolation of her loss fell suddenly and heavily upon her once more. The old man was still telling his maize grains, his figure a silhouette of dignity undiminished by misfortune.

A small boy wrapped in a wool blanket that dripped melting snow into the warmth of the room came in and crouched by the old man. The boy spoke quickly, gesturing urgently. The old man's face grew serious, then he shook his head slowly, covered his face with his right hand, and sighed. He woke up his nephew and told him the news. Sharif glanced at Elizabeth, then woke up his wife. Malolai's face grew pale with horror, and the pupils in her green eyes contracted to points of concentration as she shot questions at the boy. Finally she turned to Elizabeth, on whose face interest was strangely absent.

"The helicopter Commander Rahim shot down," began Malolai in a quavering voice, "in that helicopter was Governor Ayub of Kunar, Yusuf's brother."

It took some time for the implications to sink into Elizabeth's brain. But when they did, she felt as if she had been dealt a blow to the solar plexus, a blow so severe that she would never fully recover. There was nothing to say. All words had been rendered superfluous. Finally her voice found the absurd question, "Is he dead?"

"Yes." Malolai hesitated. "We can never know what his intention was in coming there…"

"And the commander?"

Tears brimmed in Malolai's eyes. "Amrau Tangay has been utterly destroyed. The boy says everyone there is dead. Some think the commander escaped. Others say no."

"Poor Commander Rahim," said Elizabeth, her voice heavy with ripe tears. "Two sons…" She could not finish. Her journalistic training had taught her to zealously examine the who, what, when, and where, but she had long since learned that how and why were always left up to speculation and spin. Truth was impossible to find in the debris of war, but it was no less to be searched for.

Elizabeth's eyes dried then, and the lump in her throat grew hard and dry. Determinedly, she formed a dam against the tears in her heart, and prayed the dam would not burst till she had reached Peshawar.

It was early afternoon when they left the house. The sleet flung itself at them like ice-needles, and as they ascended the mountain, became snow and stuck in patches alongside the path. Near the top the path itself was covered with a thin, slippery layer of fresh snow. By the time they reached the Durand Line they walked in a cloud, marking each step in the whiteness that surrounded them. Elizabeth shivered on the hard rock of the border, in an icy wind that leaped up from the east to tear the sky's shroud to shreds and reveal the innocent, naked blueness of afternoon sky. She looked over her shoulder to view once more the unfortunate land that had given, and taken, and saw that the clouds had parted and patchy sky blinked at the rain-washed land. Then she knew it was not only the memory of Yusuf, but the land itself that held her.

CHAPTER 54
ELIZABETH

Peshawar, Pakistan

E lizabeth sat alone on the worn gold couch in the salon of Massoud Khan's house, her back to the gas fire, which hissed like an angry insect. She stared into the glass of tea that she held in her right hand, reflecting on its rich translucence, fascinated by the bits of leaves spiraling towards the bottom.

Rebab music played on the stereo, summoning memories of other seasons. Without order they came, like flotsam bobbing on a restless ocean. How many days had she known Yusuf in this life? Altogether maybe three months? In a span of days, she had lived a whole lifetime, falling in love, marrying, and being widowed by war. Yet she had found and lost more than most people dared dream.

She sank into the comforting embrace of music. Despite the gas fire it was cold in the room, so she pulled Salima's white pashmina shawl more closely about her. She didn't know why she had wanted to wear white tonight, but some unconscious urge had prompted her to wear white *shalwar* topped by a white *kameez* printed with tiny blue flowers that reminded her of the *shin gul* of that first spring. She was somehow not surprised when Salima, seeing her choice, told her that traditionally in Afghanistan white, not black, was the color of mourning.

Despite Elizabeth's grief, the white made her dazzlingly beautiful, and her recent tragedy shined as courage on her high white brow. She wanted to command all her dignity to attend the *fatehah*, the memorial prayers for her late husband which, like all the *fatehah* for martyrs in these days, would be tinged with the bittersweet hope for a swift end to this sorrowful war.

Outside, the air above Peshawar was thick with dingy, chilly smoke from coal fires and charred dreams. Human breath further thickened the air, which hung and condensed slowly on windows, blankets, and rifle barrels. It was dark now, darker than she had imagined Asia. She glanced at the windows and saw only her own reflection, which startled her.

The door opened, and Salima came in, smiling tentatively. "*Salaam*," she greeted Elizabeth.

Elizabeth conjured a smile and murmured a greeting. Had it been two days already since her arrival in Peshawar? When Elizabeth and her companions had arrived well after midnight, Salima had arisen from her bed, knowing something was dreadfully wrong, to greet her pale, ashen-faced friend. She had not wakened the servants, but had rushed around the hushed house herself, lighting the fire, making tea, and preparing beds for Elizabeth, Malolai, and Sharif. She had tactfully asked no more than Elizabeth had told in a single sentence: "Yusuf is dead."

When Malolai and Sharif had gone exhausted to bed, Salima had sat holding Elizabeth in her arms, weeping with her until dawn's slow gray light had seeped into their consciousness. Neither had wanted to wake Massoud, knowing that the bad news would still be there when he awakened. But when he arose for morning prayers he saw light in the salon and joined them in weeping for the man they had all loved.

Massoud had held Elizabeth's hand while she looked down at the centered pattern of the carpet, recounting the little she knew, pausing now and then to swallow hard, and finally giving in again to tears. Now, two days later, all the tears had been sucked up by Elizabeth's parched spirit, and she sat dry-eyed.

For a long time Salima said nothing, and Elizabeth was grateful for the silence of understanding.

Salima's hand closed on her friend's. "We will always remember Yusuf as one of the martyrs, maybe one of the last martyrs. The price of freedom has been high. We will never know how many thousands, millions even, have died."

"I want to be happy for Afghanistan," said Elizabeth. "Happy that it's all almost over. But…" Her voice caught and she bit her lip.

"You don't have to come tonight, Elizabeth *jan*," said Salima. "It is not expected of you. It might be hard for you to be around so many people. But nor should you be left alone. I have arranged to go first, and let Malolai sit with you for a time, then I will come back and she will go."

"No, I *must* be there. Yusuf would want it."

"It is not necessary. It is not your religion. You will mourn and pray in your own way."

"But Bibi Hafizah is there, and Maryam. I'm part of the family now, however briefly."

"Yes, but…"

"I'm not Afghan. I know. Not by birth. But Afghans are not the only ones who have to face unpleasant things with courage. That's what I've been writing about and photographing all these years, in Afghanistan, El Salvador, Lebanon, South Africa. I don't know if I have the courage all these people I've met do." She faltered and her voice became small. "But I feel I need to go."

Salima squeezed her hand. "As you wish. I will stay beside you at every moment, and we will leave as soon as you need to, even if the mullah's prayers are not finished."

Elizabeth's face crumpled, then she composed herself. "I have no courage," she whispered with an effort. "I guess I'll just have to do without it."

"You have a great deal of courage," said Salima. "Courage is not being blind and ignorant and thus not afraid of anything. Courage is doing what you are afraid to do. You have more courage than anyone I know."

"I try." Hers was a small voice, all the braver for its small size.

"You've done so much for us," said Salima, sighing.

"No more than anyone else."

"But the stories you wrote, the photographs you took, they all helped to shape world opinion and change the reality. Drops of water make rivers, which flow to oceans and become one."

Elizabeth looked at her directly. "All I did I did out of love."

"And that is what is important."

"But it wasn't only love for Yusuf. It's a love that goes on. That is why I must go tonight, to honor Yusuf, his family, and his people."

"*Shabbash*," said Salima simply.

"And I have made a decision."

Salima looked at her questioningly.

"I will go to Kabul now."

"But you can't!"

"Why not? Massoud and others will go as soon as they can."

"But Massoud won't even let me go until we are sure everything is safe. That could be months, or years, depending on what happens after the Soviet troops are gone."

"I will go," she said stubbornly, her small chin emphasizing her decision.

Salima broke into a laugh. "I don't think anyone can stop you."

"Exactly. Yusuf and I had plans to go. So I want to see his home city. And yours and Massoud's. You and Yusuf have told me so much about it, and I always wished I could see it."

"It won't be the Kabul we remember," said Salima regretfully. "And what will you do there?"

"Live," she replied. "At first I'll write about the troop withdrawal and the change of government, and then we'll see. Maybe I can get a job with an NGO doing some kind of aid work. I'm learning more Dari and Pashtu and maybe some organization will need someone with P.R. skills."

"That's good. But you can't live in Kabul forever, even if you do get a job. What about your family? Don't you want to go home and see your parents?"

"Not now, not yet. I haven't even told them about…what happened. You must understand, if I'm in a familiar place I'm afraid all the memories will come back, and I can't live with the memories while they're still so fresh. I want to let them fade a little. I want to keep myself busy with something new, yet something connected with Yusuf, something that he loved that I can love too. Then by the time the memories come the sharp edges will be dulled and maybe they won't hurt so much."

Salima thought. "You can go with Massoud, I suppose. I am sure he can arrange a safe place for you, and there will be other journalists there. But still, it may be dangerous."

"I'm not particularly afraid of danger right now. Sometimes I wish I'd died at Amrau Tangay, and I could be with Yusuf now. Salima *jan*, think back on that night when Massoud was attacked, and you'll understand."

Salima nodded, her face tight and worried. "I do understand. But I don't want to lose you too. And still I am afraid for Massoud, afraid that there might be civil war, and it might go on and on. I wish he was not going into Afghanistan anymore, or that I could go with him now. But he must follow his destiny."

"And I have to follow mine. If there is really such a thing as destiny, I suppose we must automatically follow it, regardless of our own wishes. But Salima, by God, I believe we can alter that destiny, or else why are we human?"

"The Sufis say, 'Trust in God, but tie your camel first.'"

Elizabeth laughed for the first time since the death of her husband. "What a way of putting it! Meaning God gave us brains and hearts to use, so use them?"

"Yes, something like that. So what will you do in Kabul to alter your own destiny and that of the world?"

"I don't know yet. I can't think that far ahead, but I believe I'll somehow be shown the way. I can only have faith in something undefinable, and go on living the best way I know how. Some people might say I'm no better off and no worse off than I ever was, but I know that's not true. I know how much I've changed.

"I'm better off for having had a most precious spirit merge his heart with mine, and worse off for having lost that…" Elizabeth's voice quavered and tears started. "But Salima, life just isn't fair! Not to any of us, not to all the people who have lost loved ones in this war and all the wars that are still going on."

For a few moments the two women sobbed, holding each other, then Salima got up and brought a box of tissue to Elizabeth.

"It will be a long time before the pain grows less," said Salima. "In our culture it is acceptable to cry. You are brave. We all know that. You don't need to prove it to us, or yourself."

Elizabeth smiled weakly. Salima glanced at her watch. "If you are going, then we must call the driver and go now. Do you still want to go?"

A swift nodding motion, a small "Yes."

"I will get my *chadar*. We won't stay long." Salima looked as if she were about to say something else, then left the room.

Elizabeth stood up, adjusted her shawl over her head, and glanced out the window. It had begun to rain. And tonight, in the rain, they would mourn a hero and mark endings and beginnings.

She turned away, half listening to the rain, half listening to the music, which nearly drowned the sound of the rain. She walked to the wall opposite the window and examined the framed collage on the wall. Salima had culled pictures from the years of war. There was Massoud Khan with his father Mohammed Akbar at the talks in Geneva. Massoud in battle gear, a bandoleer across his chest. Massoud crouched behind an anti-aircraft gun, Massoud surrounded by Mujahedeen in a *sangar*, and visiting his men in the hospital. Then Elizabeth winced as her eye caught a recent addition to the collage, a carefully trimmed oval of Yusuf, stethoscope over his bandoleer, woolen cap tilted at a rakish angle, a devil-may-care grin on his face. A picture she had taken.

Tears started to her eyes and spilled over. She gazed on that face with love, remembering the many moods she had seen in such a short time, the animation, anger, compassion, tenderness, and love. And the terrible pride mixed with terrible uncertainty. With a hand still faintly stained with the henna of her wedding day, Elizabeth reached out to touch the image and spirit of her beloved. The picture blurred before her vision, and she barely heard the knock on the door.

She turned slowly. Through the distortion of the rain-streaked window, she saw a familiar silhouette in Mujaheed cap and woolen blanket. Her heart stopped in a freeze frame of daring hope as she heard one word.

"Elizabeth…"

EPILOGUE

"There was and there was not.
It was so and it was not so.
It may have been or it may not have been.
Either way, it is past."
– traditional beginning to stories in the Hindu Kush

It may have been that Yusuf survived, against all odds and against the witness of Elizabeth's eyes. Or it may not have been.

It may have been his figure that she saw through the rain-streaked window, or it may not have been. Perhaps there was no one there at all.

Perhaps it was his voice she heard, or perhaps not. Perhaps his voice spoke to her from the spirit world.

Perhaps her fantasy came true, and she was hugging Yusuf, regardless of the rain, the mud, the dirt of travel, regardless of the cast and the crude sling on his left arm, regardless of the pain her embrace caused him.

They clung to each other and wept without shame. Finally he lifted her face toward his. "It's wonderful to see you," he croaked, "but I have three broken ribs. Maybe a couple more after that bear hug you just gave me."

"What!" She let him go and stepped back. "Yusuf, is it really you?"

He looked down at his body and patted himself with his good hand. "The last time I checked."

She kept staring at him as if he would dissolve into illusion, shaking her head in disbelief. "I was there when the helicopter fired at the clinic, and I saw the building collapse. I started to run down to dig you out, but then the other helicopters came and the whole village was…my God, completely destroyed. I really thought you were dead."

He grinned. "So did I. My father told me everything. That's why I came straight here."

"Oh, Yusuf…" She hugged him fiercely, despite his pain. "Yusuf, where is your father? Is he all right?"

"'All right' is relative, after what happened. Come on, sit down." He slipped his good arm around her and let her lead him to the couch. "My father is filled with grief. He has killed his own son."

She held his eyes. "I know. He once told me Afghanistan was the Land of Cain."

"But this is only the beginning. Now the civil war will start. The day the last Russian leaves, the serious killing will begin."

"But can't anyone stop it? Isn't there anything we can do?"

He cradled his wounded arm, then looked at her directly. "I am a doctor. I will go back to Afghanistan and tend the wounded, as long as it takes, as long as the war goes on. Will you come with me?"

"Yes, when?" she answered without hesitation.

He patted his arm. "Not for awhile. We'll go to meet your parents first. And then…" He stopped and looked at her with naked honesty.

"Back into the fire," she finished for him.

"But fire has its own magic."

"Everything happens for a reason," she whispered, kissing him with the most tender touch on his bruised forehead. The fire of this war had honed her soul, and she did not flinch from the still fiercer fires ahead.

"But Yusuf, how did you ever survive the collapse of that house?"

"The question is not really how, but why. There's plenty of time for how. *Inshallah*, a whole lifetime. As to why…" He paused and leveled his gaze at her. "That only God can know."

GLOSSARY OF UNFAMILIAR TERMS

P = Pashtu; D = Dari (considered a dialect of Farsi, or Persian); Ar. = Arabic; if origin is not specified, the term is in general use, either in Muslim countries, or in the Indo-Pakistani Subcontinent

afarin (D) Bravo!

Ai, khoda mehrban ast. (D) Oh, God is kind.

al-hamdulillah (Ar.) Praise be to God; thank God

Allahu akbar (Ar.) God is great

Amrikai (D) American

arussi (D) wedding celebration

azadi (D) freedom

azan (D and Ar.) Muslim call to prayer, given five times a day

ba'amana khoda (D) goodbye; go with God

Baba (D) father; daddy

baklava (many languages) layered sweet made of thin dough, honey, and nuts, popular throughout the Middle East and Central Asia

bakshish (D, P, Ar.) bribe, gratuity

bas (D, P) enough

Bia! (D) Come!

Bismillah (Ar.) In the name of God

Bismillah ar-rahman ar-rahim (Ar.) In the name of God, the Compassionate, the Merciful; beginning phrase of every chapter of the Holy Koran

bolani (D) savory dish of meat and greens stuffed in fried triangles of thin dough

bukhari (D) wood-burning stove

burqa (Ar.) a woman's veil with a thick chiffon flap that covers the face; usually black cloth

chadar (D) a large cloth or shawl, used as a veil; usually worn over the head and reaching to the hips.

chadari (D) pleated veil enveloping a woman from head to toe, with only a crocheted grill for light and air.

chai tea

chai khana (D) tea house

charpoy a wooden-framed rope bed

Che shud? (D) What happened?

Chetour asti? (D) How are you?

chillum water pipe

chowkidar watchman, caretaker

Chup! Hush! Shut up!

Commandant Commander

Da khodai pah aman (P) goodbye

Dari Afghan Persian

digar (D) others; another

doorgh (D) cooling drink made of yogurt mixed with water, chopped cucumber, and dried mint

dupata (Urdu) long chiffon scarf worn by women with *shalwar kameez* for modesty and decoration

Farsi Persian language

ghazal a poetic form, always meant to be sung; usually about romantic or spiritual love

gur unrefined brown sugar in lump form

Haj pilgrimage to Mecca, a duty required of all Muslims, if at all possible, once in a lifetime

Haji someone who has gone on pilgrimage to Mecca

halwa sweet dish made of flour, sugar, and oil, sometimes with nuts and raisins mixed in

Inshallah If Allah wills it. Used frequently in conversation.

ja-i-namaz (D) prayer rug

jan (D) Persian term of endearment, "dear," "love"; pronounced with "ah" sound

jehad Holy War; really "the struggle against the darkness within ourselves"

jezail a long, heavy Afghan rifle used in the nineteenth century

Kaka (D) paternal uncle; used as a term of respect for elder men

Kalashnikov Russian-made automatic rifle, AK-47; the main weapon in the Afghan war

Khala (D) maternal aunt; used as a term of respect for elder women

Khalq (D) "the people" or "the masses;" a faction of the People's Democratic Party of Afghanistan, formerly led by Noor Mohammed Taraki, later by Hafizullah Amin

Khalqi (D) a member or supporter of Khalq; also a pejorative term for a collaborator with the Communists

Khan Chief; king; now used as a title of respect; also a common last name, particularly among the Pashtuns

khoda hafez (D) goodbye; literally "God is your friend"

khosh shudam (D) Pleased to meet you; happy to meet you

kohl (Ar.) black powder used as eye make-up; antimony

Koran Holy Book of the Muslims; also spelled *Quran*

La ilaha illallah, Muhammadur rasulullah (Ar.) "There is no God but God, and Mohammed is his Messenger;" Muslim profession of faith

Madar (D) Mother

malik landowner, headman

Mashallah (Ar.) well done; used in the sense of "Thank God"

mehrbani (P) thank you

memsahib (Urdu, Hindi) mistress

muhajirin (Ar.) refugees; the first refugees were the followers of Prophet Mohammed who fled from Mecca to Medina as a result of persecution

Mujahedeen (singular *Mujaheed*) freedom fighters; literally "holy warriors," those who fight a *jehad* (a battle against the darkness within themselves)

mullah Muslim religious functionary who performs rites, leads prayers, and teaches religious education

namaz Muslim prayers, required five times a day

nam-e-khoda (D) "In the name of God;" often used to indicate that one is absolutely telling the truth

naseeb (D) fate, luck, "portion"

nikah wedding vows; religious ceremony conducted by a mullah

noql (D) sugared almonds

Parcham "The banner;" a faction of the People's Democratic Party of Afghanistan, led by Babrak Karmal, and considered hardline pro-Soviet

Parchami a member of the Parcham wing; also a pejorative term for someone who collaborates with the Communists

Pashtu the language of the Pashtuns, also known as Pathans, who inhabit southern and eastern Afghanistan, as well as Pakistan's border province of Khyber Pakhtunkhwa (formerly Northwest Frontier Province), and parts of Baluchistan

Pashtunwali (P) "way of the Pashtuns;" strict code of tribal law that provides for hospitality, asylum, and blood revenge

Pathan a Pashtun (Anglicized term)

pilau rice cooked with onions and spices, and usually with vegetables, or raisins and nuts, and sometimes with chicken, lamb, or goat

purdah literally "curtain;" the practice of keeping women separate from men outside their own families

qila (D,P) fort; a fortress-like compound with high walls

qismet (D) fate, luck, "portion"

rebab Afghan folk lute with a wooden body, a stretched skin face, and three plucked strings, plus drone and sympathetic strings

rickshaw three-wheeled motorized taxis

sahib master, sir; often appended as a term of respect

Salaam aleikum (Ar) greeting of all Muslims; literally "Peace, God be with you."

Salaams greetings

sangar (D) bunker; camp, often a cave, where guerillas are based

Shabbash! Well done!

shalwar kameez (Urdu) name for men's and women's garment, consisting of wide, loose trousers (*shalwar*) and a loose shirt (*kameez*) falling to at least the knee.

sheitan Satan

shin gul (P) "blue flower;" a tiny, five-petalled wildflower the color of lapis lazuli

Shuravi Soviets; term of contempt in those days

Staray mashay (P) Pashtu greeting; literally "May you never be tired"

surmah (D) black powder used as eye make-up; antimony

tabla skin drums used to accompany *rebab*, flute, and other instruments

tobah repentance; often used in conversation as the equivalent of "God forbid"

Urdu the national language of Pakistan, also spoken by Muslims in India; a mixture of Arabic, Persian, and Hindi, it became a lingua franca during the Moghul era

zamindar landowner
zargul (P, D) "yellow flower" or "golden flower"

ACKNOWLEDGEMENTS

This novel, and all my work, was made possible by the generosity of my late parents, Maria and Joseph Denker. I thank them in Spirit for their unstinting support and faith in me through the years of writing, filmmaking, and energy healing. Both of them read many versions of the manuscript, dating back to the first draft in 1983, and often hosted and housed expected and unexpected guests from Afghanistan and Pakistan.

Thanks to my dear friends and fellow writers Jennifer Heath and Tara Waters Lumpkin for reading the manuscript and offering heartfelt suggestions.

Thanks to Emily Tippetts and her team at E.M. Tippetts Book Design for her wonderful reworking of my original cover design, and for her formatting of this edition.

Special thanks to Sandra Phelan for her generous, wise, and thorough copyediting and proofing of the final manuscript. Any remaining errors are my own.

I could not have experienced Afghanistan without the love and support of my dear friends Syed Ishaq Gailani and his wife Fatana Said Gailani. Both have worked tirelessly for human rights and women's rights for over 40 years, risking their lives daily. Although I've been able to support the Afghanistan Women's Council from time to time, I can only dimly conceive of the dedication and sacrifice they and so many other Afghans involved in rebuilding their country go through on a daily basis.

The late poet laureate of Afghanistan, Ustad Khalilullah Khalili was also a great inspiration, and an embodiment of the Sufi ways.

My late friend, architect Nader Khalili, always supported my writing aspirations, and I can just see him Sufi dancing in heaven.

I could not have experienced the hospitality of Pakistan without my "brother" Abid Zareef Khan, his late parents, and his large and lively family in Peshawar.

Finally, I invoke and give thanks to the Sufi spirit of ONENESS.